A LIVING TARGET

"He's got a gun!"

Who? was Link's first thought. Then he *knew*. The smirking terrorist had come to kill Maggie. He instinctively rolled away from the front of the house, shielding her in his arms, Maggie grunting with the burden of his weight. *Bam!* The explosive report of the gunshot reverberated and stung Link's arm.

"I've got my pistol in my hand," Maggie cried. "Under the towel." She kept pushing the towel-shrouded revolver at him until he felt metal. It took some fumbling before he located the trigger guard. He raised the pistol. The terrorist took another step . . .

Also by Tom Wilson

Desert Fury
Final Thunder
Black Wolf

BLACK CANYON

Tom Wilson

A SIGNET BOOK

SIGNET
Published by New American Library, a division of
Penguin Putnam Inc., 375 Hudson Street,
New York, New York 10014, U.S.A.
Penguin Books Ltd, 27 Wrights Lane,
London W8 5TZ, England
Penguin Books Australia Ltd, Ringwood,
Victoria, Australia
Penguin Books Canada Ltd, 10 Alcorn Avenue,
Toronto, Ontario, Canada M4V 3B2
Penguin Books (N.Z.) Ltd, 182–190 Wairau Road,
Auckland 10, New Zealand

Penguin Books Ltd, Registered Offices:
Harmondsworth, Middlesex, England

First published by Signet, an imprint of New American Library,
a division of Penguin Putnam Inc.

First Printing, September 1999
10 9 8 7 6 5 4 3 2 1

This one's dedicated to my father—
a man, a builder, and a pioneer—
who passed away bravely, following an especially
difficult time

ACKNOWLEDGMENTS

I make it a point to experience the places I write about. This time that proved to be an especially pleasant task.

Colorado is not for wimps. To penetrate into the heart of the state you must cross barriers so inhospitable that the toughest of mountain men and pioneers chose to go around. Those who approach from the featureless eastern plain are stunned by the spectacular sentinels of the Front and Sangre de Cristo ranges. Then, as if those were mere primers for the real thing, come the soaring Park, Sawatch, and San Juan barrier ranges. Together those giants—fifty peaks reach more than fourteen thousand feet—make up the Rocky Mountains of Colorado. To discourage intruders from the west are the rugged and ghostly-in-appearance Roan and Uncompahgre plateaus. Coming from the south, you encounter the thousand-feet-deep trenches, canyons, and gorges of the Gunnison and Arkansas rivers.

I've lived in Colorado—two of my children were born in Denver—and I'm constantly drawn to return, regardless of wherever else I may hang my hat. To remind me, each year my favorite ski group heads for Steamboat Springs—when we're not going to Aspen or Vail. The snow is the kind skiers dream about, and the recreation is superb year-round. Yet a friend who lives there explains that Colorado is not a place but an attitude. That's easiest to understand when you're breathing the crisp air and observing some of the most spectacular scenery in the world.

In gathering background details (I've altered, subtracted and added landmarks to satisfy the needs of the tale, and populated the story with people dredged entirely from my fancy), everyone I interviewed went out of their way to be helpful. I have noted that Coloradans are singularly self-sufficient and proud of the fact. A few who were of special assistance in the writing of this book were Jack and Anita McEncroe, Robin Olds, and Tom and Kathy Wilson.

Thanks. I'll be back.

Prologue

1995—Mountainous Region of Sinaloa State, Republic of Mexico

Except for the black tape securing his elbows and ankles the man was bared, lying on his back on the waist-high altar stone. The police sergeant barked out an order for him to stop jumping about, and despite his obvious terror he complied. Behind them the priest moved with deliberateness, watchful but silent, ignoring the frightened sounds of this and the other prisoners.

He carefully picked up the obsidian masterpiece. It was ancient, tailored for its specific purpose—the handle comfortable in his grasp, the blade thick, heavy, and sharp. Perhaps his own ancestor had used it for the first time.

The priest approached the offering, turned and surveyed in the four holy directions. Finally he placed a hand lightly on the man's chest and whispered: "For you, Tezcatlipoca," dedicating the offering to the Aztec god of the masses. He raised the ceremonial knife. Brought it down hard, but immediately realized that the force had been insufficient. The man grunted as the thick blade wedged in his chest, and made a gurgling sound as the priest levered it back and forth. As he pulled it free, blood frothed within the ugly wound from air escaping a punctured lung. He raised the knife in both hands, and again brought it down. This time so harshly that the sternum separated.

He dragged the blade downward for six inches, then

pulled the knife free. Finally he delved in search of the living organ. He felt it, pulsing and throbbing.

Quickly! he urged himself, and viciously wrenched and pulled—hacked away arteries with the knife—and then was able to rip it free. He held it up, blood running down his arms, his chest heaving with effort. As he felt the thing moving in his hand, he experienced a sensation not unlike the onset of orgasm. The ancients had sometimes eaten the hearts of enemies as a gesture of honor and respect, but the priest had felt neither for this man.

When the heart was still and of no further use, he discarded it into a nearby trash pit.

The priest motioned the sergeant toward the woman who would be next. And as he waited for her to be dragged to the altar, he remembered how it had begun only a week earlier.

Benito Juarez International Airport, Mexico City

The jet touched down, skittered, and rolled as Axel Nevas stared out at the big airfield. He had been recalled from his office in Washington by the minister of external affairs; asked to return to "attend to a minor matter."

Like the other presidential candidates the previous year, Luis Donaldo Colosio had promised an end to corruption. When he'd been assassinated prior to the election—whispers said his mistake had been a promise to limit the flow of drugs into the US—his campaign manager, Ernesto Zedillo Ponce de Leon, had humbly stepped forth. After he'd won with the sympathy vote, the cleanup had been "postponed." Mostly there were celebrations about the passage of NAFTA that would *ease* border restrictions with the US.

Another year passed before the opposition parties reissued their demands to eliminate official abuses, and Axel Nevas had learned that his recall had *something* to do with the investigation. He felt little cause to worry. He was a lifelong member of the Institutional Revolutionary Party, and Zedillo himself had seconded his appointment as director of "the Agencia," Mexico's pitiful answer to the US's National Security Agency. He had known the Mexican President for several years, and there were commonalities. Both had attended the National Polytechnical Institute and then graduate schools in the US. Axel remembered him as a somewhat slick fellow, and certainly no zealot of integrity.

Axel's people in the Agencia used communications listening devices to uncover foreign trade secrets, with a budget that limited them to minor efforts in the US, Canada, and Brazil. He was surprised that the investigators were even aware of their secretive work.

When the seat belts sign was switched off, Axel stood—he was gangly, all knees and elbows, had a thin blade of a nose, and a balding dome and solemn appearance despite his relative youth. He took an impatient step toward the door of the Aero Mexico jet. At his level he was authorized to fly first-class, but preferred the austerity and anonymity of economy.

Inside the terminal, he'd just turned toward the customs area—his luggage would be exempted due to his diplomatic status—when four men in plainclothes intercepted him. A heavily muscled man displayed a leather case. A gold badge showed an eagle perched on a cactus, devouring a snake. They were federal policemen.

"I am Captain Torré. You will accompany my friends and answer their questions."

"How long . . ." Axel began—his voice deep, like two bars of rusted iron being scraped together—but another man introduced himself as Sergeant Someone or Other and rudely led him toward an exit. Axel turned to complain to the captain, but he was pushed along.

Outside he was shoved into a sedan. He had been wrong. The authorities were indeed interested in his Agencia. The questioning continued all the way to the Zocalo district, where offices of nation, district, and city were located. There he was escorted into the rear entrance of an obscure old building, and down ominous flights of stairs to a dank basement.

The interrogators knew about the "other" thing Axel
Nevas directed, that had nothing to do with international
trade. How the Agencia obtained tapes and photos of various diplomats in Washington and blackmailed them.

There were rationalizations. The practice had begun with
predecessors. The Agencia's budget was so paltry he was
forced to either supplement it or cut back even farther. He
considered telling them all that, but instead waited, admit-
ting nothing and requesting a lawyer.

"We know everything," the sergeant said as if bored by
the repetitions.

"My lawyer's number is in my briefcase." *How had they
found out?*

Two policemen held him while the sergeant pulled on
leather gloves, slammed a fist into his stomach, and as he
doubled over, grasped and squeezed his testicles, and twisted
as if he would pull them off. When he screamed another
man beat him until he stopped. "We already know everything," the sergeant repeated, and took pleasure in explaining what a woman and two men at his Mexico City Agencia
office had revealed to government investigators.

They'd said Axel had done it all, and had taken everything for himself.

He quelled a surge of hatred against the turncoats.

"All you have to do is confirm what they said."

Axel admitted nothing. Just continued to ask for the
lawyer.

"I hear you are an Aztlan," said the sergeant, referring to
off-beat admirers of the ancient culture, a proclivity among
the trendiest Mexico City inhabitants.

Axel's ribs ached and he feared they were cracked. His
tongue encountered the snag of a broken tooth. His nose was
bloody. Yet he bristled. "My family is descended from . . ."

He stopped, angry at himself for saying anything at all.

The sergeant smiled at discovering the nerve. "Ahh. One
of those lunatics who cut open dogs and leave their guts
hanging out for others to pick up."

Axel's mouth had become taut. He had surprised himself

at his utterance, for he'd never displayed much interest in the things his grandfather and father had revealed about his heritage. The sergeant was looking for weaknesses. He would give him no more.

After a while they took him to a windowless cell that smelled like old garbage, and left him with pencil, paper, and instructions to provide a confession before they returned.

There was only a dim light, a bed, table, and filthy chamber pot. No food or water. No conversation. Time passed. Days perhaps, but he did not know since there was no hint of sunlight. When it became obvious that he would languish until he confessed, he spent his time resting, using as little breath as possible to minimize loss of bodily liquids. Now he knew the arrest was no mistake. He was to be one of Zedillo's examples.

He withdrew into his mind, perhaps because of the sergeant's taunting, and remembered his grandfather's explanations. They were descended from high priests. The A, X and L of his given name were similar to certain pictographs that explained the origins of gods and men. During his eighth year his father had demonstrated rituals of offering, sacrificing goats and dogs.

He recalled old beliefs and rituals that were not at all known to the public.

If delivered from his awful predicament, he vowed to change. No, that was bribery!

He spoke aloud: "I will believe in the gods of my ancestors, beginning *now*!"

High priests honored all Aztec gods, but selected one who would guide his life. He had not yet made such a choice.

So in the putrid cell Axel began praying to those gods that he could remember—they totaled more than a hundred—for a sign. Periodically he would be distracted by thoughts of the employees who had caused his grief, and wonder why they'd turned on him. But then he would force his consciousness back to the gods, and find himself remembering more of his childhood teachings. Ah, there were so many. Which one should he pick to follow?

He had no idea how much time passed before he heard another person's sound, only that his beard had grown an inch and he was so thirsty he had difficulty restraining himself from drinking the brown scummed liquid at the bottom of the chamber pot.

The sound of the door was ear-shattering. He opened his eyes and felt an overpowering dread. It was Huitzilopóchtli, the squat and ugly god of war. Staring at Axel with his bug-eyes, mouth splitting his blocklike head with a taunting, malevolent grin. Hissing and swinging his ax to and fro in anticipation of . . .

"You didn't confess, I see." The image altered, became the police sergeant.

Axel's resolve faltered. He was about to tell him he would sign anything. Do *anything*.

The sergeant motioned in two hefty and blank-faced women. As they lifted and stripped Axel, he emitted a groan, for he was still sore from the beating. They helped him to his feet, led him out of the cell and down a corridor, and placed him under a shower of tepid water. He gulped like a fish, taking in precious liquid as they scrubbed him. Finally one held him upright as the other soaped his beard and shaved him.

When they pulled Axel from the shower—the taciturn women as wet as he—the sergeant handed him a cool *cerveza* and a handful of crackers. "Good, eh? But drink and eat slowly so they will be gentle on your stomach," he cautioned.

After the first nibble Axel crammed them into his mouth. Gulped the beer down and belched. The sergeant gave him more crackers. Then, "Come. We have an appointment."

An interrogation? Axel wondered. Should he beg?

The women had fresh clothing taken from his luggage, including shoes, slacks, and a delicately embroidered Panamanian *camisilla*. They tugged at him, but Axel pushed them away and dressed himself, periodically looking at the sergeant, whose countenance had lost its former antagonism. He wondered but did not question.

"Follow me, please."

As he trailed behind the sergeant, Axel learned that he'd been in the cell for seven days. It seemed longer. He had to rest often as they climbed stairs to the ground floor, but the sergeant waited patiently. Outside Axel shaded his eyes from the harsh glare of daylight.

As he was helped into the back of a dark Chevrolet sedan he discovered Torré, the muscular police captain, in front. The sergeant got in next to Axel. "There was no confession," he said as he closed the door.

The captain directed the driver to the National Palace, the residence of the President of Mexico. Axel did not ask why, although his head spun with possibilities.

Would he meet with the President? Was it all a mistake? More questions?

The palace was not far. They were waved through a side gate and proceeded around to the rear, where they parked at a helipad. A tremendous helicopter—dung brown with the green, white, and red markings of the Mexican Army—waited, huge twin rotors turning slowly. Torré got out and led the way, and Axel followed.

There was an interrogation technique he'd once been told of where prisoners were given a choice between admission of guilt or being tossed out at a thousand feet. Would they use Zedillo's personal helicopter for such a task? He dared not question. Not yet.

As they entered the helicopter a uniformed crew member showed Axel into a seat in the very rear of the fuselage, opposite a woman with severely swept salt-and-pepper hair. She observed him with a calm and serious mien as he belted in.

Torré and the sergeant made their way forward and took seats in the midsection.

Axel Nevas gave a start—for Torré had joined the Agencia employees who had turned him in. The three had seen him, for they studiously avoided looking in his direction.

The engines surged, and they rose, dipped, and were away. It was surprisingly quiet, the vibration not nearly as great as Axel remembered. Of course that might be expected when flying in El Presidente's helicopter.

The woman leaned forward, and spoke in a monotone: "I am Marta Fuentes."

Axel's heartbeat quickened with the recognition—she was the eldest sister of Amado Fuentes. Among the many stories about him was one that she was the only human who had seen his face and survived. That was undoubtedly exaggeration, but there were few photographs and no recent ones. Yet it was said that he was easily recognizable.

He tried to keep his voice steady. "I am Axel Nevas."

"Yes. Director of the Agencia, and an expert with the electronics?"

"Yes, Dona Fuentes." If the Agencia still existed. The remainder of the statement was correct. He held a graduate electrical engineering degree.

She gave a curt nod, and looked out the window, obviously unafraid of his proximity despite the fact that he'd been a prisoner only a short time before.

Twice during the next three hours they climbed through mountain passes, then descended as the terrain dropped. Finally a few miles ahead he could see the Pacific Ocean, and below them a large, arid, and isolated valley. A treeless, stubble-grass expanse called llano.

Rancho Fuentes.

Twenty years before, Amado Fuentes had been a teenage mule humping cocaine across the Texas border with a thousand others. He had eliminated some competitors, intimidated the rest, and begun a spectacular rise. As soon as he'd felt at ease with a position, his superiors had had a way of disappearing, and he of filling the void. At twenty-two he'd controlled the border from Brownsville to Yuma, getting a percentage of everything passing through. To reduce risk he had purchased, through third parties, properties on both sides of the border. Mostly farms in remote locations, but also homes in Laredo, El Paso, and Nogales to be used as way stations. Mexican officials were either bought or killed. Americans bought or circumvented. He had set up villages as methamphetamine manufacturing centers, others to grow cannabis or poppies, and shipped their product along with Colombian and Peruvian cocaine, and Thai heroin and hemp.

As his successes multiplied he'd returned to his birthplace and purchased the valley, paying landholders twice their price. Rancho Fuentes measured twenty by twenty-five kilometers, and on it were raised Mexico's finest Arabian thoroughbreds. Don Amado, as he was called by then, built a church for the adjacent community, bought the local political structure and ordered that the local citizenry be fairly represented. No one went hungry or without work. Orphans and widows were succored. No one spoke badly of their *padrone*. There was talk that he had secretly met with the Pope and received his blessing.

The helicopter dropped toward a pad a hundred meters from a sprawling multitiered home. It was white stucco with blue tile roof, a sculptured swimming pool extending along one side, a reflecting pool with large fountains in front. An emerald lawn covered the gently rolling hills, tended by an army of gardeners. Beyond the green, barren llano stretched into the distance. Nothing could approach unnoticed. A radar antenna nodded back and forth at the end of a paved runway. The Mexican government had declared the airspace above the rancho a restricted flying zone. Uniformed personnel drove topless jeeps about the perimeter. Two Range Rovers waited at the pad. An honor guard wore the uniforms of the Mexican Army, and carried automatic weapons with muzzles raised. The VIP helicopter was normally assigned to the President. It was said that Amado Fuentos held the government in his hand. Here was confirmation.

Marta Fuentes walked toward the house, purposefully slow. Axel limped at her side, feeling he was living a dream. He turned to watch the helicopter lift off, the other passengers still aboard. Taking them to another destination?

His hostess spoke without looking at Axel. "You should thank those two. Captain Torré brought you to our attention. The sergeant said that you refused to bend."

Axel still ached in too many various places from the beating to feel charitable toward the policemen.

They entered the house and her shoes made *tic-tic* sounds as they crossed the tile. She led him to a door, opened it, and Axel Nevas met the most dangerous man in the hemisphere. He stood a few feet away examining Axel, and then a cigar. He lit it and looked back up.

You could describe Amado Fuentes as porcine, for he was jowled, had a thick belly, a large neck, and small lobeless ears. His eyes were hard, and he wore the sneer of a bully accustomed to getting his way. But none of those things distinguished him. Rather it was his *nose*—large, round as a plum, and turning various shades of blush red according to his mood. The bulbous mass so dominated his features that when you looked away, you forgot the rest.

All but the unforgettable nose.

It was said that he'd killed a man who had committed the misfortune of laughing, so Axel was careful not to stare as Marta introduced him.

Don Amado puffed the cigar once, and minced not a word. "Tell me, Senõr Nevas, since you are so smart with all those technical things. There are people in Mexico City I wish to know about, to hear everything they say. Can you arrange this thing?"

Thus began a meeting that altered both men's lives, and those of many others.

The following morning, after they'd taken a morning meal on the veranda, Amado Fuentes asked Axel Nevas to accompany him on a helicopter ride, this time in a much smaller, unmarked copter. When airborne, Amado nodded out at the featureless llano. "Every morning my sister and I go for a horseback ride. It is my only true pleasure."

He pointed northward. "I control the entire US border. Little crosses that I do not know about, and once you are operating your listening posts for me, *nothing* will get by."

"That is impressive, Don Amado."

"Every few months another important person from one of the families in Colombia or Peru or Uruguay comes to sell me another distribution network in the US, tired of the constant pressure by the Americano agents to extradite them. Now I am the prisoner. If I step from this prison, I might be kidnapped by Americano agents who act like this is *their* country."

Axel Nevas waited.

"That is why you are here. We are going to change things. I have the money, and you"—he tapped his head—"have the brains. When we are done with them I will live in their country and build a big home and fuck their daughters."

"Not their wives?" Axel asked mischievously.

Don Amado released a peal of laughter. "Them too."

He sobered some.

"But first you will tell me everything my friends and enemies in Mexico City are saying."

When they landed on a hillside helipad, Axel was surprised to see the muscular police captain, Torré. He nodded pleasantly as they walked past, then followed at a respectful distance.

"I visited this place as a child," said Don Amado as they climbed a stone stairway. "It is very old, and no one who lives near here tells outsiders about it. Some say it was the birthplace of the first eagle men and the first gods."

They came upon a weather-aged carved-stone wall. Axel stopped to examine it, lightly ran his hands over faint but intricate pictographs. "You are Aztec too?"

"Perhaps. Does it matter?"

"Blood is important. From your abilities, I believe you must be descended from the greatest speaker-kings of the Aztec. If you wish I can find out for you."

"I had rather people ask no questions about me." The previous evening, tongues loosened with much wine, Axel had told about his reawakening, how he intended to honor his heritage. In return, Amado had revealed very little about himself.

Behind them the helicopter lifted off. "I told the pilot to return in two hours," said Amado, leading on up the hillside.

"You are a priest, but have you ever made an offering? Not animals, the real thing?"

"No," Axel breathed. Getting a glimmering of what was to come.

The stone steps ended at a large, flat pedestal stone. At its center was a waist-high weathered block with grooves etched into the top. The police sergeant waited there with the three Agencia employees. All had been stripped naked and bound with tape at ankles and elbows. The woman looked stunned. She had obviously been raped, for her breasts were bruised and swollen, and blood and mucus were smeared on her thighs.

"Look, it is Senõr Nevas," one of the men cried in falsetto, as if he hadn't betrayed him.

Axel felt a roaring in his ears, and considered the thought that everything that had passed before had been leading to this single moment of awakening. Whatever would come would be a result of what he did here.

"I don't know much about these things, but you may need this." Don Amado handed him a hand-crafted obsidian knife, its thick blade tapered to a razor's edge. "After we spoke last night, I telephoned Mexico City. It was taken from the National Museum."

Axel was still admiring the knife when Amado added a small, ornate automatic pistol. It was deep-blued, inlaid with silver filigree, and had mother-of-pearl grips.

"Gifts of our new friendship," said Don Amado. He waved at the humans. "And those."

On the altar was a cotton wrap. A blood apron. Someone—Marta Fuentes?—had researched the needs of high priests.

"Would you prefer for us to leave?" asked Don Amado.

"It's not necessary." Axel's deep voice was filled with new authority. As he began to remove his outer clothing, he asked the sergeant to position one of the male prisoners on his back on the stone. The woman began to choke as she sobbed—and she and the remaining man urinated where they stood. Axel was interested in the reactions, but not overly so.

When he'd placed shirt, trousers, and shoes in a neat pile, he wrapped the cotton apron about his midsection, and took the obsidian knife with him.

The first offering was to Tezcatlipoca the all-powerful, and due to Axel's unfamiliarity with the task, it took two harsh strokes to split the victim's chest. Since the woman was impure, he offered her to Mictlantecuhtli, ruler of the dead, who was not offended by such things. He swore that she continued screaming after he'd pulled her pulsing heart from her chest.

The third one was incoherent as the sergeant dragged him toward the stone and the corpses with gaping chests. Blood had filled the channels and flowed down the sides of the altar.

"There's no need to put him on the altar," said Axel. "Have him stand beside it." He put aside the obsidian knife and approached with the pistol.

"Thank you," babbled the man in misunderstanding. "Oh, God. *Thank* you."

The last offering was most important, for Axel no longer doubted which god he was to follow. The sign had been given when the sergeant had come to free him.

"For you, great Huitzilopóchtli," he said, voice rasping on the brittle word as he grasped the man's hair and held the handgun firmly to the back of his head. *Pop!* A spray of unignited gunpowder scorched the victim's hair, creating a pungent odor as the body shuddered and kicked and sank to its knees. More ritual was unnecessary.

Deadly Huitzilopóchtli—he'd slain his own family as he'd leapt from his mother's womb—did not give a peso about ceremony or blood or living organs. Only that his victims be offered no mercy. He preferred war prisoners and traitors. Axel vowed to never pass by a chance to make an offering to the god who had provided him the new life.

The agreement with Don Amado worked well. Axel and his Agencia answered to no one in government, although millions were spent on the most modern electronic eavesdropping

devices. He was assisted only by a small group of technicians and listeners, and the captain and sergeant who were
placed at his service. Don Amado Fuentes became aware of
every utterance spoken over Mexican radios and telephones
concerning his operation.

As for Axel Nevas' unique services, not only did he provide comprehensive information, but a number of Don
Amado's enemies met their end by sacrifice. When Amado
was convinced of the quality of his work, he called Axel
Nevas in for another meeting at Rancho Fuentes.

Another dramatic expansion was planned for the Agencia. This one northward, and requiring enormous invest-
ment. But by then the Fuentes were supplying the vast
majority of the drugs to the Norte Americano markets, and
still expanding into distribution.

Within six months they had captured Denver, Vancouver,
and LA. In Seattle five former drug distributors were discovered arranged in a pentagon, each with a gunshot wound
to the back of the head. In San Jose four were similarly slain
and arranged in a square. Some policemen believed it was
the work of a satanic cult, and others toyed with ideas of
citizen vigilantes. After each mass slaying there were fewer
arrests and less contraband drugs intercepted. That, of
course, could be interpreted in different ways.

While he was suspected to be at or near the pinnacle, no
one was sure of Amado Fuentes's role in "the trade," and
certainly no one knew of Axel Nevas's involvement. With
the expansion going so smoothly, it was time to withdraw
from the "prison" at Rancho Fuentes.

In the spring of 1997 a male body was delivered to a mater-
nity hospital in Mexico City, with chin, cheeks, and nose
sliced off, and several liters of liquid body fat suctioned
away. Both sister and mother tearfully claimed it was the
pitiful remains of Don Amado Fuentes, who had died under-
going plastic surgery. Authorities in the US were logically
skeptical, but then the fingerprints matched those taken by
US border authorities twenty years before, and a DNA sam-

ple delivered to the laboratory of the federal police further confirmed his identity. Finally a disbelieving US Embassy agent picked up from a HUMINT source that at Rancho Fuentes there were no more morning horseback rides, all Mexican Army troops had been withdrawn, the skies there were no longer a restricted flying zone.

The funeral was a spectacle, the coffin open so mourners could see the way the great man had been ravaged. REMEMBER ME read a huge spray of flowers. The files on Amado Fuentes, considered by some to be the richest and most powerful man in the world, were closed.

Soon there were unproven rumors that an unseen female called "the Voice" was now taking care of business north of the border.

Winter, 1999–2000—Denver, Colorado

Axel Nevas answered the cell phone's angry buzz. "I've been *seen*," said the nervous caller.

Axel was immediately attentive. "Where?"

"New York. Last night. I was leaving the meeting I told you about when the ambassador's daughter and her friend got a look at me."

"I thought you were going to postpone it until after your operation."

The man paused, a reminder that he was still exceedingly dangerous. "There was business," he finally said evenly.

Axel removed all reproach from his tone. "Were you seen clearly, or just in passing?"

"We were face-to-face." He took a breath. "The ambassador's agreed to have his daughter sent home and institutionalized, rather than the—alternative."

"Good. And her friend?"

"She's the problem." He named her.

She would be extremely well protected.

"It must appear to be an accident," the caller decided.

Axel thought about it. "Or perhaps a kidnapping?"

"That's even better. Use whatever resources you need. I'm on my way to surgery, and I don't want to have to worry."

"You *don't* have to worry. Have I ever let you down, Amado?"

PART 1

Steamboat Springs

1

Abraham Lincoln Anderson was at his desk, staring at the
skyline, mind idling and considering mundane thoughts
like why so many people were gathered in this particular location in the world. He was a westerner—shamelessly wore
western boots and western-cut suits, even owned a good
mare that he kept in Boudie Springs, Montana, on loan to
the North County Search and Rescue Team. Out there when
one was unhappy with one's surroundings one moved on.
Here people complained incessantly. It was New Yorkers'
favorite pastime. Yet they remained and had the temerity to
feel sorry for those who lived elsewhere.

But Link was bound to remain because of a promise made
to Frank Dubois that he'd be there to help when the need
arose. They'd made the vow while flying combat in Desert
Storm, and thereafter when one had called, the other had
honored the pledge. When Link Anderson's stepfather suffered a heart attack and his company was threatened, Link
had phoned Frank to ask if he knew of anyone who needed
the services of a charter airline. Now the firm was thriving,
operating the Weyland Foundation's fleet of airplanes as
well as their own. When Frank had been promoted to chairman of the foundation, he'd known that Link would assist.

Which was why an outdoorsman like Link Anderson was

staring out over the city. Why a half-Blackfoot Indian who had studied the old, stealthy ways until he could sneak up on a bull elk and reach out and touch it, was sucking up coffee and thinking about the high country two thousand miles distant instead of being there. Why a pilot who loved to fly was behind a desk.

Erin Frechette entered from the outer office. The widow of a lieutenant who had served in Frank and Link's squadron in Saudi Arabia, she'd learned to balance home and career— earned a master's in computer sciences, and worked in industry, running a team that programmed missile computers. Here she was uncanny at wringing intelligence about any subject from their networks and archives, or anyone *else's* networks and archives. Link did not ask, just took the information and used it. His title was—take a deep breath— executive vice president for special projects. She was his technical assistant.

Most Weyland Foundation business was known to the public. Habitat Earth worked to improve the world's ecology, Mankind Earth nurtured society's well-being, and Cultural Earth promoted the arts. The scope of their undertakings were vast, and Frank Dubois had to concern himself with all of them. But he entrusted Link and Erin to supervise the personnel working on floors 24 through 27—who in their turn managed many of the most secretive projects in the world. While these were often suggested by the American government, all projects had to be deemed appropriate by the *handful,* the five guiding souls who made up the financial committee. For the past fifty-six years they had, through their covert projects, helped to nurture democracies and topple despots. Frank was their chairman, occupying the position previously held by his grandfather, Cyril Weyland. Like Frank, the others of the handful were heirs of the original five.

Link knew that the world was a better place because of the Weyland Foundation's projects, yet under other circumstances he would not have pursued, or have accepted, the position that he held. The fact that he enjoyed working with Erin helped.

"Johnny's got a heavy basketball game tonight," Erin said. "He needs a cheering section, so I'll miss dinner at the Duboises.' " Her son would soon be eight.

"How about I cancel dinner and go along." There was more than a modicum of friendship and mutual respect between the two.

"Katy would be upset. You promised her, remember." The occasion was being held for the Duboises' sixteen-year-old daughter, about to leave on a ski outing.

Erin poured coffee—he liked his blistering hot—and deposited herself into a chair. The standard motif for Weyland Foundation executives was Old Musty. She had done their offices in southwest style, with cacti, Remington bronzes, and Charles M. Russell and Bev Doolittle paintings. Link liked it, regardless if Frank Dubois called it gauche. His friend had a stuffy side.

"Ready for the update briefing on 311?" Erin asked.

"Sure." He turned his mental switch to business. In two weeks he'd fly to northwestern Canada, then Siberia, next to Australia, and finally to Bangladesh. Those were tied together in an immense project labeled Green 311, green meaning it involved capitalization of an enterprise to promote democracy. Blue projects were to assist the US Government. Black ones involved the deposing or disruption of tyrants. Scarlet denoted emergencies with the potential of dire consequences, and assumed the utmost importance. Few had been so designated. The fact that the foundation even participated in most of the international projects was confidential.

Link was interested in the undertaking, but as a pilot he was more intrigued with the mode of transportation to be tested, called the MCP. The US Army had specified it and Lockheed Martin, with Boeing as a primary subcontractor, had designed it with rapid reaction command and control in mind. The MCP—or Mobile Command Post—was short, fat, and ugly, but it was light, had long legs, was suitable for

all-weather short field operation, and carried a drive-off
Grumman van with full housekeeping features. The army
had been unable to afford it. The Weyland Foundation
would try out a prototype on Green 311 and decide.

As usual, Erin began her briefing as mother hen. "When
you leave it's going to be brutally cold, so pack warm clothing and extra telephone batteries."

They worked together smoothly, as if they'd been doing
it for much longer than a year. Regardless of location, Link
could press MEM and 1 on his flip-top phone, and she'd provide answers to keep him going in the proper direction.
Global Star and Motorola were *still* launching satellites,
while the Weyland Foundation had quietly fielded their system three years before. It was low power, directional and
used smart satellites that shuttled messages back and forth.
The encryption circuitry and codes were considered un-
breakable, thus they spoke with assurance that no one was
listening.

The desk phone buzzed and he picked up. "Interrupting
anything?" asked Frank Dubois.

"Erin's bringing me to speed on Green 311."

"A lady just arrived up here carrying a letter of recom-
mendation signed by a Lieutenant General Paul Anderson.
Thought you might be interested."

Link's stepfather was a retired three-star. "What's her
name?"

"Margaret Tatro. She works for an executive security
firm."

He smiled at a memory. "She's a childhood friend. Her
father was shot down over North Vietnam and didn't come
back. My family sort of looked after hers until her mother
remarried."

At age four Link had been adopted and taken from Montana to Washington, DC. Some of his earliest memories
were of playing with the two Tatro sisters. When he'd last
seen them he'd been twelve and no longer had time for girls,
especially brash redheaded troublemakers like younger sister Margaret, who had hung around him entirely too much.

"What's the subject, Frank?"

"All I know is that Gordon Tower called yesterday and advised me to increase security on my family. The Tatro woman's here to explain."

Supervising Agent Tower was assigned to the New York regional FBI field office, and periodically visited the Weyland Building. The foundation and the Bureau worked closely on projects of mutual interest. Tower was no alarmist, so *something* was up.

Frank went on. "She wanted a private meeting with just Tower, her boss, and me, but I've asked our security gurus to sit in. Care to join us?"

"Be right up." As he disconnected, Link recalled more about Little Margaret Tatro. The last he'd heard she'd been with the FBI, married to an employee there name of—oh, yeah—*Brown*. Since she was back to using her old name, the marriage obviously hadn't worked.

Fifteen minutes later, the time it took to travel the various hallways and elevate the fifty floors separating their suites, Link stepped into Frank's empty inner office. An oaken door was ajar, so he slipped into the briefing room.

The meeting was under way. Shown on an oversized computer monitor were the words: "WESCOR Personal Security—a division of Wolverine Executive Security Corp."

Frank Dubois's wheelchair—two years ago he'd been crippled in a civil aircraft accident—was parked at the head of the conference table. Seated on either side were his senior security managers: the director of safety—who presided over security and held the equivalent of a vice presidency—his deputy, and the chief investigator, all clad in blue blazer uniforms. Next was a craggy black man wearing a light tan suit: FBI Supervising Agent Gordon Tower.

Link found Margaret Tatro standing at the side of the room in an aqua pants suit. She was short and busty—petite and cute—and although she wore her rust-colored hair neatly coifed rather than in a ten-year-old's pigtails, he would have known her despite the years. Mmm? Except she was either a lot sexier or he was viewing her through more appreciative eyes.

A meticulously groomed executive-type male was pitching WESCOR's services. "We've not lost a client in our thirty years of existence. That includes some high-profile folks in places like Lebanon, the West Bank, Cairo, Medellin, Mogadishu, and Sarajevo. Our success lies in our belief that to err is human, but let the other guy do it. If we slip up, it's on the side of prudence.

"Our trademark is the fact that our contracts invariably begin with a study, at which time we learn everything possible about our clients' environment, routine, and any threats they face. To do that we use experienced analysts such as Miss Tatro. You'll note on her bio sheet that she has degrees in criminology and psychology, worked as a special agent for the Federal Bureau of Investigation, and taught investigative procedures at their national academy. She's been with us for two years, and was recently promoted to department supervisor. Yesterday she . . ."

The Weyland Foundation director of safety, who had been with the foundation for thirty years, raised a hand to stop the WESCOR executive. "I suggest that you run this past my office rather than take up Mr. Dubois's time. He undoubtedly has more important business, and as you may know we have our own protective and investigative security professionals assigned to . . ."

Margaret Tatro interrupted just as rudely as he had. "Look. Yesterday I discovered two bits of information that Mr. Dubois should be made aware of. One, members of his family are in jeopardy, and two, there's an obvious information leak within your organization. When I'm done you can toss me out, whatever, because I've gotta get back to work anyway."

The director was startled into silence as the diminutive redhead took the podium.

Link allowed a smile to flicker. This was the girl he recalled. *Still* as tough as a prickly pear. He noted that her boss looked about uneasily as he took a seat. The Weyland Foundation was immensely wealthy, and he obviously had no desire to get into a rock fight.

Frank Dubois teepeed his hands as if intrigued. "Please continue, Ms. . . . may I call you Margaret?"

"Maggie, please. My mother only called me Margaret when I was in trouble."

"Go on with your briefing, Maggie, and we'll listen."

She did so smoothly, as if the confrontation had not occurred.

Last week she'd begun an analysis for a contract involving protective measures for employees of a plant located in a nice area of Brooklyn that was fast becoming infested by drug dealers. She'd familiarized herself with the neighborhood, studied police statistics, spoken to merchants and postmen and delivery people. Then she'd rented a second-floor apartment with a street view, and enlisting help from one other person, prepared for a general surveillance. To cover all bases she had brought in a video camera, a parabolic acoustic dish, and a frequency scanner/recorder to intercept cell phone transactions between distributors and runners.

"That's illegal," snapped the chief investigator, still sour from her put-down of his boss. He'd come to the Weyland Foundation after a stint with the Secret Service and was known as a rising star in security. Perhaps the next director.

Maggie did not pause. "Possessing a scanner or tape recorder is not illegal. If we discover a crime in progress, we report it. Same if one's being planned. If someone's threatened we warn them. Otherwise the *accidental* tapings are erased. We can't use them in court, but these are not nice people and normally no one complains. Would you rather *not* hear about what we heard?"

"Please continue." That came from Frank Dubois.

She nodded. Yesterday she'd visited the stakeout and took over so the other surveiller could take a break and have a hot lunch. They were expecting a cocaine distributor to drop in for a sort of spot inspection of the neighborhood operation. Maggie explained, "We're talking about a guy with a *big* income. Ferrari, mansion, yacht, *that* sort of big."

Sure enough, ten minutes later Maggie got a video of the guy getting out of a limo and going into a building. Seconds afterward she'd intercepted an incoming call on a cellular number.

A woman had identified herself as "the Voice" and the distributor answered in subdued tones, like she and not he was the heavyweight. That seemed odd. Here's this tough guy running a multiple-million dollar dope business in two of the meanest boroughs in America, and he was nervous? The Voice passed on firm information: There would be a narc squad raid at a specific warehouse—and gave the time, the precinct, and the name of the officer-in-charge. She wrapped up by saying that someone called Axel would be in contact and to do what he said.

"As soon as she disconnected I called Gordon to tell him what I'd heard," said Maggie.

"Why not the local police?" asked the chief investigator.

Supervising Agent Tower spoke up. "This one's our baby. For the last few years we've had rumors about this 'Voice' taking over portions of the drug trade from LA to Maine. Mostly it's in bits and pieces, like the Mexican Mafia's involved, and some high-placed public officials have been bought off. Every time we get onto something solid it seems to disappear, like they're reading our mail and listening to our office conversations."

"Should we be talking this openly about it?" Maggie asked Tower.

"Yeah, Maggie. Everyone here has security clearances you wouldn't believe. I work with the foundation often, and we get more information than we give."

She eyed the security officers coolly, as if not sure. Finally she continued, saying that Gordon Tower, whom she'd known in the Bureau, had agreed to call up a senior DEA agent and come over to listen to the tape. Hoping that just *maybe* they had a break regarding the Voice.

Then, after he'd hung up, Maggie had intercepted another call.

The man called Axel—who spoke in incredibly deep tones—told the distributor about a family he wanted followed. He named Franklin S. Dubois, his wife and daughter, and provided seed information to get him headed in the proper directions. For instance the daughter was at a meeting of the Diamond Snow Bunnies . . ."

"*Double*-Diamond Snow Bunnies," Frank corrected with narrowed eyes.

Maggie made the annotation on her notepad. Looked up. "Axel explained it's a ski club. He said your wife was at a fund-raiser planning session."

"Setting up an art festival for AIDS patients," Frank said softly, eyes riveted on her.

Next Axel had described Frank's chairmanship of the Weyland Foundation, and explained how he would be difficult to track because he often went by helicopter. As, in fact, he was about to do to attend a meeting with the secretary of commerce at the World Trade Center.

The director of safety looked surprised. "Do you remember the time of that conversation?"

"It was twelve-ten."

The chief investigator gave a snort. "I would very much like to hear the tape." Snapping out the words as if Maggie were under interrogation. "Is it time-marked?"

"It was. It's not available," she added, and continued. "While Axel was talking I kept wondering why a huge-income guy like the distributor would rock his boat and go up against someone as big and as organized as you guys."

The chief investigator shook his head vigorously. "We've heard nothing about a planned kidnapping, and we have extremely good intelligence. And you're also telling us that this—Axel fellow—knew about the World Trade Center meeting half an hour beforehand? Impossible. Not only are our communications impenetrable, Mr. Dubois's destination wasn't even given to the helicopter pilot until just prior to takeoff."

Maggie then enunciated very clearly: "You just made two mistakes, buster. One, I haven't once mentioned kidnapping, and two, I *hope* you're not calling me a liar."

Gordon Tower pinned the investigator with a hard look. "A bit ago I vouched for you. Let me add that I've known Maggie even longer, ever since she came to the Bureau, and I've never known her to lie or exaggerate. When she says something, you can take it to the bank."

The director of safety spoke up. "Perhaps she was mistaken about the timing."

"It was *precisely* twelve-ten," she said. "I even wrote it in my notebook."

"But the time-marked tape was destroyed?" asked the investigator. Dubious, half smiling.

"I did not say destroyed. I said it was not available."

"Go ahead and explain, Maggie," urged the FBI agent.

"Are you kidding? Knowing there's a leak here?"

The Weyland Foundation security bosses shuffled and glared. Maggie scanned the room, and paused as she regarded Link. Recognition softened her expression and she mouthed, "Hi."

"You can trust us," Link said with a grin. "Spit in my hand and cross my heart."

She laughed, removing a layer of tension from the air. "Yeah, but maybe I'm too embarrassed to go on. Not everyone gets to crawl around in a stinkin' *dumpster*."

There was a low ripple of laughter.

"Now let me go on and maybe we'll get back to that part. After this Axel described Mr. Dubois and family, he paused for a minute and then changed his mind. He said he'd pull some people together to deal with *the bitch*. In the meantime, he told them to forget the rest of the family and just keep an eye on *her*."

Frank grew a lighter shade of pale. "My wife?"

"He didn't specify. Your daughter's sixteen? He could have meant either of them."

He looked no happier. "Go on please."

"Axel was about to disconnect when suddenly he yelled to the distributor that their phone call was being monitored. *That* grabbed my attention, especially when he gave my address and ordered him to take care of the woman there who was just talking to the FBI."

"I don't understand," said the chief investigator.

"He meant *me*! He told him where I was! You want to hear impossible? *That* was impossible. How the hell did he know I was doing it? How do you know when someone's listening to the radio, which is what I was doing?

"I look out then and see all these bad actors pouring out of the other building heading my way. Do I pause? Unh uh, not me. I run out in the hall, set off a fire alarm, and head down the back stairs. When I get to the alley I do a half-gainer into a dumpster and burrow into garbage."

Her audience digested the events, the assistant chief of safety not hiding his smile.

"Did you think to bring your cell phone?" the investigator asked. Not as nasty now.

"Yep. And I tried calling the closest precinct. *Nothing*. I tried 9-1-1. *Nada*. It was like my battery was dead although it checked okay. When I heard voices in the alley I turned it off."

Gordon Tower picked up her story. "When we arrived the stakeout room was empty. No Maggie, no scanner or tapes. Not even the parabolic. Just a fireman all upset about the false alarm, a broken door, some wrappers from deli sandwiches, and a couple of full ashtrays."

"Soon as I heard the firemen out in the alley," said Maggie, "I started yelling and they helped pull me out. Upstairs, I told Gordon about it and said I figured there was a bug in the apartment. We looked but couldn't find it. Also, NYNEX swore there was nothing wrong with 9-1-1 or the precinct's numbers, and said I must have misdialed. And finally, my cell phone worked like a champ."

For the next few minutes the same arguments kept recurring. Regardless of Tower's assurances, the Weyland

Foundation's security supervisors were suspicious of Maggie, and upset that she insisted there was a leak in their office.

Frank Dubois brought them to earth. "For now accept it. *Somehow* they learned what they learned about us," he said. "With that in mind, I'm concerned about my wife's safety."

"Or your daughter," corrected Maggie Tatro.

"Either way, we can handle *narcotics* dealers," said the chief investigator.

"Be careful there," Maggie Tatro said as she opened a briefcase and replaced her notes. "They're better organized than ever."

Frank looked past his people and down the table to the FBI agent. "Gordon?"

"Maggie's right. We're intercepting a fraction of the hard stuff we did a couple of years ago. Justice likes to say it's because we're winning the war, but the narc agents know better. It's like the distributors know everything they do. When they take down a big distributor, which is seldom, someone's in his place by sundown. So beware these guys."

He looked around. "Which brings up a final item. Last night the NYPD went searching for the distributor and the three runners Maggie IDed."

"Why?" asked the investigator, his nastiness showing again. "Looking for corroboration of Ms. Tatro's story, like I'd be doing?"

"Call me Miss, not Mizz," Maggie snapped back. "My sister feminists kicked me out of the movement because I still intend to trap some lucky guy into committing."

"Poor bastard."

"Yeah. And you want corroboration of my story? This morning they found the bad guys."

"In a playground," said Agent Tower. "All four with a bullet in the back of their head, and laid out like we've been seeing happen in the trade. This time in a nice, neat square."

"Now you know the story," said Maggie, closing her

briefcase, "and I've got to get back to Brooklyn to try to put this Humpty Dumpty analysis back together."

Frank regarded Maggie's boss. "A question before you go. I'm concerned about my family, and your business is protecting people. Is there something we're not doing?"

"Every situation is different, Mr. Dubois. That's why we begin our contracts with an analysis of situation, environment, and . . ."

"We track *all* of those things," interjected the chief investigator. "*All* of the time."

Frank Dubois gave him a jaundiced eye, and turned to the director of safety. "Until we know the threat's over, I want airtight protection for my wife and daughter."

"Of course, sir."

He pointed at the chief investigator. "I want to know why this is happening and who's involved. I want you to begin looking today."

"Yes, sir." It was no time to argue.

The chairman of the largest benevolent foundation in the world regarded the WESCOR executive. "Can Miss Tatro be made available to conduct an independent analysis to ensure our security measures are appropriate?"

"Certainly, sir."

"I have to finish in Brooklyn," Maggie injected.

"Another analyst will take your place." Her boss's eyes glistened with dollar signs as he regarded Frank Dubois. "We'd be *very* pleased to perform the study."

There were disbelieving looks from Weyland Foundation security people.

"I'll demand absolute cooperation for Miss Tatro from all of our people," said Frank, his glare lingering until all three men nodded.

"What about you, Gordon?" he asked the FBI agent. "Can you give us an official hand?"

Agent Tower looked at Maggie. "What do you think?"

"I think I want out of this."

He chuckled.

"It might be smart to get VICAP involved. See if there've

been similar events in the recent past. Like good guys disappearing off of drug surveillance posts. Also, whether they think we're looking at a kidnapping or something else."

The Violent Criminal Apprehension Program was headquartered at Quantico, and was as good as its reputation, manned by the finest criminal behavior science specialists in the world.

"Sure," said Tower. "They move ponderously, but they're good at that sort of thing."

"And maybe get the communications guys at the lab to go over my story and find out how that Axel guy could have found out what he did. Something else too. I keep thinking there's something I'm missing. Maybe something I ought to remember about this Axel."

"You said that last night. So far there's nothing from the databank."

She nodded, then glanced at Frank. "I'll start with a look at your family's routines and vulnerabilities. Then . . ."

"For God's sake, we *know* all that," exploded the chief investigator.

Frank regarded his man with a hard and silent gaze, held it, and let him suffer until his anger had melted into self-pity. It was said that Al Capone had been able to do the same thing with a mere look. Finally Frank turned back to Maggie and nodded. "When can you begin?"

"Umm. Day after tomorrow?"

"My wife has no trips planned, but Friday morning Katy leaves for Colorado with the young skiers you mentioned. How about you? Do you downhill ski?"

"I haven't for a while." She looked thoughtful. "How long has her trip been planned?"

"It's an annual event."

"Then it's predictable. It might be judicious if she cancels for this year."

"You really think it's Katy they're after?"

"No way to know. Until we do, let's hedge our bets."

"This is Katy's year as president, and her heart's set on the trip."

"We'll protect her," said the director of safety. "Instead of a single bodyguard, we'll send more."

Frank Dubois was thoughtful. He turned to Maggie. "Let's present the problem and let her make up her mind. In fact if you're not busy this evening, you can meet both of my ladies."

"I've got an eight-thirty engagement." Her date had tickets for a show. "Before?"

They decided that she'd drop by the Dubois home at seven, meet his wife Paula, try to convince daughter Katy, and depart by eight.

"I do think she should reconsider."

"Fine," Frank said. "But if I were you I'd dust off my skis."

As the meeting broke up, Link walked over. Maggie was even shorter than he'd guessed. Five-two or five-three. She was also more voluptuous and attractive.

She smiled. "Mother heard you worked here somewhere, but I didn't expect you in the briefing. Something about you being Mr. Dubois's private pilot?"

"Nope. That was a one-time thing two years ago. My folks didn't tell you?"

"When I saw them last you were in Montana. They explained how you'd gone to the Air Force Academy and been a fighter pilot and saved America from Saddam Hussein."

"Congratulations on your contract."

"Thanks, I *guess*. If I'd known I'd end up working for 'em I would have gone lighter on those guys. Mmm. Maybe. Any advice on how I should handle the Dubois girl?"

"Don't get caught calling her a *girl*. She considers herself modern woman with a big W."

"Understood. *Girl* has a vulnerable ring, and warrior maidens despise weakness. I felt that way until my senior year in college. And sometimes, when I'm nose to nose with a guy like your investigator, I still do."

"Once you get past her big front, Katy's a pussycat. Sort of a paradox."

"That's just being a female and having the prerogative of changing one's mind. The condition never really goes away." She smiled.

"There's something else you should be aware of. Two years ago Katy was confronted by a truly evil man. Attacked. Beaten. Sexually abused. For a while she didn't remember much. It was slow coming back."

"Traumatic block." A statement not a question.

"If she's hurt again . . . ?" He shrugged, as if to say *Who knew?*

"Let's try to make sure she's not. Will she take advice where her safety's concerned?"

"Probably. She's had bodyguards around all her life." Link found himself talking more than normal. "Will you be around for lunch?" he asked.

Maggie's superior was looking. He started over.

"Rain check?" she asked. "I have to fill out reports for both NYPD and the company, then transfer the contract over to a replacement so I can get this one started." A nice smile played games at the corners of her lips. "How about when I get back from Colorado?"

"We can talk it over this evening," Link told Maggie as she was spirited away. Likely wondering what he'd meant by the last words.

2

Maggie arrived at the Duboises' apartment tower with time
to spare, and counted five plain-clothed security people in
the vicinity. Good, they were taking the threat seriously.

After her identity was established and her purse pistol
retained for safekeeping, she was ushered through a metal
detector. Waiting at the elevator, she continued to protest to
herself that she didn't *want* the damned Weyland Foundation contract. For one thing, she would be working too
closely with the FBI, and if Bozo the Ex heard about it, as
he might, he could make mischief. Like he had done every
time he got the chance after she'd told him to go find someone who didn't mind competition about who wore the
frilliest undies.

To get even he'd put out rumors that she was doing everything from spreading AIDS to taking bribes. She'd switched
jobs, moving from the Hoover Building a few miles to the
Quantico Academy. The stories had followed and become
more vicious. Like she leaked information to other law enforcement agencies, which in the Bureau was high treason.
When other instructors confided that they'd received phone
calls from Bozo the Ex about her mental instability, Maggie
had officially complained. Her boss, Agent-in-Charge Gordon Tower, had taken the matter up with the deputy director
for professional training. The deputy director, a friend of

her ex's, had called her in and demanded to know if there
was merit to the stories.

Maggie had quit the Bureau despite Gordon Tower's efforts to set the matter straight.

She'd worked hard for the promotion at WESCOR—not
that assistant department supervisor was more than a fancy
title, but she'd earned it—and did not want to fail. If she did,
she might as well get out of law enforcement. And this particular contract was not the sort to make her look good, with
half of the foundation already angry at her.

Someone on the inside was leaking information to some
very nasty drug people regarding the Duboises. Her task
would be to discover who was doing the leaking, and to get
there she'd have to choose between two routes. Easiest
would be to work from the inside. Find the culprit in the
haystack, then determine the purpose. Yeah, working from
the inside was preferred, but would take the cooperation of
the security folks at the Weyland Foundation. *Ho, ho.*

Or . . . she could learn who in the drug business was getting the info, and how, and try to backtrack to the source.
More difficult, but it was the way she'd have to approach it
because she could get more from druggie gangsters than the
assholes in Weyland Foundation security.

It would be one, two, three. Learn the family's routine, also
how well they were protected and their vulnerabilities. Then
try to plug the holes. Next, get out there and dig around in the
druggie community and find out what the hell was going on.

Maggie knew about perseverance. When applying for the
FBI, she'd run into snags. One was stature, for five feet five
inches had been the minimum height for special agents. She
would have to stretch three inches, and while her degrees
might seem perfect, J. Edgar had preferred lawyers and
accountants. She was offered a clerical position. It was no
putdown. Almost twenty-five thousand personnel were employed by the Bureau, and only a fifth were agents.

The accumulative no-no's had seemed to be a death knell
for her application, but Maggie had learned there were power
buttons in every bureaucracy and had gone for the right ref-

erences, such as ones from General Lucky Anderson, and
General Ben Lewis, who was running the Desert Storm Air
War, and another from a guy named George H. W. Bush, un-
der whom a friend of her father's served as liaison officer.
With those in hand, the Director *himself* had intervened.

She had trained diligently, graduated a fully qualified
special agent, and become one of those rare folks who had
smiled all the way to work. Due to the great recommendations, she'd been pulled in to work at the Hoover Building,
and spent her time coordinating information between the
sixty field offices and the various operating locations, making sure no bad guys slipped through the cracks.

Between trips she'd started seeing a handsome guy who
worked in the protocol office. They'd gone on an outing to
Atlantic City, and come back married. *Mistake!*

After she'd taken him home for their first Christmas, her
mother asked about the Bozo who kept sneaking into her
and her other daughter's bedroom and sorting through their
undies. The name stuck, although it was soon modified to
Bozo the Ex.

You know the rest. The escape to Quantico. The following whispers.

Aww. Lighten up, Maggie told herself. It had been two
years since she'd left the Bureau, and Gordon Tower said
he'd married a woman with big bucks. But it was kind of
just that everyone still called him by the name her mother
had started: Bozo the Ex.

As she rode up in the elevator, she switched gears and
posed an important first question. Who was being sought by
the druggies? Mother, or daughter?

Likely the mother, she thought, but following the daughter on the ski outing would be a good thing. She'd learn how
the foundation's security people handled a difficult situation, like trying to protect a full-of-herself teenager on a
wide-open ski slope.

Maggie stepped from the elevator into a foyer, noting the
single door. Meaning they owned the entire floor of a
considerably humongous building. She'd rapped only once

when a uniformed woman answered and ushered her in, taking her fur wrap.

Maggie fought off the urge to gape, for the Duboises' apartment was even more lavishly appointed than she'd anticipated. Done in crystal and gold, with scads of old art.

Frank Dubois waved from the next room. "Welcome, Maggie," he said, and introduced her to his wife, who was blond and willowy. Katy was on her way. "Sorry to desert you, but I've got to change." He wheeled himself from the room.

Paula was quick to compliment. "You look lovely."

Maggie thanked her. She was dressed for the play, wearing a spaghetti-strapped black dress. Overkill since her date was more friend than romantic interest.

"Frank says you're a longtime acquaintance of Link Anderson's. He'll be here for dinner, so if you can possibly stay . . . ?" She smiled and cocked her head.

So *that* was what Link had been talking about. "I really do have an engagement." Maggie told her about the play.

"Frank said you overheard a threat."

"Yes, ma'am."

"No reflection on your professionalism, but let's hope it's a mistake. Also, my name is Paula, not ma'am. And since you're Link's friend—and he's as close to family as anyone can get—I fully intend to call you Maggie."

"Great." It would be hard not to like Paula Dubois.

Katy Dubois burst into the room with the excitement and clamor of a freight train, and immediately began to regale her mother with details of the final meeting of her ski group before they embarked. "Thank God I got the new ski outfit," she said. "Forget skiing, it's going to be a fashion statement. And now Julie Cordellons' been sent home to Mexico because of some silly family thing, and since she was my vice president I'm stuck with all the work."

The bubbling sixteen-year-old was on the verge of being gorgeous. Paula introduced them, then immediately slipped away to "check the kitchen."

"You're here for dinner?" Katy asked, eying her evening clothing.

"To meet you and your mother, actually, then I'm off to a play." She mentioned she was a friend of Link's, which was an obvious good start, then used a shot of the ammunition he had provided. Mentioning how she was surviving just fine in a male-dominated occupation.

"You're a personal security analyst?"

"The best." After she'd talked about her education, her years in the FBI, and her decision to break out and try industry—no reason to add the role played by Bozo the Ex—Maggie broached the real subject by apologizing for the invasion of space during the coming week.

That drew Katy's attention. "I'll be in Colorado, skiing."

"Umm. I'd like to discuss that too."

Five minutes later, after she'd outlined what she'd overheard on the druggie's cell phone and suggested that Katy postpone the trip, the squeal could be heard throughout the apartment.

"No *way!*"

After Maggie butted her red head against a degree of obstination worthy of Lieutenant General Thomas Jackson, she said fine, she'd pack for Steamboat Springs too.

"I've already got bodyguards," Katy said evenly, "and my parents are overracting as usual. I feel like a fish in a bowl—as usual."

"That's the penalty for being Katy Dubois. I'm sure there are some great benefits too."

"Name one," Katy said ruefully. "When I visited my grandparents in South Carolina, I used to hang around with a girl who's got an old Chevy. Anytime she wants she can go swimming, get a hamburger, you name it so long as she doesn't do anything dumb. But when we go together, my bodyguard tags along. She's stopped inviting me because it's so spooky."

Maggie raised her hand. "I won't be spooky. Promise."

Katy *almost* cracked a smile. They were on a kindred wavelength.

Maggie tried another tack. "Another thing. I'm single

too. Sometimes bodyguards scare off neat guys, right? I'll only run off deadbeats with a little gun I carry in my purse."

When Katy grinned, Maggie was pleased. The ice barrier was melting.

As Paula Dubois returned to the room, a chime sounded. Link Anderson was shown in, and Paula immediately pecked at his cheek.

"Link!" Katy called. "Your friend wants me to postpone the best ski trip of the century." There was a lilt in her voice, and Maggie noted that her cheeks had flushed.

"Listen to her. You should have seen her dismantle a couple of guys today."

"I'm going to take her to Steamboat and we'll chase guys together."

Link Anderson laughed. He was a certified sexy guy, and Maggie realized that she too was grinning idiotically. At age ten she'd fantasized about Lincoln Anderson. Skip twenty-odd years and you'd think things might change.

Ten minutes later when she left, saying she'd see Katy in Steamboat Springs on Friday, she and Link exchanged looks—and wow! Lots of mutual stuff there from both sides. For the first time in a long while she wanted to be alone with a man.

What a day. Adventure—emotion. She hoped the show would be half as interesting.

8:15 P.M.—Boca Raton, Florida

A coded e-mail message was received and displayed on a personal computer screen. A woman with severely swept salt-and-pepper hair simultaneously pressed the letter "d" and the Ctrl key. The hard disk drive growled as it decrypted—and a few seconds later the screen was transformed.

To zzz.V.com from zzz.T-Can-E.com /d/
STOPPER: A nu player has been assigned to monitor Kitten beginning Friday. Female, Tatro, Margaret A.,

auburn hair, green eyes, 5'2", 111 lbs., DOB 12/26/66, BS Criminology & MS Psych U of So. Caro., FBI 91 to 97, WESCOR-PS 97 to Present, Title: Personal Security Analyst. This changes Weyland Foundation security people at Steamboat to five (5).
Phil: Lcl antidrug task force meeting called for 1000 on March 9th
Nwrk: Competition from Thai group is eliminated

The woman read the STOPPER information, and immediately called a number in Colorado. "You have the message about the Tatro woman?" she asked.

Axel responded in his deep voice. "Yes, Marta. The T-Cans work for me, remember?"

"Is there a problem with her?"

"What would you like to know? She wears size seven shoes, a thirty-four double D bra, and carries a prescription for hay fever. Her friends call her Maggie, and she poses no threat to my plan or to you."

She felt foolish for questioning. "Our friend is uneasy," she explained.

"Tell him it will be done as I said. Good bye now. I have work to do to make it happen."

She knew she should be reassured. The Aztec priest might be odd, perhaps even crazy, but the partnership had paid off beyond their wildest dreams. The campaign they called STOPPER would succeed, as all the others had done.

She went back to the message. The remaining notes from T-Can East were business as usual, and soon the woman became embroiled in the routines of daily business. Warning distributors. Setting up shipments. Running an empire which in scope and revenue rivaled the largest in all the Americas.

6:20 P.M.—Steamboat Springs, Colorado

Axel watched as the new arrivals stalked into the chalet. Nine of them, all heavyweight distributors from various cities. All with a lot to lose if they failed. He liked that part of it.

He and Captain Torré and Sergeant Santos had arrived from New York a few hours before. Then the ski instructor from Vermont. Torré had wanted to pull her into a bedroom. He had once procured young women for Amado Fuentes, and had a preference for using females against their will. So long as it didn't affect business, Axel did not mind. This time he said no.

"Everyone take a ski mask, " he told the new arrivals. "Any time you go out, wear it."

One of them—his name was Guteriez and he ran the Denver operation—said he had ten untraceable snowmobiles on their way, as he'd been told to do. "What's this about?" he asked.

"You're here to kill a sixteen-year-old girl."

"All of us?" He sounded incredulous.

"Yes. Show everyone to their rooms," Axel told Sergeant Santos. "Then we will gather for the briefings."

There was work to do. A girl to kill. Kitten was her code name at the Weyland Foundation. Axel had decided to call her Kitten-bitch to further dehumanize her.

3

Maggie Tatro was sore all over and had a well-earned hang-over. It had begun the previous afternoon when she was met at the airport by a longtime family friend named Anita Crow.

"Better pace yourself, hon. The Aspenauts are here," Anita had said, an announcement which baffled Maggie.

She'd soon learned more. After depositing her bags in the Snowbird Luxury Condominiums, where the Weyland Foundation had reservations, they went next door to the Snowflower, a carbon copy of the Snowbird. There she met a mob of mostly retired fighter jocks who had just come off the ski hill and were sipping various whiskeys and telling war stories about dogfights and flak and shootdowns from World War II to the Persian Gulf War. Some were legends like Robin Olds, a multiple ace who had downed enemy aircraft in both World War II Europe and Vietnam. And Billy Sparks, who had dive-bombed surface-to-air missile sites in Hanoi. And Bob Lilac who could *still* stand on his head and drink a martini.

A good number remembered Maggie's father, although he'd been killed thirty-two years earlier. The fighter pilot community was small and shared unselfishly, and considered her a full member. Billy Sparks was bartending—he and his wife Dell had been family friends from Maggie's

earliest memory—and mixed her a concoction he insisted
was no stronger than mother's milk. In the small kitchen a
grumpy old retired lieutenant colonel named Tom DeBerre
was cooking for fifty. He gave her a hug, said her dad had
been a great guy, then ladled hot chili and told her to eat up
because the fighter jocks would pour booze down her and
bore her with their lies. He also said to get on down Montrose way—in southwestern Colorado—for a visit.

At 2 A.M. Maggie found herself still sipping "mother's
milk" and listening to their tales and wishing her father
could be there. Most were departing the following morning,
which was one reason she'd remained so late. When she
rose unsteadily to return to her condo, she mentioned to
General Robin Olds that she was expected to ski with a
bunch of expert kids and had not been on a slope since age
twenty. Olds, who lived in Steamboat, turned to a one-time
Marine fighter pilot, now Delta captain, named Jack, who
was Anita Crow's other half.

"Have her up on Tomahawk soon as the lifts open."

Jack had peered at Maggie solemnly and slurred, "Will
do, bosh."

So at seven that morning there'd been a knock on her
condo suite door, and after a quarter hour of listening to the
banging she'd answered, opening only one eye because of
pain brought on by all that bright daylight, to see Jack
Crow's smiling face, asking if she was ready and offering a
handful of aspirin and vitamins.

"You gotta be kidding me," she'd muttered, having just
enough strength to hold her robe together *and* reach for the
pills.

"This too," Crow had said, handing her a tomato juice that
tasted suspiciously as if it was mostly alcohol. She hadn't
the strength to argue.

As soon as she'd changed into ski clothes—new for she'd
bought them the day before—he'd escorted her to the Grubstake Restaurant, forced her to eat a plate of eggs and bacon,
then led her to the Sport Stalker rental shop next door to out-

fit her with boots and skis. While she was still protesting and dreaming of returning to bed, he'd dragged her to the gondola, where they'd boarded the car, and halfway up the mountain she'd realized that she was going to ski and there was no way out of it.

And ski she had. First slowly following Jack down an easy run so they could ride lifts to the top of the mountain. There meeting Robin Olds, trying to understand while he explained the new types of skis and skiing in powder. Wishing her head would stop pounding as he said to follow him, then heading downhill with her eyes glued on his skis, because she'd have chickened out if she'd looked elsewhere.

After four grueling hours she was getting the hang of it back, listening hard to both Crow and Robin. They were different birds from different eras—Jack Crow one of the youngest Phantom pilots in Vietnam, Robin Olds one of the most experienced—and they skied as well as they'd once flown. Maggie decided if the seventy-six-year-old Robin could do it, so by God could she. But after twenty-odd runs she was the one who was dog tired.

At one o'clock Crow had to leave for Portland, where he'd captain a Delta run to Tokyo. Robin led the way down the mountain, slaloming between spruce trees in dry powder. At the halfway point Maggie tried to beg out and ignore the direction he was pointing. Finally she took in a breath, slipped over the side, and followed them down the hairy expert ski run called Rolex.

In the world of skiing the various runs are assigned either a green circle—meaning the run is for beginners—a blue square, for intermediate skiers—or a black diamond for the expert daredevils. Rolex is a solid black diamond, steep and studded with tricky bumps called moguls. Maggie's performance was not great, but her mentors had preached enough about bump-skiing that she made it without a bad fall. She passed a number of others who were not so lucky.

"I'm ready for you, Katy," she then said happily to no one.

Ski Town, with its condos, hotels, and restaurants, and

specialty shops, was nestled into the base of Mount Werner.
The golf course was lower and immediately north of Ski
Town. Old Town was several miles farther, with its authen-
tic western flavor, established businesses, and historic
buildings. Steamboat Springs was a sprawling combination
of it all: Mount Werner, Ski Town, Old Town, homes around
the golf course, and the outlying areas.

Maggie was bone-weary, and let the skis run all the way
down to the condo, resting as she went, vowing to get in a
shower and nap. Praying she had time, because the girl
should arrive shortly. *Just one hour of sleep. That's all.* But
as she stopped across the blacktop from the Snowbird, she
let out a groan. Katy was standing in front, clad in a knockout two-piece silver-and-black ski outfit, a smile on her
face, skis on her shoulder.

Maggie's heart plummeted, for there was no earthly way
she could go back up the mountain. She watched as a
woman approached Katy, under the scrutiny of two obvious
bodyguards. The new female wore the red, green, and black
colors of a ski instructor. Katy's private tutor? The instructor shook Katy's hand as if they didn't know one another.
Maggie told herself to check out her credentials, then decided it had likely already been done.

Menacing clouds were boiling in from the west. Heavy
snow was forecast at Aspen, but was supposed to pass south
of Steamboat. Now it looked like the storm might veer
north. Maggie was not unhappy. A good blizzard might shut
down the skiing long enough for her to sleep in.

As she passed by, Katy seemed preoccupied with her
conversation. If she could, Maggie decided to take the elevator up to the third-floor suites where they were all staying, shower and catch a nap, and *then* talk to the bodyguards
setting up shop next door.

Tomorrow was soon enough to ski with Katy, and look
over the security measures.

3:10 P.M.—Boca Raton, Florida

Marta was as close to nervousness as she got, and felt it was warranted. After all, Axel's task was to silence the one person who could spoil everything.

All of the Aztec's operations cost great amounts of money, and they were worth every penny. Take the two T-Can listening posts here, and the one in Mexico. As her brother had once said, they knew when every government agent farted.

For instance, Marta knew that the Dubois girl had arrived in Steamboat Springs, that contact had been made, and that STOPPER was about to enter its active phase. Everything should go quickly. Then she could relax.

She was outside, at a lawn table using a laptop computer-cellular telephone combination. Her brother wanted to take the motor yacht out for an evening cruise. She would accompany him, with the laptop. They were never out of touch of Tin Can or her networks of distributors.

The computer beeped. A message blinked: **You have mail.** She pressed ENTER, and then went about decoding the message.

> To zzz.V.com from zzz.T-Can-W.com/d/
> STOPPER: WF bodyguards and security are in Suite 324 as planned. Kitten in 323. No one has discovered Lucille or Rene. No complaints about our snowmobiles on the hill. Sheriff dept., municipal police are at skeleton manning level preparing for crowded weekend. Bad weather approaching but forecast to pass south of Steamboat.
> LA4: DEA Raid planned at Warehouse 91 at 2200; AIC—SA Ryan.
> StL: General goods shipment will be 4 hrs late.

She picked up the cell phone and punched in a present number.

"Yes?" responded Axel's deep and calm voice.

She spoke in her soft monotone. "There are no surprises?"

"None." Axel took a raspy breath. "We're about to begin."

"Axel?"

"Yes?"

She started to say, "Don't fail," but halted. Axel could hardly fathom failure. He communed with his god with the difficult name, and went to gruesome ends to appease him. Who knew? Perhaps it was what made everything work. "Good luck," she said.

Her brother came outside and approached the lawn table. Much of his face was swathed in bandages.

"Axel is about to proceed," she said.

"Good!" His voice was exuberant. He issued a rare laugh as he turned toward their private beach a hundred yards distant. Then he hissed a curse. They'd had trouble with people climbing their fence and using their sand—which was very fine and uniformly white and expensive, trucked in from Key West.

For the first time Marta noticed the leggy blonde with a deep tan—there were a million like her in southern Florida—lying on her stomach, sunbathing.

"I'll call the security gate," Marta said.

The intruder pushed herself up to observe the beach. She possessed small, pointed breasts. The kind her brother preferred when very young girls were unavailable.

"I'll speak to her," he said. Marta watched him walk toward the sunbather, carrying a drink, belly sucked in and strutting. He was acting younger and leaving more business to Marta. She didn't mind. Axel had things set up. He might be crazy, but he was effective.

The T-Can listening posts informed her of shipments, payments, and every possible problem. Marta called the distributors, and arranged necessary actions. If they were difficult she called Axel Nevas and they stopped breathing. All was done smoothly. Profitably.

The beach girl eyed the approaching owner. Sat up, an arm raised in a casual attempt at modesty. She smiled sheepishly and said something as he stopped. Marta wondered if he was grinning under the bandages? She wondered why the girl was fawning over him even though she couldn't see his face? She knew the answers to both questions.

The laptop buzzed, and she turned to business. T-Can East was keeping her abreast of a development in Syracuse where a SWAT team chief was briefing a drug bust. The merchandise had been moved, just enough left behind to get the chief promoted. After all, he was their man.

1:15 P.M.—Snowbird Luxury Condominiums, Ski Town

Katy Dubois had spotted Maggie across the street, getting out of her skis and looking like she was about to fall over from exhaustion, but she'd carefully paid no notice. She liked Maggie and felt they'd be friends, but she needed a good workout and no hindrances. Katy told the new ski instructor she wanted to get up on the mountain and put in a couple of hard hours. Her friends would be here tomorrow, and she wanted her ski legs firmly under her.

Too bad about Rene. Her normal tutor had left a message that she was down with a gimpy leg, and sent a replacement. Katy had tried to call to offer her sympathy and ask more about "Lu for Lucille," which was the name embroidered on the breast of the replacement instructor, but could only raise her answering machine. That was okay. Rene had been at Katy's side on various ski slopes since age four, and had undoubtedly sent the best.

They walked across the square to the gondola building, her bodyguards doing their steely-eyed bit to stare down scruffy-looking people, regardless that that was the trademark of every living snowboarder. As they headed for the Ski School express line, Lu for Lucille—the bodyguards had embarrassed Katy by verifying the woman's identification by phone *right in front of her*—handed her a lift ticket that was good for all week.

"We'll start by working on form. An intermediate, then a couple steep runs?"

"Sure," Katy responded. Looking good was as important

as performance, and she wanted both. Still she wondered if Lu had talked with Rene, because her usual drill was to start on long, gradual runs and do everything just right. It was easy to be graceful when the hill was steep and did the work for you, more difficult in slow motion.

They started with Buddy's Run, an intermediate slope where Katy found her skills were fast returning. Lu for Lucille stayed by her side, shouting an occasional compliment but offering no criticism, which was what she needed. Lu just kept looking back at the bodyguards. There was a man and woman, and they were following easily—meaning this time someone had actually thought to pick skiers. Still, Lu was casting looks that said she wasn't pleased.

What was it Maggie said? Bodyguards were the price of being Katy Dubois? Kinda neat. She asked the male if he could carry her jacket, since he had a small backpack. He smiled a little like Harrison Ford, who she thought was sexy for an ancient guy.

After their second run, at the bottom of High Noon, Lu leaned toward her. "I dunno 'bout you, but I need to get off this crud and ski some *powder*."

It seemed an odd statement from someone who was being paid extravagantly to offer an occasional hint. So far Katy was not impressed with Lu.

But surely Rene wouldn't send her a bummer. "How're my turns?" Katy asked.

"Too good for dumb slopes like this. We oughta go get in some heavy-duty carving."

"Look. The only reasons I ski with Rene my first day out is she takes me where she feels I need the practice and tells me what I'm doing wrong. So *take* me and *tell* me, okay?"

The sarcasm went over the head of Lu for Lucille, who looked back at the bodyguards. "Hon, those guys don't fit in on tough slopes. They might get hurt, you know."

Katy bristled at the "hon." "You pick the run. I'll follow you, they'll follow me."

Lu did that. She went to the top, started down an intermediate, then slipped over the side of a steep one called Three

O'Clock. Katy had no trouble. In fact it was Lu who made a turn to slow down when they got to a slick chute where the answer was to tuck and go. Even the bodyguards did better than Lu. When she caught up as Katy waited at the Sundown Express chairlift, she mumbled something about a cramp in her leg.

Katy didn't care that Lu was not much of a tutor. She was getting her legs back and by tomorrow she'd have her wind. All she needed was to ski a few more slopes.

They took the lift, the chair wide enough for three but with only the two of them aboard.

On the ride to the top the temperature plummeted, and Katy wished she had her jacket. But the bodyguards were in the chair a hundred feet to their rear.

Katy stared out to their right, where dark storm clouds were roiling. Lu for Lucille was grumbling again. "Won't be long before that stuff hits. Why don't I take you down a *good* run?"

"That's what I want." She let the sarcasm back into her voice.

"When we get on top, let's drop over into the back bowl."

Katy had seen the warning signs. "That one's roped off. It's restricted."

"That's for tourists. There's a cornice way over to the right to avoid, but the left side's safe. It's loaded with virgin powder, and there's just enough trees to make it fun."

"But it's off-limits."

"That's what the sign says." She grinned. "I skied it this morning."

"The bodyguards would pitch a fit."

"They see us go over the side, they gotta either follow or not, right?"

"They'd follow. It's their job."

"So . . . you game, kid?"

Katy despised being called kid even more than hon, and decided she did not like the instructor. It seemed odd that Rene would pick someone so—different.

"I don't think so," Katy answered.

"Scared?"

She bristled. Saw that Lu for Lucille was wearing a superior look. "Of *course* not."

"Then just follow me. Don't worry, I'll keep us out of trouble. We'll stop a couple hundred yards down the slope so the bodyguards can catch up."

They were approaching the top. Below them a purple snowmobile was parked, and beside it a man in a black ski mask was staring up at the chairs. Lu for Lucille lifted a hand in a sort of wave, and he lowered his face into a mittened hand, as if speaking into a radio.

"You know him?" Katy asked. She'd said she was from Vermont and had only worked at Steamboat for a couple of weeks.

Lu gave a vague nod.

Katy almost chickened out, almost told her she'd wait for the bodyguards. But of course if the guards had anything to do with it, they'd stop her from taking any kind of restricted run. They were at the top of the chairlift, and had to drop off.

"Follow me," said Lu.

"I don't think . . ." Katy began, but Lu ignored her and headed straight for a sign reading, AVALANCHE POTENTIAL, TRAIL CLOSED, and zigzagged around it.

The bodyguards will see me, Katy thought, *and they'll follow.*

She schlussed around the sign, and started down.

Katy did not see the chairlift behind them stop, or know that the bodyguards were not in view as she and the instructor dropped over the side. Back at the bottom of the lift an out-of-control skier had crashed into a threesome at the red line, just as they were loading. The attendant had hit the stop button and gone to their assistance. The lift was stalled for a full minute.

When the bodyguards arrived at the top, their ward in silver and black was nowhere to be seen. They made a right turn onto a long and rambling intermediate run called Tomahawk, hoping to catch up at the chairlift below. Katy was normally more considerate, and it was quite unlike her to try to ditch them.

The woman radioed their base station, set up by the two other security officers in the condo in Ski Town. "There's a problem. Kitten's out of our view."

"Will you have trouble catching up?"

"Don't know. We'll call from the bottom of the run. Snow's starting to fall and the temperature's dropping, so she'll need her jacket."

The closed ski run was rated a *double*-black diamond, meaning that even in normal times it was off-limits to all but the very best. It began with a ten-foot jump from a ledge into a narrow chute. Oddly there was none of the powder promised by Lu. It was more like ice, and the chute would have been treacherous if Katy hadn't leaned forward, kept her skis headed downhill, and let it all hang out.

While it looked scary—especially with the humongous cornice on their right, which actually was a buildup of ice holding back a few hundred tons of snow—it was not *that* difficult, even though Katy had been away for a year. But it was well beyond Lu for Lucille's skill level. Halfway down the chute the instructor chickened out, leaned back, flailed, and lost it, and then sprawled. The hill was so steep that she hardly slowed down, but instead zinged along with only her butt in contact with the ice.

Katy held up at the first moderately level area, turned, and gawked as she watched the ungraceful slide. She caught one of Lu's skis then the other, then observed as she came to a halt a dozen feet away. She made a pained sound, but as far as Katy could see all that was bruised was her ego. And maybe her bum.

As Lu struggled upright, Katy stomped over with her skis. The instructor laboriously clicked boots into bindings, with Katy providing a steadying hand. Then Lu held on to *her,* huffing and frantically scanning about as Katy tried vainly to pull free.

Lu spotted a pair of snowmobiles parked another hundred

yards downhill. Both were purple, like the one they'd seen when riding the chairlift, and one towed a stretcher sled.

Like that driver, these too wore black ski masks that covered their faces. The snowmobile engines revved, and they started toward them.

Lu for Lucille grasped Katy's hand firmly. "I'd like you to meet a couple people," Lu said in a nasty tone. That was hint one. Other alarms rang as Katy noted that the bodyguards were nowhere in sight. She had really, *really* screwed up. A kidnapping effort!

Katy was determined not to make it easy for them. No *way*. She'd gotten herself into the mess, and would get herself out. As the snowmobiles grew closer, one of the drivers delved into his snowsuit. She tried to pull loose from Lu's grasp, but the instructor held on to her mittened hand with surprising strength. Katy squealed and twisted, and pushed her off balance. Lu flailed, and found herself holding an empty mitten. She clawed as Katy turned, and grabbed the leather strap of her fanny pack. Katy lashed out with a ski pole, heard Lu's curse, and lunged hard.

The strap broke. She was freed. Katy pushed off, noting in the corner of her eye that the snowmobile drivers were waving pistols. A plume of snow kicked up nearby, then another. One weapon was silent, but the other made tremendous, concussive sounds.

The idiots were shooting at her! Katy had no time for proper fright as she crouched and skied diagonally across the wide run, heading for the steep area beneath the massive cornice, the danger zone where the rim of ice held back tons of snow.

The engine sounds grew louder, and there were more pistol reports.

At the steepest point she would turn downhill to get up a bag of speed. Only a cretin would dare follow down the treacherous run to the only ski lift in the back bowl.

She peeked to her rear. Sure enough, both snowmobiles were in her wake, bouncing wildly, drivers waving pistols like cowboys, *gaining*. Lu for Lucille following. Not an instructor at all. A fake! Katy had sensed something was amiss and had *still* gone with her.

"Fool!" she screamed at herself. Fear gathering like a thick ball in her throat.

There were more gunshots, and Katy's concern grew as the snowmobiles drew closer. As soon as she turned downhill there was no way they'd be accurate. No way, José, while bumping down a supersteep slope.

Another thought: how could they kidnap her if they killed her? So were they *really* shooting to hit her?

She made a sharp kick turn, headed straight down the hill, and heard more gunshots.

There was an ominous rumble from behind, then a loud crack, and Katy knew that one had not come from her pursuers. Their shooting had triggered an avalanche.

Her heart pounded. She was grateful that Lu for Lucille had been wrong, that instead of powder she was skiing on ice. No good to carve on, difficult to turn, but she could go *very* fast.

She tucked, head, knees, and hands forward, streamlined to offer minimum wind resistance—then wanted to go even faster because in the periphery of her vision she saw chunks of ice bouncing and tumbling, catching up and bringing even more terror into her throat.

The noise of the avalanche grew to a deafening roar that filled her senses. It was likely she only imagined the terrified screams from behind. The icy surface beneath her skis lifted and then tossed her, and she was caught in the roiling, tumbling mass.

4

Link was at his desk, tense as a drawn bow. A thought echoed: *Someone close to you is in danger!* Sweat gathered on his forehead, although the office was not warm.

He stood on shaky pins and looked about, wondering, thinking that something was happening *right now*. Something bad. Something involving . . . evil. And to someone dear to him. He took a few steps from his desk. Seeking activity, wanting to normalize things. The sensation remained as he opened the door to Erin Frechette's outer sanctum.

"Two-seven-seven-five," she said into the phone, then listened. "I'll tell him," she said, disconnected, and peered at him. Frowned. "Everything okay?"

Link paused as the sensation began to subside.

"Yeah." He rubbed at his temple, wondering what it had been.

"That was Frank. Security's about to provide a status report on the threat to Paula and Katy. Five-thirty, in Frank's office again. Do you want me along?"

"Go ahead and pick up Johnny. I'll brief you tomorrow."

She tidied her desk. "I'm on my way, pardner. Got your sat phone?"

He patted his shirt pocket. "Yeah."

The troublesome sensation returned so quickly he had to brace himself.

"Link?" Erin's voice sounded from a distant tunnel.

Two years before, Link had been plagued by dreams that had had the habit of coming true. He had never determined the source, although his fiancée, now deceased, had been convinced it had to do with his Indian ancestry.

That smacked too much of the occult. Link did not believe in ghosts or smiling ETs with puppy eyes. Yet the dreams had come from *some* source.

His sense of foreboding was strong—and he was shaken. *Ridiculous,* he told himself.

"Link?" Erin repeated. On her feet now, with a supportive arm around him.

"I'm okay." The emotions receded. He took a breath. Exhaled it. "It's over."

"What's over?"

He fessed up. "A strong feeling that someone close to me is in trouble."

She examined him through suspicious eyes. "Take a seat while I check on your family and friends." He laughed somewhat nervously, but sat down as she'd directed. He noticed the time. Five-oh-two in the afternoon. With a certainty not born of logic, he felt that someone was in grave danger.

3:02 P.M.—Mount Werner, Steamboat Springs

Eerie silence followed the tumult, and Katy wondered if she was alive. Then a few sundry bruises began to throb, and she discerned a chunk of ice an inch or so before her nose.

She was obviously buried, but did not know how deep or have a reference to up or down. *Then* she remembered the rest, Lu for Lucille, people on snowmobiles shooting at her, the avalanche.

Get out! her mind cried, and she tried to recall Rene's "If you're buried in snow" lessons. It came back in steps: Stay calm. Take stock. Create an air pocket so you can breathe. Dig out.

If you can't reach the surface, make an air vent with a ski pole.

Katy flailed wildly to form the pocket, and suddenly the rest no longer mattered. She sat up, sputtering snow and chunks of ice.

The storm had arrived with a vengeance. It was snowing hard, already in white-out conditions. She started to yell for help, then remembered Lu and the snowmobiles.

She felt around, found both poles but only a single ski. Took stock. Nothing seemed to be broken or terribly bruised. Her right mitten had been pulled off, but she had both glove liners. Also missing was the fanny pack with goggles, money, identification, tan lotion, and lip balm.

All of those were replaceable when she got back, which was what she had to concentrate on doing. She did not want to take long because the bodyguard had her jacket and it was getting colder by the minute.

She *could* continue on only one ski. Would have to.

Katy struggled to her feet, noting the ghostly snowmobile a few feet distant. The exposed hood and single runner made it looked like the shark in *Jaws*, about to leap out of the snow.

Then her heart did a pitty-pat, for there was movement. An arm emerged, then a head and torso. The ski mask was missing, revealing a male face. Long hair. Swarthy features set in a pained expression. Scar over his right eye. His teeth were clenched, exposing a gold incisor as he released a groan. He continued wriggling free, babying a left arm that was bent at an odd angle. He dropped something, dragged himself farther out, and lay panting. Ten yards distant and staring directly at Katy as he lifted the dropped object, a radio.

Blowing snow obscured him. "Axel—nghh, Madre de Dios!—ngghh, Guteriez es . . ."

The response was immediate. Incredibly deep. Too faint to understand all the words. Something about using English.

"Nggh . . ." Guteriez gasped. "I'm in the back bowl. The fuckin' mountain fell on us."

". . . heard a rumble . . . thought . . . thunder . . . everyone okay?"

"Shit no. My arm's broke and Jorge and Lu are buried."

"How . . . Kitten-bitch?"

"Just below me. Doesn't look hurt. Can't see her now and couldn't do anything about her anyway 'cause I lost my gun. You better send someone."

"Two shooters . . . enough?"

"More. Somebody's gotta find Lu and Jorge. The Kitten-bitch can't get to the other side long as the lift's covered. She's here, and hey, I'm in *pain*." He added a moan for emphasis.

"Hang tight . . . help. Get a chance go ahead and kill her, then . . . everyone out."

Kill her? The word had been distinct. Her mind churned as the man pleaded for them to hurry. She overheard Axel talking to others on the radio.

Get out of here! Katy's second ski had not turned up, so she'd have to go on without it.

Guteriez was obscured, but he said he'd found his gun.

Katy pressed to make sure her boot was locked in the binding, and pushed off with both poles. Felt awkward at first, but picked up speed. She heard the man's voice, sounding more excited. He'd probably discovered she was gone. She leaned into the snow unable to see due to the ghostly flat light. Everything, falling snow, surface, looked the same.

Unlike the front of Mount Werner, the back side was uninhabited. No condos or hotels. No homes. Not many ski hill people either, for all runs led to a single, central chairlift. When they shut it down, anyone left behind had to use an emergency telephone there. So all she had to do was get to the chairlift. Right?

But what about Guteriez saying the lift was *covered*. Were bad guys waiting there?

She had to decide very quickly, for with all the snow the lift would soon shut down, leaving only the telephone.

If the phone was left operable.

Katy heard sounds ahead, turned in an awkward arc and planted her poles as she stopped. Listened to the rumbling of an engine that had revved to life just below and was now idling.

The wind had picked up, blew a chill and a shudder through her. If the snowmobile was at the lift, it was close. Katy looked up, trying to see lines or dangling chairs. Nothing.

She had to do *something*. They were trying to *kill* her. She wished Maggie Tatro were here with her "little gun." But no one was here, and whatever was done would be up to Katy, so think!

She'd disliked Lu for Lucille, and a feeling had told her something was wrong with it all. Her mother said women were often intuitive when it came to danger. Why hadn't she listened?

No more mistakes. She could not afford them. So, where to next? If the chairlift was being watched, she'd have to make it to safety some other way, and leave no trail to follow. Link Anderson had shown her how to be stealthy in a forest. Move like the wind, he'd told her. Like a cat. When they'd selected a code name for security purposes, her father had picked Kitten.

Katy liked Snow Cat even better. *Stealthy* Snow Cat. Talking it over like that built a façade of courage, and some of her fear evaporated. Aside from the one below she heard the engine sounds of more distant snowmobiles, two up the slope behind her, others farther away.

The shooters sent by the deep radio voice named Axel?

Or a safety patrol examining the avalanche? She would not know until they were close.

A vague voice wafted up from the idling engine. A deep voice responded.

Axel.

A gust cut though the fake-fleece like it was not there. *Think smart!* Katy told herself. *Make an escape plan.*

She didn't know how many there were or, except for Guteriez and Lu for Lucille, what they looked like. They knew her, though. Even her code name. She felt a flush of hopelessness.

Stop that! It would soon be dusk. Perhaps two hours of light remaining. That meant she had to be more watchful for that long. Maybe hide somewhere. Link had taught her that searchers see what they believe should be there. They'll look for things they relate to humans. If there are trees around, become foliage. If there are rocks, become a stone. But all that had been in the summer. Here she was stuck on the wrong side of a ski mountain, freezing her boobs off.

And she had to make sure she *didn't* freeze. She had to find something to layer herself with. Like paper or fabric. A newspaper could save you.

And finally, which way to go? *Come on, pokey, think!*

Back to Link's instructions. Searchers expected their quarry to be predictable. Or at least to use logic. So do the unexpected and go where they wouldn't believe.

Katy took in a breath, consciously evened her pulse rate, and imagined that Link was here, guiding her.

"Use your head and fake them out."

Where would they expect her to go? Answer: to the ski lift to use the telephone. She'd heard them say they were covering it. She'd heard the snowmobile. So she couldn't go there.

Next they might expect her to find a place to hole up. They would search every hut, nook, and cranny, and mound of snow. So regardless of how good that had sounded, it was out.

If she did neither of those they might think—although it was slippery and steep—she would climb the mountain to get to the restaurants and buildings on the other side.

So what was left? Go around the mountain? If she tried

that, they'd think she would head north, where after a few miles she'd find homes.

Which left the longest and least likely option. If she went south and got lost, she could walk all the way to Rabbit Ears Pass, and then maybe even to Denver before reaching civilization. Also, going south around the mountain was a long trek and she'd likely freeze.

Nope, they'd certainly not suspect it. It would be dumb to go that way.

Katy would do it—walk around Mount Werner the long way.

Do not get lost! Answer: Remain at the same elevation, traversing on the ski when possible, and she shouldn't wander off the mountain. The route would eventually lead to homes, and then to the condo in Ski Town, where she'd get gloriously warm, and never again get out of sight of her bodyguards.

Without waiting she pushed off in an arc to her right, and angled across the open slope. And *just* as she approached the middle of the wide run, in the most exposed position, the sounds of two snowmobile engines blared from above, coming toward her and coming *fast*.

She wanted desperately to turn downhill and flee, but the driver of the snowmobile at the chairlift would see her, and with no slope remaining, there'd be nowhere for her to go.

C'mon, ski! Go faster! Katy gritted her teeth, poled hard, and continued the traverse, hearing the machines drawing so close they might even run into her. Mind begging that the drivers would be looking in other directions. She stopped, froze, pulled in a breath as they roared past like specters— one to either side!

They were immediately out of sight, but two male voices raised above the din of the engines, screaming: "That was her!" "Get the bitch!"

A driver yelled shrilly for the other to "Watch out!" then, "Don't . . ." And then "Aw *shit*!" There was the screech and scrape sounds of collision. Next the thump, thump, thump of a snow machine rolling down the hillside. Simultaneous angry yells. A pained squeal.

Katy dug in with both poles, levering forward, traversing the hillside. Except for whimpers and groans there were no new sounds from below. No idling engines. The two drivers had collided, then tumbled with their snowmobiles into the one waiting at the lift.

"Thank you," Katy whispered fervently as she entered the trees. From up-mountain she heard the sounds of more snowmobiles, and her shivers were not only from the chilling cold.

5:25 P.M.—Weyland Building, New York City

Link was on his way up to the meeting, still thinking about the mental alarms. After the previous incidents had turned out to be true, a psychologist had explained that it had to do with short-and long-term memories working together, mulling through inconsequential tidbits that when put together had meaning. Fighter pilots called it situational awareness, women intuition. The phenomenon occurred more frequently among identifiable ethnic groups, such as certain North American Indians. Like the Piegan Blackfeet, Link's ancestors.

Today's discomfort had indicated something amiss, but left it to him to sort out.

Supervising Agent Gordon Tower had dropped by room 2775 as Erin was leaving, and she'd ratted on Link about his déjà-whatever-it-was, asking Tower to keep an eye on him. To his credit Gordon had not blinked, although he likely believed Link was a relative of the Mad Hatter.

Now he accompanied Link down the final hall toward Frank's office, telling him that Maggie's information about the Voice's phone call had borne no fruit. With the distributor dead and no new leads, they knew no more than before. There was a rumor that the distributor had been replaced.

"Efficient," Link said.

"Yeah. The Mexicans are more organized than the Colombians ever were. The DEA guys like it that now the bodies are so neatly laid out. The old crimson necktie bunch were sloppy."

"Anything new about the threat against the Duboises?" Link asked.

"Not yet," said Tower. "Hopefully it was a false alarm."

As they walked into the massive office, Frank Dubois was chatting with the director of safety and chief investigator. Good. It was to be informal.

Frank was smiling. "Good news. Looks like it was a false alarm."

The chief investigator was smug. "We ran it by every contact, including the FBI. Nothing. The NYPD has nil. Same with the DEA, even though Ms. Tatro said it was a plot by the—ah—drug community." If his voice had been an expression, it would have been a sneer.

"With your concurrence, and assuming there's nothing new, I would like to reduce the number of security people at Steamboat," said the director of safety.

A shudder trembled through Link's body. *Frigid!* Someone close to him. *Cold!*

"Not yet," he said, breaking into the director's soliloquy about false alarms.

"Wha . . ." began the director of safety.

While it was cool in New York, what Link had just experienced was bone-chilling.

"Katy," he erupted aloud, suddenly sure. He drew a ragged breath and got to his feet. Feeling better now that his intuition had a target. There was no doubt in his mind. It was Katy Dubois who was in trouble. In Steamboat Springs. In peril and cold.

Frank was growing pale.

"Do you know something we don't?" asked the chief investigator. Almost accusingly.

"A feeling. I'll call you from the airplane, Frank."

Frank's secretary came in. "A call for Mr. Dubois. Line one."

He took the call, and regarded Link. Whispered, "Katy's missing," and handed the phone to his director of safety.

"I wouldn't worry until we're sure foul play is involved," cautioned the chief investigator.

Link needed no more. "I'm going to Steamboat." He reached into his shirt pocket for the sat phone. Pressed MEM and 1. Erin was still in a taxi, traffic-bound as she headed for home. He told her the problem and his intention. She told him to go to the rooftop for the helicopter, that she was setting up her laptop and would arrange everything.

"We have security people at the ski hill," said the director of safety, as if Link might get in their way. He ignored him. "I'll call from the airplane," he told Frank.

"I'll accompany you." His friend's voice was shaken.

"I'd prefer if you stayed here and ran things," Link told him.

"Gentlemen," said the director of safety in a soothing voice. "There's no reason for alarm. All the bodyguards are saying is that they've temporarily lost contact. There's a snowstorm, so that isn't unreasonable."

Link started for the door. "Mind if I tag along?" asked Supervising Agent Gordon Tower, catching up as Link reached the hallway. As the two men called for an elevator, the satellite phone buzzed in Link's hand.

He flipped it open. "Anderson."

Erin spoke in clipped tones. "The Lear jet's in Washington and both Gulfstreams are out of town. Did you want to wait, or take the MCP." The prototype mobile command post.

He was not anxious to try something new. "How long if I wait for a G-four."

"Fifty-minute wait plus the time to refuel."

"We'll take the MCP if you can find the crew?"

"Be back at you." She was off for the following thirty seconds. Then, "The test pilot's on his way to Teterboro now. No response from the other crewmembers, but they shouldn't be long."

"He's all I'll need." Link had received two check rides in the airplane. The test pilot had been a Lockheed-Martin safety engineer on the MCP project, and was an expert on the aircraft. They would be enough.

"Gotcha," said Erin. "I'll file a flight plan for Steamboat Springs." She was off the phone for a few more seconds, and came back on as Link and Gordon reached the rooftop. "You're filed with the FAA. I also got an update from security. There's still no sign of Katy."

The helicopter on the rooftop pad was starting engines. "Tell me more," Link said as the two men strode toward the bird. Erin explained what had happened on the ski lift, how when the bodyguards got to the top, Katy was gone. About then there'd been an ice slide in the back bowl.

"Could she have been caught in it?" he asked.

"They don't think so, but now the mountain's shutting down because of the storm, and they're having trouble getting any of the skiers down. It's a bad scene, Link. Everything's in whiteout, the temperature's dropping, and Katy's somewhere there in light clothing. Security's saying it's not the first time a teenager's ducked her bodyguards, and she's probably fine. They even feel she might even be off the hill, maybe with friends somewhere."

"If that's the case, I'll turn back." But it would not happen. His apprehension lingered.

"Darn. I'm looking at the weather on my laptop. The Steamboat Springs airport's shutting down. There's an all-weather runway at Routt County Airport, thirty miles west."

"Yeah." It was called Hayden Field, and he had landed there before. "File us for there."

"Damn," she exclaimed. "Now I show that all landing aids at Hayden were just declared inoperable. With this weather you'll need them. Link, I don't know if you're going to have anywhere to land."

3:40 P.M.—Snowbird Luxury Condominiums, Ski Town

No one intentionally awoke Maggie, but there was no way to sleep through the clamor from the adjacent suite, where security had their computers, phones, and radios.

She pulled on the same ski outfit, and went next door. "Something up?" she asked as she slipped past the bodyguard who had responded.

The security supervisor was at the table, wearing a headset. "Stay out of it," he snapped.

"Get real. I've got a contract says I work with you guys."

"Still a no-show," lamented a woman's voice over the radio.

Maggie yawned. "They're paying me to follow the kid around, remember."

"Like you did today?"

"Hey, friend. It says *starting* today so I'm punching the clock now." She hoped Katy hadn't eaten. She was famished. "Where is she, so I can start my tagging along?"

The supervisor pointed at the window, where the snowfall was horizontal. "She ditched her bodyguards, and now she's up there *somewhere*."

Maggie's voice sobered. "Talk to me about it." *Damn!*

Somewhere between the explanation about the substitute instructor and the lift being shut down because of a wild skier, she lost her appetite. When he explained the ice slide in the back bowl, she felt sick. The supervisor took more negative radio reports, yet did not seem concerned. He called it "probable willful evasion."

"Bull," Maggie said under her breath.

The two bodyguards had been positioned at key points on the ski hill, checking out all female tourists the ski patrols were bringing in. The supervisor kept a phone circuit open with his office in New York, who were tracking events.

"How can I help?" Maggie asked, worrying even more now that the light was beginning to fade. Her headache had returned, every bit as bad as it had been that morning.

The supervisor took a call on the scrambled satellite

phone, grunted a couple of times like he was taking orders, then turned to her. "That was my office in New York. You're no longer in the game. Just stay out of the way until we find her," she was told.

"Yeah, right." Her voice dripped with sarcasm as she took a seat.

Damn!

5

Axel Nevas was uncharacteristically intense, for things were not going as he'd intended. He enjoyed discipline. Each morning he exercised his body, then his mind by detailing the day's schedule. He accomplished those things in their listed order. Predictability was something you either expected or made happen—or how could you master your world.

As an Aztecan high priest, Axel knew that predictability was often the discriminator that set great men and wise gods apart from the rest. Take Centeotl, the god who was concerned with corn, or Tonatiah, who fussed over the brilliance of the sun and making sure time remained constant. They knew the importance of being predictable. His own Huitzilopóchtli could be relied upon to be fierce and warlike.

But all of that changed when it came to weather. The Aztecan gods Tlaloc and Ehecatl, lords of rain and wind, were often fickle. And meteorologists? As Henny Youngman might say, "Take them *please*." Even with all of their schooling, their satellites and radars and computers, they could not foretell the path of a simple low-pressure-generated storm system.

Axel stared out. A carriage lamp was illuminated at the corner of the chalet, just thirty feet distant, but the snow was so obscuring that it might as well be off. The TV announcer called it the storm of the decade. They expected a two-foot accumulation by morning.

But the storm was not all that was wrong. The plan had been to take the Kitten-bitch on her very first run. They'd been forced to alter everything because of the ineptitude of the ski instructor, who had taken the girl to the wrong trail!

A man came in, stomped his feet to knock off the ice, and angrily pulled off his ski mask. He'd been outside working on a balky snowmobile and had come in to warm up.

Axel kept his mind on the project dubbed STOPPER. Reviewing errors.

Although he'd had everyone looking, they'd lost track of the instructor and the Kitten-bitch for an entire hour, had not spotted them again until they'd been in line for the express lift. The woman had absently touched her ear—a signal to change to the backup plan—and they'd frantically begun to reposition shooters, snowmobiles etc., hoping she wasn't screwing up again.

Now Axel had a worse mess on his hands. The instructor and Jorge, his snowmobile expert, were buried on the mountain. They'd not looked for them. Their fate was obvious since they'd been caught in the jumble of ice and rocks.

But where the hell was the Kitten-bitch?

On his belt were two cell phones that he wore in holsters like a gunfighter. He should call Marta, who liked to be called "the Voice," but failure was not something he admitted to easily.

Guteriez, the distributor from Denver, sat nearby, arm in a sling fashioned from a towel until he could get to medical care, casting hard looks because he needed someone to blame for his injury. In his other life he was a mean bastard who could snap his fingers and make people die. Here he and the others answered to Axel. All were neatly groomed, with no earrings or telltale body jewelry to draw attention. Except for the instructor, all were men. Their business was male-dominated. There were no equal opportunity boards in the drug trade.

He had reliable people. The two who were not drug distributors, the captain and sergeant, had worked for Axel for four years. The distributors were intelligent managers of personnel and critical assets. In their positions they routinely considered demographics and supply and demand and power structuring. They empowered and set goals for subordinates. On an average, seventy people worked directly for each of them. Indirectly, on the streets, in neighborhood laboratories and related businesses, hundreds more. They controlled banking investments, and scheduled vessels and aircraft, and interstate trucking rigs.

"Snow's coming down *heavy*," said the one who had just come in.

"I can see that," Axel replied, voice rumbling like angry thunder.

The distributors were able to hone their management skills because there was no excuse for failure. The Voice provided accurate information, the key to success in any business.

It was all made possible by the Voice.

Ha! If you believed that, you might believe that pigs flew.

The god Huitzilopóchtli made it happen through the work of his servant and priest, Axel Nevas. Who had established the listening posts called T-Can East and T-Can West. Who between them heard everything of any slight importance to the trade. Which was passed on to the Voice. Who passed on all of importance to the distributors.

If a distributor was out of line in a way that irritated the Voice or the dead man, he and his top men became offerings to great Huitzilopóchtli. Axel Nevas sacrificed freely.

Business was up. Problems were down. As long as the distributors were effective they were kept rich. If they grew greedy and Axel or the Voice or the dead man were made angry, they might as well start slicing, because they'd lose their balls and their ability to breathe. Or more likely, Axel would make them part of a triangle or square, or another symbol.

Keep the Voice and the dead man happy.

Now they wanted the Kitten-bitch dead, so dead she must become.

On Wednesday, after the ten distributors had arrived and been shown their bedrooms, Axel had gathered them for a motivation step and said in his rasp, "Being important business people, you may think you can argue with me." He'd looked around as though he were making up his mind, and settled on a big, gangsta-looking tough guy from New York named Garcia they all knew. He had beckoned, and Garcia had come up. Grinning, strutting, and preening, because he was that kind of person.

Axel had acted as if Garcia had not been specifically selected. Reached behind him like he was his buddy, and smiled to the group. *Pop!*

The tough guy had dropped, kicked a few times, and was still.

"For you, great Huitzilopóchtli," he had intoned, which went unheard because the others were shuffling and staring with open mouths.

Axel had replaced the small ornate pistol into a hidden belt holster. "From now until you get home, do what you're told."

They'd understood the motivation step.

With himself, Torré and Santos included, there were an even dozen. A powerful number. Numbers and geometry were important to the Aztec priest.

Axel had next shown photos and videos of the Kitten-bitch on big-screen TV, and told them they were gathered to kill her. "Make her disappear so it looks like a kidnapping, but that isn't as important as killing her. Get away clean and leave no traces, but *kill* her."

One girl? Most of them felt it would be a cakewalk.

He'd explained the girl's schedule. Told them the condo and suite and room she'd stay in. About her security detail that would set up next door. He'd given names and profiles of her regular ski instructor and the bodyguards and the local law enforcement people who had already been briefed on the girl's arrival.

He'd introduced the woman from Vermont, who would replace the girl's ski instructor and lead the Kitten-bitch to the attack site. There they would isolate the Kitten-bitch from her bodyguards, strap her to a medical litter, and haul her away. Fast! The others would block the bodyguards and confuse things while a mile away they rendezvoused with an unmarked helicopter. Later Axel would toss the girl out somewhere over the Rockies.

The remainder would ditch the snowmobiles and snowsuits, and melt into the crowds at the bottom of the hill.

He had them memorize radio codes. "Memphis" meant it was done, time to abandon the suits and masks and gloves and become model citizens. "Frisco" meant the opposite, to kick ass and make blood. Take out cops. Make examples of citizens. Anything it took to accomplish the objective. As he explained it, grins came to faces, because the distributors had another thing in common. They enjoyed hurting people.

"Takin' *over*!" Guteriez had said with a smirk. "I like Frisco."

"Well I don't," Axel told him, "because that means things have become difficult."

"New York" was the recall word. In the event they had to get out *tout de suite.* Calm Memphis, Wild Frisco, and Hurry-up New York. Remember them.

He went over alternative plans, in case something went awry. The last one was to shift operations to the back bowl. And during all of that Axel left the unlucky Garcia on the floor, leaking blood. A reminder they had to periodically step over.

The following morning had begun early. Preparing, just as Axel did in his personal life. They'd rehashed the plans and radio codes. Then went out to the snowmobiles.

Private machines weren't permitted in the mountain's ski areas, but these were purposefully similar to those of the ski patrol, and even if discovered the authorities often went light on tourists. They could get away with it for a single day.

Jorge gave the snowmobiling lessons, and most had a good time. They wore dark, unremarkable snowsuits and knit caps and ski masks whenever outside. Even when riding in boring circuits around the chalet.

Then back inside where he issued weapons. They'd all have pistols, and either a short shotgun or Ingram machine pistol. He'd displayed and explained a map of Mount Werner and Ski Town. A final practice jaunt on the snowmobiles, this time carrying the secreted weapons. Jorge helped them top off their gas tanks.

That evening Axel showed more video clips of the girl. Blonde, pretty, tiny mole on her right cheek, walking out to a limo with bodyguards fore and aft. "Kitten-bitch," they were all now calling her. Not a human, but an objective. Kill her and go home to the big bucks.

It seemed unlikely that it could have gone *that* wrong.

Now Axel went down the list written neatly into his notebook. On the left were names. On the right locations, which he erased and penciled in as they moved about on the mountain.

It was maddening. All those people, all so capable and tough, acting like a group of clowns. Two had been lost in the ice slide: Jorge and the instructor. Guteriez was reduced to whining about the broken arm. Two others hurt when they'd seen the Kitten-bitch and tried to turn, and ran into *another* snowmobile and knocked the driver loopy. One was now looking on foot because his snowmobile was too damaged to drive.

They'd been left with seven operating snowmobiles, and one idiot on foot.

He'd drawn a grid on the map, and was trying to direct them, but a half hour before one had radioed that he was lost. Another machine had broken down in front of the hill. That one had been driven by the man who had come in to warm up.

So now they had five operating machines and *two* idiots on foot. It was like a comedy, with clowns running around sticking their thumbs in their eyes while the Kitten-bitch laughed.

A radio crackled: "This is Torré."

Good. Captain Torré was rock-tough and *listened.* "This is Axel."

Torré told him his snowmobile was giving him trouble.

"Well *fix* the damned thing," Axel thundered, exasperated.

A cell phone buzzed. A report from T-Can West, in Denver. Axel pulled the map over and penciled X's here and there on the mountain. "Those are ski patrols," said the contact. "They're asking everyone coming off the hill about the girl."

"How about up higher?" Axel asked "And on the back side?" Oddly it did not seem strange to be getting information about the situation here from so far away.

"Your own people are the only ones back there. When the ski patrol hears a snowmobile—they can't see them but they hear them—they call on a bullhorn for them to come down"

Axel knew that was true. They periodically heard the broadcasts.

The contact gave more locations, these in Ski Town, which was just down the hill from the chalet, and Axel annotated the positions of law officers. One on-duty city policeman in a cruiser. There were two others, but they were in Old Town. Two deputies were at the county prison, even farther away. Two off-duty highway patrolmen were drinking in a local bar.

The Weyland Foundation security people had telephoned for assistance from the chief of police—called the supervisor of public safety. He'd be along after dinner.

Axel looked at the X's on the map. "What are the bodyguards reporting to New York?"

"The one in charge believes the girl's willfully evading them. When the weather clears he feels they'll find her, possibly with the instructor somewhere in Ski Town."

"Then there's still no declared emergency?"

"Yes and no. Frank Dubois seems worried, and one of the Weyland Foundation vice presidents, Lincoln Anderson, is flying out with an FBI agent named Tower. Did you want more about either of them?"

The Aztec felt a tug of uneasiness. "Two men?" he considered. "When will they arrive?"

"Eight o'clock your time, but I doubt they'll be able to land. The airports are closed."

"Keep track of them." he said, and disconnected, wondering about his uneasiness since the foundation seemed to be even more screwed up than he was.

Except for the one named Lincoln Anderson. There, the feeling again.

"Axel?" came a radio call. Ortiz said he couldn't find his partner.

"You're not here to hold hands. Keep looking for the Kitten-bitch."

"We can't see screw-all. No one will find her in this stuff."

Another man grumbled. "Colder'n shit up here, man."

"Who said that?" Axel snapped, voice rumbling with fresh anger.

After a moment Torré's heavy accent came on the air. "I got the snowmobile running, but I'm freezing like ever'one else."

"Axel, Ortiz here again. Look, the Kitten-bitch doesn't even have a coat, she's a fucking icicle by now. It's just snowed so much we can't find her body."

He had a point, "Keep looking," Axel said, staring out, seeing nothing but blowing snow.

Ortiz again. "We gotta do something to get warm. Maybe it would be better to put this off until morning, when we can see"

"That is not going to happen," said Axel. "We'll look until we find her."

"Then let us break into one of the buildings up here so we can warm up."

Axel glared out the window, listened to more complaints on the radio.

He opened a holster on his belt, and withdrew the special cell phone. It was on a new crystal and a new number, which changed at noon, his time, wherever he was. The same precaution was made with the Voice's cell phone number. He was serious about security.

Axel heard a buzz, then a click, and then the Voice's monotone.

9:30 P.M.—Off Boca Raton, Florida

The boat owner leaned back in the hot tub, looking out at the lights of other anchored yachts and shuddering with sensations. Careful not to get the bandages on his face wet, for they were pressure sensitive and must not be tampered with. Contemplating his new name.

The one he would use until his death at an elderly age, when friends would come from the corners of the world to commiserate with his young widow and try to impress all the heirs he had produced. He would have all those friends, for he'd not only be handsome, but ebullient and outgoing. A moral man who contributed to good causes. The kind of person people respected.

For a while he might continue as a bachelor, but certainly not the reclusive type the last person with this name had been. No, he would seek out world-class females like Dodi and Ari had done, and lavish gifts upon them. Sooner or later he would pick one to marry. Someone worthy, who would bear fine sons.

He spoke the words "Carlos Alfonse David," and liked the sound. Anglo friends here would call him Carl David (Day-vid), Carlo David (Duh-'veed) when in his Mexico City penthouse or one of the beach homes in Rio or Cannes or Majorca.

He would assume the reclusive man's heritage as a Jamaican planter. Forget the rubbish that Axel Nevas spouted about being descended from the Lord Speakers of a vast kingdom.

He smiled. It would be enough to be known as the wealthiest

man in the world. The investments were being made even now under the new name. Industries purchased.

He groaned with an especially exquisite sensation, and returned to the present, holding firmly to the sides of the gurgling hot tub, feeling *good* as the blonde did her underwater business. *Almost there,* he thought, offering mental encouragement. The college girl from Madison he'd discovered sunbathing on his beach had a definite talent.

His sister came out on deck and started over. He hit the button that shut off the bubbles, so he would be able to hear her.

The blonde came up for air. She had pointed breasts that turned him on, and boasted that she could hold her breath for a very long time. To his pleasure he'd found it to be true.

Marta looked evenly at him, her face only a shadow with the deck light turned off. "We must talk," she said, meaning the blonde should not overhear.

He reached for a Cuban cigar, lopped off the end with a razor-sharp guillotine, popped it into his mouth and looked at the blonde. "Go back to work."

The girl wrinkled her nose. "With her watching?" When he nodded she took a resolute breath, and went under. The submerged tub lights illuminated her sufficiently that they could see her approach her objective. He found that humans would do anything for money. He'd promised her ten thousand dollars if she succeeded. He made a grunting sound as she made contact, and put a hand on her head to steady his ship.

Marta flicked a gold-inlaid Zippo and held the flame to his cigar. "Axel is calling."

"Mmm. He's still there?" he puffed the cigar and leisurely pressed his underwater hand up and down on the blonde's nape. "I thought he would be done by now."

"They're having difficulties because of snow and cold. He wants to allow his men to break into buildings so they can become warm. Otherwise they may freeze."

"So? Why is he asking?"

"They may have to confront policemen.

"So *kill* them. I want it done with. If he needs more people, more guns, airplanes, whatever, all he as to do is tell us. Give him whatever it takes."

"There'd be no way to get anything to him. Transportation is shutting down. Airports, roads, *everything*. He's worried about losing more of his people."

"The girl?"

"He feels she is already dead, but he must find out."

"Yes." As he thought it over the blonde began running out of air and tried to surface. He was not finished with the discussion, so he held her firmly in place.

Marta looked with interest as the blonde's legs began to thrash.

"Tell him to do what he must. Just *kill* the girl."

"Shoot policemen? We're not speaking about a Mexican village, Don Amado. It is. . ."

"Don't *call* me that!" he said angrily. "*Never* use that name again."

She winced and pulled back. "I apologize"

"I have decided upon Carlos, remember. Carlos David."

"Yes. *Carlos*." She nodded dutifully. "All I meant was that it is an American city with many tourists. If people are killed, there will be anger."

"What do we care if people are angry? If we lost every man there, if they were captured and tortured, the authorities could never trace them to us."

She hesitated. "Axel could," she finally said. "He knows us."

"Axel is a lunatic, but he is loyal. He would never turn on me." He snorted a laugh. "He thinks he is a priest and I am his king, remember?"

"Of course." Marta was staring at the spectacle under the water.

"Tell him to do whatever he must."

She walked from the deck, pausing to glance back as he released the blonde's head. The girl bobbed to the surface, clawing, snorting, and coughing up torrents of water.

"You didn't finish," he complained.

She had her mouth open and was gasping wildly for air. She began gagging and crying.

He leaned forward. "I said, you didn't finish."

It took her several tries. He'd smoked another cigar before she succeeded.

6

The flaps were down and the landing gear extended; the engines howled and the airplane sank earthward. Four eyeballs were glued straight ahead, staring out the windscreen.

Two of those belonged to Link Anderson, who was increasingly sold on the MCP. Not only was it airworthy, but the avionics were downright magical. A particular new technical concept—tuned aperture radar, or TAR—was most helpful. There were three of them, all relatively compact and having no moving parts. Good stuff.

One was housed in a bulbous pod on the top of the tail and looked skyward, another was mounted along the belly and stared toward the ground. Those two provided much of the capability of AWACS (airborne warning and control) and J-STARS (joint surveillance, targeting, and reconnaissance), although they did not have the range or full function of the larger systems. After all, the MCP was a small fraction of the size of AWACS or J-STARS birds.

But in their present blind visual conditions, with absolutely no help available from the inoperable systems at the airfield, it was the TAR located in the nose that was of particular help. The MCP test pilot, presently Link's copilot, had tuned to precision high-definition mode, and had the heads-up display on.

Although they could see only a blur of snow, electronically superimposed on the windscreen was an electronic picture of the runway two miles straight ahead. The same picture was shown a few inches below on the multifunction display, should they wish to lower their eyes to change a switch or read a dial.

"Whiskey Foxtrot Five-One, this is Hayden, break off your approach and climb out," came a gruff radio call from the ground.

Link broke protocol by arguing. "Hayden, Whiskey Foxtrot Five-One would like to continue the approach. We have a good visual on the airfield."

"Thirty seconds until touchdown," said his copilot. Beads of perspiration on his forehead betrayed his concern.

"Negative, Whiskey Foxtrot Five-One. Break it off," Hayden repeated. "This ain't a request, buddy. Don't matter if you can see through weather, I just measured five inches of new snow on the runway, so unless you got skis you're gonna bust your butt."

That they could *not* see on any scope.

"Whiskey Foxtrot Five-One acknowledges," radioed Link, applying full power and starting the flaps up as he pulled back smoothly on the yoke. "We're breaking off the approach."

Erin had pulled every possible string to call out the Hayden fixed base operator and get him to have the runway plowed, but the snow was coming down far too heavily for them to keep up.

"Thanks for trying, Hayden," Link told the operator. "We'll be back at first light."

Link nodded to the copilot and released the controls. "You've got the airplane. Take her to Laramie, and put her down."

"Will do." The copilot exhaled a long breath of relief. Same with FBI Agent Tower, riding in the military-style web jump seat between them.

Link chose SECURE COMM on the communications wafer

switch. The call would make use of the same circuitry and satellites as his flip-top telephone. If someone tuned to the frequency, all they'd hear would be a series of squeals.

"Mind if I listen?" asked Gordon Tower, and Link switched him on.

Erin picked up on the first ring, although it was late there. "Were you able to land?"

"No, but it wasn't the airplane's or the airfield operator's fault. Mother Nature's dropping too much snow. We're heading to Laramie for the night. Any new developments?" he asked.

"Security feels that Katy's probably with friends. Also, all roads into Steamboat are closed. They'll send a gang of snowplows at first light, but nothing gets in or out until then. Umm. Your Miss Maggie Tatro called a few minutes ago, asking for a number to reach you. I told her I'd need your permission."

He had been thinking of the short redhead. "Go ahead and connect me."

"She was at a pay phone. I thought she was under contract to us."

"She is. Let me talk to the security office at Steamboat." He'd spoken with the supervisor earlier, but hadn't thought to ask for Maggie.

"Security," came the tired voice of the on-scene supervisor.

"Anderson here. We couldn't land, so we'll try again in the morning. Anything new?"

"No, sir. Like I just told Mr. Dubois, Kitten may be with friends, maybe even dancing somewhere. There's certainly no reason for you to become involved."

Link wanted to tell him to drop the bullshit. Instead he asked about the weather.

"Sixteen inches of new snow and still coming down. Now returning to our previous conversation, the police and the sheriff's people are all helping, and I feel confident that . . ."

"Don't," Link interrupted, unable to keep his irritation from showing.

"Ah—pardon me, sir?"

"Don't feel confident about anything until you know. Frank's fed up with the bull too."

The voice dropped. "Of course, sir. I was just . . ."

"Do you have any slightest clue to where she might be?"

"No, sir. But the ski patrol has dispatched two Sno-Cats to search the mountain, and the city police are looking in all the restaurants and discos."

"Sno-Cats? Where are they looking?"

"We figure Katy and her instructor would be savvy enough to try to make it to a lower elevation, so we're starting at the bottom and working our way up. It's a slow process because there's so much mountain to search, and we're in blizzard conditions."

"How about the avalanche? Have you searched the back bowl?"

"It's low on our priority list. Kitten knew to stay away from restricted areas."

Link had no further questions for the man. "Let me speak with Miss Tatro."

"She's . . . ah . . . no longer in the room."

"Why not? She's under contract."

"I was . . . umm . . . led to believe this was outside the terms of her duties."

"I don't have time for arguments. Get her, would you?"

The voice fell. "Yes, sir."

As Link waited he was increasingly displeased at the infighting. Security could become part of the problem. *Don't overreact,* he told himself, but he knew he had to correct the situation.

"Mr. Anderson?" Maggie's voice.

"Call me Link so they'll know we're friends."

"Sure . . . Link."

"What's going on?"

"They're giving me the mushroom treatment, keeping me in the dark, and refusing to let me participate."

"Put the supervisor back on."

"Yes, sir?" came the male voice, sounding strained.

"Miss Tatro was employed by the chairman of the foundation. Cooperate with her."

"My instructions are to exclude her until they've completed a background check."

Link controlled his temper. "Consider it completed. I'll personally vouch for her. If anyone has trouble with that, have them call me on their way out the door. How about you? Do *you* have trouble with it?"

"No, sir."

"Good. Make sure your office knows about this conversation so I won't have to hold it again. My patience is wearing thin on the subject. Now give me back to Maggie."

"Yes, sir."

"I heard," Maggie said a second later. "Thanks."

He gave her his sat phone number. "I have to terminate. Call if you learn anything."

Link switched off and watched as the copilot descended toward an airport just west of Laramie, Wyoming. They were beyond the periphery of the storm, and the night lights of the small city winked merrily, not at all in harmony with Link's mood.

11:10 P.M.—Suite 324, Snowbird Condos, Ski Town, Steamboat Springs

Maggie hung up, and waited on the security supervisor, who was instructing the bodyguard to relay his new instructions concerning Miss Tatro to New York. She typed the message into a laptop computer, connected via modem to the Weyland Foundation.

"Sorry it came to that," Maggie said.

"I don't have a problem, it's the office. Me, I wish you'd take over so I could rest."

"Just treat me like one of the crew."

"So what is it you want so bad you called in a code one-one?"

"What's a one-one?"

"Out of twenty thousand employees at the foundation, there are five code ones who run the place. Mr. Anderson is a code one-point-one, which means he answers to them—only. He's about as high as you can get without wearing oxygen."

From Link's relationship with the Duboises', Maggie had guessed he was a mover in the organization. She gave the supervisor a good-buddy smile to smooth feathers. "How about you just clue me in on what's developed, and include me in decisions from now on?"

"Sure." He held up a finger. "One, we're in constant contact with New York, and they're running the show, not me. Two, they're not convinced Kitten's in danger. Her group's been coming here for years, and she's made contact with the local crowd. She may be with friends."

"I don't think so. Katy's . . ."

"We'd prefer if everyone uses her code name."

"Sure. *Kitten* is a very normal, very presentable young woman, and wouldn't be seen dead off the hill without wearing a new outfit. I looked. She brought five, all of 'em knockouts."

He looked at her.

"She's either still on the mountain, or she's dead. And now I'm a full partner, I'd like to ask a favor of the sheriff."

He captured the attention of the woman at the laptop. "Check downstairs for the sheriff."

"Sure." The female bodyguard hurried out.

"While we're waiting," Maggie said, "fill me in on all the unauthorized snowmobiles I heard were running around the mountain."

"The safety patrol says it happens. Tourists get off the authorized snowmobile trails and take off on the ski slopes. And by the way, they're *still* up there."

"This late, and in a blizzard? Don't you find that odd?"

"Yeah, but they keep saying tourists do odd things."

"Until we know better, maybe we should consider them hostile."

"Until we *know* better, there's no reason to think they're anything but tourists."

She had a troublesome thought. "You sent the Sno-Cat crews out unarmed?"

"No way. Even if they're just dealing with liquored-up tourists, they could get in trouble. Each Sno-Cat's got a driver, one of my people, and a county cop."

"What are they carrying?"

"The deputies have nines, and our people have Ruger three-fifty-seven hideaways. They're issue, and about all our people can take on this sort of outing."

"You have anything bigger here?"

"No." His tone was regaining a defensive edge.

The bodyguard returned, ushering an older, brown-uniformed officer with an impressive handlebar mustache.

"Sheriff Davis, Miss Tatro is a part of our effort, and has a request."

Just then the sheriff received a radio call. The Safety Patrol reported a silent alarm from the gondola building on the mountain.

He told them to send a Sno-Cat crew. "Might be your Kitten," he told the supervisor.

"Sure hope so."

The sheriff regarded Maggie Tatro. "Better be quick, miss, 'cause I'm headed for my office on the other side of Old Town. There's people stranded on the highway both west and south of here, and the snow's still building."

"I'm concerned about an earlier development. Could you send someone to check on Kitten's normal ski instructor, the one who's supposed to be sick."

"Rene Clark," said the security supervisor. "I've got her address. We tried phoning earlier."

"And could you do the same," Maggie asked, "for the replacement instructor?"

"Lucille Shepherd," said the supervisor. "We have hers as well." His words were clipped.

"I'd like someone to drop by," she said.

The sheriff radioed for a deputy to check on both instructors, and then frowned at something he said. He looked up. "Another break-in's being reported on the mountain. Farther up, at the Saddle Rendezvous."

Fifteen minutes later an announcement came over the radio. "This is security in Sno-Cat one, at the gondola building. There are four snowmobiles in front and some lights on in the restaurant. The deputy and I are getting out to investigate."

"Tell them to be careful," warned Maggie. "Maybe draw their weapons."

The supervisor looked displeased, but he relayed her words.

"Will do. We're both outside, next to the building. Looks like the door's been jimmied."

The supervisor was lifting his microphone to respond when . . . *Bra-aa-aa-aat—pop, pop, pop, pop—Bra-aa-aa-aat—pop—Bra-aa-aa-aat.*

They turned in unison, gawking in the direction of the ski hill. "Is that what I *think* it is?" the female bodyguard asked in a tremulous voice.

"Yeah," said the sheriff, hurrying toward the door.

The security supervisor tried to contact his man in Sno-Cat one, but received no response. He phoned the ski safety patrol and advised them to order the Snow-Cats off the hill.

They'd heard the gunfire too, and Sno-Cat one was not responding.

The female bodyguard was already typing a new report on the laptop computer, informing New York that the search had entered a new, more dangerous phase.

Axel had heard the shooting, which had come as no surprise. T-Can had kept him informed about the Sno-Cats, and he had relayed warnings to his men on the hill.

A minute before Captain Torré had radioed that a Sno-Cat had pulled up in front of the gondola building where they'd broken in and were warming up.

Torré came back on the radio, gloating. "They didn't get

off a shot. Deputy and another guy were at the door with their pistols raised. I kept their attention while Santos went around and behind. He took them out, then the Sno-Cat driver."

Axel stared out at the still horizontal snowfall. He had been told to do whatever was necessary. He'd announced the code word "Frisco" and said they could break into buildings to warm up. He paused, adrenaline pumping like he'd been up there shooting. "Did you all hear what they did?" he radioed. "Do not look for trouble, but if anyone interferes, take care of the problem." That was the new rule of thumb. "Torré," he called. "Check the Sno-Cat. We may be able to use it in the search."

"Sure. Santos didn' shoot the motor or nothing."

Axel's contact at T-Can West called. Exuberant. "That got their attention. They're pulling the second Sno-Cat back."

"You did well too," Axel said. He felt pleased, and so did others. The gloves were only halfway off, but already they were back to telling jokes on the radio. He pulled the big map out and wondered if they were searching for the Kitten-bitch in the right places.

11:40 P.M.—General Brees Airfield, Laramie, Wyoming

Everything was shut down in the old hangar they'd rented, and the single light that remained on cast long shadows. Link had changed into rougher clothing, taking it from the B-4 bag he kept at Teterboro for just such purpose. He wearily took a chair at the side of the open office, intending to lean back and snooze so he'd be fresh in the morning.

First, though, a call to Steamboat. He was reaching for his pocket when the satellite phone buzzed. He flipped it open. "Anderson."

Erin's voice was sleepy. "New word from Steamboat Springs. There was gunfire on the mountain, and a Sno-Cat isn't reporting."

Link sat up, very awake. "Anyone hurt?"

"I've got Maggie Tatro on the line."

Maggie brought them up to speed. They'd heard sounds of gunfire, then no radio response from the Sno-Cat. "The other one's been recalled. Also, we just received word about the ski instructors." Rene Clark and Lucille Shepherd had been found in their separate apartments. Both executed, a small-caliber round administered to the back of the head.

Katy's new ski instructor had been a fake. She was up there alone.

"Seems crazy," Erin said, "that they'd go to all this trouble just to eliminate Katy."

"It's like they're desperate," Maggie said in agreement.

Link spoke up. "The snowmobiles are still running around on the mountain, right?"

"Yeah," Maggie said. "They're guessing seven or eight of them."

"Then they probably don't have her."

"I agree, but the police aren't about to send more people up there, not knowing what or who they're facing."

Link felt weariness settling in his eyelids. "I've got to sleep if I'm going to fly in four hours, but give some thought to something. If Kitten's trying to get to safety, do whatever you can to make it easier for her."

He went to the office next door to tell Gordon Tower. Then he intended to crash.

7

2:50 A.M., Saturday, February 26th——Mount Werner, Colorado

Katy had heard only a single snowmobile for a long while, so she'd not had to hide. Meaning no burrowing into deep snow or crouching behind bushes as she'd done earlier. Hiding and praying she wouldn't be seen in their wavering headlights. Listening as the riders stopped and spoke on their radios. Hearing people use names like Santos, Ortiz, Torré, and Axel.

Santos had killed three people in a Sno-Cat that had stopped at the gondola building. She'd been well into her trek and had hardly heard the faint gunfire, but she'd heard a rider talking about it on his radios. Victor spoke in a high voice. He was lost, and was still going the wrong way, thinking he was on the other side. Next stop Denver? She didn't feel sorry for him.

Sometimes the shadows played scary tricks on her. Or rather not shadows but the darkest of the dark places, since there was so little light. Katy had gone on for so long she felt like a robot, beyond fatigue, and keeping on with what she'd started because she was too stubborn and frightened to stop. She was determined not to freeze. She kept moving, burning calories and keeping her system charged, but the real secret had come early in the trek when she'd found a two-by-six feet plastic banner announcing the periphery of the ski hill. After tearing it into strips, she'd steeled herself, pulled off the sweater, and hauled down spandex. She'd rotated, wrapping the stuff around her arms and torso and upper legs, then pulled the sweater on and the stretch pants up. A final strip went around head and face, leaving a gap at her eyes so she could see. The wrappings had periodically unraveled, until she'd learned how to secure them in place. She looked mummylike and as if she'd gained fifty pounds, but the thick layers paid off.

Still she worried about frostbite, and had gross images of waking up in an operating room with some cackling fiend in a white smock carving off various protrusions, leaving her a featureless lump. "Take off the nose, ears, and the icy chin . . . Oops, missed a toe here. Oh yeah, gotta get that finger. Hmm. The nipple's got to go. Ah . . . did I just see her stick out a tongue?"

Katy had laughed at the vision, but it was no longer funny so why was she *continuing* to think about it? Comic relief? Fine, but think of something else.

She still had the dumb ski, which was dead weight when she was floundering along. But then she'd come to a field of snow, laboriously position it and get aboard and teeter—didn't matter if she attached her left or right boot at first, then only the left one worked—lock the binding and push off with the poles. She would traverse, going directly across and hardly descending at all, which took a lot of effort with the poles. Still, when she was on the ski she felt she was zipping right along. When the snow would run out she'd grunt and shove harder until the way was blocked by trees or boulders. Then remove the ski and lug it until there was another field.

Katy was enjoying a respite in the storm, even thinking that the worst might be over and she'd at least be able to see as she mushed and floundered across a chest-deep pocket of snow, when it started again. Slowly, in big flakes, then more densely, then so hard-driven she had to squint, then turning into small kernels of grit that lashed her face as the wind grew in intensity. Making tinkling sounds as it struck the plastic wrap.

She shoved the ski ahead and churned her way to it. Again. On an on, like there was no end. Thinking she'd run entirely out of energy at *some* point. Peering at her watch from an inch or so away and trying to see the luminescent dial.

Five more minutes and it would be eleven hours since she'd begun the trek. With it coming down so furiously, unless she ran smack into a house she wouldn't know it existed. Maybe she'd passed a dozen already and not known it. Perhaps she'd gotten turned around and was veering into deep wilderness. Approaching the suburbs of Nome, Alaska?

She thought of turning downhill. Who knew? Perhaps civilization lay just below.

No way. Stick to your plan. Try to keep going around the mountain at the same elevation.

Yeah? For how long? Wasn't eleven hours enough? How much farther could she go?

Doesn't matter. You'll eventually get . . . *somewhere.*

The ski boots hurt, the tops had chafed her shins for so long she was sure blood had crusted there, yet she dared not loosen them. They'd fill with snow and her feet would freeze. With them secured it would be next to impossible to break a leg. That's what they were for. But they *hurt!* Katy felt a new urge to stop, maybe throw a tantrum and scream for help.

Instead she began to hum a really old tune by Hootie and the Blowfish. It had begun in a vague recess of her mind and was becoming louder.

And louder yet.

She could see very little, but knew she was at the edge of yet another snowfield. Time for the old balance on the ski trick. She'd push along with the ski poles, and make better time.

Eleven hours and counting. Cold, cold, cold coldcold. She kept humming to the song.

The tune changed. Not her subconscious. The tune *itself*
had changed when the next song began to play. She *had* the
CD. She *knew* it. It wasn't just her mind, she was actually
hearing it.

Yes, yes, yes. Yes!

Katy was up on the ski, pressed her full weight so the
binding clicked and locked. Good old ski and binding!
We're close! She pushed off with both poles, heart pounding, heading toward the source of the music. Then even in
the driving snow she could make out the glow of a light, that
became brighter and ever brighter. The music grew louder.
And Katy Dubois, although still numbed by the chill, dared
to feel victorious! She began to smile.

4:15 A.M.—Genera Brees Airfield, Laramie, Wyoming

Katy materialized at the opposite end of the room, walking
toward him with a smile and a rash of white spots on her
cheeks like she'd been very close to frostbite. She had been
exposed for too long, but at least she was now safe and free
from danger.

Bzzzzzzzzzzz.

Cold, she silently mouthed to him, holding herself and
shivering.

Behind her a dark figure materialized, moving slowly,
threatening, arousing Link's suspicions. He wanted to reach
out to shield her, but it was impossible to move.

Bzzzzzzzzzzz.

Link tried to warn her, but couldn't speak. Tried to motion at it so she'd at least be aware of the apparition but his
limbs would not respond. Katy yawned sleepily, holding
herself more tightly and smiling as if she were pleased. He
tried to warn her that the shadow was wafting closer, and finally managed a meaningless croak.

Katy smiled and mouthed: *Did you say something?*
Bzzzzzzzzzzz.

He tried to speak again, to call out, but all that emerged were guttural noises.

It's good to be safe, she mouthed wordlessly. But she was not safe. The shadow-figure was upon her, tall and gangly, awkward in appearance, balding, and with a thin bird's beak, outstretched hands snaking about her throat . . .

Link thrashed, reached out desperately as the buzzing sound repeated.

He came awake, tense, sweating despite the coolness of the room. The sat phone buzzed urgently. He managed to slip the instrument from his pocket and open it, answered with a slurring semblance of his name. "Anderson."

Maggie Tatro's happy voice announced, "Link, we've got Kitten!"

He sat erect in the chair, blinking into the darkness and trying to focus his thoughts.

"I tried to call you earlier, but the sat phones were tied up."

He remained groggy. "How is she?"

"Katy's one smart girl. Led the bad guys into an avalanche and escaped, then wrapped herself in a plastic banner so she wouldn't freeze, and just skied and walked out. On *one* ski!"

"She's not hurt?"

"A doctor's coming over, but she seems okay." Maggie laughed merrily. "You were right about helping her help herself. She made it around the mountain, twelve miles according to the map, and found one of the homes where we'd asked people to play music and turn on lights."

Link began to recall segments of the nightmare. But was it a dream, or another warning?

"A deputy picked her up and brought her straight here. As soon as . . ."

"Where are you?" he blurted.

"In the third-floor condo suite they're using for a security office."

"And you've got Katy?"

"Yeah. Thawing out and talking to her mom and dad." As she continued talking the dream returned and became vivid. Link remembered the awkward specter. Felt uneasy again.

"Katy's about to crawl into the tub now. You know how . . ." she was saying.

"Maggie!" he interrupted. "How many people are there besides Katy?"

"Three bodyguards and myself. There's a couple of deputies in a cruiser downstairs."

"Do you have a fix on the terrorists? Where they are or how many are involved?"

"Not yet, but the sheriff called the governor. Soon as the state troopers arrive . . ."

"Maggie, that's fine for then, but how about now? Get out of there! Relocate somewhere safer and more defendable."

She paused for only a tiny moment, then spoke with urgency. "Oh, damn, Link. Everyone was so busy celebrating I just joined in."

"Move everyone. Kitten, yourself, and the others."

"Stand by," she said brusquely. He heard her yelling for Katy to forget the bath and get into something warm. Now! They had to move. He heard arguments, and Maggie responding there was no time to screw around. Just do it! She had orders from the top. The others listened. He heard sounds of discussions over radios and telephones, of rustling clothes and quick footsteps. Nervous laughter once, but the conversations had an urgent undertone.

Maggie picked up the phone. "She's dressed now. We're moving to the courthouse in Old Town. Both the city police and the sheriff have offices nearby, and they're calling in off-duty officers. Here, talk to Kitten while I organize the caravan."

"Good work, Maggie," he tried to tell her, but she handed the phone over.

"Link?" Katy's voice was unsure.

"Yeah, it's me, Kitten. You gave us a scare."

"Me too. I walked forever, and a whole lot of people were trying to kill me. The only thing that kept me going was remembering what you told me about . . ."

Link stiffened as the sensations returned tenfold. "Katy!" he started.

A tremendous boom sounded, followed by a cacophony of automatic gunfire.

"Oh God!" someone screamed. He heard the phone clatter to the floor, then Maggie's hoarse voice. "Katy! The balcony!" There was the *pop, pop, pop* of a small-caliber hand gun. Another loud boom—a shotgun's report—followed by a shrill scream. The rattling chatter of AK-47 fire, and the low *brrrrrp sound* of a silenced Ingram.

Link's consciousness switched to a cold, harder, more analytic mode he'd learned in combat. Those who did not have the knack often proved inept during times of crises. The troubling sensations were gone, replaced by an urge to act. Since he could not he listened carefully, cataloging everything he heard.

"No!" A mix of desperation and fear.

Boom! Boom! Boom! A shotgun.

Quiet moaning. Cautious footsteps. A guttural voice asking: "Anyone seen the Kitten-bitch?" More shots, these distant.

A different voice, pained, with an indefinable accent. "This one is alive."

First voice: "Talk to her."

Second voice: "Where is Kitten?"

A low, gurgling response, then a high-pitched moan.

"Tell me or I do the other eye. Where's the Kitten-bitch?" A series of whimpers. Another low gurgle that faded.

"Damn it, you killed her." First voice. Deep and rumbling.

"Wasn't very alive and she wasn' gonna talk."

Another voice. "The bitch isn't here, Axel."

Sounds of movement and rustling. "She can't be far."

A new man's voice, with a heavy accent. "Man, she got lives like a cat."

There was a cell phone's buzz, and the first, guttural voice answered. He sounded surprised, then said: "Everyone look for a small telephone on the floor."

Someone picked up the sat phone. "This it? Red light's on. H'lo?" It shut off.

How had they known? Link listened for several more seconds, until he was sure the connection was broken. He switched the phone off and on, got a tone and hit MEM, then 1.

Erin's response was immediate. She'd been told that Katy had been rescued, but not the rest. When he explained, her voice became horrified. "What about Katy?"

4:25 A.M.—Snowbird Condominiums

Axel looked about the room, still speaking with his contact at T-Can. A pilot at the Laramie airport had overheard everything during the attack.

"What is his name?" Although Axel suspected he already knew.

"Lincoln Anderson," the contact confirmed. "The Kitten was talking to him. She was the one who dropped the phone."

So close! Axel disconnected and looked about as if she might be hiding in a corner, took a machine pistol from a man, and stalked out onto the balcony. He pointed the muzzle out and sprayed a dozen rounds at nothing, just to vent his fury. After a moment's staring into the falling snow he went back inside. Motioned at the bodies. "Get rid of those."

They began dragging the corpses toward the back balcony, tossing them over the side.

She was somewhere here.

He had nine men at his disposal. Make that seven, with Victor still out there running who knew where, lost in his snowmobile, and Guteriez only good for complaining about his arm.

Torré and Santos had been left to take out the deputies in the basement parking lot, and then guard the building. That left five, plus himself.

He formed two search teams. They would start with the Snowbird, where they were. Herd the people into a room and check them out. Look for a blond girl with a mole. Kill anyone who came close to the description. They'd check the building next door and do the same. Then the next.

"Find her," he said, his anger simmering. Wanting to make another example, to offer one of them to Huitzilopóchtli. Not daring to because he needed more people, not less. "Remember," he said. "You can make blood and hurt anyone you wish. Just find her and kill her."

Katy had run for the balcony as Maggie had urged, scrambled over the bars and without hesitation leapt into the snowdrift far below—it was head high, thankfully, with the first couple of feet fluffy new snow. As the sounds of shooting had continued, she'd rolled off the drift and scurried down the side of the building, then into the basement parking lot. Crouching between automobiles, trembling, numbed, and unbelieving that it was happening.

Awful thoughts arose. Maggie was still up in the room. So were the bodyguards.

Run! Katy's eyes were drawn by flashing blue and red lights reflected against a basement wall, and it took a moment to realize that she might be viewing her salvation. She ran blindly toward the source, turned the corner, and saw— just as she'd prayed—a police cruiser.

Katy could make out a shadow in each front seat. She wanted to cry out for help, but hesitated. Two steps closer, and as the scene unfolded she crouched between two parked cars.

Several hastily clad people were huddled at the glass-enclosed stairwell, gaping at the cruiser. Blood was splattered on windows—the windshield shattered by shotgun blasts. Inside were headless torsos still strapped in place. Bright gore and matter were clotted on the windows.

Katy backpedaled farther, and leaned over. Vomit spewed forth, spattering her legs.

More shouts from upstairs, and while death was certain if she lingered, a grand spasm purged more of the contents of her stomach. She gasped and drew in precious breaths.

Two of the ones gaping at the horror—a young couple—came to life and hurried toward the driveway exit. Beyond was the gondola plaza, and beyond that Ski Town, where they might lose themselves among the condos and mobs of tourists.

Katy started to follow, then held up as a man in a nylon ski mask and wild black hair came in through the exit, pushing the two back with the muzzle of his weapon. Another man, this one muscular and wearing a knit mask, joined him, saying, "Oh, *yes.*"

The gawkers looked on as the men backed the couple against the police cruiser. The muscular one pulled the woman's cap off, displaying blond hair. "Is that her?"

The one with the thatch shook his head. "The Kitten-bitch has the little mark."

"What is your name?" The larger one asked. He had a heavy accent.

"M—Melanie?" her voice quavered.

He pulled down a zipper and felt her. Smiled. "You are right. This one's breasts are too big." The woman was trying to pull away as he spun her around and prodded her toward the glass-enclosed stairs. "We will find a quiet room so I can examine her more."

The young man's voice cracked. "Leave her alone. She's my . . ."

The muscular man prodded her, "I said *move.*" She stumbled and hurried.

"Do not let Axel know about it," the wild-haired one said.

"He told us to warm up. Can you think of a better way? I always share with my men, so you can have her when I'm done." He shoved again when the woman balked. She let out a squeak, and scrambled.

"Please don't hurt her," yelled the young man, but Wild Hair jammed the muzzle of his wire-stocked weapon into his abdomen. He oofed and bent over, and began to cry.

A trio of ski-masked men trotted down the stairs and walked toward the exit.

"Please help us," the young man cried after them. "They're molesting my wife!"

The wild-haired gunman lifted his rifle in one hand, and fired a bullet into his head. His victim went down like a stone and was still before the sound of the shot stopped echoing.

The men who had walked past did not look back.

Katy slithered between a vehicle and the concrete wall, making her way toward the open side door where she'd entered the basement.

The gunman's radio crackled to life. "Anyone . . . out of the building?

"Santos here. We have the entrance closed. No sign of the Kitten-bitch."

"Fifteen minutes . . . other police . . . in a cruiser."

"I will take care of it." He lowered the radio, and cocked his head at the terrified tourists. "I will ask only once. Have any of you seen the blond girl? She has a little mark in her cheek."

Katy prayed, for she'd been in their view. No one answered.

Santos motioned at the cruiser. "While we wait, take off their uniforms."

Katy edged ever closer to the exit, careful to remain unseen. Knowing that detection meant death, and that the terror being visited upon the others was because of her. If she was bolder, she might even have tried to think of a way to distract the killers. She was not. She duck-walked to the exit, slipped through to the dark world outside, and almost sobbed with happiness.

Brraaat! Someone screamed and began to thrash behind her on the concrete floor. "You do not learn. When I say to do something, *do* it fast!"

She was startled by other loud, ripping sounds. Noises of automatic weapons fire issuing from Ski Town. Katy hurried down the side of the building, finally stopped, and listened.

Another gunshot sounded from the basement. Upstairs a man screamed in pain, terror—or both. Katy scrambled onto the giant snowdrift that had formed under the eaves, and tumbled down the other side. Skirted the tennis courts, then thrashed directly away from the building. When it became so deep she could hardly continue, Katy pitched forward onto her belly and just lay in the snow, wanting to cry but knowing she could not afford the time. Still, for a while she just lay there feeling abjectly sorry for herself, listening to periodic screams from the condo. Similar sounds from the next building, where they were obviously searching as well.

The highway was a couple of miles distant, and it would be impossible to wallow through that much chest-deep snow. Like before, she considered finding a drift and burrowing. She was better prepared, in insulated parka and snow pants—mostly white, so she'd be hard to spot. Silk underwear and turtleneck. Thermal socks and boots. She'd even stuffed a Turtlefur neck warmer in a pocket. She had glove liners, and could keep her hands warm in her jacket pockets.

The security supervisor had said it was twelve degrees outside, a manageable temperature if she burrowed. But there were questions. How long would she have to remain there? Would help arrive before the bad guys discovered her nest? And to just lie there?

Nope. She'd head for Old Town, where off-duty policemen were gathering like a Wild West posse. Katy made a calculation. A couple of miles to the highway, then three more to Old Town. It was four-forty-five and daybreak would come at about seven-thirty. Meaning she'd better hurry.

So far she'd heard no traffic. If a vehicle approached from Ski Town, she'd hide. How about traffic coming from Old Town? It was unlikely any bad guys were there. She decided that if anyone came from Old Town, she'd flag them down.

Katy began thrashing her way toward the street, hands in pockets for warmth but having to remove them now and then to maintain balance. Floundering and using up precious energy. Stopping periodically to huff and puff and rest.

She felt numbed, had been frightened for so long now that there was little room for more than desperation, yet careful not to forget that death could come at any moment.

8

They'd defied gravity once more. "We're flying," Link advised the copilot. "Gear and flaps coming up." Center had cleared them to eighteen thousand feet, so they'd be well above the Snowy Range peaks when they turned southwest.

A light on the SECURE COMM panel blinked. The copilot took the call. "New York, for you," he said over intercom.

"We're through ten thousand feet, climbing to flight level one eight zero," Link told him. "Take the airplane." He released the yoke and switched to SECURE COMM. "Anderson," he said.

Frank Dubois's voice was grave. "Security gave me a rundown on what you heard."

"She got away, Frank. The bad guys were upset and looking for her." Link wanted to reassure his friend further, but could not. Gordon Tower had learned from the police in Steamboat Springs that *someone* had taken over the entire condo building. There was no answer from either the office or rooms, or from a patrol car parked downstairs. Now there was no response from the condo building next door or a hotel a block distant.

"Erin's got some ideas," Frank said. "In fact, we're calling from her office."

She came on, her voice carefully businesslike and neutral. She felt it might be someone's way of getting even for something the foundation had done. They'd dealt with powerful people and gained bitter enemies. She was researching the vast Weyland Foundation databanks. It would take a while. Link did not agree. There was an urgency about the attacks that did not seem appropriate if the perpetrators were merely seeking revenge. Yet it was *an* idea.

"Where are you?" she asked. "My GPS tracker shows you south of Laramie."

"We're headed for Hayden."

"You'll have company. Law enforcement people from all levels. Tell Gordon that's he's been placed in charge of the FBI effort, by the way."

"He knows. He's in back, talking to Washington about the Hostage Rescue Team that's on the way."

"The problem's going to be getting them on the ground while they can do some good."

"Yeah." The radar showed more massive cloud buildups to the south.

Frank spoke up. "I told the President's chief of staff that we want action and no roadblocks in your way. DOJ's activated the joint contingency program."

With that declaration certain officers of the Weyland Foundation gained official government status. For instance Link carried the identification of, and had just been instated as, an assistant attorney general. It was intended to add to his authority, should he require it.

"Link, don't hesitate to use any possible resources you need. And I mean *any* resources."

"You don't have to tell me that, Frank."

"I know." He was quiet for a moment. "The director of safety feels the bad guys may be working with someone on the inside at Steamboat, since they seem to know everything in real-time. For instance they had to know the moment Katy showed up, because it would have taken that long to prepare the attack. And you overheard them using her code name."

"Maggie thought the leak was there at the Weyland

building. What if they're both right, and someone's broken our encryption codes?"

"That's improbable. They're the best in the world, Link. The NSA set it up."

"So who does security think might be the source?" Link asked, thinking he knew.

"Truthfully, they're not fond of the way Maggie Tatro came aboard."

"Frank, I heard her trying to save Katy's life when the bad guys attacked, and she may have been killed for the effort."

"I hope not." Frank released a weary breath. "Stay in touch, Link."

"Try to get some sleep. I'll do whatever has to be done."

When Link broke the connection, the copilot was on the radio. "Whiskey Foxtrot Fiver One is level at 18 thousand feet, turning to a heading of two-one-five degrees."

"Whiskey Foxtrot Five One, you are cleared direct to the Hayden Airport. Give us a call ten minutes out and we'll add you to the pile."

"Will do. How many in the barrel at Hayden, Center?"

"Four holding, and more on the way."

6:04 A.M.—Snowbird Condominiums, Ski Town

Axel checked and replaced the battery of the cell phone he'd used almost constantly, and took a call from T-Can West: "The FBI hostage rescue team is en route, and Anderson is already orbiting. There are eleven aircraft trying to land at Hayden right now."

Axel felt the indefinable tingle course through him, as had been happening whenever Lincoln Anderson was mentioned. Was it excitement? A challenge to his abilities?

"No one can land until the weather clears. All landing aids are still shut off."

"Fine," said Axel, a little let down that he wouldn't get to face Anderson. He might be a true adversary, worthy of sacrifice. "Your people did well, T-Can, Torré and Santos intercepted the last police cruiser precisely where you led them. There are fewer officers left now."

"You're left with the county sheriff, supervisor of public safety, five deputies and city police, and a highway patrolman. Oh yes. *Plus* twenty members of the citizen's posse."

"The more of those the merrier. Amateurs will only add confusion."

Axel disconnected. His men were going through apartments and condos. Kitten had to be nearby, and they had plenty of time to find her.

6:30 A.M.

Katy was on Werner Road, leaning into the wind and trudging toward the highway, measuring her breathing and making herself remain as alert as possible although she was so foot-dragging weary she'd stumble every few steps. Several times she'd heard vehicles and fled off of the roadway to dive into the snow, too frightened to try to view the drivers as they passed.

She had learned to remain in place, because a short while later there'd be another coming the other way. The same vehicles, bad guys out looking for her?

For warmth she'd pulled the neck-warmer over her face and ears, which was scary because it muted her hearing. To ensure no one was coming up behind unheard, every ten paces she'd stop and listen for engine sounds. She was careful to walk in ruts left by vehicle tires, so her trail was minimal. The bad news was that with the stops and the slow pace, getting to the highway was taking much longer than she'd anticipated—and it would soon be full light.

On her right she could see a Taco Bell, which she remembered was near the highway.

A few times she'd heard diesel engines, coming from Old Town then heading south on the unseen highway she knew was closed. Sure enough, all the trucks had halted farther down the highway, making loud airbrake sounds. Meaning there was a lineup there waiting for the highway to open. She supposed it was the sounds of a truck on the highway that made her sloppy, like she'd be able to hear traffic on the street just as easily. But for whatever reason, Katy went too long between stops, and when she heard engine noises behind her it was *close*!

She scurried off the street, and dove headlong over the four-foot embankment left by the snowplow, heart thumping wildly.

Behind her the vehicle stopped. "I saw something," said a man's accented voice.

When both car doors opened, Katy held her breath, too frightened even to crawl down the embankment lest she make noise, yet knowing she couldn't just stay there.

"Yeah," said the man. "Somethin' lef' a trail in the snow. Maybe the Kitten-bitch?"

Darkness was fast turning into gloom. Katy prepared to rise up on all fours and crawl, wondering if she could do that in deep snow.

"Probably a fockin' animal." It was the familiar voice of Sergeant Santos, who had done the killing in the basement lot. "All kinds of animals here."

"Could be the Kitten-bitch," the other man repeated.

"Or maybe a big lobo wolf that's gonna jump out and bite off your *cajones*. She didn't come this far. We're almost to the highway."

It seemed odd that he was curt. She'd gotten the idea that the other man was in charge.

"You forget she walked all the way around the mountain. We should check it out."

"Maybe *you* check it out. You're the one spen' an hour warming up with the woman while I had to kill her man and all those police."

The other one's voice turned cool. "I told you you could take a turn with her."

"There wasn't time. Axel was angry about the police car. He kept saying why did I shoot the windshield on that one too? I didn' tell him because I had to take care of that entire carload of police all by myself. You forget you aren' a capitan anymore, Torré."

"Sure I am, and Axel was right. You weren' supposed to shoot the windshield."

That really riled Santos. "So what should I do while you were . . ."

There was a loud *thump,* followed by the sound of shattering glass.

"What the hell?" exclaimed the already irate Santos.

"Park in the road, somebody's gonna hit you, Sergeant." Torré sounded smug.

Katy heard sounds of a vehicle door, then a new male voice, high-pitched and angry. "Why in hell's name did you stop here? Snow coming down like this, someone could be *killed*."

"Who the fock are you?" asked Sergeant Santos, belligerent.

"If you don't mind I'd like to see your insurance card."

Katy took the opportunity to crawl down the side of the snowbank, putting distance between herself and the men. She froze during a silent lull, fearing they'd hear her. The snow was falling less fiercely, the morning brightening, and visibility was rapidly improving.

The new voice changed as the possessor began to plead. "Jesus, don't point that thing." Katy rose up and could make out three shapes on the street.

"Say one more fockin' word, I'm going to *shoot* you."

"Okay, okay. Whatever you . . ."

Bam!

Katy flinched and watched one of the shapes drop, heard a squeal and thrashing sounds. The smallest of the upright figures pointed his arm downward. *Bam!* No more squealing. Katy continued crawling, trying not to think of what she'd seen.

Torre sounded curious. "Why did you shoot him?"

"I told him to shut up his mouth, *that's* why. I mus' do all the work. I shoot all those police, those people in the basement. I figure I mus' shoot him too."

Torre laughed. "The way you think, we should shoot ever'body in this town."

"Maybe." A door opened. "I thought you wan' to check if that was the bitch's tracks?"

"No time. Axel said the police are sending another . . ." They were still talking as the doors slammed. A moment later they drove on, yet Katy remained frightened beyond words. Beyond thought. All she could do was huddle against the snowbank and hold herself and blubber and think of how close she'd come to dying. Again.

The vehicle's sounds slowed as they turned onto the highway.

Katy drew a ragged breath and tried to think out her best option. *Get the dead guy's car keys and drive to Old Town?* Yeah.

She forced herself to calm down, wondering how long it would be before the pair returned. The snow was intermittent— moments of calm interspersed with flurries. Enough visibility to easily follow her trail in the snowfield, not snowing hard enough to cover it.

Katy crawled over the bank and hurried to the street. She went to the dead man's vehicle, a late model pickup, and leaned through the open driver's door. No keys in the ignition. She went to the body and knelt. Not wanting to look at the face, just get his keys and drive away. As she reached for his pocket a tremble shuddered through him, followed by a twitching of his legs.

Katy let out a squeal. Not a loud one, but piercing enough to scare herself. She'd observed a bodily reaction from beyond death, she knew, but it had frightened her nonetheless.

She made herself look. There was blood on his coat, and a dark hole in his forehead. He was irretrievably dead. She made herself reach into the trousers pocket, but found nothing. In the other pocket she discovered loose change. Where were his keys?

Katy looked about the street where he might have

dropped them, found nothing and finally reasoned that one of the killers had taken them. She resumed walking toward the highway, staying in the rut the killers' car had left, the neck warmer pulled down so her ears were uncovered. They were cold, as were her hands and face, but she had to be able to hear.

Pop, pop—pop, pop. She froze in her tracks. The sounds came from the direction of Old Town. The bad guys had run into the law, or *someone*. And *someone* had fired a weapon.

The roadway split, with branches to right and left. Ahead was an underpass, with the street traversing beneath. She started to follow the lane that veered right, toward Old Town. Wondering about the shots, and if the bad guys hadn't been captured or even killed. Thinking too how the weather was lifting and she could see and be seen, and it was fortunate that she wore white and blended with the world about her.

Katy heard engine sounds approaching from Old Town, and remained calm and still until in the distance she could make out a vague shape. It was coming slowly. She was at the merge point, where traffic from Ski Town joined the highway. If she remained still the vehicle would pass only a few feet from where she watched.

Don't take the chance! Katy decided, and backed down the turnoff ramp a dozen feet. She knelt on a narrow concrete ledge of the overpass. Waiting, praying it wasn't the dark car she'd seen earlier. If it was the police, she'd wave and shout her heart out. But there was also the chance that things had gone the other way.

The vehicle hove into view, and she felt giddy, for it was not the one driven by the killers. As it drew closer and turned into the off ramp labeled MOUNTAIN VILLAGE, she made out the light bar and the neatly barbered appearance of the driver. A police car!

"Help!" Katy immediately called, but it was a hoarse croak, too low for the occupants to hear. She waved, still below their line of sight, and began to rise up and yell again.

An inner caution stopped her. Her vision narrowed. There

were no ski masks as before, but the passenger had a stiff thatch of dark hair, like she'd seen in the basement.

The one called Santos was staring in her direction.

Katy dropped down, lost her footing, and slipped along the icy concrete ledge, reaching out to grab hold of *something*— then dropped off and slid down the slippery incline. She put out her hands, lost her balance completely, and tumbled all the way down onto the road beneath the overpass. The road to Ski Town, where Torré and Santos would be in about three seconds.

She scrambled and flung herself behind the only thing around, a marker guide for snowplow drivers, and into the accumulation of snow there.

There was no time for fear. The cruiser passed by not ten feet distant.

They had to see me! Katy's mind cried out. Santos had killed the driver of the pickup just because he'd argued, and would delight much more in dealing with her.

Katy remained dead still, heart pounding in her throat. Forced herself to listen. Heard nothing at first, then only the diminishing sounds of the cruiser proceeding toward Ski Town. After a moment she released a shuddering sigh, slowly gained her feet, and then carefully climbed back up the incline to the highway.

She stood there, rubbing the knee and staring in the direction of Old Town, where policemen gathered at the courthouse. Could she make it before Torré and Santos returned?

Katy remembered all the trucks she'd heard. How they'd stopped, likely waiting for the highway to open. They were much closer than the courthouse.

She took a soulful look toward Old Town and the protection she might find there, then turned and began to trudge southward, remaining in the tracks left by the last truck.

9

Lincoln Anderson had spent the previous two hours in a racetrack holding pattern five miles above the earth. When they'd arrived they'd been fifth in the stack. Since then, several more had been added. The modest-size county airport was transformed into one of the busiest in the country, despite the fact that the scheduled airlines had canceled their flights because of inoperative landing aids. There were an impressive array of state and federal government aircraft. Several others had been chartered, for the media had leaned of the anarchy in Steamboat Springs.

Gordon Tower was relieved, for two Boeing 737s had arrived with his Hostage Rescue Team, the FBI professionals trained and equipped to deal with terrorism. Link wanted to go in immediately on their heels.

Throughout their first hour Erin had grilled Link about every nuance he'd overheard on the phone, plugging it all into her computer so she might determine the elusive who and why. Link desperately wanted to know those things, but his first step was to get to Ski Town. And *that* meant he had to land.

The Hayden operator called the orbiters. They were making headway with snow removal, but with the airport instrumentation inoperative, the pilots would have to visually

see the runway in order to land. That might be minutes, or
even hours, away.

7:12 A.M.—Snowbird Condominiums, Ski Town

"Axel," he responded.

The T-Can West contact spoke rapidly. "You wanted to
know when the FBI team arrived. They're about three miles
over your head right now, in contact with the mayor and his
people in the courthouse in Old Town. As soon as they land
they'll join with a local group called the county posse, and
head your way.

Axel wondered for a moment. "How many on the HRT?"

"Forty-six."

The hostage rescue team was one of the best-trained special tactics groups in the country. It might be smart to deal
with them early.

"Eliminate them," Axel said.

7:20 A.M.—Holding Orbit, 14,000 feet, East of Hayden Airport

The kills were handled professionally, and quickly done.
The two Boeing 737s carrying the FBI hostage rescue teams
and their complement of prepackaged winter equipment, including parkas, protective gear, special surveillance devices, comm systems, and an array of weapons, used the
call signs of Hawk 22 and Hawk 24.

Hawk 22 was circling in a right-hand racetrack pattern at
14,000 feet. Hawk 24 doing the same, but one thousand feet
higher. They had been placed at the bottom of the orbiting
mob, and when the weather broke for even a moment they
would be first on the ground.

In front the pilots were alert. Weather flying was not for
wimps. In back the team members were dressed and ready
to go. The HRT team chief in Hawk 22 was in continuous

contact with the Steamboat Springs courthouse, and had as good a picture of the situation as could be expected.

Supervising Agent Gordon Tower monitored it all from a console in the rear of the MCP aircraft that was piloted by Link Anderson. While he would be the senior on-scene agent, he would leave the initial attack to the HRT tactical team chief.

Neither Tower nor the team chief knew when the 737 pilots received individual calls to change to different radio frequencies, for they were made on entirely different wavelengths.

On his new frequency, Hawk 22 was told to descend to ten thousand feet and set up a new orbit to the south of the airfield. Still a racetrack pattern to his right. Hawk 24 was, on his own frequency, told to descend to ten thousand south of the field and to establish a left-hand orbit.

Seven minutes later, a single radio call was heard on emergency guard frequency, 121.5 MHz, which was hardly distinguishable above the squealing sound of air rushing through a cockpit. "Mayday! Hawk two-four has had a midair collision. Mayday! We are . . ."

Nothing more was heard from either aircraft.

Link listened grimly from his own orbit as Hayden Tower repeatedly and without results, called for Hawks 22 and 24. Neither aircraft responded.

When Gordon Tower settled into the jump seat aft of the copilot, Link gave him a grim shake of his head. It did not look good for either 737, although the collision seemed bizarre since the last he'd heard they'd been a thousand feet apart.

He contacted Frank Dubois on the sat phone, told him about the probable midair collision, and asked him to apply leverage to have the safety rules bent.

Frank was hesitant. "You really want to try a blind approach?"

"This airplane's got more tricks than Houdini." He motioned for the copilot to turn on the magic. The copilot switched to an electronic map of the earth within two hundred miles. He moved a cursor to the airfield, zoomed in. Pressed a button for high definition. *Wow.*

The airport operator had them change frequencies. Then: "Five-One, I just received a fax from the FAA gods. You may land as soon as the runway's cleared, which should be in ten minutes. Be advised that all navigation and landing aids are still inoperative."

"Yes, sir. We have self-contained capability. Anything on the two Hawks?"

"A rancher ten miles south of here heard an explosion in the mountains, but nothing's confirmed. Seemed odd that both airplanes would be that far off course."

They were instructed to fly east for fifteen miles while descending to twelve thousand feet, and set up a new orbit. Local altimeter setting was 29.83, surface temperature was minus 6 degrees centigrade, winds were light and variable. They would land on runway 28.

The forward-looking TAR was on now, augmenting the lower one. The symmetrical lines of runway and taxiway returns were vivid. They could even see a snowplow.

"We have the airfield in sight," he radioed. At least sort of, he told himself, wondering if he really trusted the systems that much. Thinking about the two Boeing 737s and hoping they would not be next. So far the experimental MPC aircraft was making it look easy. Sort of an airborne Swiss Army knife, capable of anything. At least he hoped so.

7:48 A.M.

"Axel," he responded. Pleased about the elimination of the FBI team.

The T-Can West contact spoke rapidly. "They're letting Anderson land despite the weather and the airport equipment being out. He may not be dangerous, but he has the FBI supervisor with him."

"Anderson is the *most* dangerous of all." It was a fact that he *knew*. A natural enemy?

"If we stop him it might be too much coincidence. They'll suspect something's fishy."

Axel finally decided. "Let him get close, then destroy him." He felt a rush of excitement that Lincoln Anderson would die. He'd wanted to confront and defeat him but nothing must interfere while they determined the Kitten-bitch's location.

7:50 A.M.—Highway US 40 South, Steamboat Springs

For half an hour Katy had stared at the dozen-odd rigs from behind the highway sign, seeing everything from vans to semis parked along the highway, all with engines rumbling and white smoke billowing. She did not know where the highway led, except for the vague knowledge that Vail was in this direction. As she drew closer she thought how the cabs appeared like cozy nests on wheels. While she knew nothing about trucks or truckers, she supposed they were awaiting the opening of the highway.

As she walked, she'd periodically peer back toward Old Town, where there was safety, and Ski Town, where there was sure death. Now she observed the lineup, wondering what to do. Ask one of the drivers to take her to the Old Town courthouse? Did the truckers know what was happening in Ski Town? She decided they did not. Otherwise they wouldn't be waiting here as if nothing mattered except getting their loads to wherever they were headed. She was not about to tell them. Who would help if they knew a bunch of killers were after her?

A paunchy middle-aged man crawled out of the cab of the last truck in line—hauling two trailers with ROCKY MOUN-TAIN CARTAGE CO. printed on their sides—swung to the ground beside a front tire, and began working a ratchet lever. Adjusting chains, Katy supposed.

He wiped a glove across his forehead, leaving a smudge.

From toddlerhood she'd been warned about strangers, yet she had to trust *someone*.

His attention remained on his task. *Should she just walk up to him?* she wondered.

"Whatcha doing, kid?" a female voice called, and Katy turned to view a shapeless mound hunkered by the next tractor-trailer in line, checking tire chains as the man was doing.

Unless absolutely necessary, don't give your identity, she'd been told during countless security briefings. *The first things people visualize when they hear your name are dollar signs.*

"Hitchhiking," Katy replied, and walked toward the truck, which was painted pink beneath layers of road grime. The woman was fortyish, with a florid face and squinted eyes. Not at all pretty, wearing unbecoming dirt and grease-streaked winter coveralls.

"Your momma know you're ridin' your thumb?" The woman was giving her a look-over.

"Sure," Katy said lightly, as if she did it all the time.

"So where you headed that's so important you gotta freeze your butt off?"

"Home." Katy read the address painted on the side of the cab, ANDORA TRUCKING, MONTROSE, CO, and decided she'd be better off with the woman than the man, regardless of her oddity. "We live near Montrose," she said, wondering where that might be.

"Oh? In Black Canyon?"

"Yeah." Katy wanted the conversation to end, nervous she'd get caught in the lie, or worse, that Torré and Santos would decide to check in this direction.

"Damned if I ain't headed there too." The woman gave a semblance of a smile as she began removing the coveralls. "Gimme a hand," she said, and Katy helped her maintain balance. Beneath the coveralls the woman wore jeans and a woolen shirt, both of which had been around for a while and bulged at every possible seam. Katy could not help staring, for everything she had on, even the low-heel western boots, were hot pink. Mostly faded now, but her clothing had once been the same color as the gaudy truck, with a bit of grime around the edges. Even the long johns that peeked from the neck of her blouse were pink—and soiled.

"They call me Annie," she said. "Or Roadkill Annie—whatever." She pulled a flamingo-colored droop-brim hat from the running board, wiped off the sooty slush, and put it on. "Might as well climb in. Colder'n a witch's third tit out here."

Annie crawled up, opened the driver's door, and waited for Katy to get in. "That's how they tell witches, y'know. Got a third tit somewhere on 'em. Armpit, back, *some* where."

Katy held on to the mirror to pull herself up.

"You gotta name?"

"Katy—uh—Katy Smith."

"Well soon's the snow plows get here Mizz Katy Smith, we'll head for home."

As Katy climbed up, she paused to observe the highway for a final time.

The police cruiser was only fifty yards distant. This time it was the shadow figure of the driver that had Santos's wild hair.

Katy scrambled inside, heart fluttering and praying she hadn't been spotted.

Annie peered at the highway, then at her. Wearing a calculating look, as if wondering why her passenger didn't want to be seen by the police.

7:55 A.M.—7 Miles East of Hayden Airport

The runway was clear and they'd begun the straight-in approach from the east. The copilot had the airport on the heads-up display, superimposed on the windscreen.

Amazing, Link kept thinking.

"It's no longer forward-looking radar alone," said the copilot. "We're integrating everything into the digital map. GPS from satellites. Radars from the top and belly."

"Amazing," Link repeated.

The radio sounded. "Whiskey Foxtrot Five-One, break off your approach! Another aircraft is on the runway!"

Link cocked his head, wondering. He did not answer, just continued the approach.

"You heard him," said the copilot. "Pull out."

"That wasn't the operator. The voice was wrong." He pointed at the image on the windscreen. "Anyway, I've been watching the runway. See the airplanes on the apron? But there are none on the runway unless it's a stealth fighter, and I doubt they've got those?"

The copilot stared hard and nodded. "You're right."

"Let's hope I'm right. If you see anything, yell."

The frantic radio transmission came again. "Five One, climb out *immediately*. Heavy equipment on the runway."

"I thought it was an airplane," Link responded. "What is it that's on the runway?"

The tower radio went dead. Link switched to Hayden ground control. Nothing.

He called anyway. "Hayden. Whiskey Foxtrot Five-One's four miles out, gear and flaps are down. We *will* land."

As the wheels touched, solidly and not with the feather-kiss he normally strove for, Link was careful about applying the brakes, and let the bird roll. The MCP took only one of the ten thousand available feet before coming to a rest. Versatile, indeed. He followed a snowplowed route, parked in an open area near the tower, and told the copilot to shut down the engines and put the bird to bed. He'd give him a call later. Then Link unbuckled and hurried back, pulled on hat and coat, and swung open the entry hatch.

Gordon Tower joined him. As soon as they were outside—the two big turbofan engines just beginning to wind down—they hurried toward the operations building.

"Let me tell you something," said Gordon. "I *hate* flying in bad weather."

"Me too. Scared me to death."

"Don't *tell* me that."

As they entered the flight management room, Tower said, "So you won't worry about it, I just got the word from the Hoover Building. You're running the show now."

"Nope. The feds are in charge, and you're in charge of the feds. I'm here to make Katy safe. The only reason I accepted the assistant AG appointment is to move anyone who tries to get in my way."

A big man of indefinable age, wearing a huge chocolate-colored Stetson, awaited them with an angry expression. His voice boomed: "My name's Bob Titus—I'll spell that if you wish—and I don't give a *damn* who your bosses are. What the hell's going on with my electronics? You government boys have anything to do with that?"

"Innocent," said Link. "We need to rent a vehicle and we'll be gone, sir. Whoever's screwing with your airport electronics tried to get us to abort our landing, but we don't have time to worry about that right now. We'll pay for the vehicle."

The big airport operator paused to try a radio, to no avail, then turned back. "Before their phones went out I spoke to a sheriff's deputy in town. Not with the sheriff, who's a friend by the way, because he and the chief of police drove into Ski Town and are no longer responding, just as the two policemen they went to check on are not responding, and two deputies before that. Now they've lost contact with *another* cruiser. So where were you headed?"

"To Ski Town," said Link.

"I had three buses all ready and waiting for that FBI team, but I doubt the poor souls'll be needing 'em." He nodded to a rawboned male, western hat pulled low on his forehead, lever-action carbine propped casually against his leg. "Higgie here'll drive you."

"We won't need a driver. I know the way."

"Bad idea. You'd have to pass by the Routt County Courthouse in Old Steamboat. Forty legally deputized men and women are gathered there, armed with rifles, pistols, and shotguns, mad as hell that someone's shooting their police and has more or less taken over Ski Town. Now there'll be no FBI team, so they feel it's up to them. They're called the County Posse and while they're mostly trained to donate money and attend policemen's and firemen's ball, they know they gotta do something."

"We'll stay out of their way."

"You don't understand. They're nervous, they don't know you, and you'll look suspiciously like strangers who may have been shooting their cops."

"We'll take all that into consideration."

"What'll you do if a uniformed officer waves you down?"

"Stop and cooperate," Tower said impatiently.

"You're not listening, son. *Someone* has four police cruisers and a lot of uniforms and they're heavily armed. Stop for the wrong folks, you'll get yourself *killed*. If the posse sees you, you'll get yourself *killed*. Higgie, being a social lion hereabouts, knows everyone, including the local police and the posse members. You don't want to get killed, let him drive you to Old Town."

Higgie was chewing tobacco, nodding solemnly.

Link asked a final question, "How long before the others can land?"

"Can't say. I just had every radio, that's four VHFs and four UHFs, shut down on me. Not one of them works. We're out of business here, son."

"Odd."

"Forty years in aviation and I've never seen anything like it. They don't build coincidences that can handle this one."

They followed Higgie out to a gray bus. As they climbed aboard, Gordon brought up the Hostage Rescue Team.

"It appears that both airplanes crashed in the mountains. Those were our best-trained antiterrorists. Washington's going crazy."

"Who's calling the shots there?" Link asked as Higgie started the engine.

"There was an executive NSC session this morning after the attack on the Sno-cat, but all they did was confirm it's a bona fide act of domestic terrorism. That put it into the federal ball park, no matter that no one's eager to get it. So I'd say it's being juggled between our FBI director and the attorney general."

Higgie drove toward the exit.

"My bosses at the Bureau weren't sure if I should do the reporting or you."

"Like I said, you're stuck. I'll only use the title for leverage."

"You don't realize how powerful the Weyland Foundation is with Washington insiders. That's why presidents tread lightly. You have a reputation for getting things done and keeping a high degree of moral sanity. You really do wear white hats."

"Yep." Link touched the brim of his cream-colored John B. Stetson. "But sweet talk all you want, Gordon, you still have to run the feds and do the reporting."

Tower chuckled. He had tried. "Ah the heavy yoke of authority." Then he sighed. "I hate it about those poor bastards on the HRT. I knew most of them."

"Let us know if you see anything odd," Link told Higgie as they pulled onto the highway.

"Don't you worry none about that."

As they rode—it was twenty-two miles, Higgie said—Link thought about the carnage he'd overheard on the sat phone. Had it been Maggie he'd heard gurgling. Dying. And did they have Katy? It seemed improbable that she could evade for so long.

8:07 A.M.—Highway US 40 South, Steamboat Springs

Santos thought Torré was doing a good job of scaring the truckers. He was in a uniform stripped off a dead cop, and the silly shits did not notice the blood. The captain would crawl onto the step on the passenger's side, get them to open the door, and say they were looking for a runaway girl involved in a robbery. If there was a sleeper, he'd have the driver open it. Since every other trucker west of China had a stash of speed, they did not like that. But when he'd say, "Just a peek so I know there's no girl, otherwise I will call in people who'll tear the truck apart," they opened up. One look was much better than a thorough examination.

Torré got away with it because he looked the part of the captain he was, with his short hair, muscular build, and hard smile. And the way he had killed both of the last two policemen after they'd gotten out of their cruiser? Santos had no more complaints about him not carrying his load, just wished he'd been able to use the woman to warm up on too.

Captain Torré crawled up the next cab, looking official and asking about the girl. "Let me see behind the seat," he said officiously. They'd come to suspect the trucks after they'd driven the newly acquired cruiser back to the dead man and his pickup. Whoever had left the tracks before had returned to look at the body, and Santos admitted it could be the bitch. They'd tossed the corpse in back of the pickup, and gone looking.

They had decided to check out the trucks, and Axel had readily agreed. They'd begun with the one in front. Torré was now looking in number seven. There were six rigs to go. The last three—a green one, a no shit *pink* one, and a white one—had sleepers.

8:11 A.M.—Suite 324, Snowbird Condominiums

There were only the two of them—Guteriez and himself—remaining in the suite. The two search teams were still out looking through condos and apartments.

"How long until I call the chopper?" asked Guteriez, whom he'd placed in charge of *extraction* and took the job seriously. He also wanted to get away somewhere he could have the arm looked after.

Except for the huge fact that they'd not yet found the Kitten-bitch, things had gone smoothly. The teams were methodical in their hunt, and as they finished with each building Axel marked it on his map.

Despite the intervention, Anderson had landed at Hayden, but neither he nor the FBI supervisor posed the level of threat they would have faced with the HRT. T-Can West had just informed him that the next attack would be made not by police, but by the so-called County Posse. The fact that they were a group of loud amateurs allowed Axel to keep searching.

He got another radio call, scratched off another condo complex. Two more civilians killed. Still no sign of the Kitten-bitch, and they'd searched all the obvious places.

Aside from the fifty FBI agents and pilots, thirteen body-guards and law officers had been killed. Also about twenty civilians, some as examples, most because they'd been in the way. His people had worn the ski masks, and Axel did not believe anyone had been identified. The only ones not wearing them were Torré and Santos, who were posing as deputies and checking the lineup of trucks for the Kitten-bitch.

"How long until this posse gets here?" Guteriez asked. More nervous with each minute.

"They're still organizing," he told him. "There is no big concern. The ones who would have been real trouble are dead." He looked at his watch, unwilling to admit defeat. "We'll keep looking."

Guteriez spoke into his radio, on a different frequency from the ones they used for the search. He lowered his handset. "He wants to know how many passengers?"

"Nine," he said, and Guteriez echoed the number into his radio.

"He can't take that many."

Axel studied the notepad. They'd leave the two buried on the mountain, and Victor, who was still lost. The last time they'd talked, his snowmobile had run out of gasoline, and he was speaking slowly—freezing. No loss with any of them, as long as they were dead.

He ignored gunshots from the direction of the search. A voice was loud on the radio. "Ortiz here. Someone shot at us from the next house up the hill. Want us to skip that one?"

"Perhaps they're shooting because they have the Kitten-bitch," Axel said, thinking Ortiz possessed the intelligence of a doorknob. He made up his mind about who should be eliminated. "Let the others continue, and you and Garcia come back. I've got something for you to do."

"Axel?" Sergeant Santos's voice queried. "We're almost finished looking in the trucks."

"How many more?" he asked.

"Ummm . . . only four." Santos laughed over the radio. "There is a pink truck and a donkey-ugly woman in a pink hat, you believe it?"

"Go ahead and finish. Then I'll need you and Captain Torré here as well."

10

"Here he comes," Annie warned from the front. "Scrunch down."

In the sleeper, Katy did not need encouragement, for her heart was pounding so furiously it threatened to burst. She lay as flat as she could possibly make herself, scarcely breathing, thinking how lucky she was to have picked Annie. The colorful truck driver had not questioned why she wanted to hide from the police after Katy explained they weren't genuine, that they'd killed the officers and taken their cruiser and uniforms.

"I trust you, kid," was all Annie had said as the fake policeman worked his way down the line of trucks, even after she'd switched on her CB and heard the other truckers saying they were looking for a runaway girl who'd robbed a store. Annie hadn't seemed concerned, just told her to climb into the sleeper, remove the only working lamp bulb, loosen the top of a jar wedged in the corner, and burrow under the mattress.

The place had not smelled wonderful before, but after a few seconds with the jar opened, the interior reeked so noxiously that Katy thought she would be sick. She was thankful that Annie kept the hatch cracked, so at least some of the fumes could escape.

After an eternity, Annie hissed, "Cop's coming, kid. I'm gonna button you up."

Katy lay flat, head at the end of the enclosure immediately behind the driver's seat. The only light was that which filtered past an ill-fitting cover of the overhead port.

She felt movement, and knew the killer was on the step. Scarcely breathed as she heard muted conversation, inaudible through mattress, blankets, and closed hatch. She heard him getting into the cab—and began praying, as she'd done a lot lately.

There was a metallic sound as the hatch was pulled open.

"Jesus. What's that smell?" Torre's familiar voice. Hearing it made Katy wonder if he'd kill her outright, or use her to warm up with like he had the other girl.

"Kept a cat in there," Annie explained, "and she weren't particular where she went. Kept on pissin' on ever'thing so I got rid of the thing."

"You *sleep* back there?"

"It ain't easy," Annie admitted. "I'll hose it out soon as I get home."

He made a grunt as he leaned inside. "You didn't see a girl out there?"

Annie laughed derisively. "Sure, and I'm hidin' her."

"The light does not work."

"Needs a bulb, but there's a flashlight next to the door."

"Yeah. Got it." There were sounds of him tapping it on something so it would illuminate better, then a rustling noise as he leaned farther in.

Katy almost screamed at the weight of his hand on her leg. It took every ounce of her forbearance to remain still as he felt about the periphery of the mattress. After a lifetime, lasting no more than fifteen seconds, she heard rustling as he withdrew.

"Jesus, it smells in there."

"Ain't your worry, is it?" Annie said as the hatch slammed closed.

A moment later Katy vaguely heard, "Relax, kid. The asshole's gone."

She wanted to cough and gag from the awful odor, but also felt a wave of relief. "Thank you, thank you, *thank you*," she whispered to the woman who had saved her life.

Annie watched in her side mirror as the muscular piggie walked to the next rig, the wild-haired deputy following in the patrol car. She despised cops, and had felt like getting her gun from the junk bin and shooting him the second he'd opened the door. If he'd found the girl she might have, except she'd of had the problem of what to do *then*. Maybe kill the girl with *his* gun, then plant hers on the kid? Say the kid must of snuck into the cab when she was out doing the chains, and the cop and kid shot it out? Annie decided it was best none of that had happened.

She hadn't liked the looks of the spike-haired driver in the cruiser either, staring at her and laughing like he had. Leroy called deputies "county mounties." And while they were generally better than state cops, and definitely better than *any* of the federal pricks, she and Leroy despised law officers no matter what shape they came in.

Cool it, she told herself, and keep on hauling. She cracked open the hatch and called back. "Put the lid back on the stink pot. I can smell it even with the door closed."

She kept it filled with odiferous things like rotten eggs, human shit, and a dead rat. While various inspectors might not think highly of her hygienic habits, they seldom spent much time examining the sleeper compartment with the lid off the stink pot. She could of hid a dozen wetbacks there and they wouldn't do more'n glance and say "close it!"

"That smelled *awful*," she heard from the kid. Then, "Are they gone?"

Annie looked in the mirror, saw muscle piggie getting into the cab of the next semi. "Nope," she said. "Stay put. Another rig just pulled up and he'll be checking him too. Might be more checkin' too. Cops are like rabbits. Got a way of multiplyin' when you least want 'em."

"They're not policemen. They killed the officers and took their car."

"Oh yeah. Forgot," Annie said, wondering at the crap the kid was trying to lay on her. Annie did not have her figured, but she knew things weren't as she'd heard. The kid had come strolling up the highway looking peaked, wearing a outfit like something outen a fashion magazine. Sure as hell hadn't been bought in Montrose. More likely from some expensive shop at Aspen or Beaver Creek. Everything fit so well she musta looked it over before she stole it.

Said her name was Katy Smith, but pausing on Smith. The initials "KAD" were etched on her bracelet and embroidered on the collar of the outfit. Meanin' either her initials were KAD or she'd stole 'em from someone with those initials. She also said she was riding her thumb, unusual for a girl who was a good-enough thief to lift a gold-plate bracelet. A smart thief would know better than to hitch wearing it, since it would be taken by the first hustler to come along. In fact it was one of several things Annie intended to get her hands on before they parted ways.

Another scam was when the kid had read the side of her tractor and said she came from near Montrose. Then she'd said yes when Annie had suggested "Black Canyon," which was not a town but a no-shit *canyon*, and the only home there was the cabin used by her and Leroy J. Manners, Annie's old man. The kid did not come from anywhere *near* Montrose, and wasn't hitchhiking because she *wanted* to, but because something had gone bad and she had to get out of Dodge. So was the deputy's story true about the kid being involved in a holdup?

That didn't ring quite right either. Maybe the cops were fakes like the kid said. It seemed unlikely, although a few times during the morning Annie had heard sounds above the noise of the idling engine that might have been gunfire.

As if preordained, she heard a faint *bra-aa-aa-aa-aat* echoing from the hills. Bingo. She identified it as an SKS Chinese rifle on full auto-fire. She was sure, for Leroy J. Manners had given her one for her birthday. She stared toward the mountain—for the first time she could distinguish the base of it—with narrowed eyes. Who was shooting? Then she made herself relax, for come to think of it, did it matter? Even if the girl was in a barrel of shit up to her neck, or muscles and bushy-hair were fake cops, it could only bode well for Annie.

The two searchers left in their police cruiser, taking off fast like they had someplace to go, and she thought again about the gold bracelet. "Hey, kid," she called back.

"Are they gone?" The girl's voice was clearer. She'd moved closer to the partially opened hatch, probably gagging on the lingering smells of the stink pot.

"Nope," she lied. "Still there. I was thinking about that pretty bracelet you're wearing. Mind if I have a look?"

The kid dropped it into her hand. She examined.

"My grandmother gave it to me," said the kid.

"Yeah?" Annie placed it around her wrist. It was a tight fit.

"I can't give you that one, but I'm sure I can have another one made specially for you."

Can't *give* it to her? Annie laughed. "Did I see you wearing a watch?" she asked.

"Sure . . . here."

Annie held it up. It was gold-colored, like the bracelet, and looked new. She had a friend with a fake Rolex sent from her brother in the Navy. This one seemed heavier.

"It was a birthday present," the kid said. "Go ahead and keep it. I owe you, Annie."

She tossed the watch in the junk bin under her legs. "Wearing any rings?"

"No."

Annie held up her wrist, admiring the bracelet, thinking she'd get someone to grind off the initials and change them to her own. The thought made her feel so charitable she decided to let the kid stay a little longer before kicking her butt out.

"Go ahead and snooze." Annie closed the sleeper hatch, looked in the mirror and saw that the deputies' cruiser was out of sight. She reached for the radio, deciding to listen to music on the local radio station while they waited for the snowplows.

8:31 A.M.—County Courthouse, Steamboat Springs

Link Anderson remained in the background as Gordon
Tower spoke with the peace officers and deputized amateurs fortifying the courthouse. Now that the FBI's rescue
team were not coming, they were not impressed with the arrival of a single fed.

A quietly resolute city councilman named Jeff Cliver was
the one in charge, and he had already formed a squad to lead
into Ski Town. When Gordon tried to talk him into waiting
for state troopers who were coming from the interstate behind snowplows, he shook his head.

"We have no choice, sir. They're killing our citizens.
We've got to stop them."

Cliver was methodical about his task. A middle-aged, retired Marine officer who had served in both Vietnam and
Desert Storm, he knew they mustn't rush headlong into a
situation they could not handle. They would go in in some
force. Fifteen men now wore old-style Kevlar vests from
the police armory and carried hunting rifles. Ammunition
had been stuffed into parka pockets. Most of them were
relatively young, and all wore an identifying blaze orange
cloth tied around their left knee, a skier's trick so they could
be picked from the crowd.

They would communicate by radio, since the phone system was intermittent. A retired telephone executive said the
problem was due to so many simultaneous calls over-
whelming the system. A repairman said that was bull when
considering the new digital modules, so for the moment the
matter went unsettled.

Councilman Cliver offered a final few words. Remain a
unit. Do nothing without his approval, or if he was incapacitated, the approval of his replacement. At latest count,
eleven law officers were not responding, and a much larger
number of citizens were feared harmed. They wanted no
more casualties.

The County Posse filled the main hall of the courthouse,

and every man and woman offered encouragement as the squad filed out.

"Mind if we tag along?" Gordon asked the ex-marine.

"Sorry, sir. I've been briefing the people here for the past hour, and we don't have time for last-minute changes. You can follow, but I'd prefer you stay well back." He directed a woman to supply them with two-way handheld radios, and pointed out a city-owned pickup.

It was the best they could hope for and neither of them argued.

Link's sat phone buzzed. Erin said the Steamboat Springs radio station news team had called the foundation, saying they'd identified Katy as being one of those involved and wanting more. Could he stop them from announcing it? He told her they'd listened to the radio on the drive in and Katy's name was already being used. It was too late.

He explained the posse and the assault squad.

"Keep your head down, pardner."

The convoy was formed. In front was a bus like the one they'd taken from the airport, modified with quarter-inch thick sheets of steel inserted to protect driver and passengers.

"Is that Higgie?" asked Gordon. A bystander said the original bus driver had suffered a cut installing the steel armor. They needed someone who knew the bad guys from the good, and Higgie was a logical choice. Several passengers were also aboard.

A stocky, mature woman, brandishing a pen and pad that identified her as press, came over to Link. "You're with the Weyland Corporation?" she asked.

"Let's do this later, if you don't mind."

She gave him a shrewd look. "The manager of the Snowbird Condos escaped and he's inside, telling everyone how your people are involved."

Link narrowed his eyes. "Involved?"

"You know—through the Dubois girl? The one they're after?"

With the cows out, it was too late to close the gate. "I'll

have someone from the foundation call as soon as we know anything." Link nodded politely, and walked to the bus.

Councilman Cliver was leaning in the bus door. "It may get dangerous."

Higgie grinned back. "*Dangerous* is when you get between a big, mean two-thousand pound bull and a sassy heifer."

One of the assault squad chuckled, although a bit nervously.

"Ain't funny. Heifer's likely to run right over you gettin' to that big boy."

"Sounds like a lot of bull," said the squad member.

Councilman Cliver called for a radio check, and twelve men and three women checked in. Among them were three of the remaining peace officers, and the best marksmen in town. Except for Cliver, who was Chief, and the two who answered as Shooter one and Shooter two, they used last names. Like Clark, Murphy, Wilson, Box, and Walsh.

Four-wheelers were lining up behind the bus, and Link and Gordon headed for the white pickup. It was almost time to roll.

8:35 A.M.—Snowbird Condominiums, Suite 324

Axel was brooding, listening to the radio reports and losing hope. They were into the critical period. He was down to cutting fine lines, getting every possible minute added to their search time. The brutality had worked. There were no problems with his people getting their way as they looked through every nook and cranny. The word was out about what they did to people who would not cooperate. Still, they could not stay much longer.

Ortiz and Garcia came in from the search, bragging how they'd made an example of a family trying to escape. Garcia, laughing about beating on the wife while the man begged for them to hurt him instead. Ortiz: "So I shoot the kid, then his woman, *then* him. Right there on the street with

people lookin' out windows." He laughed. "No more problems with *that* street."

Behind them Santos and Torré came in, silently shucking
off deputy uniforms.

"You examined every truck?" he asked.

"She wasn't in any of them," said Torré.

Axel caught Ortiz's attention. "You two. Put on their
uniforms."

A call arrived from the T-Can West contact. "The posse
is sending their squad. Fifteen of them, plus Anderson and
the FBI agent. He too seemed increasingly nervous as Axel
delayed the departure.

"Another half an hour and we will be gone."

"They know you're at the Snowbird. They have
marksmen."

"Yes. Call if there's something new."

His other cell phone buzzed. The Voice, concerned that
he hadn't found the girl.

Axel replied stiffly: "I understand what must be done."

There was nothing more he could do except keep looking
until the final available second. After all, the next radio call
might be someone saying, "Hey, we got the bitch."

Ortiz and Garcia had on the deputies' uniforms and were
grinning and posing like children. He took them to the window and pointed, told them what he wanted, and where.

Ortiz frowned. "What if they shoot first?" he asked.

"You'll be wearing uniforms and they'll think you're
friends."

"But after we start shooting . . . ?" Ortiz asked warily.

Axel drew back like he was surprised. "Do you think I
would send you without backup? These two men and I will
be looking out for you."

Ortiz looked at Torré and Santos, who had pulled on
sweaters and parkas, and appeared somewhat relieved.
"Where will you be?" Ortiz asked.

"Close by. Don't question more. Take some extra clips
and *go*."

Guteriez was back at his elbow, wanting to proceed with the

"extraction," reminding Axel that they needed fifteen minutes to make it happen. "I *know*!" Axel said too forcefully.

He still had a three-man team searching. Axel called and told them they only had twenty minutes, then to go to the parking lot where they would all meet. Until then, keep looking.

Ortiz and Garcia were zipping up brown twill jackets with fake fur collars. They picked up SKS automatic rifles and shoved ammunition clips into their oversized pockets.

"They'll see our faces," Ortiz complained to Axel.

"If you kill them they can't talk. Now go on or I'll shoot you and do it myself."

They laughed as if he were kidding and went out.

Axel thought of Anderson. It was time to confront the increasingly pesky man. He motioned Torré and Santos over. "One is a tall man in a merino coat and white hat. Leave him to me."

"There will be enough to go around," Torré said. Santos was mean, but Torré was the fearless one. A near-perfect killer, his weakness keeping his hands off women.

Axel hefted a rifle and checked that the scope was securely mounted, sighted through it to make sure it was clear.

"When we're done, we will separate." He handed Torré a key. "Go to the house I showed you. They'll be searching here in town, not out that far."

He told Guteriez the time for the extraction, and left with Santos and Torré. It had been a particularly frustrating morning. He was looking forward to watching Anderson die.

8:43 A.M.—Routt County Courthouse, Steamboat Springs

The procession was under way. It was only a five-minute trip from Old Town to Ski Town, but they were traveling cautiously and would take close to twenty. Councilman Cliver quite wisely refused to take undue chances. In the lead, precisely in the middle of the highway, was the ar-

mored gray bus, with darkened windows to dull the glare of
the snow and mask the interior from casual observation.

Fifty yards back, driving at cospeed and using the right
lane of the empty highway, came the first four-wheeler, carrying two squad members with hunting rifles and shotguns.
Another fifty yards back, on the opposite side of the road,
was the next vehicle, and so forth, a total of four. A "shooter,"
the best of the marksmen, was in each of the final two vehicles, with their spotters driving.

Much farther behind, Link was at the wheel of the white
pickup, Gordon Tower in the right seat. They were to stay
out of the fight while Gordon reported events to Washington.

Councilman Cliver's idea was simple. If attacked, Higgie and the passengers would duck behind the armor as the
others fanned out and pounced. The fanning out part might
be difficult with snowfields on either side of the highway,
but they knew snow a lot better than most.

If they encountered light resistance, they would respond.
Anything really heavy, they would withdraw and set up farther back to wait.

No heroics or acting like John Wayne. It was to be a team
effort.

They passed the first patrol car, and the frozen bodies of
two policemen who had been stripped of their uniforms.
Councilman Cliver grimly radioed for them to proceed.
With each passing moment, another civilian might be dying
at the hands of the terrorists.

11

Link and Gordon Tower trailed behind the small convoy, watchful for sign of the terrorists. When the bus and its entourage took a turnoff marked, "Mountain Village," Link continued ahead, and stopped at the center of an overpass, where they stared left, toward Ski Town. It had been several years since Link had skied Steamboat, but Mount Werner was one of his favorites. It was big, diverse, and had great snow and warm people.

"Base, we just turned off the highway, toward Ski Town," radioed Councilman Cliver.

Link watched the procession continue. Now on a narrower street, the bus remained in the center of the road, but the smaller vehicles were immediately behind—more difficult to spot from ahead. They would continue like that into Ski Town.

Higgie announced a pickup on the side of the road, with the snow-covered form of a human body in the bed. "It's Jules Weaver. Looks pretty dead," he said sadly.

"Let's keep going and remain alert," Cliver radioed.

Link had promised the councilman that he and Gordon would remain on the overpass until cleared to proceed.

Behind them was Old Town, from which they'd just come. A mile ahead was a lineup of trucks, likely waiting for the highway to open. To their left they could barely see the base of Mount Werner, but Link knew there were ski runs, and condos and homes on its side. Ski Town proper, with its hotels and stores, would be hidden behind two small hillocks.

The convoy continued. They'd gone half a mile on the street when a transmission broke the silence. "Higgie here. A vehicle's parked in the road ahead."

Cliver's voice sounded. "How far?"

"Four or five football fields, sittin' crosswise in the road."

"Keep going, and keep talking."

"I think it's a . . . yeah . . . a police cruiser with a light bar." Pause. "There's two officers standing on the other side of the vehicle."

"You know 'em?"

"Still too far." Pause. "Both are toting long arms." Pause. "They're in deputies' uniforms, but they don't *look* like any of the deputies I know."

"How far are they now?"

"Maybe a hundred yards. Yeah. I'm confirming it. These are *not* our guys. One of 'ems got long shaggy hair, and the sheriff would pitch a fit."

Cliver's voice seemed even calmer: "Then it's a trap. Don't get too close."

"I'll do like we planned." For the first time Higgie's voice wavered. After all, he was the one in front, closest to the hostile guns.

Gordon watched through binoculars, Link squinting. The slow-moving bus continued forward, then veered right, hard left, and halted. Slanted in the street and blocking traffic as well as the terrorists' view of the smaller vehicles in its wake.

All but the two rearmost vehicles pulled up close and stopped. Cliver's voice remained flat. "Everyone in the bus stay down. Everyone in back, deploy."

The squad members were out of their vehicles. A hundred yards behind the bus the final four—Link noted that they and cautiously moving into the snowfield. A shooter and his spotter to each side of the road.

"This is Higgie. The fake cops are trying to look into the bus. One's trying to pull the door open, and yelling for everyone to get out."

"We can hear them, Higgie. Hunker down with the others and quit talking."

"You betcha."

"Shooters, get out far enough to get a scope of 'em."

The men in white, spotters and marksmen, were difficult to distinguish in the flat light.

Weapons fire shattered the quiet. *Bra-aa-aat. Bra-aa-aa-aa-aat.*

"Who's doing the shooting?" Cliver's voice, still calm and conversational. The marine showing through.

Higgie's high voice replied: "The bastards in the uniforms, and they're shooting at *me!*"

Bra-aa-aa-aa-aa-aat. Another long burst of gunfire. *Bra-aa-aa-aat.*

"Darn it, the bus is Swiss cheese!" Higgie squealed. "Would someone please stop them?"

"Shooters?" asked Cliver. "Can you see 'em yet?"

"Shooter one has the left one in the scope."

Bra-aa-aa-aa-aat.

"Yeah. Shooter two has the fake deputy on the right."

Bra-aa-aa-aat.

"Go ahead and take them out," said Cliver, a slight emotional tremor in his voice.

"Now," breathed one of the spotters. There were two shots, both louder than the anemic 7.62-millimeter rounds being fired by the terrorists.

"This is Murphy. Both aggressors are down." That voice held no trace of elation.

Higgie was not so nicely composed. "Hot *damn!*" A pause of silence followed. Then Higgie again. "You sure you got both of 'em?"

A full minute later Councilman Cliver reported to the courthouse that the two impostors were dead. Then he called Agent Tower. "It's clear. You can come on up this far."

"Good job, councilman."

"I'll step aside gladly, soon as your people arrive."

Link drove warily as they approached the first buildings, located on access roads that paralleled the barren main street. He felt the paranoiac and hair-prickling sensation of being watched, and from the way Gordon was seriously staring about, he was not alone.

Tower advised Washington about the shooting and what they'd seen. He put his cell phone away, and said what Link had been thinking. "That was too easy. The terrorists were whipping everyone in sight—foundation security, police department, sheriff's deputies. Then this bunch shows up and takes them like that? Too easy."

They passed the spotters and shooters, the latter standing with rifle muzzles raised, the former observing across the fields, scanning the buildings. Experienced hunters all.

"But then, maybe Cliver is better organized," Gordon tried.

"Maybe," Link said. Wary as he drove onto the shoulder and squeezed past the bus, and approached the police cruiser, which the squad members had pushed to the side of the street.

He parked. Gordon got out first. Link followed.

"Got enough photos?" Jeff Cliver asked a woman who was photographing the bodies, still sprawled in the middle of the street where they'd fallen.

"Let me finish the roll," she said, clicking away.

Each terrorist had been shot only once, one low on his forehead, the other squarely in the chest. The woman was photographing them from every angle possible to dispel all future doubt about what had happened. In the land of milk, honey, and the ACLU, even terrorists had rights.

Link observed the closest buildings of Ski Town, anxious to get on with it but honoring the deal with the councilman. "If the bad guys are around," he told Tower, "they know we're here." He pointed at the first large structure. "That's the Snowbird, where I heard 'em break in."

"And that's where I'd still be if I were them," said Councilman Cliver. "They'd have a view of the only two approaches."

The photographer finished. "All done," she said. "You can move the bodies."

As team members grasped arms and legs and lugged the gunmen to the side of the road, Higgie called out from the idling bus. "Holes and dings everywhere, but she's still running."

"Good," said Cliver. "We'll put the six back inside with you, and the rest of us will trail along on foot and keep the bus between us and the Snowbird. Ready to drive?"

"Might as well."

"Shooters and spotters, come on up," the councilman called.

Link heard a shout from one of the spotters in the snowfield. "Watch out for . . . !" was all he got out before a burst of gunfire exploded from that side. *Bra-aa-aa-aat.*

Link dove for the shelter offered by the pickup, hat lost and rolling down the street.

Bra-aa-aa-aa-aa-aat. Metallic *thunk-thunk-thunk* sounds as the vehicles were holed. Other bullets skipped off the concrete pavement. He heard screaming from where he'd just been, and another chatter of automatic gunfire. *Bra-aa-aa-aa-aat.* They were in a crossfire!

Ahead of him three squad members huddled, protected on one side by the patrol car, on the other by the bulk of the bus. A man dashed from behind the bus. *Bra-aa-aa-aat*—he twisted and wilted as sprays of steel issued from first one side of the street then the other.

Link chanced that the terrorists would not be able to switch aimpoints sufficiently fast—and dove toward the protected area. He was wrong, for a rifle round thumped into the police car inches from his head, as if someone had singled him out! He rested for a few heartbeats, chest heaving as jolts of adrenaline surged through him.

Bam. Again a rifle shot meant for him, although he was out of sight. *Bam*.

The wounded man remained in the open, writhing and shrieking—his life's blood draining, missing a portion of jaw and chin. They did not bother more with him. Beyond the jawless man lay the now-still auburn-haired photographer. There was no obvious blood, and as he watched she began to collect herself, as if about to rise. He decided that she'd been hit but saved by body armor, and was about to emerge from the shock that often followed.

"Lady," he called, not too loudly. "Stay down and play dead."

Bra-aa-aa-aat.

"Lady," he repeated. "*Please* just stay down."

Councilman Cliver was huddled beside him, holding a bloody shoulder and speaking into a collar mike. "Base, we've been ambushed and have people *down*."

Link made an assessment. None of the spotters and shooters were standing and had likely been taken out by the first bursts. Two others lay prone and unmoving in crimson puddles. Then there was the jawless shrieker, horribly wounded but still writhing.

Bra-aa-aa-aa-aat.

The woman had neither moved nor released another audible sound since he'd called to her. Crouched with him between the vehicles were an able-bodied man and woman, and Cliver, still talking to the courthouse in Old Town despite his wound.

A few had obviously made it into the bus, but where was Gordon Tower? *Bra-aa-aa-aat*. The senior FBI agent was nowhere to be seen. In the bus? No way to get there so quickly.

Bra-aa-aa-aat.

Link heard a familiar voice mutter "dirty bastards," and looked about. He stared at the pickup parked in front of the bus. Looked lower and noted a drooping butt—touching the snow-covered street and reflexively drawing higher. He was relatively sure the bum belonged to Gordon Tower, clinging to the undercarriage.

The woman beside Cliver applied pressure to his shoulder wound to stanch bleeding. He was pale, his voice trailing off, obviously in shock, likely from a combination of situation and wound. "We need help," he managed to croak into the mike.

Bra-aa-aa-aat.

"I can see a rifle barrel poked through a window of the white office building," said the man huddled farthest from Link, peeking around the back bumper of the riddled police cruiser. "Third window from the left." He leaned out, fired a quick shot with his rifle.

Bra-aa-aa-aa-aat. The return fire was immediate. Ricochets skittered off the roadway with spanging sounds. *Bam.* Yet another round punched through the metal near Link's head.

"Damn!" yelled Gordon Tower, pulling up so far he disappeared from view.

There were new gunshots fired from the bus's windows, the ones inside coming to life.

Link leaned out and looked past the front bumper at the building. A face was framed in the window. Swarthy and thin, with a cruel blade of a nose. The sensations he'd felt in New York and later in the hangar in Laramie, returned. The word that had come to him then returned.

Evil!

The eyes stared back, reptilian in intensity. The lips become bared, teeth clenched in a hateful grimace, a snake lusting to strike. He moved so the *0* of a rifle scope hid his right eye. Preparing to shoot. It took willpower to regain his senses. When Link pulled back, he hardly heard the sound of the shot that struck the bumper, but felt a spray of metal grit sting his cheek.

Axel Nevas released a guttural curse. He had met the one who caused his emotions to soar with such primeval and raw hatred. He'd been eye-to-eye with Lincoln Anderson.

He and Torré were on one side of the street, Santos on the other. The so-called "squad" was being decimated, yet he felt no sense of achievement. Would not until he had killed the man he'd just seen. A true enemy. An offering worthy of Huitzilopóchtli.

A radio call. Guteriez was anxious to initiate the extraction. "Not yet," he replied, excitement churning within. Not until he had killed Lincoln Anderson.

He had fired several times at what he'd *believed* was Anderson. Now he knew. He had looked into the eyes of a man he had instantly despised. Felt hatred welling from some timeless past. For the moment even the girl no longer mattered.

A cell phone buzzed. In his intensity he ignored it, fired his rifle again, and did not answer the call. The sound was insistent. "Axel," he finally muttered into the instrument. Staring hard at the chromed bumper where he'd seen the hated face.

The contact at T-Can West said a large force of state troopers were entering the town in buses that were following snowplows. They would be there in minutes. "No!" he muttered in his deep voice. T-Can did not understand, so he disconnected. He took a deep breath, waited for a long moment, but Anderson did not reappear.

The tension-filled moment faded. There must be another time, both for Anderson and for the Kitten-bitch. He radioed Guteriez, his voice very calm. "Call for the extraction."

Then he looked to Torré, crouched at his side near the window. "End it," he told him. "You know what to do." With that he backed away.

Link dared not allow himself to be so shaken, yet the image of evil was still etched into his mind. It was only the face of a terrorist, he tried to tell himself, but knew it was more. Someone he must cope with. He peered again, ready to react to another rifle shot. There was nothing where the face had been. Nothing in the window at all. His adversary had moved, but where? He saw a flicker at another window, but instinctively knew it was not the evil one.

Bra-aa-aa-aa-aat. That burst sounded from the other side, along with spranging sounds of metal being penetrated. The men in the bus fired back.

Link listened carefully, and after a moment called, "I only hear a single weapon on each side!" He'd decided there were only two of them, and something inside told him the evil one had departed—if the face had been real and not some figment of emotion.

"Take your time and take the bastards *out*," directed Cliver as the woman continued pressing a hand against his wounded shoulder, trying to slow the bleeding.

Then: *Bam, pop-pop-pop, brrr-brrr-brr-brr-brrr, bam-bam, pop-pop-pop* . . . There was a dramatic increase both in types of weapons and numbers of rounds fired. Deafeningly loud! All running together, like an army was shooting at them. On and on it went.

"Jesus Christ!" a squad member screamed.

"They're reinforced," sounded a faint voice in an unnecessary observation.

"Gotta be fifty of 'em!" yelled another from the bus.

Then the same thing happened on the opposite side, more gunfire, if anything even louder. *Bam-bam, pop-pop, brrrr-brrrr-brr-brrr, bam, pop-pop-pop-pop* . . .

"We're surrounded!" The men could hardly hear one another over the continuous din, but there was little to be said as they huddled and stared at one another in stark fear. Link hugged the street as heartily as the others, wondering if the terrible hail wouldn't soon reduce both sedan and bus to tiny shards. Cliver was barely audible as he spoke into his microphone, the ex-marine showing through. "We're receiving heavy fire, I repeat *heavy* weapons fire."

Above the din Link heard a faint thunka-thunka sound . . . stared up, saw a low flying helicopter, painted a spectral gunmetal gray, looking eerie against the background of flat light.

Brrrr-brrrr-brr-brrr, bam, pop-pop-pop-pop . . .

"Understand," Cliver was saying, having to repeat everything because of the noise. "State troopers coming through from I-70. Tell them to proceed with extreme caution. The terrorists are reinforced and throwing everything at us. We need an armored personnel carrier. Hell, a tank."

A huddled man poked a thumb skyward at the helicopter, as if to say, "*O-kay!* Help is here!" The chopper was descending—its diminished noises now drowned out by the terrific sounds of the firefight—as if about to make a firing run on Ski Town.

Bam-bam-bam, pop-pop, brrr-brrr-brrrr, bam-bam, pop-pop-pop . . . the gunfire continued as if the shooters took no notice of the helicopter.

Link turned and stared at the bus. Something was wrong with it all.

The helicopter dropped ever lower. As if the pilot was *landing!*

Bam-bam-bam pop-pop-pop, bam-bam-bam-bam, brrr-brrr, pop-pop . . .

Although the din was terrific, there were no new bullet holes in the bus. He looked at the pickup, beneath which Gordon Tower clung so desperately. No new holes there either. He'd not seen a single hole punch its way through the patrol car or felt it rock from an impact since the gunfire had so dramatically increased. Another puzzle—there were no telltale rattling noises, such as had been made by AK or SKS assault rifles.

Link raised up and stared over the trunk of the police cruiser. *Bam-bam, pop-pop, Bra-aa-aa-aat, bam-bam, pop-pop-pop* . . . The sounds were still coming from both sides.

The woman beside Cliver grabbed for Link as he stood and took a few steps, looking first one way then the other as the terrible noises continued.

He picked up a fallen police shotgun and started for the building on the access road sixty yards distant, where they'd believed an army of terrorists were hiding. Two squad members were motioning frantically but he ignored them, wading into the snow until he was waist-deep.

Another man picked up on what he had divined and also stood, peering at the building on the opposite side, the other source of the gunfire.

It took Link several minutes to thrash across the field and approach the office building, feeling more trepidation than he displayed. The windows of the building were all shattered, but he went to the third one from the left, where the squad member had first observed the gun barrel. He leaned in, saw the thing he was after, poked the shotgun's barrel inside, and fired a blast into the rectangular plastic block there.

The awful noise immediately ceased.

He looked across to the opposite access road, watched until the man going there approached that building. A moment later, that awful din was also stilled.

Electronic noisemakers. The military called them firefight simulators. They'd been used in the Persian Gulf conflict by Special Operations aircrews, dropped from airplanes to confuse the Iraqis. So effective that entire battalions had surrendered without a fight.

With the terrific noise abated, the sounds of helicopter blades were clear, coming from the direction of Ski Town. The engine surged, and rotors clattered. The helicopter hove into view, dipped, and disappeared southward.

The terrorists were escaping.

Link began to trot along the access road that paralleled the street where the squad members were beginning to attend to their wounded. Jacking another round into the shotgun. Running toward Ski Town and answers he hoped to find there.

12

Katy had known she should not sleep, but she'd been up for too many hours, was too physically exhausted, too mentally drained from being so frightened for so long. So in the presence of warmth and relative safety, and despite the pervasive odor of the stink pot, she'd allowed her cheek to nuzzle into the threadbare blanket. Then she'd pulled a lumpy pillow over her head to shield her from the world, and dropped into a state of deep slumber.

Later, very faintly through the pillow she had heard sounds from outside. Once she thought she heard her name. Then she almost came awake at noises not unlike the booming explosions of a combat video game. Each time she drifted back into deep slumber.

Annie rode a tumult of emotion. When she'd first tuned in the local radio station the announcer had warned listeners residing on Mount Werner not to venture out. Violent criminals were roving the streets, and were suspected of murdering law enforcement officers. Their identities were unknown, only that they wore ski masks and were slaying anyone who got in their way.

"They are heavily armed and *very* dangerous, and the sheriff's department urges citizens not to challenge them," said the announcer. "Remain in your homes until authorities deal with the situation, and stay tuned to this station for the latest information as the emergency continues.

"The reason for the confrontations are still unknown, although a local businessman, the manager of the Snowbird Luxury Condominiums on Apres Ski Way, has stated that kidnappers are seeking a potential victim identified as Katherine Dubois. He has identified Miss Dubois as being sixteen years of age, of average height, with blond hair and blue eyes. It is unknown whether the group is now holding her, but if anyone out there has seen her, call the station and we'll relay the information to the authorities. *Please* do not dial nine-one-one, for those lines have been saturated for the past several hours."

The announcer's voice had raised, his words coming in rapid fire. "We have just received verification of heavy gunfire near Ski Town."

Annie had heard the distant shooting clearly and had shrank down in the cab. She was no stranger to automatic weapons fire, and knew what it could do.

The sound went on and on, the announcer calling for Mount Werner area residents to lie flat on the floor, like a Vietnam War veteran at the station was suggesting.

Four heavy-duty snowplows rumbled past the trucks from the south, coming one after the other and going fast. Two-dozen white buses trailed behind them. Inside each the muzzles of assault rifles were raised, and grim, unsmiling faces peered out.

The shooting had then stopped as if it were switched off.

Yeah, she told herself. Something *damned* big was going on.

When the shooting had increased, the announcer's voice had risen dramatically. Now he cleared his throat a couple of times, tested his mike, and his voice no longer trembled. He could not give details, but help was only minutes away. To fill in until he knew more, he explained that Katherine Dubois, whom the kidnappers were after, was the daughter of Franklin Dubois, chairman of a big foundation back East, and . . . *one of the richest people in the world.*

It took a while for that one to sink in. Annie reached for the junk bin, pawed through it and found the wristwatch. She held it up, wondering. Annie was not lucky. She'd never won anything in her life, not in any drawing or lottery or even a poker game. It was her lot in life to finish last, and she'd grown to accept it. If there was a good and a bad consequence, she knew which one she'd reap. Thus when the description of the kid came over the radio, Annie knew she'd either heard wrong or there was another who looked like the blond girl. There had to be a catch. It had been too easy, the way the kid had just walked up and crawled in.

She switched on the CB, keeping the volume low, listening as the truckers talked about what they'd heard on the radio, and the white buses going by. The guy in back of her thought he'd seen a girl walking the highway. He'd just woke up when the cop had come, and been too sleepy to think straight. He asked if she'd come from another truck, or maybe was the girl the announcer talked about. Another guy laughed and said he'd likely seen Roadkill Annie, who was in front of him and was *maybe* a female, but sure to hell wasn't no teenager.

Annie started to respond as usual, tell him at least she wasn't back home spreading AIDS like his wife, but she thought better. The other thing just kept running through her mind. How the kid's father was *one of the richest people in the world.* She couldn't help grinning, thinking Leroy would tell her she'd done something smart instead of slapping her cross-eyed for screwing up like he often did.

Annie listened to the truckers jabber, talking about the crazy things happening in Ski Town. A couple of them were betting the radio announcer had cranked up on meth to make it through the morning. Others said the gunfire they'd heard had sure sounded real.

She squinted at the closed hatch, wondering how she should handle it. If she took the kid back to Old Town, there might be a reward, but there'd probably also be questions, like asking what Annie had been hauling and where, and what was she doing here on the back road. Things that Leroy J. Manners did not want anyone knowing, since both the feds and state officials already suspected he was connected with a lot of thefts.

Maybe she was wrong. Maybe they'd just pay her a bag of money and not ask a thing, but few of her experiences with those who wielded power—like the kid's father—were happy ones. They'd cheat her out of her reward, or pay her less than they would anyone else. And if she wanted it kept quiet, they'd pounce on that weakness. Maybe learn about Leroy and the things she'd just hauled.

She tried to think it through but quickly became confused, as she was apt to get when Leroy wasn't around because she was scared of what he'd do. Annie just knew that what she had back there had to be worth *something*. As she admired her new watch and bracelet she decided to call Leroy and ask him what to do.

Someone ahead in the lineup said now the road was open, he had to get back to Golden. If the guys up front weren't going to lead, he would. Finally a trucker pulled out and passed the others, and one by one the rest followed. Annie dropped the transmission into high-low, revved the engine, and eased forward, giddy at her good fortune. There was a pay phone at a store ten miles down the road, where she'd stop and call Leroy.

Katy slept with the pillow over her head, muting the world outside. She was gently rocked in her cozy cocoon, and at some level of consciousness knew they were in motion. She did not associate that with danger. Leaving the terrible place did not seem at all bad.

Ski Town

Link approached the first structure—a sprawling three-story, L-shaped building with SNOWBIRD LUXURY CONDO-

MINIUMS painted in script on the front—at a steady dogtrot. While he was relatively certain the terrorists had flown out, they'd not been predictable in other of their actions. Perhaps the helicopters had brought in reinforcements. That seemed unlikely, but he constantly shifted his gaze to detect signs of danger.

The contrast between the previous terrible din and the present quiet was eerie. It also seemed incongruous that the gondola cars and lift lines were so still, and that the normally crowded square was so deserted, with none of the normal bustle of skiers clomping out to challenge the hill.

As he drew close, he noted movement behind windows on the second floor, and instinctively crouched to make a smaller target as he kept up the pace. He wished he had borrowed one of the Kevlar vests. A chilly gust made him huddle into the coat. He slowed enough to pull up the sheepskin collar, and realized that somewhere in the melee he'd lost his hat. Slowed again as he entered the basement parking lot, holding the shotgun—cocked, a round chambered—at the ready. In the center of the basement was a glassed-in island housing the elevator and stairwell. He continued past several frozen corpses. Two had been stripped. More lawmen, he decided, whose uniforms had been taken.

The bodyguards had set up shop on the third floor, in suite 324. Link took the stairs—made of pierced steel grating so skiers wouldn't slip in icy boots—trying to make little noise. On the first floor, he found a woman lying in front of a registration desk, throat cut and mouth open in an unheeded plea. Dried blood scabbed a ten-foot radius of carpet around her.

He returned to the stairwell and went on. At the second floor—where he'd noted watchers at the windows—sounds came from behind a door marked HOSPITALITY ROOM.

Hushed voices spoke in frightened tones, producing an incomprehensible polyglot of sound.

Leaned against the wall opposite the door were a dead man and woman, knife wounds slashed across faces and torsos, a section of gut bulging from their bellies. Grim warnings of what the people inside faced if they dared to emerge?

". . . don't hear him out there." "Maybe he went somewhere else." "How do we know he's not one of them?" "We should wait for the police, period, and . . ." ". . . all boarded the helicopter . . ." ". . . shooting right up to when they took off, so . . ." ". . . don't trust any of the . . ."

When Link knocked the voices fell silent.

"Is everyone okay in there?"

Man's voice: "Don't answer." Then, "Who are you?"

"My name's Anderson and I'm here to help. How many of you are inside?"

A woman's voice: "Forty-four adults and nine children. I'm one of the staff. They killed my boss while she was phoning for help, and brought the rest of us in here with the guests. The two out there tried to escape. They brought them back, and . . . and killed them, so you can understand we're frightened."

"Is anyone hurt?"

"We have three rape victims, and most of us have bruises from not moving fast enough, but no one's critical." Pause. "Are the killers *really* gone?"

"That's what I'm trying to determine. So far it looks like they've left."

"Thank God!"

"If you want, I'll lead you out to safety."

Dead silence for a moment, then the woman's voice again. "We were told if we tried to get out we'd be killed. We'll wait in here."

"One more question. Is Katy Dubois with you?"

"Hell no," the man grumbled. "The terrorists were asking for her."

"She's the *reason* for this," said a bitter female voice.

Link left on that sour note, returned to the stairs, and continued to the third floor. A man's body lay sprawled near the elevator.

Placards identified the suite numbers in the two wings. To his left were 305 through 325—he crept down the outside walkway, shotgun at the ready. The next to last door, adorned with a plastic NO SMOKING sign and the number 324, was ajar. Link entered cautiously, weapon poised, remembering the sounds of mayhem and death he'd heard from the room.

The living area was a mess, with trash and the remains of food littered about. Radio transmitters and a laptop computer—like those used by the Weyland Foundation—had been swept off a table and left in a jumble. The carpet was soaked with congealed blood. The killers had not been tidy. Bloody prints were tracked everywhere.

Link explored from front to back, unlatching doors, using the business end of the shotgun to push them open. The bedrooms and baths were messy, but empty. Back in the main area he followed bloody smears where bodies had been dragged, stepped out onto the balcony, and stared down over the railing. Three corpses had been tossed into the snowbank below, now covered by a few inches of snow. One was female, sprawled and head cocked upright so the features were visible. The eye sockets were bloody, identifying her as the one he'd heard being tortured.

It was neither Katy nor Maggie.

He looked toward the street, to where the bullet-riddled bus was parked, the squad members moving about. Identifiable by the orange flags tied about their left legs. Three bodies were laid in a neat row, on the opposite side of the road from the fake deputies. Good news, for he'd believed many more had been killed. A seemingly endless column of buses approached the ambush site from the highway.

"Katy? Maggie?" Link called out, not expecting an answer. He moved his gaze back to the snowbank, where the killers had discarded their victims like yesterday's trash. The silence was heavy. He leaned the shotgun on the rail, cupped his hands and called louder. "Katy Dubois? Maggie Tatro? It's Link Anderson!" The words echoed as he scanned the fields with dark and narrowed eyes, remembering what he'd heard when the killers had shot their way into the suite. Maggie had urged Katy to go off the balcony.

In the distance the convoy halted at the ambush site. State troopers in both white and olive drab uniforms dismounted. Two-person weapons teams hurried into protective positions about the riddled bus, kneeling and taking aim at nothing in particular.

"Katy!" he called again, squinting. "Maggie!" Again his eyes were drawn to the snowbank. He was about to look away, when he noted the slight movement of one of the bodies.

"It's safe," he said in a hushed voice, staring in disbelief. The one who had moved was the oldest of the two males—the supervisor he'd decided—riddled with gunshot wounds, and with two sizeable gouges missing from his chest.

The body shuddered again, and from its side appeared a gloved hand that did not belong, grasping up from the snow like a specter reaching from a grave.

The body shifted again. He heard a faint feminine cry. "Link?"

Someone was trapped under the corpse! Calling his name! Link spun about, hurried through the messy room, and rushed out the door. He ran to the stairs and then down, taking them three at a time, wanting to rejoice yet unwilling to think about what he might find.

He'd burst out the basement door, hurried past the bodies, and squirmed between vehicles before his heart dared to speed up . . . and he dared to hope.

Link ran until he saw a body—arm draped over the side of the snowdrift—and knew he was in the proper place. He left the shotgun, clambered up the side of a ten-foot bank, then paused for fear he might somehow harm the survivor.

There. He'd dared to think it. The *survivor*! When he had drawn himself up sufficiently to peer over the top, the spectral arm had become a torso and head. a bloody scarf covered the face. He reached out, hand shaking with excitement. "Let me help," he said.

She pawed the scarf aside, but he was slow to recognize the crimson-streaked features.

She frantically pushed at the supervisor's corpse, at the

same time trying to extricate herself from the ice-crust that had formed about her hiding place.

"Thank God," Link whispered, voice filled with raw emotion. Then he realized that the red streaks were not confined to her face. She was covered from head to waist with blood.

Joy turned to despair. "Oh God, Maggie," was all he could say, and felt like crying.

13

Link was gentle with the extraction, so he wouldn't harm a wounded limb. At first Maggie cooperated—then she began to whimper and thrash for she'd seen the horror of the young woman's face, with its eyeless sockets and agonized scream frozen into place. Link grasped her hands, and pulled. She held on as he dragged her off the bank, felt himself slipping, and clutched her protectively as they fell together.

Link gained his own feet and cautiously drew her up. Maggie's clothing and exposed skin were soaked with crimson—and he tried to determine the source of her bleeding.

She had trouble standing. "Be careful," he warned. "You're injured."

"Not . . . not my . . . blood." The words emerged in a rasp. She was so wobbly he had trouble holding her upright.

"Katy . . ." he began.

"Told her . . . go off the balcony . . . then I kept . . . shooting at the door until I . . . ran out of bullets." Link remembered the reports of a small-caliber pistol, puny compared to the sounds of shotgun and automatic weapons fire.

She shivered violently as her words tumbled forth. "Ran after her and jumped. Then had trouble . . . getting off the bank and I could . . . hear 'em up there . . . so I wiggled down in the snow." A ragged breath. "One of them stood up there and . . . and . . ."

"You're safe," he said gently.

". . . was shooting, so I was . . . lucky he missed. Then they . . . someone . . . dropped the bodies, and . . . and the supervisor landed on me and I was . . . I was under . . ." She shuddered violently, swayed, and began to crumple.

He steadied her. "Let's get you inside."

Maggie attempted to pull free. "Gotta find . . . Katy."

"First let's get you warm." He carried her toward the entrance, still unsure that she wasn't badly wounded. She didn't fight him, held on to his neck.

"When I heard you . . . nothing ever sounded . . . so *good*." Her face crumpled. "Oh, shit!" and she started to bawl.

"Good for you," he said softly, thinking of the horror she'd endured. "Don't keep it in." Maggie buried her face in his neck, her nose and cheeks cold as icicles on his skin, and continued blubbering. As they entered the basement, Link heard vehicles out on the street and voices barking orders. The state troopers had arrived.

He was pleased she didn't see the corpses. She'd had her share of horror. He started up the stairs. As they approached the second floor, she shuddered again, but had stopped crying. Someone called out from the hospitality suite, but Link went on without answering.

Maggie wiggled in his arms. "How're you doing?" he asked.

"Trying out my equipment. I kept moving the whole time, hoping nothing would freeze."

"Good." He was concerned that her core temperature might have dropped too far. Ninety-five degrees was okay. Ninety was dangerous. Eighty-five was critical. The good part was that he'd never seen anyone with severe hypothermia as lucid as Maggie seemed to be.

As he stepped onto the third floor he felt her tense, and understood. No one would wish to return to hell. "Which is your room?" he asked.

She spoke into his neck. "Three-twenty-three. The k—key's in my jacket p—pocket."

The suite was adjacent to the one he had inspected. Link juggled her as he retrieved the key—nestled in the pocket with a small pistol—opened the door and stepped in. While a few things were overturned, likely by the terrorists in their search for Katy, it was neater and warmer than the suite next door.

"In there," Maggie said, and he nudged open a door and deposited her on a king-size bed. She curled up as he pulled off gloves and heavy coat.

"We've got to get you warm, Maggie."

"Y—yeah." She was shuddering as he stepped into the bathroom.

He ran water, waited. "Good news," he called out. "The hot water wasn't shut off."

Outside bullhorns were blaring, announcing the arrival of the state police and telling citizens to remain inside until a unit arrived at their building.

As the tub filled, Link returned to Maggie. She'd shed gloves and scarf and was trying to unzip her blood-soaked parka with fingers that refused to work properly.

Link opened a closet, pulled out spare blankets, and took over the disrobing chore. He began by pulling off her boots. Followed with parka, ski pants, and heavy socks.

She began to fade and wilt.

"Damn it, hang in." He pulled her turtleneck over her head and added it to the heap. She was down to thermal underwear—made of a new synthetic wonder-fabric touted to be warmer than silk. Her clothing had been so blood-saturated that even those were red-streaked.

As he lifted her, she became a mass of jelly. Her teeth stopped chattering, her shuddering slowed, and Link wondered if she wasn't worse off than he'd imagined. He'd heard of hypothermic victims' hearts that had simply shut down, as if without reason. He carried her into the bathroom, and as they entered the steam-filled room Maggie emitted a low moan.

"Talk," he told her. "Complain. Call me names. Anything."

She released another moan as he knelt with her and felt the water. It was tepid, as he wanted. Too warm and she might not handle the shock. He lowered her.

"Oh God!" Maggie came alive, body tense as a board, lips drawn. "It's *hot*!"

"It's not, but keep talking," Link said gently, cautiously pleased at her lucidity. He rolled up shirtsleeves and removed his watch, and began moving his hands over her. Lightly, inspecting for a consistency of hard rubber. The water, now a rosy hue from all the blood, was up to her abdomen. He'd keep it running until she was immersed to her neck.

"It's like l—lightning bolts are shooting through my legs! Does that mean they're frozen?"

"No." He felt very protective. "The circulation's returning. Your blood's cold. It thickened and slowed down, but thank God it didn't freeze and stagnate."

"No frostbite?"

"A little. Light frostbite creates white speckles, like you have on your nose and cheeks."

"They sting."

"Good. That means you can feel them. It'll go away." He continued running his hands over her, pausing here and there. She relaxed a little. He avoided her legs. Do them too early and he might send a blood clot to her heart. "Your cheeks and nose will turn bright red. Also your sinuses will flow, but don't be embarrassed. That's everything coming back to life."

"I don't c—care."

Long minutes passed, and she was increasingly alert.

"I thought about you when I was down there, Lincoln."

"Yeah, well I worried about you." Should he be saying that? In her condition?

Link kept the water running. Exchanging it, letting it flow down the drain as he continued running the tap. He finished exploring, pleased that he'd found nothing terribly wrong. Her muscles were firm, but he'd encountered no hard rubber, which was how frozen flesh felt to the touch.

She'd gotten very cold and was hypothermic—but she was responding to warmth.

He was rubbing her neck lightly. Maggie peered into his eyes. "You've done this before."

"A few times."

"Darn. I was hoping I was your first."

He allowed a smile. She was coming around.

"So where'd you get your experience with this sort of thing. A back seat in high school?"

Link laughed. "I worked on a ski patrol, and a search and rescue team. I've seen people worse off, and I've been where you are. We'll thaw you nice and slow. From here on it keeps getting better." He eyed her, and had trouble dispelling inappropriate thoughts.

She gave a small shiver that agitated the water. "Thanks for being here."

"It's the other way around. I'm thankful I found you alive."

Her voice dropped to a purr. "God you've got wonderful hands."

Half dead and she was flirting? At which time he realized that he was admiring her exquisiteness, a fact that was readily apparent, for the water-soaked thermal underwear had become transparent. He was running a hand over her rib cage and wondered . . . and forced his eyes away, ashamed of his thought.

Link made himself concentrate on her right hand, on the fingers he kneaded and rubbed in turn. He switched to the other hand.

Catching himself looking again. Stop! He was trying to save her life, for God's sake. The water was to her breasts. A harmless glance? He felt for the plug, staring. Heard his voice emerging in a sort of croak. "I'll let the water drain faster. Get it warmer."

"You were right, Lincoln," she murmured. "It just keeps getting better."

They heard sounds of people running on the walkway outside.

She tensed. "Friendlies?"

"State police. A *lot* of 'em."

They heard them crashing into the suite next door. Loud yells, then more noises as they battered their way into various bedrooms.

"God that feels good," she said as he massaged her feet.

"And you can feel everything I'm doing?"

"It hurts when you first touch something, then it stings, and after a bit it just feels nice." Maggie made a happy face and groaned as he began with the second arch. She grew a cute lopsided smirk. "Here I am stark naked in front of a nice-looking guy I like, who's just felt me from top to bottom, and I'm thinking about how great my *feet* feel?"

"You're not na—" He realized he was admiring a stiff and rosy nipple; went on working with the foot, fastidiously keeping his eyes there. He changed the subject, trying to sound more clinical. "Are you having any chest pain?"

"No."

That meant it was unlikely there was pneumonia. As her core temperature returned to normal she would remain vulnerable, but he was generally pleased. "Lean forward," he said. He took a minibottle of shampoo and a plastic cup from the sink; repeatedly poured warm water over her head, then worked up lather, loosening congealed blood so it would rinse away.

"Wonderful," she whispered, eyes closed.

"Any ideas about who the bad guys might be?"

"It's like it was all a vague dream, but some of it's starting to come back. There was a man on the balcony talking on a phone. His voice was distinctive. Low and deep, but like he was using a stage whisper. You know, quiet but it carried? He spoke to the Voice and to something named tee can. Katy heard him on their radios, and said he was in charge." She paused. "Axel! His name was Axel, and something about him kept trying to ring a bell in my brain. But"—she sighed—"I'm not sure if he was real or I was hallucinating."

He was real. Link had heard the deep voice on the phone.

Seen the face across the street in the window. Sensed the evil. "Axel," Link repeated. Feeling his anger rise.

Maggie's eyelids were drooping. She tried out her frown. "Is my nose red like you said?"

"Yeah. Rosy cheeks too." He felt an urge to hold her, even wondered how she would react. "Any ideas about how the terrorists know everything we do almost before we do it?"

"Just that it's eerie. Like how did they know we had Katy in that room? And how did they handle the cops so easily?" Her speech slowed. "Tough cops too, and not amateurs."

Maggie sat up a little, moodily eyed her body, then looked at him. "Would you get my suitcase? It's the blue one in the next bedroom. My purse should be next to it."

"I'm harder to get rid of than that, Maggie."

Her voice was soft. "There's no one I'd rather be doing this with. Scout's honor. I've been having unladylike thoughts about you since I saw you the other day. But everything's working again, and we've got to find Katy."

"You don't think the terrorists have her?"

"I don't know, but they were sure looking right up to the end." Maggie sighed. "I'm also worried that if she's still hiding, it's awfully cold out there."

"Agreed." Link got to his feet. "You're hypothermic, Maggie. your temperature's still much lower than it should be, so keep soaking." Her breasts were exquisite.

"You're looking again."

"I am not."

Subtle smile. "Go get my purse and my suitcase, would you?"

"Keep the water circulating, and make sure you don't go to sleep no matter how badly you want to. When you get out, wrap up in blankets. We don't want pneumonia settling in."

She listened carefully. Nodded.

Link went next door and retrieved her blue suitcase, returned, and opened it on a luggage stand. He rapped once on the bathroom door. "I'm going out to see what's going on."

"Would you come back in for a minute?"

He did, and she motioned him close. When he knelt she put her arms about his neck, and smooched him on the lips. "Thank you for coming for me, Lincoln." Her voice was throaty.

"You'll be okay?"

"Yep. Don't forget your watch, and bring my pistol."

He went back out, reloaded the snub-nose .32 Smith & Wesson revolver with rounds he found in her purse, and placed it in her reach. "I'll send a doctor."

"If you get a choice, could you make it a woman? I'm going to get out of this invisible suit." Maggie slid down in the water and sighed as he closed the bathroom door.

As he emerged, a dozen SWAT team members pounced, leveling various weapons.

"He's a friendly." Supervising Agent Gordon Tower ambled down the walkway, carrying a badly crushed Stetson.

Link nodded a greeting. "Last time I saw you, weren't you humping a driveshaft?"

"I'd just as soon you didn't spread that around." He handed over the flattened hat. "I think you lost this when you were crawling around on your belly out there."

Link examined, wondering if the hat was terminal.

"I take it he's one of yours," said a SWAT team member wearing captain's tracks.

"Yeah. Stetson beret and all."

The SWAT captain reluctantly motioned for his men to back off, let down at losing the only potential bad guy they'd encountered.

"Maggie's alive," Link told Tower.

"You found her *here*?" The FBI agent looked surprised.

"Where'd you think she was?" Link said archly, and explained she was inside thawing.

"I'd like to talk with her. She may know something critical."

"Until her temperature's back to normal, no one's going

to talk to her except a doctor. She just spent five hours in a snowbank under a frozen corpse." He explained.

"Jesus." Tower looked uneasy at the thought.

"If anyone asks, she was *definitely* hypothermic, which isn't something you can fake. Now she's trying to get her body temperature back to normal. Is there a doctor around?"

"State guys brought a half-dozen EMTs and a doc with each one." Tower waved the SWAT team leader back over. The captain looked at him so oddly when he mentioned Maggie's name, it was obvious that some kind of communication had been passed around regarding her.

When the captain called for a medic, Link interrupted. "Get her a real doctor, okay? And at the risk of sounding like a sexist pig, make it a female."

As he complied, Gordon Tower regarded Link. "What does she say about Katy?"

"She hasn't seen her since she went off the balcony. She followed pronto, but Katy was already gone and she spent her time burrowing and getting bled on."

Link asked about the people in the hospitality suite, and learned they were on the way to the hospital. Some were still blaming it all on Katy.

"How many dead so far?"

"Two dozen and climbing. The electronics is back on at Hayden Airport and a planeful of FBI agents are finally on the ground. Soon as they're here I'll send them out with the state guys to keep score. There's been nothing like this since the Civil War. The terrorists hurt a lot of people."

Link was staring at the low clouds, tossing an idea around in his mind. "Anyone know where they might have gone?" he asked.

"Not a clue. The FAA's got everyone in the state looking for the helicopter."

The doctor arrived, and Link let her into the suite. "Go cautiously," he told her, and explained the pistol. When he closed the door, she was prudently calling Maggie's name.

His idea continued to form. The terrorists might still be

airborne, but Link did not believe so. A layer of angry clouds blanketed them, and no sane helicopter pilot would fly in such a storm.

An older man wearing a star on the epaulets of a down-filled coat came out of suite 324 and addressed Gordon. "The helicopter lifted off from the local airport. I'm sending people there. Care to go along?"

"I'll pass. My agents should be here shortly."

"I'd like to go," Link said. A visit to the airport fit with his idea. While Hayden had safer all-weather approaches, the Steamboat Springs facility was much closer.

Gordon Tower introduced him to the state police commissioner, then added, "Mr. Anderson is also an aviator who knows his stuff."

"That's what we need." They shook hands. "I'm sending the SWAT team captain and a couple of his men, but there's room."

While the commissioner made the arrangement, Tower turned to Link with an inquisitive look. "Something at the airport you're particularly interested in?"

"Maybe. Could I get you to check on Maggie after the doctor's done?"

"I'd planned to. She may have insights, which is something we're short of."

"Take it easy on her, Gordon. She's been through a lot." Link started down the stairs, feeling unsettled and very protective.

PART 2

Black Canyon

14

The Ford Expedition was one of scores of vehicles brought in by the state police. Two troopers were in front, Link and the SWAT captain in the second seat. Higgie, who had asked to be dropped off in town on their way through, was in back.

The captain regarded Link. "You're an aviation expert with the *Justice* Department?" He continued looking, as if inquisitive as to where Link stood in the hierarchy of things.

"A pilot," was all Link said.

"How'd you like to have to fly in this crud?" asked a police sergeant looking up at billowing clouds.

"I'm thinking of doing just that. It's according to what the weather does between now and when we get to the airport."

Higgie spoke up. "Wouldn't leave you any maneuvering room. Cloud ceiling's only three, four hundred feet."

"I'd have to find the right airplane," Link agreed. "Something maneuverable and slow, with good vision."

"Who'd you take with you on this hypothetical flight?"

"I'd go alone." He would not want to have to worry about a passenger.

As they passed the bullet-ridden bus, Link noted the blood still bright on the snow.

The captain shook his head sadly. "They should have waited for more firepower."

"They did what they had to do," said Link.

They approached a growing lineup of vehicles.

"I knew they were checking the vehicles going out," said Higgie. "Looks like they're inspecting the ones coming in as well."

"Have to," groused the captain. "The idiot radio announcer told everyone the missing girl's Daddy Warbucks' daughter. Every redneck around's headed here lookin' for free money."

"Roadblock won't stop them," the sergeant added. "They're swarming in in snowmobiles and ATVs, asking how much reward they'd get to bring in the girl."

As they waited, Link examined his hat, a ten-star John B. Stetson that had set him back a considerable sum. Regardless of the generous salary received from the Weyland Foundation, it was not in him to toss it aside. He smoothed it into a dome with his fingers, regarded it from one side, then the other. It was badly askew. He did it again, with the same results.

"How long we gotta sit here like this?" Higgie asked from the back.

"Be a couple minutes before we can get around 'em," said the driver.

"Give me that," Higgie told Link with a trace of disgust. "And let me out." Outside, he sauntered to the rear, and bent down. Thirty seconds later he returned, holding the hat carefully, the felt steaming from the hot exhaust. He gave the crown a few deft strokes, bent the brim in a hint of a curl, waited for a few seconds, and handed it over. Except for dark smudges, the Stetson was perfectly formed, right down to the three cattleman's creases.

"Trick I learned," said Higgie. "Better'n new now 'cause it's got a history."

As soon as he was seated, they were treated to another of Higgie's bad jokes, explaining how local sheepherders were distinguishable because they wore wide-topped boots to accommodate ovine rear legs, then how they distinguished between ugly and pretty ewes.

"Yous?" asked a city-boy policeman.

The traffic moved. When they were close the driver pulled around the remainder of the line. The state trooper inspectors waved their brethren through.

On the other side, the vehicles extended all the way to the Highway 40 intersection. The sergeant snorted in disgust. "Most are treasure hunters." There were also lawmen, and in one of the vehicles the Weyland Foundation's chief investigator was talking animatedly.

Link wondered if he still harbored antagonism toward Maggie.

At they turned north on the highway, Link looked back. "Where are the trucks?"

"I saw 'em too," said Higgie.

The SWAT captain spoke into his collar radio, said "Roger," and switched off. "The highway terminates at Interstate 70. They'll all be stopped and searched there."

With that, Link forgot about the big rigs. He had enough on his plate.

"You're actually thinking of flying in this crud?" Higgie asked.

"If I can find the right bird and the weather holds."

"Mind telling me why?"

"We're surrounded by mountains here. There'd be no way to fly anywhere without getting into heavy storm clouds."

Higgie was thoughtful, nodded. "That's true."

Link explained that the helicopter was likely headed for Denver or Salt Lake City, but it was unlikely they'd cross the mountains in severe weather. Since the helicopter did not have an unlimited supply of jet fuel, it made sense that they'd land to wait out the storm.

"I'd like to go looking."

"So happens, my brother and I keep a two-seat Tri-Pacer Colt at the Steamboat airport. He gives lessons in it, and we rent it out and such. I got my private license in it fifteen years back, and I get in a few hours. Like to visit friends or locate a stray during the calving season."

A Piper Colt would be perfect. He had another idea. "You must know what the area looks like from the air."

"About as good as you know your wife's right bosom."

With no wife handy, Link squelched a vision of Maggie in her transparent underwear.

"I'd like to use your airplane *and* your help, Higgie."

Higgie raised eyebrows. "I wouldn't treasure flying in this weather."

"Just help me find out where to look." Link explained.

"Might just work," said Higgie, nodding slowly. He told the police sergeant he'd go on to the airport with them, then asked if anyone had a cell telephone. Link handed over his satellite phone, which also worked on both analog and digital cell systems.

Higgie punched in the numbers for the radio station.

11:35 A.M.—Highway 131

They were making slow time. Although the road had been cleared enough that they had no problem getting through, there was considerable ice and convoy after convoy of official vehicles coming the opposite direction. When Annie heard the truckers in front of her talking about the roadblock, it was too late to avoid it. The cops had set up a mile short of I-70, and she was in sight of it before she could pull over and think things over, and maybe try to wait them out.

She'd stopped at the market south of Steamboat to call Leroy J. Manners and find out what to do about the girl. He might have even told her the cops would do something like this, and to ditch the girl or even try to collect a reward. But the phone had been out of order.

Leroy seldom trusted her to do the right thing. Not that she was much better at the trust game. He cheated on her when he got the chance, but he came home most nights and kept up her supply of Jimmy Beam sour mash, so she wasn't going to squeal so loud he booted her out.

Annie slowed, then stopped at the back of the lineup. Trying to be gentle and not wake up the kid in back. Thinking about what to do about the situation.

Before she could ponder much on it, a highway patrol-piggie was at the side of the tractor, motioning for her to roll down her window. She knew him, an overeager asshole assigned to the stretch of I-70 between Gypsum and Glenwood Springs. She did not like him, but he was as good a choice as she could expect. Once before she'd used the stink pot to dissuade him from checking too closely, and he'd not been eager to crawl up there since.

But would the kid hear? Maybe try to get out? Annie set the brake and opened the door. She grabbed on to the mirror and swung to the ground, letting the driver's door swing shut.

"You alone?" he asked, snappish and looking past her at the cab.

"Yeah. Got me another cat so it's kinda ripe, but you wanta look, go ahead."

He dolefully squinted at the cab, then at her. "Where you coming from, Annie?"

"Yampa," she lied, indicating a one-horse town halfway to Steamboat. She bent over the front wheel as if there were something there of interest. "Lookin' for something?"

He ignored her question, just looked her rig over with the superior kind of look that only cops could give. "See anyone walking on the road?"

"In this weather?" she asked incredulously. Wondering if he'd ask for a bill of lading, and wishing she'd brought the fakes she'd prepared showing she'd hauled boxes of toilet tissue and paper towels. Certainly no stolen motorcycles and guns like she'd taken to Cheyenne, using back roads and driving nights to avoid weigh stations.

The driver in front revved his diesel and released his brakes. Started to roll.

The cop was looking at a rig that was pulling up behind her. "Go on," he said.

"How's the interstate?" she asked, no shit wanting to know.

"It's clear to Grand Junction." He knew she was from Montrose. "Might be a delay after you get on Fifty." He was backing away, anxious to see her gone. *Good piggie,* Annie thought.

Annie traveled only ten miles of interstate before pulling off into the town of Eagle. She left the engine running, intending to cross the street to a small café with a pay phone in the back.

She heard a steady thumping on the hatch, and leaned close. "Whatcha need, kid?"

"Where are we?"

Annie started to tell her, then thought better. Scrunched her nose as she considered various lies. "Not far from where you climbed in. Those two cops followed us and they're out there looking again."

"Still?"

"Yeah." Annie grinned at her own cleverness. "You just settle down and keep quiet, and I'll get out and talk to 'em some more."

The kid worked the handle. "The door's locked."

"So it'll look right, dummy. Hey, you want I'll say screw it and you can get your young ass out. Those guys are up just ahead, and they're looking back here right now."

The kid remained quiet, likely thinking about it. Probably hearing the occasional car passing on the street, which Annie could do nothing about, and wondering.

"Like I told you," she said, "we didn't go far."

"What time is it?"

Annie figured the less the girl knew the better. "Hey, kid. I gotta get out and talk to 'em. You stay real quiet. They hear you and . . . you know."

She got out, locked the door, and went across to the café, and headed for the pay phones in back. Used up sixty cents calling the cabin and talking to the stupid answering machine they had stolen off a K-Mart truck. She hated talking to the thing, but told the machine she was on her way, and if Leroy came home to wait for her. She had something he should see.

Next Annie called the Conoco Station where Leroy

worked in back pumping propane, and wasted another sixty cents because the owner said things were slow and Leroy had taken the day off. "Try the Cowboy," he said. So she used her last quarter calling the bar where they hung out, where she should have called first, seeing it was a Saturday.

"I'll get him," said the mixologist, which was what the bartender with no tits wanted others to call her. Annie felt jealousy warm her ears despite the fact that the mixologist was married to her own nephew, for she'd been known to cozy up to Leroy when Annie was on the road.

She heard someone shouting as they jostled a pinball machine that was clanging back.

"Yeah?" came Leroy's sullen voice. He did not like her calling him at the Cowboy.

"I'm in Eagle, on my way home. You been listening to the news?"

"You want the news, turn on your radio. I'm busy."

"About what happened in Steamboat, I mean. You hear about all the shooting and such?"

His voice filled with admiration. "You mean somebody kicking ass big-time, yeah I heard. So far they's forty dead in town and fifty feds in a crash. You there when it happened?"

"Yeah, I got stuck there on the way back." She took a breath. "I got something with me."

He laughed. "Better be green and it better be more'n two thousand."

She'd gotten twelve hundred dollars from the dealer in Cheyenne. Leroy had said to demand two thousand, but the dealer laughed in her face.

"Not that. Something else." She paused, looked at a waitress talking on another phone just three feet distant. "Or maybe some*one* else."

"You drinkin' on the road again? You get caught, don't come whinin' to me."

She was increasingly nervous, not wanting to explain about the kid because the waitress might overhear. How could she get him to understand?

"Annie, you fuck up again, and I'm . . ."

"Dammit, Leroy, listen!" Her outburst shocked him. Annie did not talk to him like that and might well get a thumping for it, but the more she thought about what she'd done, the more nervous she became. She took in a breath. "Did you hear what those people was looking for?"

"Some rich kid. They're talking about it at the bar now." His voice sort of trailed off.

Annie looked at the waitress, hoping she was so wound up with her own conversation she would not listen to theirs. She lowered her voice. "I've got her out in the truck."

Leroy was silent, digesting what she'd said. Then, "In your truck?"

"Locked in the sleeper."

He digested again, then exploded. "Jesus. You got her in . . . Jesus!"

Annie cringed, even though he was not in striking distance. "You ever hear of kidnapping?"

"I wasn't thinking, hon. I been bullshitting her. I'll let her out and she'll be happy."

He was quiet.

"Should I try for the reward?"

"Naw, you'd just fuck it up. Just a minute. I gotta think." He paused again.

She waited. Biting her lip and thinking of what he'd said. Kidnapping was serious stuff. People had always said she had more guts than good sense. Dummy, she called herself. Dummy!

"She see you?"

"Yeah." How'd he think the kid had got in her sleeper without seeing her?

"You tell her about me?"

"I wouldn't never do that."

Another pause. Then, "Take her to the cabin. Time you get there, I'll have it figured out."

Relief flooded over Annie, and she almost laughed with happiness. "I done the right thing, didn' I, Leroy?"

"We'll talk about it."

"You hear about her daddy? Hon, she's the big chance we been talkin' about."

"Maybe." But he sounded more and more pleased. He asked when she'd get there. Shouldn't be more than four hours, long as the road from Grand Junction was open. He said to call him from the cabin. He was talking to Shag and they had business to clear up.

12:10 P.M.—Steamboat Springs Airport

Link listened as the airport operator explained how two weeks earlier arrangements had been made to rent the empty hangar at the far end of the field. A man of medium stature, with a mustache and ponytail, had explained he was working for the DEA, and had shone a badge, although the operator had not thought to examine it.

The agent had needed a place to hide a helicopter from public view, part of a covert operation to intercept a load of drugs coming over the Canadian border. He could tell him no more, but the operator had been happy to cooperate.

Yesterday midmorning, before the storm had arrived, the helicopter had shown up and landed beside the hangar. It was a tight fit, but the two men had squeezed it in. When no one had come to the operations shack after a couple of hours, he'd driven down to check them out. Not suspiciously, but he'd been interested. The agent had emerged wearing dark coveralls and a knit hat, waving him off and shaking his head like he wasn't supposed to come closer.

That had been his only contact. He hadn't questioned the government men, and as instructed, he had not told anyone else they were there.

Early this morning, when he'd arrived behind his snowplow to open up the operations shack, he had heard about the craziness in Ski Town from the local radio station. Thinking the government pilots who had obviously spent the night should know about the events, he'd gone there. They hadn't responded to his banging on the door. Still it

had never occurred to him that they might be involved with
the terrorists. At eight, he'd seen the doors opening, and the
helicopter being pushed out. No more activity for a while,
as he'd listened to reports about the missing rich girl and the
shootings and such. Then the helo pilots had started engines. At precisely 9 A.M. they had taken off. No call to the
operations building, nothing about clearance. Just taken off
and disappeared.

He'd checked the hangar. They'd left not as much as a
cigarette butt. He'd still believed they were on a secret
dope-stopping mission, so he had not even mentioned their
departure to the FAA, until the troopers had called, asking if
he knew anything about a gray helicopter.

Link finished inspecting the Piper Colt. The 38-year-old,
108-horsepower, tube and fabric two-seater had a high-
wing and offered excellent visibility of terrain. Also, it had
been hangared during the storm, which meant he did not
have to remove accumulated snow.

The radio station was airing the message Higgie had requested, explaining that he was working with state authorities trying to track down the killers who had terrorized Ski
Town. The announcer asked all ranchers residing south of
Mount Werner, and anyone else who had seen or heard the
helicopter, to call Higginbotham at the airport.

Higgie and the state trooper sergeant were taking a steady
stream of calls, trying to narrow down the search area. The
ranchers liked the idea of capturing terrorists. So did the
SWAT captain, who returned to Steamboat Springs to organize an excursion team, in case they were located.

15

12:35 P.M.—Bob Adams Airport

The moment Link was airborne he knew it was a good choice. The Colt was a slow but maneuverable workhorse, a stable platform with superb visibility. But those attributes also meant he was vulnerable to ground fire, so he must remain out of shooting range of the terrorists.

He turned back toward Old Town and called Higgie. They need not worry about radio interference. The Colt was the only airplane using the field.

According to the Weather Service, the storm would linger, and for the next few hours the cloud ceiling would drift up and down. Link felt the helicopter pilot would likely wait to escape, hopefully long enough for him to learn *where* they were waiting and call in the state troopers.

Link flew past Old Town. "I'm abeam the courthouse," he announced to Higgie.

"We've had close to three dozen calls, mostly from ranchers south of Ski Town. The helicopter flew past the Clark and Blaisdale spreads. Mike McGinty lives seventeen miles out and they went smack over his head. But the Ace-High Ranch is just six miles farther, and no one there saw anything. They heard 'em, but they didn't go over. Where are you now?"

"Flying south on Highway 40. Mount Werner and Ski Town are off to my left."

"Look about five miles straight ahead. See where the road forks?"

"Not yet." Link estimated the visibility to be only a mile, and to make matters worse there was little visual difference between objects and background. The world was without depth, a condition of nature that skiers and pilots alike call "flat light" due to the odd polarization. Nor was there adequate room for maneuvering, only the meager space from the surface to the bottoms of the low, roiling clouds. Although he could not see them, not far to his left the terrain rose abruptly—the base of the high Rockies, some of which soared to fourteen thousand feet.

Link was sweeping his vision about when he spotted an irregularity on a rolling hillside. He turned for it. "I've got something on my left, about half a mile off Highway 40."

"Don't get close," Higgie warned.

"It's not the helicopter. I'm throttled back and flying slower, and . . ." He passed it, then turned a wing up to observe. "It's an abandoned snowmobile. Maroon-colored, like the terrorists used. The helicopter was obviously here because the rotor-blast dusted it off and left a circular snow-blown area. Yeah, there's the marks left by the skids where they put down. Looks like someone got out and . . . there's a human body with blood around the head like he was shot. Better advise the SWAT captain."

"Sure will," Higgie said. He asked about landmarks and fixed the position on his map.

Link returned to course. "I can see the fork in the highway up ahead."

"The left branch is US 40. State 131 meanders to the right. When you get to the fork, split the difference and fly due south. The first ranch is Rip Blaisdale's. He said the helicopter flew over going very fast." Higgie called out terrain features, like a streambed—the dwindling Yampa River—visible only because of stark cottonwoods that grew along its banks. He approached the McGinty ranch, where the helos had last been seen, and Higgie unnecessarily cautioned him to be careful from there on, because he might be getting close, and to *definitely* avoid overflying the next house.

"That's the Ace-High spread. Paul and Barb Chase live there, and she gets upset when anything disturbs her layin' hens. You might think those terrorists are bad, but Barb can be downright mean when someone disturbs her layin' hens. Paul starts up his tractor at the wrong time and she gives him what for. This morning she heard the helicopter comin' their way, but she thinks they veered off, because she kept hearing it, but no one ever saw it."

Link scanned the snowclad countryside, found nothing except rolling hills, fields of snow, and a few small wind-blown structures scattered about.

"I got Barb on the line," Higgie said. "She says don't come much closer. Better listen, 'cause she keeps an old .44 revolver, and doesn't hesitate using it. Took after a wolf last year and scared the pee outa the thing shootin' up the countryside."

Link was smiling. "I won't go much closer."

"She's saying this morning's sounds came from east of where she hears you now."

East? He looked leftward toward invisible mountains, saw nothing of note but turned there anyway and told Higgie what he was doing.

"They couldn't of gone far because of the terrain. They're either close by or turned the other direction."

After another full minute Link was running out of maneuvering room.

"Still no helicopter?" Higgie sounded disappointed.

"Nothing." Link eyeballed the diminishing space between clouds and earth, then scanned again for sign of the chopper. Wondering if they had somehow camouflaged it.

"There oughta be a big old hay barn close by."

"Just passed it off to my left." He had noted that it was starting to fall in on one side.

"Sure thought they'd be there," Higgie complained. "Don't try going no farther. There's a steep hill directly in front of you. Maybe you oughta go back and check around that old barn."

Link spotted the solid gray mountainside. "Will do." He rolled sharply left, pulling back on the yoke and coordinating the turn with a little rudder so it would be smoothly done and he'd neither climb nor lose altitude. Also wanting to slow down to examine the hay barn.

He completed the one-eighty turn and rolled out wingslevel, flying slow, the decrepit barn offset slightly to his left. There was nothing of note to see—only a large, weathered building with missing boards and doors hanging askew. Then his eyes narrowed.

The snow in front of the big swinging doors appeared trampled, as if people had walked there. Closer and he could make out skid marks.

Too close! Before he could react his world changed from tranquil winter serenity to an inferno of gunfire—from a world of quiet white to one where brilliant fireflies flashed and winked furiously from every opening and shadow of the old structure.

"They're in the barn," Link said over the radio. "Shooting." No response. He called again. *Nothing.* Link had the nose down and was diving, although at a much slower rate of descent than he'd prefer. He could hear the *pfft-pfft* whispers of bullets passing through the cockpit like hot darts cutting through butter, two of them holing the windscreen, another thumping into the overhead.

"I'm taking hits," Link announced, his tone even although his pulse was pounding.

Higgie's radio had gone out, and now sparks flashed from the Colt's radio console. No way to contact anyone, but that did not concern Link nearly as much as a pair of rounds that punched through the canvas seat on his right, leaving gaping holes.

He skimmed over a stand of cottonwoods, dropped even lower, and was finally out of their sight. Beyond was a flat expanse where he hugged the earth, the Piper engine churning out its paltry horsepower as he fled, still wary and alert, for while he was out of the range of their small arms, he did not know if they'd deployed other shooters.

Link eyes his gauges, and as he dwelled on a particular one, his olfactory senses confirmed that the tank was punctured. Next question—how fast was the fuel draining?

Very fast, he concluded, for he could actually see the needle dropping. There'd certainly not be enough to make it back to the airport—and after a longer look he wondered about reaching the highway! He would have to put it down soon.

As he looked for a suitable place for an emergency landing, Link wondered why the terrorists hadn't fired the first time he'd passed by. Only after he and Higgie had discussed the barn had they fired, and then with all they had, as if they knew when he was onto them. And again an airport's radio had gone out at the critical moment. *Another* coincidence?

Where to put down? Hopefully somewhere that wouldn't destroy the airplane. A field of snow might work, but considering the tricycle landing gear, a plowed road would be best.

The Ace-High Ranch was close, but Link rejected the thought. If the terrorists decided to follow, he must not draw them to others. He climbed until he was skimming beneath the swirling clouds, continuing westward toward the highway. The low fuel light flickered, came on as the needle dipped to E. The highway was still not in view when the engine coughed, and he knew he must pick a suitable snowfield. The engine sucked in a vestige of fuel and revved to full torque—as he discerned the highway in the distance.

Could he make it? The Colt was light and nimble, and had a fair glide ratio.

The engine sputtered, and the prop flailed a few more times and stopped. The world became silent and he could hear only the whistle of the cold wind.

He made the right turn into the wind, gently and not daring to overdo it. The airplane floated around the corner until he was aligned with the roadway. He let it sink, flared just a little, and touched down. Skittered once and then was firmly on the surface. The bird rolled for only a hundred yards. As it slowed to a crawl, he guided it to the far right side of the highway.

Link switched everything off and climbed out. He released a long pent-up breath, turned to look—and stared. Holes were stitched along the length of the fuselage, several rows of evenly spaced and symmetrical perforations punched into the fabric. A hasty count showed fifty-odd hits, and there were undoubtedly more on other surfaces. Yet with a patch job and a new fuel tank, the airplane would fly again. Willie T. Piper had built tough airplanes.

He pulled out the flip-top satellite phone, pressed MEM, then 1. Erin picked up. "Extension two-seven-seven-five." Her voice was cheerful, as always.

He asked if she'd hook him up with the Steamboat Springs airport.

"Sure." She went off line. A few seconds later he heard a buzz as the telephone rang. "Where are you?" she asked conversationally as they waited.

He looked around. "I'm not really sure."

"Mmm. How about the highway next to the Ace High Ranch, owned by Paul and Barbara Chase."

"You're amazing." He meant it.

When he picked up, Higgie could hardly believe his ears. "You're alive!"

16

The convoy of police buses and four-wheel drive vehicles arrived just forty-five minutes after Link landed. The SWAT captain, first out of the lead pickup, took in the airplane.

"You're a lucky man, Mr. Anderson."

Link nodded into the worsening weather. "They're in a barn seven miles that way."

"How many?"

"Enough to make all those holes."

"The helicopter's in the barn with them?"

"Yeah. The area around the doors was trampled, and there were skid marks where they'd pushed it inside. I should have noticed it the first time I went by."

"Think they've left?"

"I doubt it. They probably knew they hit me and I couldn't go far. And even if I made it all the way back, so what? We can't get to them on the ground, and the ceiling's too low to fly back there again. The good news is the weather's still too cruddy to get over the mountain, which is where I think they're heading."

His cell phone buzzed. Higgie said that so far the people at the Ace-High Ranch hadn't heard the helicopter start up. Also, the airport's radio systems were back on the air.

"What's the latest weather forecast?"

"Two more hours of scattered flurries, then it'll lift."

"Sorry about your airplane but we'll have it repaired or replaced. Your call."

As Link shut off the phone the SWAT captain was looking eastward. "How about roads?"

"Nothing's plowed within five miles of the barn."

"And you don't think they'll take off in this stuff?" the captain asked again.

"They'd have to be crazy." Link looked and found the captain smiling.

"Let's bank on them not being crazy," said the captain.

They heard sounds of diesel engines, then of large vehicles shifting and slowing.

"That's a dozen Sno-Cats I asked for from Steamboat Springs. Also two M-60 machine guns. No way they'll outgun us again. Can you point out the way?"

"You bet." Link's smile had grown to match that of the captain. If the snow continued for another hour and the terrorists stayed put, they'd catch them.

Only minutes passed before the Sno-Cats were unloaded from the flatbeds and lined up on the highway. The fields were covered with four feet of snow. Drifts reached higher. The flexi-track Sno-Cats handled such accumulations with ease. In each were four heavily armed state troopers. The SWAT captain and Link Anderson were in the lead vehicle.

"Check in," the captain called over radio, and one by one the drivers reported that they were ready to go. Their own driver revved the Sno-Cat's diesel engine and released the brakes.

Link had told them the terrain was open most of the way. The captain had advised the state police commissioner that they should be at the barn in twenty minutes.

2:40 P.M.—Abandoned Hay Barn

The men were grunting and cursing as they manhandled the helicopter through the doors. It had been a tight fit, and Axel did not want to damage the craft by being hasty. Yet he also knew that time was critical.

He took a call from T-Can West, and announced, "We have fifteen minutes."

The first pilot was staring at the sky and the tiny flakes. "You want to fly in this?"

"There will be fifty state troopers with machine guns. If we stay we'll end up as dead as if we fly and don't make it. You said you could do it when we were planning."

"I said we could get out blind, like at night, not during a *blizzard*."

"We have no choice."

"I'd rather wait for a lull and fly a few miles down the valley. There's more old barns."

"Perhaps there will be no lulls. All of the ranchers are listening now, and the state police would just come for us again. So prepare to fly."

The second pilot was even gloomier. Also looking at the weather. "Jet helicopters are fragile, and they sure aren't designed to fly in blizzards. They ice up. And to try to get over the mountains in a storm when there's pockets of turbulence and wind shears and every other kind of air agitation you can think of?" He shook his head. "It would be suicide to try it."

"But you *will* try it," said Axel. "Once we get on the other side, we'll be safe."

"That's a fourteen-thousand-foot mountain between us and the other side. With this load we can't even *get* that high."

Axel sighed. "One last time I will tell you your business. If you go the right away, it is only ten thousand-five. And you have the best and most expensive navigation systems . . ."

"GPS receivers," said the first pilot, trying to convince himself. "The military version that pinpoints us within twenty feet."

"See, and you have maps that give accurate elevations."

"Yeah," the first pilot echoed. "Great maps."

"Then you should be able to fly blind."

The second pilot remained gloomy. "If the icing doesn't make us crash, our weight will."

The first pilot nodded. "We're carrying too much fuel and gear, and too many passengers. We didn't expect to haul *everyone*."

"How long would it take to offload enough fuel?"

"Maybe half an hour?"

"Too long. We'll leave the weapons behind."

"That'll help, but not enough."

"How much more weight would you like to be rid of?"

"I tell you there's no safe way to fly in that stuff," argued the second pilot.

"Damn it, how much weight?" Axel glared fiercely.

"Four hundred pounds."

Axel looked around. Battise, the pudgy distributor from Newark was standing by the barn door, huddling in his coat. He was a big man in Newark. Here he was dead weight.

Axel palmed the pistol, then walked over and took the guy's arm. "Come into the barn for a minute. I've got something for you."

"We gonna get out of here okay?" he asked nervously.

"Yes we are," he said as Battise pushed his hands deeper into his pockets, and stepped inside with him. *Accept my offering, great Huitzilopóchtli.*

All the others heard was the pop of the .22 round.

Axel went out and waved the two pilots in. Their eyes bulged at the sight of the dead man. "Will that be enough?" he asked them.

"Jesus," whispered the second pilot. He closed his eyes and shook his head.

Axel raised the pistol. *Pop!* The second pilot fell like a stone.

The first pilot backed toward the door, wide-eyed. "Prepare to leave," Axel said as he solemnly arranged the bodies into a T. Neither was a true enemy, but his god was insatiable.

He set off the flare he'd left in the barn, and went back out, the small automatic tucked back in his pocket. As the fire began to spread they all stared at Axel in abject fear. More than they felt about flying in weather.

"We should start loading, don't you think?"

2:52 P.M.—Open Range, Ace-High Ranch

"Anything new about Katy Dubois?" Link yelled to the captain as they rumbled and bounced across the snowy fields.

"Nothing, and they've finished checking all the condos and homes. It's like the earth swallowed her. Personally, I think the bad guys have her. I've told my people not to shoot into the barn or the helicopter, or anywhere else they might be holding her."

"There's a row of trees up ahead," the driver yelled back to Link.

"The Yampa River's just this side of the cottonwoods."

They nosed into the shallow streambed, emerged and went on.

"Slow down. We're only a mile away."

"Think they'll hear us?" the driver asked.

"Probably. It's open from here on."

The captain had been studying the map Link had brought from the airplane. He radioed the other Sno-Cats. "Time to spread out."

Four vehicles angled left, the next four to the right. Almost immediately the crew in Sno-Cat number two reported that they smelled smoke. "Yeah," said their own driver. "So do I."

They approached cautiously. The barn was blazing brightly, already fallen in on one side. As they stopped a wall collapsed in a bright shower of sparks.

Everyone dismounted, and walked the final fifty yards. Wary, weapons up and ready. The going slippery because the fire was fierce enough to create a good deal of ice.

A series of pops and bangs issued from the embers.

"Stand back," someone called. "Sounds like ammunition cooking off."

The police captain scowled as he turned to Link. "Any ideas?" he asked.

Link's head was cocked. "Have the Sno-Cat drivers kill the engines."

The captain made the call. They listened, heard the distinct *whuppa-whuppa-whuppa* coming from high above.

"Guess they were crazy after all," Link muttered.

With each passing second the sound became fainter.

"Come on," one of the troopers said. "Hit a mountain, you lousy bastards."

3:01 P.M.—Airborne Near Rabbit-Ears Pass, Rocky Mountains, Colorado

Axel hung on as the helicopter rocked and tilted. He observed the others, whose expressions were drained and frightened. He might have been no better if he had not made the offerings. Huitzilopóchtli would watch after him. The knowledge sheltered him from any fear of crashing into one of the craggy mountaintops that they knew were around but could not see. And, too, his mind was filled with hatred for the man named Anderson.

If not for Anderson, he would have had more time to search for the Kitten-bitch. He would not be in this helicopter— would be relaxing and waiting in the hay barn—were it not for Anderson.

There were bright points. He'd succeeded in taking over a city, and been responsible for the deaths of dozens without fear of consequence. The storm had helped, but it had been the information from his listening posts that had made it possible. Would that matter to the Voice or the dead man? No, they'd still fear the only person who could prove that he lived. Axel still must give them success. Gather a new army, since this tiny one was depleted. As seed, there were Torré and Santos back in Steamboat, in the event he needed something done, someone killed there.

Quite suddenly they broke out on top of the boiling clouds. There was a layer of weather not far above, a snowy mountainside off to their right and another to their left, but the pilot could see, and they would live. He felt a rush. Great Huitzilopóchtli had once again protected him.

He made three calls on the cell phones. The first was to T-Can West to let them know his destination. He asked if the authorities had found Kitten. No. They had not a clue where she was.

The second call was to the Voice, to tell her he would set a new plan into motion.

The final one was to T-Can East, ordering them to learn everything possible about Lincoln Anderson. Who was he? What were his vulnerabilities?

17

Fifty-one men and women waited impatiently to learn if the girl's body would be found in the ashes of the barn. They'd still been listening to the diminishing sounds of the helicopter when the ammunition had begun to cook off more fiercely, and they'd had to back off. While burning ammo is seldom propelled with the intensity of bullets fired from a weapon, accidents happen.

The SWAT captain remained in contact with the commissioner, who was on the phone with the FAA people in Denver. None of the radars at the numerous airports, among them Buckley Field, DIA, and Colorado Springs, had detected the helicopter crossing the mountains. Meaning they'd either crashed or were hugging the terrain with their identification systems shut off. Police had been dispatched to logical landing places, and all flight facilities were alerted to watch for and report the gray-colored unmarked craft.

They'd been at the fire for half an hour when the captain asked, "Smell it?"

"Yes." Link had experienced the sick-sweet odor before, visiting a bunker into which his flight had dropped BLU-1Bs. The Iraqi soldiers had refused to emerge, and there'd been no time to wait them out. The problem was solved when Link's flight had dropped eight cans of napalm into the bunker's vent holes. When he'd visited the smell had been unpleasant.

War is hell. Don't start one unless you're prepared to suffer.

Now the same odor wafted from the ash and embers of the hay barn.

"Might be livestock," a trooper said. No one answered, for no one believed it. The troopers had smelled humans burning after car crashes.

One tried going closer to try to get an ID. He called out that he could see a torso and charred limbs, but he could not tell the gender. A flurry of rounds cooked off: *Pop-pop-pop-pop.*

"Don't press your luck," said the captain, and the trooper retreated.

Link was asked if he wanted to return in a Sno-Cat. The SWAT captain said he'd call as soon as they knew. Link decided to stay. If it was his friend's daughter, he should be there.

At four o'clock Erin called for a status report.

"Still nothing," he told her. "It's too hot to get close enough for a good look."

"What do you think?"

"It's not her."

"You've done well with your guesses so far."

A pair of troopers were cautiously advancing into the embers.

"Anything new from Ski Town?" he asked Erin.

"Forty-four confirmed dead there so far. It's getting a huge play in the media."

"It should. Have they identified the terrorists?"

"Some promising partials were found in the condo, and they've printed the dead snowmobile driver and the two at the roadblock. ID's working it."

The FBI's Identification Division would use their Automated Fingerprint Identification System to electronically search for a match among the one hundred eighty-five million prints on record.

"What about Maggie? Does she remember any more?" He watched the two troopers cautiously approach the charred remains.

"Maggie's no longer with us."

The revelation shook him. "What happened?"

"She quit. She was offered a polygraph test and . . ."

"Offered a *poly*graph?" He blurted the words.

"Hey, I wasn't the one who offered it. I liked everything I heard about her."

"Sorry. It's just that she's run into obstacles from the first. Who wanted the lie detector? Our security people?" He did not withhold a hint of sarcasm.

"Yes, and they said Gordon Tower had a part in it."

Link bristled more. The FBI agent had *known* what Maggie had endured.

The state troopers called out that a second charred corpse lay perpendicular to the first. They examined closer, looked back and grimly shook their heads.

"They've discovered a second body. Neither of them is Kitten."

"Good news!" she exulted.

Link good-byed, switched off, and told the police captain he'd take him up on his offer of transportation.

5:15 P.M.—Ski Town

Supervising Agent Gordon Tower had taken a room in the Sheraton, only half a block from the Snowbird crime scene. He answered the door knock, said a few more words into his mobile phone, and disconnected with a sigh and shake of his head. "They've located the wreckage. They're all dead. Everyone on the hostage rescue team."

"That's terrible but I'd guessed it. Where's Maggie?" he snapped.

"I don't know. Congratulations. From what I hear, you're lucky to be alive."

"Maggie went through hell, and you ganged up on her?"

"That's not the way it was." He frowned. "In fact, I think she ganged up on us."

"Just tell me where she is and then stay out of my way for a while."

"She gave me something for you. Hear me out and I'll hand it over. Otherwise, you can wait while I run it past every office between here and Washington."

"That's ridiculous."

"So is not listening. I'm your friend, remember? And I'm Maggie's friend." Gordon held the door wide until Link stalked in.

Gordon took a seat, leaned back wearily and put his stocking feet on the coffee table. "I'm too old for this crap. I turned forty last week."

Link waited.

"When the doc came out after seeing Maggie, she said to give her a while to warm up, which I did. When Maggie answered the door an hour later, first thing she did was ask about you. I didn't know you were flying, so I said you were fine. I've known Maggie for almost ten years, and I've never seen her eyes sparkle like that. She's got a serious case of attraction going."

"Damn it, what happened?"

"She told me what Katy had told them, then about the shoot-out and going over the rail and hiding. Then she acted like she'd remembered something, and asked if I'd call Washington and have them fax us a subject's file. I called, but they had nothing."

"First name Axel?"

"Yeah. Axel Nevas. When I told her the people in ID didn't have anything, she started brooding, like she was thinking hard about something, so I settled down to wait. About then is when the Weyland Foundation's chief investigator and her boss from WESCOR showed up. I asked Maggie if she felt like talking with them. Sure, she said, but I warned them to go easy because she'd been through so much."

"And the investigator wanted a polygraph?"

"It wasn't like that. They waited very politely while Maggie went to the desk, wrote a note, and put it in an envelope. Then when she came over to join us, everyone was considerate. The chief investigator even apologized for getting off on the wrong foot the other day, but Maggie was only half listening, the other half off somewhere in her mind. That was when she told her boss she hoped he'd understand, because a girl's gotta do what she's gotta do. Something like that, as if she was warning him."

"That's all? For him to understand?"

"Yeah. Then your investigator . . ."

"Not *my* investigator."

"The foundation's chief investigator, okay? Anyway, he asked very politely if she'd relate what Katy had said, and Maggie took a breath like she was about to jump into the deep end of a pool and said if early homo sapiens had been half as dumb as he was, Neanderthals would be running things."

Link almost smiled.

"That's just one I remember, but there were a lot more. She was giving him hell. Insulting his manhood and mentioning things that would set anyone off. Her boss said to back off. I tried to get her to go rest, and told her we'd come back later, but she kept calling the investigator more and more names, until he stopped sputtering long enough to ask just how she was able to survive when all the others in the room had been killed."

Tower gave a shake of his head. Amazed at what he'd heard. But that wasn't all.

"She smiled like he was a good boy, just dumb as a stump—in fact she said that, and he croaked something about wondering where she'd really spent the night."

"He was wrong," Link said. "The doctor could have told him."

"Yeah, but you should have heard her insults and seen the way she was enjoying it. I stepped in and told everyone we'd come back and talk when she was feeling better. Maggie said she was fine, thank you, that the fool just didn't know how to listen."

"Damn," Link muttered, but in an awed tone.

"Yeah. The investigator didn't know what to say, so when he gets quiet *she's* the one to bring it up. I suppose you'd feel better if I took a polygraph, she said, and he said it was not a terrible idea."

"I heard you got into it too."

"Not then. But he'd taken the bait and said he wouldn't believe anything she said until she took a polygraph. She said polygraphs are only accurate seventy percent of the time, which is true, and there was no way she'd accept those odds. That was when I put in my two cents and made my mistake, saying I'd get her the best polygraph operator around.

"Maggie ignored me. She got her little smile, like she uses when she's made a point, and asked the investigator if *he'd* take the test to see if he was diddling his male secretary."

"Damn," Link repeated. He winced.

"Yeah. He said, That's enough. You're terminated. Her boss said he'd replace her on the contract but the investigator says no thanks. Her boss ordered her to return to New York, and *she* says no thanks." Gordon gave a nod of finality. "End of story."

"You're saying it was all her fault."

"Nope. I'm just telling you what happened. At first I figured she was feeling bad or her temperature was still out of whack, but then I realized it was what she was after. She'd kept pressing until she was kicked off the job. One minute she was raving angry, the next she'd been terminated and was calmed down and packing because she had what she was after."

"Is she still in town?"

"Probably. The airlines are all stuffed with tourists trying to get away from here."

"How about a rental car?"

"She had one. A white Ford Explorer parked in the basement. When she'd packed, she asked if I'd help with her bag. I took it down, even offered to have one of my guys drive her, but she said she'd be fine. When I asked where she was going she said she'd be in touch."

"The highway's open all the way to the interstate."

"I can't imagine her driving that far. She was dog tired, like I am right now."

Link tried to make sense of it.

"Something you should know, Link. Maggie Tatro was an exceptionally good agent when she was with us. Very intelligent and always willing to go the extra mile. You can bet she got herself fired for a reason, and it has to do with what's happening."

"She gave you something for me?"

The agent handed over an envelope. "You don't mind, I'd like to know what she wrote."

"Tell me you haven't opened it."

"Gentlemen don't read other gentlemen's mail, remember?"

Link opened the envelope, and read her note.

Lincoln,

By the time you read this I will have been officially removed from the search. I will orchestrate that, so don't fault Gordon or your investigator. I realize it doesn't make sense, but for now just go along and don't try to change it. Another request. Remember Axel, the fellow with the deep voice? Please don't mention him until I've learned more.

I will stay at an empty "nest," and meet you there at nine tomorrow morning for coffee and explanations. If you don't remember what I'm talking about, a Mrs. Brown will contact you. She est moi. Subtract one and a half hours from any times she gives you. Spooky, huh? In the meantime, remember that the terrorists really do know everything.

I should feel bad about the way I'm about to treat your investigator, but instead I've decided to have fun. Poor guy.

Bye for now.

Maggie
P.S. I forgive you for peeking. ~~In fact I rather enjoyed it.~~ *Forget that part.*

As Link folded the note, he drew a frown from Gordon Tower.

"Anything new?"

"Nope." At least he knew where she'd gone.

5:25 P.M.—Cowboy Bar, Montrose, Colorado

Willard S. Creech, who was more often called Shag, was drinking with Leroy J. Manners, his sometimes-buddy. Sometimes being when they weren't fighting over a woman or some point of honor, or stealing from one another. They were both muscular and large, both so unkempt they smelled like dirty socks, both shaved their tattooed heads—although Shag only razored it halfway back, and wove the mop in back into a fat braid. A girlfriend liked to say instead of him being a "skinhead," he was a "foreskin."

They were also about equally tough. They'd run across one another at a roadside bar years back, and gotten into a fight when Leroy called Shag's girl a dumb cunt, which she was but nobody but Shag could call her that. Leroy had got in a lucky swing and staggered him, then had beaten him to the floor and given him the boot. Shag had tried to get away, but Leroy had caught him and flung him back down. For most of an hour, between beers and until Leroy had given out, he'd kicked and followed and kicked Shag Creech. Pulverized his balls. Broke his jaw, arm, and ribs. He'd departed with Shag's girlfriend, leaving him choking on his own blood.

Shag had spent the next couple of weeks in the hospital, and it was several more months before justice was served. Leroy J. Manners had been drinking with Shag's old girlfriend in a tavern near Grand Junction, bragging to a drunken cowhand about men he'd whipped and women he'd fucked, when his eyes were drawn to the Coors mirror behind the bar. Shag, holding a number twenty-three pool cue like it was a bat, swinging it like he was trying for a big league home run. Leroy's skull had been cracked, and he had not been aware when Shag had kicked him in the face until he was lopsided and his left eyeball was perforated. Booted him in the balls until blood seeped from the crotch of his jeans. Stomped until he snapped an ankle. Then just pointed at the door, and his dumb cunt girlfriend had known what she was in for.

That was twelve years ago, but both men still showed signs of the encounters. Neither of them had more than a half-dozen teeth left, and they had to collect themselves to think things through before answering questions. Big as sides of beef. Not smart, but so tough that it didn't matter. Everyone just stepped aside. Leroy was a Klan member, and both belonged to the local skinhead group. People seldom argued, and if Shag decided to poor-mouth niggers or Jews or anyone else he wanted to come down on, he did so. Leroy liked to talk about the feds and their kids that had been blown up in Oklahoma City, and look around a bar to see if anyone dared to say they hadn't deserved it. He'd add that he'd met Nichols and especially respected Tim McVeigh, and confide that his Aryan Nation brothers were looking after the two men and would break them out when they got the chance.

Leroy lived with Roadkill Annie, who parked her truck and trailer at a shack on a back road in Black Canyon, which was a state park where you were not supposed to squat. They were usually low on funds because of a liking for Red Dog beer, Speedy Pete meth, tequila slammers, and crack cocaine, which all together got expensive. And of course they had to buy fuel for Annie's sorry rig so she could haul and sell what they stole, such as motorcycles from local bikers, and stuff from breaking into seasonal homes in Telluride, Aspen, or Durango. They did not have much to show for their lives. Annie a few trinkets of fake jewelry. Leroy a World War II M-2 heavy-barrel machine gun that was next to impossible to get ammunition for, and a half-dozen hand grenades he claimed were live and sometimes wore attached to his flak vest to show off at skinhead meetings.

There had developed mutual respect and shared secrets.

Leroy J. Manners, who was six-five and weighed maybe three hundred, had once got so mad he'd turned a guy's head *completely around on his neck*. Shag Creech had killed two bikers at a house party in Gilroy, California, and never dared to return to the state.

But now, in the Cowboy Bar, Leroy had been acting odd since getting a phone call from Annie, and was brooding about something he didn't want to explain.

"I run out of money," Leroy said, and looked over at Shag. "You gotta tab?" Leroy's credit had been shut off by the management.

Shag pondered it, and waved at the skinny bartender who called herself a mixologist and put out for anything that crawled through the door. "Coupla Red Dogs," he yelled.

"Come on over tomorrow afternoon," Leroy said. "I'll have Annie get some beer, and we'll talk somethin' over that just might get us rich."

Shag suppose he was talking about stealing something. Maybe robbing a store.

"Sure," he said, his eyes on the TV at the end of the bar, tuned to CNN and showing a reporter standing next to the gondola at Steamboat Springs. So far forty-three bodies had been found in and around the city, plus the fifty feds in the airplane.

They showed a shot of the girl the kidnappers had been after. Prime stuff.

18

They were in Guteriez's home in Cherry Creek, an upscale, old money section of the city. The mansion—on three acres, with a circular driveway, sheltered by fifty-odd old oaks—had been built by a man who had hit it big in the mining boom, not as a miner but as an entrepreneur, where the real money was made. A century later, in the *nineteen*-eighties, the place had been modernized by a now-obscure multimillionaire Denver Bronco running back.

Once over the mountains the helicopter pilot had hugged the terrain all the way to a small airfield thirty miles south of the city, disgorged the passengers beside a Chevy van, and rolled the helicopter into a hangar beside a huge warehouse, all of it owned by the construction company which also owned the private airport.

Guteriez, like other heavyweight distributors, was into businesses. He owned auto dealerships, trucking firms, and a credit union he called his washing machine. The construction firm was another subsidiary, the proprietorship murky and untraceable. The helicopter would be repainted and flown to another building site.

Periodically during the forty-minute van ride, Axel had taken calls from T-Can West, telling him what was happening in Steamboat Springs.

As they dismounted outside Guteriez's huge home, the

owner called out to two of his household staff to get ready to take him to his doctor. He was home, in charge of his life again, and likely felt it was time to revert to the old pecking order. The Voice was at the top. The major distributors like Guteriez fell just beneath. Axel was somewhere he could not define, out of the normal scope of things.

Still standing outside, somehow reluctant to go in—as if it might somehow seal the failure—Axel took a call from the T-Can contact. "The Tatro woman, the one helping the foundation bodyguards?"

"Yes?" Axel remembered his surprise that they hadn't found her in the suite.

"She was fired. I would like to remove her from our targets list."

"Go ahead," Axel said. He pressed the END button, opened his notebook, found her name and scratched through it. Then Axel got another call, and after a moment handed the cell phone to Guteriez as he was about to crawl into the back of a limo.

"The Voice wants a word with you," he said.

On the phone Guteriez's attitude immediately changed, and he did a lot of humble yeah, sures.

He gave the cell phone back to Axel and smiled ingratiatingly. "Consider my place is yours. Do you mind if I get my arm looked after?"

"Do so." Axel motioned in dismissal. "And return quickly."

"This is Axel again," he said into the phone, and walked to a nearby island in the driveway so he could speak to the Voice in privacy.

"We're pleased you made it safely over the mountain."

Axel did not comment.

"The girl is still missing?"

"Yes. So far they don't have her, or have an idea where she went."

"Our friend wants to remind you that the girl can't be allowed to return to New York. If that happens . . ."

"It will not happen," Axel said.

"How long will you stay at Guteriez's?"

"Only until I've determined a new plan of action. If Kitten shows up in Steamboat Springs, Torré and Santos are there to slow them down until I can handle it."

"When will you be able to share your plan with us?"

"One hour," Axel promised. It was all he would need.

5:45 P.M.—Cowboy Bar, Montrose, Colorado

Shag felt Leroy was acting strange. Drinking on Shag's tab yet much less than normal, as if contemplating something important. Leroy J. Manners was not a discreet person. He kept hinting that there was big money involved, but would not confide the source.

The mixologist told Leroy he had another phone call, and her unhappy look told Shag it was Annie. She was married to Annie's nephew but she put out for Leroy when Annie was on the road, sometimes even stayed with him in Annie's cabin, regardless that he called her a titless wonder in front of the whole world.

Leroy came back, saying he had to get home. Which was also odd because Leroy J. Manners never lifted a finger to please Annie. She must be bringing back something special.

"Tell her to remember my share," Shag said. He'd liberated a Harley for her to sell.

"Yeah." Leroy reminded Shag about coming over tomorrow, and started for the door.

"How about a beer on me this time?" the mixologist called to him.

"Next time," Leroy said, and Shag knew something *really* heavy was on his mind.

7:05 P.M.—Denver

Axel called the Voice to tell her his plan.

He said it made sense that Kitten was still somewhere

around Steamboat, but he wanted to be ready for anything. No matter where she surfaced, he wanted to be able to go after her.

The Voice did not comment.

Axel rubbed weary eyes and regarded his notes. He would need specialists, like pilots and a television announcer, but mostly a much larger number of expendable shooters. After ten more minutes of explanations he paused, examined his notes, and decided he'd forgotten nothing important.

"What do you think?"

"It's too much. The entire country is outraged over the killings in Steamboat Springs. This would just make it worse."

"Why should we care, unless they can do something about it? As long as we have the T-Cans, we know everything they say, and they can never find us."

"But now you are talking about forming an army."

"Not an army, only fifty men. Ask the dead man about my plan and let him decide. He knows the risk if the girl tells about him. Regardless of what he looks like in the future, his face was unforgettable then."

He paused for effect. Knowing that not long before, to bring such attention to the man's prominent feature would have brought death. Now he was indispensable.

"My plan before was good, and I had only twelve people. If I'd had more, she would be dead. Present all of that to the dead man, and ask what he wants."

She spoke in a more subdued tone. "He's already said to give you whatever you want."

"Good." He told her he would position his forces at Glenwood Springs, squarely in the center of the state. A subsidiary of one of the dead man's companies was building a resort there. They would open a month early. Tomorrow.

Sooner or later one of the T-Cans would determine Kitten's location. He would pounce even before the authorities could respond, and in sufficient strength to overpower whoever he faced.

"I don't need more details," said the Voice, "only what you will need."

He outlined requirements. Personnel, radios, equipment, weapons—this time shotguns, handguns, and UZIs as well as silenced Skorpions—and cold weather clothing. He wanted four-wheel drive vehicles and helicopters.

"When can you get it all to me?"

"Guteriez's companies will provide your vehicles and aircraft. The rest will arrive early tomorrow." She was no longer arguing.

Before they finished she asked, "Will you be making more—sacrifices?"

"Offerings, you mean? Yes. It keeps them respectful, and Huitzilopóchtli is insatiable."

She put him on hold, but returned in less than a minute. The dead man had approved everything, as Axel had expected. She gave him the name of a candidate for his next offering.

Axel joined the other survivors in the great room, and except for their destination, explained what he'd told the Voice. He told them to be ready to move in the morning after the others arrived. Guteriez—who was back from the doctor, his arm casted and in a sling—would arrange for the people to be picked up. He would also provide two helicopters and ten vehicles.

As the group broke up, Guteriez told Axel about a television announcement that had been running every fifteen minutes. They went to another room where one of Guteriez's maids was watching a big screen television. She saw them and fled.

They did not have long to wait.

A spokesman for the Weyland Foundation asked the television audience to help find sixteen-year-old Katy Dubois—Kitten's photograph was shown—whose present location was unknown. Any persons providing information leading to her safe return would receive a substantial reward. If desired, no questions would be asked. An 800 number flashed as the voice-over was repeated. A reporter added that the governor of Colorado had promised the Dubois family all possible assistance.

Axel called T-Can West and spoke with the contact. He learned that both a Weyland Foundation representative and an FBI negotiator were manning the 800 number phone, at the FBI field office in Denver.

After consideration, Axel directed that should any caller have credible information concerning the girl, T-Can was to intervene and take over. If done properly, neither the caller nor the FBI would know it had happened.

The contact felt it was a superb idea.

19

Katy had no idea where they were, only that Annie had disconnected the tractor from the trailer and shut off the engine. Within ten minutes she found herself growing cold. With the engine off, there was no longer a flow of warm air from the heater vent. Only the chill radiating from the sleeper's plastic shell.

She heard the driver's door open.

"I'm cold," Katy called. "Please let me out."

"You sure complain a lot," Annie responded, "for a runaway kid."

"I'm not running away, and those guys weren't policemen," Katy yelled. "Let me out so I can make a phone call, and I'll prove it."

Katy heard sounds like Annie was taking things from the cab.

"Keep your pants on. Come to think on it, Leroy'll be here in a bit and he might want 'em off." She laughed like what she'd said was hilarious. Then, "I better *not* see you backin' up to Leroy."

"I promise."

"Promise all you want, just don't encourage him. Tell him no, he thinks that means no stopping till he's done."

Chills ran through Katy. "I don't want that from him or anyone, Annie."

"I don't care 'bout others, but I catch you lookin' at him, I'll make you wish you hadn't."

"*Please* let me out. It's cold."

"I'll fix that, but you just stay put for a while."

Annie slammed the truck's door, and suddenly Katy was every bit as scared as she'd been the previous day. She felt claustrophobic. While the sleeper had looked big from the outside, it seemed miniscule and cramped. Like a tomb. She shivered, not only from the cold.

From behind the sleeper Katy heard scratching sounds of metal scraping metal, then the hum of the heater coming back on.

More time passed. She started feeling the inside of her cage with her hands, looking for weakness or a way she might escape. She was still at it, having come up with nothing, when she heard a vehicle pull up and shut off its engine. Someone walking over.

"Anyone there?" A man's voice.

Katy's heart skipped a beat. "Help me! I'm in the sleeper."

The same man answered. "Don't worry, kid. We'll *help* you." He laughed.

Annie's voice came from farther away, "I plugged it in, Leroy. She'll be warm enough."

Leroy? Katy cringed, remembering what Annie had told her about him.

"Jus' checkin'."

Katy heard him walking away. Then there was only the hum of the heater fan.

7:45 P.M.—Black Canyon

Annie was happy to get home and transfer the problem out in the sleeper. Leroy was walking the floor, thinking, telling her it looked like she'd fumble-fucked her way into something good. His way of complimenting.

"I picked up a twelve-pack of Red Dog in Eagle."

He was too busy thinking to answer, just went over and switched on the tube. They did not have to wait long before a photograph of the kid came on, along with the announcement of a substantial reward, same as she'd heard over the radio.

Leroy's eyes narrowed as he stared at the kid's picture. Give him a little longer and he might be hot for more than money. Go pull the kid out and bend her over.

"We oughta treat her good," she tried. "For when we turn her in for the money."

Only when the picture changed did he sit down and demand a beer. Annie might be more concerned, but the girl was out there and she was here.

She got a Dog out of the fridge—leaving the bottle closed because he liked to remove the cap—went over to his chair and hunkered. Gave him the bottle and felt his crotch like he'd told her was done by Mexican whores in Juarez.

He popped the bottle cap off with a thumb, sat back, and let her continue rubbing. Staring at the TV although the photo of the girl was replaced by a dumb-ass reporter talking about the President's ratings rising regardless that he was in Japan while terrorists were attacking at home.

"I told Shag to come over tomorrow. Said we'd get some beer and have one or two."

Annie continued to stimulate him through the denim. "Gonna tell him about the girl?"

She could not understand how he could put up with Shag Creech, when he'd been the one to blind his left eyeball. Yet Leroy said he admired him almost as much as Tim McVeigh.

He grunted. She didn't know if it was an answer or he was enjoying what she was doing.

Finally, "Whut happened in Steamboat?"

Annie started at the beginning, when she was in line with the other truckers and seen the girl. The only part she left out was about the wristwatch and bracelet, which she'd brought in. Leroy did nothing but take a periodic drink of beer and belch. By the time he finished it, she had reached in and was handling him where it counted, and he was leaning back, making grunting noises and enjoying.

"Maybe you oughtn't trust Shag with something like this."

Leroy snorted disdainfully. "Shag wouldn't fuck with me. We both got respeck."

The spot announcement came back on, and Leroy stared at the kid's image as Annie was giving him the long stroke. He was about ready, but he stared at the television so hard she knew his mind was on the girl. Either that or the money. Either way he took a good swig of beer, and grabbed a handful of hair.

Annie yelped, knowing what he was after, but wanting some for herself too. "Let's move in on the bed, hon." He ignored her, kept pulling her into position.

"In there, hon," she said, hating it when her voice turned whiny like that. Then she could no longer argue for her mouth was full and Leroy was snorting and moving around in his chair.

As Annie labored she wondered about the wisdom of letting Shag know about the kid. How with both of those guys so competitive it could end bad, and sure as hell the kid wouldn't get off easy.

Talk about *needing* it! Annie was about to go crazy. She tried to move her head away, thinking she'd somehow maneuver him to the bedroom, but Leroy knew what she was trying and held her down so she wasn't going no place at all. She stopped fighting it, just kept it up until he let out a series of snorts that sounded like a bull getting it off. Then he was making happy sounds while Annie near choked.

When she was turned loose and still gasping for air, Annie started wondering how she could keep him and Shag away from the kid. The radio had said the kid's daddy was a billionaire, and while she had no idea what that really meant, she knew if they used their heads they were onto a very good thing.

Get him a new Harley, her a new rig. Hell, maybe a *lot* of bikes and new rigs.

Annie knew the only way to get him to do something was make him think it was his idea. She would have to be smart about it.

20

In Maggie's dream, Link again rescued her from the horror of the snowdrift—and again placed her in the life-saving, still-filling bathtub. Stripped off his shirt and held her in his arms and moved his hands over her body just as before. And just as before it was incredibly pleasant.

But this time he included the forbidden places, lingering just the perfect period of time as she writhed about in his hands. After a while of it she slowly awakened, and was ashamed of what she was doing. She dropped back into slumber but it seemed only a moment before she was revived by a persistent chime. She shut off the alarm, yawned, and stretched, thinking the first awakening had been nicer.

It was still dark, yet she felt almost human after the marathon of sleep.

The town home belonged to Jack and Anita Crow, whom she'd known since childhood—Anita being the one who had met her at the airplane, Jack the one who had helped get her ski legs back. They had mutual friends, among them General Lucky Anderson and son Link, who had been guests at their home a dozen years earlier.

Jack was a Delta Airline captain, Anita a senior Delta stewardess, and before the terrorists had struck, the couple had departed for Portland, Oregon, and the Boeing 747 they'd fly to Japan. Nice people the Crows, sincere about their invitation to stay in their home, so that was where Maggie had headed after getting herself thrown off the Katy operation.

The short time between pulling up out front and hitting the guest room sheets had been spent: collecting house keys from a next-door neighbor, retrieving a phone number from her electronic organizer, and making an international call. Then she had shed clothing in a trail to the upstairs guest room, burrowed into bed, and slept slothlike for thirteen wonderful hours. Except for the dream about Link, which had been a nice interlude. Also wishful thinking since Link had been a perfect gentleman about the way he'd felt her up. Explaining that he was checking for frostbite, and if she wanted him to stop to just say so.

Stop? He had to be kidding. Link Anderson had the greatest hands since Michelangelo. Which was why she'd finally had him leave, because what kind of red-blooded American female could think straight when a hunk who was a nice guy to boot was leaned over her and seriously groping the terrain. Even after he'd left it had been hard to concentrate on—oh yeah—terrorists.

Maggie just wished he'd laid off the fact that her nose was turning bright red. Guys! *Next* time they were in a tub together . . .

She grinned as she shut off the carnal thoughts and turned to serious ones about the man she had heard while freezing her patooties off. He'd had an incredibly deep voice and she'd picked up a slight accent. When he had answered the phone as "Axel," she'd had a partial recollection, but at the time was too wrapped up in surviving to make it connect.

He'd mentioned something called "tee can," which she still didn't understand. He had discussed the killings, saying there was no Kitten and no "second female bodyguard." Then he had actually *named* her. "No Margaret Tatro," he'd said, "so keep her on the list." Then he'd said to take three others *off* the list, and told the names of the dead security officers. His voice so deep it sounded like a bass drum, like it hurt for him to talk. Then there was, "Any hits on Anderson's sat freqs? I'm interested in him."

Huh? Satellite frequencies? Hits? *Link* Anderson maybe? Was he on the list Axel talked about? Axel had spoke about intercepts and hits and interrupts and switches. Then about "the Atlanta office." And finally, for them to pass "stopper information" only to him. The normal reports would continue to go to the Voice, but no more about stopper.

Stopper? Talk about confusing!

Much later, when she was partially thawed and Gordon Tower was with her, a memory surfaced so suddenly and clearly she was amazed it had taken so long.

In a convoluted way, Maggie had thought about the deep-voiced man for the past five years. Like at income tax time or when she picked up dog crap after watching after a friend's cocker, for Maggie Tatro's memory worked best when she made associations. For instance, unpleasantness made her think of Bozo the Ex, whom she did not regard highly. Then her mind sought a more pleasant alternative and she'd recall a gentle man she'd known after the breakup, who had restored some of her faith in maledom. The gentle man had told her about Axel Nevas, and his frustration bringing him to justice. So when she thought of bad things, soon thereafter Maggie found her thoughts ping-ponging around to Axel Nevas and wondering if he'd ever gotten his just desserts. Memory by association, like they taught at the FBI academy.

She remembered what her friend had told her about Axel Nevas. Gravel-deep voice. Well educated and technically expert with electronic eavesdropping devices, but *odd*. Believed himself to be descended from Aztec priests. Director of a minor agency set up in Washington to try to obtain trade secrets—as did every country, large and small, that had an embassy there—but Axel's focus had turned to blackmail.

Maggie dragged herself from bed, pulled on her comfiest robe from her bag, found the kitchen, and put on coffee, and deposited herself in front of the Crows' personal computer. Stared for a couple of minutes until her mind revved to speed. Switched on the PC—thankfully there was no access code—and reached for the phone. After her alert the previous afternoon, her friend should be awaiting her call in his office in the federal police building in Mexico City.

He was a Mexican government agent who had attended the international course given at the FBI's National Academy. Maggie had been one of his instructors, using the name M. A. Brown since her divorce was not yet final. Socializing with the quiet and gentle man had been tonic. They'd attended concerts, gone to dinners and clubs where they could dance. They'd even talked, an activity to which she had been unaccustomed.

He had planned to propose to his lifelong sweetheart when he returned to Mexico City and not once had they considered making love, yet that was so incomprehensible to Maggie's estranged husband that he'd doggedly tried to follow them. They'd been onto him, and ditched him in a succession of hilarious locations. The last had been the courtyard of a convent for elderly nuns. When released by the Virginia State Police after questioning, his ego was so damaged that there was no possibility of reconciliation. Fine with Maggie. They'd been a mistake.

She'd found her friend's work interesting. The Mexican government was in the throes of cleaning house, and a portion of the investigative task had been assigned to his office.

In the 1980s, two intelligence bodies had been formed by act of the Mexican General Congress. The first was the Illegal Drugs Bureau, headed by an army general. The second, called simply the Agencia, was to gather foreign trade secrets and protect their own. Investigation of those bodies had been assigned to her friend's department.

The investigations were difficult, for the worst offenders proved to be those who were most highly placed. The general at the Illegal Drugs Bureau was in the pocket of the drug smugglers he was supposed to expose. And after her friend vigorously interrogated three Agencia employees, he learned of the blackmail being orchestrated by their director.

When they'd briefed President Zedillo, he had been outraged. He ordered them to build airtight cases, and then to arrest both the general and the director.

The following week her friend had been picked to replace another at the FBI course. No argument could make them understand that he had done the work and wished to be present when Nevas was recalled and apprehended. Another office, the President's own security team, was taking over and would make the arrests.

So he had not been happy to attend the course where Maggie had taught investigative procedures. Soon after they'd become friends, she had learned that he remained fixated on Axel Nevas, whose Agencia still operated from a cheap and unmarked office across town.

Nevas was apprehended getting off the airplane in Mexico City, as per the plan that her gentle man had contrived. There was no more information. Not a hint of what transpired. He'd asked the fate of the informants he had turned within the Agencia, but got nowhere there either. Instead he had received a missive from his office in Mexico City: Do *not* discuss the Axel Nevas matter further. Nevas had been working with the federal police all along. By then her friend's department had been assigned to investigate insurrectionist Indians in the southern jungles.

Her friend told Maggie that people high in the Zedillo government had become involved. Nevas had officially vanished. The Agencia too had dropped out of sight.

Maggie had checked Bureau files and pulled up a cross-reference. State Department Security had everything: Axel Nevas's technical background, the minor threats he posed to US industry, even that he worshipped Aztecan deities. It had comforted her to think that while the rest of the world's law enforcement agencies might be vulnerable to corruption, theirs was exempt.

The previous day she'd asked Gordon Tower if he'd check for the latest on Axel Nevas. There was nothing, not a cross-reference or indication that a file had ever existed. Her mind had reeled with possibilities. Nevas had an impossibly deep voice, like the man she'd overheard, and lived in a technical world that used jargon like "intercepts" and "targets" and "triggers" and "hits" and "interrupts" and "switches." Could it be him she'd heard?

His business was monitoring people with his electronics, and *she* was on his list, along with all the others searching for Katy. The fact had made Maggie feel claustrophobic, and she'd had no qualms about forcing the issue with the foundation's investigator. She'd *wanted* Nevas to call "tee can" and say she was no longer involved. She'd wanted Nevas to say, "Remove her from the list." She had— temporarily she hoped—destroyed her career, but that was the only way she could get off Axel Nevas's list and search for the truth.

Maggie dialed. Her friend had married his sweetheart, fathered two children, and gained thirty pounds. Yet his voice was as she remembered it.

Maggie called herself "Brown" and led off with a question about "the person with the deep, deep voice." He caught on instantly and shared her discretion. They spoke for thirty minutes without mentioning Nevas's name. She asked if "deep voice" could have traveled north, told him some of what she'd overheard, and asked the relevance of those things. Her friend was intrigued, and agreed to forward his opinions—unofficial ones since "deep voice" was not under suspicion for any act, trivial or otherwise—within the hour. While no form of communications should be considered secure because of the nature of deep voice's expertise, e-mail might be best. Unless someone was monitoring a specific line, the volume of traffic was too immense to intercept each message.

Maggie gave him the e-mail address taped to the front of the Crows' computer. Then she hung up and sat back, praying he would give her something positive. A lot rode on his response. If he could confirm that Nevas was involved, as she was increasingly sure, Maggie could take a giant step toward solving it all.

In an hour, he'd said, so she decided to work while waiting, and pulled out her Hewlett Packard "handheld personal computer." She'd begun with a small organizer. Then bought one with more capacity. Now the HP, which she doubted *could* be filled because of its scads of memory. She'd stored a multitude of professional contacts: local, state, federal, and international. People like the gentle man in Mexico, Supervising Agent Gordon Tower, and even Bozo the Ex, now assistant deputy director for public relations at the FBI's Hoover Building.

But it was the other database that made the organizer special, for it contained tens of thousands of names and aliases—their traits, descriptions, histories, modus operandi, and last known locations—of SUBs, whose info she'd gathered from various sources over her career.

Despite her suspicions about Axel Nevas, the identities of the terrorists were still unknowns. In FBI parlance they were *UNSUBs,* the unknown subjects who had done the dirty deed. That was her challenge, to compare available information about the *UNSUBs* with the *SUBs* in the organizer, and try for a match.

Compilers of the FBI's databases in DC and West Virginia, the CBI's in LA, New Scotland Yard in London, and Interpol in Paris, were bound by legalities regarding information they could and could not store. Not Maggie. Her SUB list included every bum, kingpin, wise guy, and shaky businessman she figured might merit any slightest attention.

She began by culling out the obviously wrong categories. Eliminating nonviolent types, like embezzlers, check writers, bunkos and lightweight thieves. Then, after considerable thought, she eliminated all who had nothing to do with drug trafficking in their histories. That whittled her list down to sixteen thousand SUBs. If it didn't work, she'd open the field back up again.

She opened a notepad, one of those two-by-three inch spiral cheapies that slip into a shirt pocket or purse, examined the list of UNSUBs Katy had met and overheard, and went to work. She ran a FIND on each, and got hundreds of matches. Quite a few expert skiers who could pose as Lu for

Lucille. Lots of Ortizes, Santos', and Guteriezes. Not as many Victors and Torrés. Only a handful of Nevases.

She was down to three hundred sixty SUBs, which she saved as "LIKELIES." A departure point to use for the next query. Guteriez was a best first bet because Katy had seen him and described him. Thin face. Dark hair. Scar over an eye. A gold tooth. Spoke with a light accent—not like he came from Mexico, but as if he had been raised in an Hispanic neighborhood.

She listed the last name, the scar and dark hair, and went for a match. Twenty-two names appeared. She added the gold tooth. All but four disappeared. *Hot* damn!

Maggie continued. Sitting in her fuzzy bathrobe, swigging sugar-laden coffee, searching for a match. After a while she paused, feeling a wave of concern. She'd made the decision to be tossed off the contract thinking it was right. Now she wondered. Unless someone was awfully understanding, if she was wrong—and there was a possibility that she was not the only sane person in a sea of fools—she was left without a job.

The chances of a lunatic getting work in her field were not promising. Who would stand by her? Certainly no one in WESCOR, and likely only Gordon Tower in the Bureau. Then she remembered how Link Anderson had worked to save her life, and how he'd listened, and her thoughts heated up again. And she was sure. Yep. She had her man.

Falling, falling . . .

She grinned happily, skimming and comparing. Also thinking how if the Axel Nevas connection was borne out, it was *awesome*.

She narrowed it down to two Guteriezes. Which one?

Maggie blinked a couple of times as noise filtered into her consciousness. An electronic chime. She looked over at the PC screen. "YOU HAVE MAIL." She retrieved it with a mix of excitement and caution, not wanting to lose it through some bonehead error with an unfamiliar computer. Only after the message was captured and saved did she read from the screen.

It was good stuff, but it was all conjecture and no hard proof.

In 1995 there'd been rumors that Axel Nevas had gone to work for Amado Fuentes, one of the most powerful drug lords in the trade. Thereafter Fuentes seemed to know everything about his competitors and enemies. Had it been Nevas's work? Had his Agencia set up shop in Mexico? No one dared to think it out loud. Most of the authorities in Mexico were in Fuentes' pocket.

Two years later Amado Fuentes had died in a botched attempt to alter his appearance. Had Nevas moved north to work for someone in the US? Possibly, for he'd not been seen again in Mexico. Next her friend spent several pages outlining what it would take to set up an eavesdropping network. Electronic modules inserted into communications lines, programmed with targets, trigger words, and priorities. The more targeted lines and words monitored, the slower the system became until you added more modules. It was an expensive endeavor.

Maggie turned on the printer to run off a copy of the message, wishing her friend had included at least some proof. Ah well. She would have to find it herself. There were three more hours before Link would arrive. In the meantime there was plenty to do.

7:00 A.M.—Grubstake Restaurant, Ski Town

Link was usually up early, doing his warm-ups and morning run. Five miles in fifty minutes was his normal goal. On this particular Sunday he was so stiff and bruised from the crash landing that he settled for walking a hundred slippery yards to the Grubstake, a local restaurant specializing in honest fare and hot drinks for skiers. The walls were covered with photos of ski champions, Indy drivers, and military heroes. Among the latter were members of a group of top pilots and scientists who gathered annually at various ski hills to discuss the year's aviation requirements, ski, and generally have great fun. At age sixteen, Link's father had brought him along, and he had been in awe of the hawk-eyed men. They'd stayed at a town house owned by Jack Crow. Which was why it had been so easy to divine the "empty nest" where Maggie was staying.

This morning the Grubstake was swarming with federal officers, investigators, and state police, but few skiers. Although selected lifts would reopen, the locals were staying home and most guests had cut their stays short. Forty-eight would be going home in caskets.

Supervising Agent Gordon Tower and the copilot from the MCP aircraft waved him over. Link slid into the booth and croaked his need for coffee.

The combination copilot/test pilot/engineer had relocated the airplane to the Steamboat airport, and detached the Grumman van. He handed over the keys. "I parked it in the basement of your building." Since he had already eaten, he excused himself and departed for the airport.

"Nice guy," said Gordon. "Smart."

"Yeah. Anything new regarding the search?" Link asked.

The agent sighed. "No sign of Katy, the terrorists, or the helicopter." He grew silent as a busy waitress poured coffee and dropped off menus.

"How about the eight hundred number?" Television and radio transmissions were made every fifteen minutes over every station in the mountain states.

"They're getting a hundred calls an hour. Mostly people complaining about neighbors and worthless son-in-laws." Gordon brightened. "But there is a development."

Link sipped coffee and waited.

"Remember the truck lineup? Last night one of the drivers dropped in on the Boulder police, and talked about a girl he'd seen on the road. He was busy with his chains, and didn't take a good look, and then figured it was the woman trucker in front of him that some of the others knew. When he got home his wife nagged at him to report it."

"So it wasn't Katy?"

"Probably not, but there's more. The trucker claimed that a deputy searched all the trucks there in Steamboat while they were waiting for the road to open. The sheriff's office here says that wasn't one of theirs."

Link sat a bit straighter. "A terrorist?"

"Probably. A second deputy was driving the cruiser. Both had on poorly fitting uniforms, and neither was in disguise, except maybe a wig on the driver." Gordon opened a folder, handed him a sheet with computerized IDENTIKIT composites of two males. One was a big, neatly shorn all-American type with eyeglasses. The other wore a smirk and had wild hair.

"After we talk to the other drivers," said Tower, "we'll get better composites."

The Weyland Foundation's chief investigator entered the dining room, came over, and took a seat opposite Link. It was the first time they'd been face-to-face at Steamboat.

Link handed the drawings back to Tower. "How will you find the other truckers?"

"The highway patrol has a list of everyone who passed through the roadblock." He sat back. "So it's your turn. Ready to tell me where Maggie spent the night?"

"She didn't say in her note."

"Yeah, but she said you'd figure it out."

"What was that about gentlemen not opening other gentlemen's mail?"

"What if only one of us is a gentleman?" Tower smiled at Link's frown. "Actually she told me that when I carried her bag down for her."

The investigator gave Link a sidelong look. "How long have you known Miss Tatro?"

"Since we were kids."

"Perhaps I should explain why I terminated her contract."

"I heard you had good reason." He remembered Maggie's Neanderthal line and fought off a smile.

The investigator looked relieved. "I've rented a conference room at the Sheraton for the duration, sort of a meeting place for the different players and officials. We're holding our first brainstorming session this morning. Care to attend?"

"Sure." Then he remembered Maggie. "I have a meeting, but I'll drop in later."

A female FBI agent came over to remind Gordon about another news conference, his third since the killers had escaped. The nation was beginning to recognize Supervising Agent Tower, and he was learning to evade hard questions and speak in eight-second sound bites.

7:05 A.M.—Denver International Airport

For the second time in a week, the domestic terminals were the focus of Axel's attention. Arriving from a dozen major cities were hard-eyed men, and this time a few women as well. These were much lower in the drugland hierarchy than the former group of distributors. These were runners and gofers. Dealers and gangstas. Intelligence had not been a factor in their selection—only avarice. Most wore their hair long and their body jewelry plentifully. Some were high on their own product, although they'd been told to abstain.

They did not remain in the terminal for long, but were escorted out to vans owned by Arturo Guteriez and driven to his massive home in Cherry Creek. There they waited in the great room. Fifty-odd folding chairs were set up at one side of the room, but they were told to wait until everyone arrived so Axel would have to give the preliminary briefing only once.

The trouble began with news Axel received over his cell phones. First, T-Can East said the Weyland Foundation's chief investigator, now at Steamboat, had made numerous sat phone calls to New York, asking about possible compromise of their secure systems. His questions were getting better and better, hitting closer to the truth. They were sending a communications expert to Steamboat. The T-Can East contact said they should consider shutting down the modules that monitored the Weyland Foundation's satellite communications.

"Not yet," Axel replied. The modules at the Weyland Building were essential to provide information about the nation's drug authorities. "We'll come up with another solution."

When Axel disconnected, the T-Can East contact—an ambitious and highly motivated young woman—called and advised the Voice, who immediately dispatched a low-level drug dealer to handle the problem with the chief investigator in Steamboat Springs.

Axel did not know about that, for his other cell phone had buzzed, and he was listening to T-Can *West* with regard to another problem, which was even more troubling.

Both in Mexico and the US, few government phone lines were monitored continuously, and even those only when key "trigger words" were spoken. This morning a telephone call had been placed to a "low priority line" in Mexico City, and would have been overlooked except for the fact it had originated in Steamboat Springs. Since they did not know what had been spoken, they had waited to see if there would be another contact. There was no call, but an hour later, an e-mail message was passed from the Mexico City office to "ani555crow.com."

The T-Can West contact read him the message, and after only a few paragraphs Axel felt a choking sensation, as if he might be ill. "*Who* was this sent to?"

"Anita Crow, an airline stewardess who's presently halfway across the Pacific. Someone's using her telephone and computer."

Axel stared, wondering why a private individual would want to know his recent history, or how a clandestine eavesdropping operation worked? He took down the address.

He called his listening post in Mexico City, and explained the information he desired to be obtained from the sender of the message. "Have my dentist examine his teeth."

He terminated angrily, decided he did not have time to wait, and made a third phone call.

Torré and Santos remained idle in Steamboat Springs. Unfortunately the police had composite drawings of them. The one of Sergeant Santos was more accurate, so he was more expendable.

He told Santos what he wanted done. First to the chief investigator, whose last name was Randall. He gave his description, his room number at the Sheraton, his rental auto's license plate numbers. Randall was a professional, he told Santos, so use care. Next he wanted Santos to set a house fire. He gave the address. Ensure destruction of the home, the personal computer, and any printed material. Most important, kill anyone inside.

And hurry!

As he switched off the phone, he considered calling the Voice to advise her and the dead man about the e-mail and the possibility of compromise. Instead he decided to wait to see what developed. Perhaps no one had retrieved the e-mail message.

He asked for the god Huitzilopóchtli to protect Santos, the man he had once hated.

21

Maggie was still in her fuzzy robe, sipping sugar-laden coffee and working at the kitchen table. Wanting to finish so she could luxuriate in the Jacuzzi tub she'd discovered in the second-floor bathroom.

She was up to the Rs in the organizer, still looking for matches with the terrorists and her SUBs. Nothing on "Axel." The woman posing as Lu for Lucille was possibly a ski bum druggie from Vermont. A possible on Ortiz, who might be a distributor from L.A.

But she had a *probable* on Guteriez's identity, and he was one of those who had most likely escaped in the helicopter.

A few years ago the DEA had become aware of one Arturo Domingues Guteriez, who had worked his way up in the Denver cocaine trade. In 1995 they'd *almost* bagged him in a scam that had pulled in several others, but since then there'd been absolutely nothing to connect him with anything. He was filthy rich now, and so lucky with shaky investments that even the limp-wristed four-star drug czar agreed that he'd become a major distributor. Still, every time they tried to intercept a shipment or raid a lab, or catch him transferring cash, they'd come up empty and the snitch would be found executed. It was as if Guteriez had someone planted in both the DEA and Denver Area Drug Task Force.

The same had been happening with other big-time distributors. The eight-page e-mail message from her friend in Mexico City explained how it might be happening.

How to prove it? Guteriez had an address in the Cherry Creek section of Denver. Just over the mountains, and *handy*. Could she somehow use him as a key to it all?

Maggie started at the sound of the door chime, and looked at her watch, wondering who it might be. She'd asked Link to drop by at nine, which was another hour and a half, and she intended to be bathed and perfumed. Maggie without a red nose, thank you.

She took her snub-nose .32 from the table and cinched the robe. Not good to get in a shootout with your robe flapping and your boobs bouncing. She tiptoed down to the entrance, gun in hand, and peeked out the view hole at a fish-eye caricature of Link Anderson looking about with pursed lips.

Her heart did a little tango, because she'd been thinking such warm thoughts about the man. "Come back later," she yelled.

He grinned. "Got a cup of coffee for a fellow in need?"

She cracked the door and showed him her unhappy face. "Later!"

"Mrs. Brown, I presume?" Playing it cute and using the name she'd written in the note. She thought of the way she looked and considered using the pistol.

"You're supposed to be here at nine."

"Nope. You said to subtract an hour and a half, remember."

"I said to come at nine, and in the future if I mentioned times to subtract it."

"Wrong." He pulled out her note. "It says here to . . ."

Maggie sighed, pushed the pistol into her robe pocket, and opened the door.

He high-stepped over unshoveled snow and entered. Stamped his boots on the mat. "I take it you're not ready," he said inanely, following as she stalked up the staircase into the kitchen.

She was about to pour him the last cup from the pot when

he *really* blew it by looking critically at her stringy hair. His frown was the final straw.

"Go away." She muttered the words.

He obviously didn't comprehend so she leaned forward and shouted: "Go *away!*"

"You want me to leave?" He had the audacity to look injured.

"I am a *female,* Lincoln. Try to think of everything you've ever heard about us being different from males. Connecting in there yet? See the smudges under my eyes that I was going to make go away with a moisturizer I spent a paycheck on. How about the spot that may be the beginning of a zit on the side of my nose? Nice?"

Link began backing toward the stairs, finally getting the picture.

"And *wow,* look at the way I look so dumpy in this fuzzy old threadbare robe, which I wear *only* when there's not the faintest possibility of being seen by another human. And see how my hair's strung all over my head? It's not normally like that unless I've spent the night working and wasn't expecting you for another hour and a half. So maybe you're right and there's no need to go away, right? You've seen every bad feature. Hey, want to smell my . . ."

Link was hastily descending the stairs, mumbling about being sorry. Maggie following, keeping the fire in her eyes.

He scurried out.

Her voice mellowed. "Love ya. Bye."

Slam.

7:39 A.M.—Sheraton Hotel, Ski Town

A woman clad in a blue Weyland Foundation security blazer answered the door to the conference room and ushered him in.

Link had driven directly there, smarting at the way Maggie Tatro had treated him like an insensitive lout. Of course it might have to do with the fact that she was lively, cute, and sexy as hell. It was more than a year since his fiancée had passed away, and he dated very little. Perhaps he *had* grown insensitive. He did not like the thought, *especially* with Maggie.

Across the room a National Guard brigadier spoke with FBI agent Gordon Tower and the state police commissioner Link had met the previous day. He was starting over when he answered another beckon and was drawn into a conversation with several local officials. Among them was Councilman Cliver, who had his shoulder bound and remained pale from blood loss.

"I'm surprised you're up and about," Link told the councilman.

"Got to keep my image as a tough marine." Cliver introduced him to the mayor, then added, "If he hadn't figured out the noisemakers, I'd still be trying to dig a standard foxhole in the pavement with my fingernails." Several chuckled.

"You were the professional," Link countered in a quiet voice. "If Colonel Cliver hadn't remained cool and collected, a lot more lives would have been lost."

That started a new round of congratulations for Cliver, giving Link a chance to slip away. He did not want the spotlight lest it detract from the job at hand: to find Katy and return her to safety.

Gordon Tower pulled him into the gathering where the National Guard general and state police commissioner were talking about working together in the event of another terrorist attack. How they'd act jointly, using the commissioner's SWAT teams—they trained regularly—and the military's mobility since they possessed vehicles, aircraft, and the people to operate them.

"A lot depends on getting the governor's approval in a timely fashion," mused the brigadier. "If we could coordinate our timing, we might even call up a ranger company that uses Fort Collins for winter training."

"That's the sort of backup we could really use."

Link listened with interest until he received a call on the sat phone.

"Hi, pardner," Erin greeted him. "As usual, woman's work is never done. While you were busy with your flying heroics yesterday, I was trying to get a consensus on what caused all the problems at the airport—losing landing aids, radios and such, everything at the wrong times, and contributing to the loss of the two FBI airplanes. I hooked up with Steffie Footwine, one of the technical people at the National Security Agency, and had her talk with Randall."

"Randall being the prima donna chief investigator Maggie called a Neanderthal reject."

"Yeah, but Steffie Footwine thinks he's onto some good ideas and decided to fly out to look things over. Which is why I called. She just landed at Hayden."

"The NTSB's already there because of the accident."

"Yeah but she wants to look for herself. She needs someone to give her a hand and Randall's number has been busy for the last ten minutes."

Link looked around. "He was here a few minutes ago."

"How about someone a little more technical, like your MCP copilot? Mind if I give him a call?"

"Good idea. Ask them to take a look at the Steamboat airport too. Their radio went out right when I needed them most. Another coincidence?"

"Lots of odd happenings. One last thing, Link. Until she's looked things over, Steffie Footwine advises that you don't use the local telephones for sensitive discussions."

7:54 A.M.

On the same floor but on the opposite wing, Sergeant Santos held his knee firmly lodged in the chief investigator's back, holding his head back so the gaping throat wound would drain into the carpeting. He'd held him like that for several minutes and there was no movement, yet the bleeding continued. He was always amazed by the amount of life's liquid humans contained.

It was good to get out of the small house where he and

Captain Torré had holed up like rabbits. No radio or television. Wondering if the police would come. Laughing at the memory of setting off the noise boxes and watching the "posse" act like an army was attacking them.

Santos let the dead man fall face forward into the thick pool of blood. Wiped the blade of the knife on the man's ratty quilted vest, and stood. He picked up the cell phone. The T-Can contact had remained on the line. "It's done," he said, looking his gloves over for red. Then peering at the dead man, who did not look like an important investigator for a big company, who would be renting a fancy room like this. This one had long hair, earrings, and carried a cheap revolver.

There was no time for questions. He had more people to kill.

"Go out the side entrance," advised T-Can West.

Santos did not hesitate, but slipped out the door and hurried down the hall. The exit door was still closing when a neatly groomed man clad in a blue blazer entered the corridor, heading for the same room he had just left.

Five short minutes later Santos drove out of Ski Town, thinking that so far his task was going well. T-Can had lured the investigator to his room by phoning his sat number, telling him a courier was coming by. Santos had waited in the bathroom, expecting a difficult fight.

The second address was not easy to find, despite T-Can's directions. After wandering around, he found himself on the very street he was looking for. Clubhouse Drive snaked around the same big mountain, around some and lower than the ski area, and he wondered what kind of person built golf courses on the sides of mountains?

Almost there. He pulled to the curb, and got out; brushed his hand on his right pocket for reassurance that the .45 caliber automatic was there. Safety off, hammer down, round chambered. A brush on the other pocket proved the two railroad flares were inside.

The cell phone buzzed.

The contact told him he had killed the wrong person. The investigator was still alive. He had discovered the dead man in his room.

"I killed the one you *told* me to," Santos argued.

"Don't you have *eyes*?" the contact said. Sounding angry.

"Why don't you come and do it?" Santos shut the phone off and tossed it onto the seat of the car, thinking now he had to finish this one, then go back and kill the investigator again.

How was he supposed to know? Then he vaguely recalled that the contact had told him something about a blue coat.

Santos's head felt cold, so against the contact's advice he pulled on the shaggy wig. He walked down the sidewalk, wondering who he had killed. It was warmer in the sunlight, but since his arrival he had constantly yearned for the warmth of Mexico. He walked slowly, feeling nostalgic, in no hurry to finish here and have to return to the hotel.

Ahead was an upscale triplex; multi-level, with sharply pitched alpine roofs and lots of angles. Each home was large, with its own yard and parking area. It seemed a shame to burn it.

He rechecked numbers—it was the first town home. A white Ford Explorer was parked on the street, meaning someone might be inside. He'd been told to kill the people, also to destroy a computer and paper printout inside. That was not a problem. No human, computer, or piece of paper could withstand a hot fire.

Santos would keep it simple. Walk up and knock, and when they answered muscle his way inside. This time it did not matter. He was to kill everyone he found there.

He headed for the porch, in his mind going over what he'd say. Maybe just shove them back in and start shooting.

Maggie was running hot water into the Jacuzzi, breathing the steam and feeling better than she had since taking the leap from the balcony. Wishing she hadn't been so hard on Lincoln because she liked him so much, but pleased that she'd be ready when he returned. She looked forward to seeing him when she had her ammunition ready. Show him she could be a looker.

Enough hot water, she decided, and was turning it off when she heard the doorchime. He'd have to wait. She had more than half an hour, and refused to be seen until she was presentable.

She pulled off the robe and stepped into the tub. The water was scorching. *Just* right. She reached for the button to activate the pump, smiling in her anticipation.

Sergeant Santos rang the bell a second time. Standing close so he'd hear whoever approached. He could make out only a rumbling noise. Nothing else, no footsteps or sounds of life, which presented a dilemma. Exposed as he was, it would not be easy to break in unseen. While the street was without traffic, he could not take the chance of being watched by nosy neighbors.

He leaned on the bell, let it chime repeatedly. Waited, and again heard not a sound. Just the gurgling of a pump or whatever. No one at home? He mulled it over and decided to go around to the side, break a window and toss in the flare. Do the same at another window. While the place burned he'd hang around and shoot anyone who came out the door. Then take off for the car.

It made sense. The only hard part might be trying to get around to the side, through snow tail-high to a tall elephant. But there was no easy way. Santos started high-stepping, sinking into snow to his thighs, grumbling as he went.

Maggie was hidden in a mountain of bubbly—she'd borrowed freely from her hostess's supply of bath beads—thinking that Cleopatra could not have been more pampered. The only things missing were music and champagne. Whenever the suds diminished even a small bit she'd press the switch—the pump would growl, a jet of water would massage her back, and the bubbles would fluff up. Link Anderson's great hands had competition.

Speaking of him, she purred and stretched all the way to

her toes, shuddered and groaned happily. Maybe she should go down and let Link in, if he would promise to get into the tub with her. Let him do his job with his hands. When Maggie was sexually aroused the soles of her feet became warm. She wondered how hot they'd be if Link were with her now.

The thought drew a wicked smile. And in reflex—knowing she did not have time for such silliness—Maggie's mind returned to business. About Arturo Guteriez and how she might pin the tail on the right donkey.

There was a tinkling sound of broken glass from the first level, loud enough to tell her that both panes of a thermal window had been broken. Maybe in the kitchen, or one of the downstairs bedrooms?

Maggie clambered out of the tub and scrambled for the counter where she'd left her pistol. Then, *Oh, damn!*

She skated and flailed on the wet tile, almost caught her balance, then felt herself falling headlong. As if it were a slow motion segment of bad video tape, she saw the marble vanity looming. Her forehead smacked solidly. She heard her own groan as her world went dark.

8:55 A.M.—Sheraton Hotel

The four—FBI supervisor, police commissioner, National Guard general, and Link Anderson—were theorizing about the terrorists and what could be done if it all happened again. Also about the dead man discovered in Randall's room, not yet identified.

The chief investigator had been ashen when he'd come to the conference room to report the dead man he'd found in his room. The state troopers had been first on the scene since there were so many around. Now the locals were joining them.

Enough mysteries to fill a barrel. The alternate riddle of the moment was what the NSA expert and the MCP copilot might find wrong with the airports' electronic equipment.

"She said to avoid using telephones?" repeated the commissioner. "Not only does that sound spooky, it's next to impossible if you want to get anything done."

Gordon Tower was interested. "But if the terrorists are listening to telephone and radio conversations it might explain a lot."

Link examined his watch and tried to slip quietly away.

"Tell Maggie hello," said Gordon Tower. Letting his smile glimmer.

Except for the headache Maggie felt glorious! She looked outside, saw Link sitting in a car, motor running, awaiting her. She opened the door and waved for him to come in, and gave him her best perky smile. Face done, but not overdone. Hair lustrous, with subtle highlights, swept just slightly to one side. Wearing gold hardware, a knockout angora sweater, and lightweight wool slacks. Wasn't that back in New York. Hmm.

She waited for him. Not overdoing it or looking eager, or betraying that she was scared. He approached wearing a look of respect. Maggie stepped out, opened her arms. She was as tall as he was. Willowy and graceful.

"You are exquisite, Maggie." Why, he even carried flowers.

"Thank you, Lincoln." She was in love.

Link cupped her face lightly. His lips moved closer. His expression adoring as he whispered, "You are lovely beyond description."

Maggie coughed.

Link said he had secretly yearned all those years. His heart had ached for her.

Maggie felt radiant, wondering if their children would be . . .

The headache worsened. She raised her head a little and gagged on thick smoke. Then she felt the heat radiating from the wall, and remembered!

She'd fallen and struck her head on the marble vanity.

Smoke was everywhere, but thickest when she rose even slightly. Best to stay low, but there was little time and she had to hurry. The flames were close, just on the other side of the walls. Couldn't see them for all the smoke, but the heat was intense.

Maggie crawled away from the heat, and banged her head against the side of the tub. She turned and went in the opposite direction, toward the door. Bumped her knee on something, felt it and found the pistol she had been going for when she'd fallen. She grasped it, then a towel she encountered on the floor, and continued crawling.

She abruptly stopped. The door to the bedroom was radiating intense heat. The fire had spread there too.

There was nowhere to go!

22

Link was in a rented four-by-four pickup—on his way back to see Maggie. Thinking she was a pain in the butt. Make that a cute, lovable, and quite sexy pain.

Turning onto Clubhouse Drive he became concerned as he heard the faint wail of sirens and saw a column of smoke. As he drew closer his feeling turned to apprehension, then to alarm. It was the Crow town home, with white streamers spewing from eaves and shingles, black pillars billowing from the back.

He nosed to the curb, out of the way of emergency vehicles that would arrive, got out, and loped toward the home. There was no sign of Maggie, only a couple in the next driveway and an overcoated, bushy-haired man who stared at the house as he slogged around from the back.

"Did a woman get out?" Link yelled to him, but he hardly noticed, just formed a half smirk that did not fit with the situation. "A woman," Link called out. "Short, with . . ."

Bushy-head ignored him. His hands were stuffed into overcoat pockets, and he continued walking toward the front, eyes fixed on the door.

Link called out to the couple in the next driveway and asked if they'd seen a woman leaving the town home.

"Oh my God. The Crows' guest." The man became

ashen. "I gave her the key yesterday. The answer's no. We haven't seen her."

"Everything's gone!" the woman lamented.

"They're just things," the man said. "The woman may still be inside."

Link tried approaching the front door, and was forced back by intense radiant heat. A look through an adjacent window showed a solid sheet of fire. It would be impossible to get in that way, and the conflagration around on the side seemed as intense.

Where in God's name was Maggie!

As he walked around the side another thought arose, and he glanced back toward the street. Bushy-head stared at the front door, looking pleased with something. Then it came to Link—he was one of the men in the composite drawings.

Unlikely, he decided. "Maggie!" he called out. As he slogged through snow grown mushy by heat, he heard heavy vehicles on the street, then the shouts of fire-fighting supervisors. They said to go for containment. The adjoined town homes were considered lost.

If Maggie was inside, the odds of her rescue had just dwindled considerably.

He examined a second level overhang and two modest-sized swing-out windows—frosted so it was likely a bathroom—wondering if he could enter there. He'd decided it would be futile, and was about to head for the front and the suspicious man when both windows flew open. Caused by the intense heat, was his first thought as heavy smoke billowed forth.

He sensed something moving beyond the outpour, and heard coughing.

Adrenaline surged. "Maggie?" he cried, saw more motion in the smoke, and heard more coughing. A flat, rectangular object skittered down the roof and fell into the mush, tossed by whomever was inside.

He scrambled up a supporting post, grasped the eave, and levered himself onto the overhang. The coughing was faint, unrecognizable.

"Reach out the window!" Link called out. He drew a breath, then kneed and elbowed his way farther up the roof and into the smoke, eyes squinted and smarting as he reached for her. He felt nothing on the first sweep of his arm, so he continued forward. On the second sweep he contacted bare skin. Fingers closed over his wrist.

He grasped the hand, pulled. She was drawn, almost yanked, through the window, and together they fell onto the rough surface of the roof. Then, before he could reestablish balance or gain a handhold, they were sliding. Link reached out desperately, searching for the eave, anything to slow their impetus, but there was nothing handy. As they went over he wrapped his arms about her. They fell, Maggie pulled close, and he tumbled in a terrible semblance of a parachute landing fall, their limbs flailing helter-skelter. They came to rest, she lying on him in the slush of melted snow, and for a moment were still, both gasping for breath.

Link could not help exulting that she was *alive*.

There was no doubt of Maggie's gender. Except for a bath towel wrapped about her arm, she was as naked as the moment she'd drawn her first breath.

"I can't see," she wheezed from atop him, wiping at her eyes with the towel.

Then Link distinctly heard, "He's got a gun!"

Who? was Link's first thought. Then he *knew*. The smirking terrorist had come to kill Maggie. He instinctively rolled away from the front of the house, shielding her in his arms, Maggie grunting with the burden of his weight.

Bam! The explosive report of the gunshot reverberated as a bee stung Link's arm. His impulse was to either charge the threat or seek safety, but he didn't dare leave her.

Maggie was saying something about "can't see—take the pistol!" when he grasped her and again rolled directly away from the terrorist. Can't be a sitting duck target!

Bam! A miss. He tried to rise in the slush, slipped, and fell beside her.

"I've got my pistol in my hand," she cried. "Under the towel."

The overcoated man was coming for them, a handgun extended in their direction, held *sideward*. Great for macho movies, lousy for accuracy.

Bam!

"Damn it, take the gun!" Maggie cried, waving the towel in the air. "I still can't see." And that was when he finally realized what she was saying. That she had a pistol under the towel!

Maggie kept pushing the towel-shrouded revolver at him until he felt metal. It took another moment of fumbling before he located the trigger guard. He'd begun to rise, intending to crouch and fire, when smirking man stopped. Aimed.

Bam! Snow erupted a couple of feet to their right.

The terrorist was still twenty yards distant—too far for a lousy shot who didn't understand a proper sight picture—his smirk now a determined glare.

Link raised the pistol, wishing he could see the sights. Facing a .45 auto with a wimp-caliber pistol was enough of a handicap. The terrorist took another step. Cool in demeanor because he didn't know about the revolver in the towel. Link waited, eyes glued to the automatic the man wielded like a kid with a toy. He would fire as soon as the trigger finger tensed, then continue shooting until a round hit.

Bad odds! he was thinking, staring at the automatic, when a stream of water, three inches in diameter, impacted squarely in the middle of the man's back. He flew forward, airborne for several feet, bushy wig and .45 automatic sailing farther yet. As smirking man slid past them, his look was transformed to one of utter surprise.

Link settled back into the mire and gawked. Three fireman held the hose. Two anchoring, one directing the nozzle. All of them grinning as the terrorist tried to rise. The stream impacted his legs, which flew comically out from under him. He flailed and slid, carried again by the torrent until he smacked into a wooden fence.

A policeman scrambled toward the gunman, his own pistol

raised, and Link heard someone yelling he was one of the guys in the drawings on television. One of the terrorists.

"*Please* make a move!" the cop yelled hoarsely to the sodden man, covering him. A second policeman joined him, and they were pulling him up and none-too-gently cuffing him.

Link shrugged out of his sheepskin, cloaked Maggie with it and pulled her to her feet. The coat reached past her knees. She was coughing and wobbly. A firefighter said something about her feet freezing and offered to carry her to the emergency vehicles.

Maggie was wiping at her eyes, shaking her head at the firefighter. "No!" she yelled to another Samaritan trying to wrap her in blankets. Exhibiting something akin to fright, holding tightly to Link's arm. "Get me *out* of here!"

"Ma'am, an ambulance will be here in a couple of minutes," one told her.

She wiped soot from her face, coughed up a glob of dark mucous. "Lincoln," she whispered urgently, "we *have* to get out of here!"

The firefighter was insistent. "We've got to get you to the hospital."

Maggie coughed again, "My *husband* will take care of me."

As Link's jaw drooped, the firefighter said, "Yes, ma'am." Then to Link, "You'd better take her, sir."

"Lincoln," she said imperiously, and held on as he lifted her.

A couple of minutes later he had wended his way past the emergency vehicles, and deposited her in the pickup's passenger seat.

"My electronic organizer!" she cried as he crawled into the driver's seat, as if she'd just remembered it. "I have to have it, Link."

"Like he said, you need medical attention."

"Damn it, Lincoln. We *need* it. It's gray-colored. I threw it out the window."

"I think I saw it." He restarted the engine and turned the heater to full blast.

"Please! I don't dare lose it."

"Get warm." Link scrambled back out and hurried along the side of the town home. Observing the police taking their time with the soggy terrorist, who glared up at them as he shivered violently. No one had offered him blankets for warmth.

Link ventured closer to the town home, ignoring shouts from the firefighters. The area where they'd fallen from the roof had been trampled into quagmire, but his luck held. The corner of a metallic device protruded from the mush.

As he recovered it one of the policemen attending the terrorist yelled for him to wait for them at the hospital. There were questions. Link waved his understanding, and started back.

As he passed by, the fire captain said the hospital had been alerted. Check her into the emergency room. They'd tend to her.

He found Maggie huddling in front of the heater, looking miserable. Her eyes were fixed on the electronic organizer that she took from his hand. "Thank God," she muttered.

23

"Take me somewhere we can talk, with a telephone."

"First you need a doctor."

"Not the hospital," she repeated. Maggie was huddled in the heater's blast. She used his handkerchief to wipe soot from her nostrils, then blew hard to rid herself of more dark mucous. "If I show up there, I'll end up back on the damned list."

"What list?" He sounded increasingly exasperated.

"I'll explain at your place." She pulled his sheepskin tightly about herself. Glanced over and caught him looking at her. "Don't look at me like that," she said. "I'm not nuts."

He braked to a halt at the Mount Werner Drive intersection. The hospital was on a knoll a few blocks to their right, Ski Town to the left. He sat for a moment, letting the pickup idle.

"If you're thinking hospital, you might as well let me out here."

He turned left, toward Ski Town.

"Thanks."

"Can't have you running around the streets naked."

She responded with a glare. Blew her nose again.

"I'm at the Snowflower," he said. "Next door to the Snowbird, where the cops are still nosing around. Lots of cancellations so it's quiet."

"Got an extra bedroom for a poor girl without a job?"

"Three. The layout's identical to the Snowbird's." He parked in the basement lot. She insisted on walking, but made it only ten feet before hopping up and down from the cold and letting him scoop her up. On the first floor they heard people in the lobby, but ran into no one. "Déjà vu again," she muttered as she was borne out the north wing. "We've got to stop doing this." She clung more or less happily as Link managed to unlock the door.

Why not? He was a super guy, *awfully* strong, and she was *awfully* attracted.

Link deposited her on the couch, knelt and rubbed her poor feet. Maggie purred, thinking how a foot massage was as good as sex any day. She watched the muscles rippling in his forearms and changed her mind. It was just close.

He finished too quickly.

"Hey," she said on impulse. "Would you hold me for a few minutes?"

He looked surprised.

"Please?" She smiled, trying for demure.

"Guess I'd better, since we're recently married."

Maggie burrowed her face into his shirt and herself into the warmth of his grasp, ignoring the fact that they looked like refugees from a tornado.

She kept her face hidden. "You didn't like me saying that?"

"I missed the honeymoon."

She started to tell him something cute, like there was no time like the present. Instead she coughed. Drew back and blew her nose. Then pulled close again, and sighed. Thinking about the unknown fate of her gentle friend in Mexico City.

Maggie pulled her mind off the bad thought and wished Link would put a move on her. Wanting a chance to say yes. It had been a long time since the soles of her feet had been heated, and she was increasingly sure of her feelings toward him.

He shifted on the couch. "Warm?"

"Yeah, but it's scary. I was warm the other night and next thing I was jumping into a snowbank. I was toasty in the

Crows' tub, then I was rolling around naked in front of the entire Steamboat Springs Fire Department."

"The only complaint I heard was from a lady fireman."

"Joke about my pink body and I'll shoot you." He'd returned her pistol.

"You've got a nasty bruise on your forehead."

"I thumped it getting out of the tub, and I was out of it for a while. Good thing. If I'd gone outside right away, I'd've had to kill the guy."

"Or him you. They have a description of two of the terrorists and he looks like one of 'em."

"He's still a lousy shot. Here's something you males should take to heart. Don't ever interrupt a woman's bath and think you'll get away with it."

Link tried to shift away, but she held on. "Not so fast. You saved my life, so you've gotta look after me. Feed me, keep me warm, take me dancing." *Make love to me,* she silently added.

He chuckled. Maggie snuggled. Then, since she had to let go at some point, she drew back and smooched his cheek. Left a sooty mark and noted his self-conscious expression, as if he entertained forbidden thoughts. *Bravo! Go right on with those,* she thought smugly.

"Be right back," he said, and disappeared.

Good. She'd needed for him to go away for a moment. Determine why was she acting like a teenager with charging hormones? Counter-argument: it was unnatural for one to wait when one was so drawn. What was wrong with a bit of lust if he was the right man?

Link returned and handed over sweatshirt, gym shorts, and wool socks.

"I take it you'd like your coat back."

"The sheep's certainly never had it so good. I'm in the front unit. You can take any of the others." He started for his bedroom. "See you when I've showered."

"We've got a lot to discuss," Maggie called after him. She carried her stack into the rearmost bedroom, wishing he'd held her longer.

She dawdled under the shower's gentle rain. Thinking it was funny how rolling around naked in snow made one cherish basic comforts. After drying herself, Maggie pulled on a huge sky blue sweatshirt that read USAFA on front and back, reminded that Link had attended the Air Force Academy. It covered her to her knees and the wool socks came that high. She drew still-damp hair back, secured it in a ponytail with a rubber band found in the desk drawer, and emerged. Except for a smoky tickle in her throat, she felt human.

Link was seated on the couch in fresh khakis and Pendleton sweater, stocking feet propped on the coffee table and staring at the composite drawings shown on the television.

"He's the one on the right. See the sarcastic expression?"

Maggie sat beside him. "I didn't get a good look."

An 800 number flashed at the bottom of the screen. Anyone who had seen the men was asked to call in. Then Katy's photograph was shown, with a voice-over saying a "substantial" reward was offered for information leading to her safe return.

"How substantial?" Maggie asked.

"Twenty million."

"That's a lot of substantial."

Link switched off the television. "Let's talk about this mysterious list?"

"Remember Axel, the guy I heard talking on the balcony? I'm pretty sure he's a communications expert in charge of a Mexican spook organization." Maggie told him about her Mexican friend, about Axel Nevas and his Agencia, about the e-mail message.

She'd believed it would be difficult to explain eavesdropping networks, but Link had visited government listening posts during the cold war.

"One was an intercept station in Ankara. There was a huge antenna farm surrounding a large building filled with radios and tape recorders. Rooms full of people monitoring the tapes."

"It's changed. Now they plant electronic *modules* with banks of processors—think of them as small computers—in communications lines. No more big rooms filled with operators either. They use supercomputers and can extract a thousand times more data."

"Modules?" He brightened, onto a recollection. "Would they put one at an airport?"

"Sure, to control their electronics, but they're mostly used in communications." She explained automated modules. How they were programmed to listen for trigger words. "Like *Katy,* or *Link Anderson.* I was on the list, so I got myself fired and pulled off. That's why I didn't go to the hospital. Someone mentions my name and bingo, I'm back on Axel's list."

"How big are these modules?"

"The size of a cigar box. They're also efficient. Someone installs a hundred modules, and someone else mans a supercomputer at a listening post. That's it. They know everything."

"Then there must be a listening post here somewhere?"

"Or maybe a thousand miles away. Axel was telling "tee can" to remove names of the dead people from the *list*. He also talked about targets and triggers. That's the right jargon. He spoke about an office in Atlanta and a local one. Maybe one of those is a listening post?"

"Would he go to all that trouble just to find Katy?"

"I'd suppose the network's set up for a bigger purpose, but my problem's trying to prove *any* of it. My friend suggested checking telephone switching stations and microwave and cell phone towers for unexplained modules, and said Señor Deep Voice prefers those made by a Czech company. But despite everything I said, I couldn't tell a module from a French poodle."

He told her about Steffie Footwine. "Nevas may be good with electronics, but the NSA's the best in the world."

"An expert is precisely what we need."

"It was Randall's idea."

"He's not a complete cretin." She sighed. "I'm worried,

Link. My Mexican friend's in danger and I don't dare call him. Axel Nevas is bad news when it comes to mercy. He claims to be some kind of Aztec priest, and those folks spent a lot of time cutting people up."

Link offered the flip-top phone. "This is secure."

She shook her head. "There's something I didn't recall yesterday. Axel mentioned you a couple of times. He said you were very dangerous, but he also asked if they'd picked up anything on Anderson's sat freqs."

He stared dubiously at the device.

"Things like that are still coming back to me. It's bugged, Link."

"Then we have a major problem. The foundation's not the only group using these. We provide instruments and satellite time for the government's most sensitive communications."

Maggie's heart pumped faster. "Such as the DEA?"

"Among others like the FBI, Secret Service, State Department Intelligence, and certain CIA-owned companies. I didn't say any of that, by the way. It's very classified."

"Shut it down. Have your people turn off the satellites or whatever."

"That can't be done lightly. We're talking about critical communications. Presidential and key officials' movements, negotiations with foreign governments, life and death situations with deep-cover agents." He paused. "And we don't *know* the system's compromised."

Maggie picked the Hewlett Packard from the coffee table.

"Then let's find out."

She explained the handheld computer as she worked the small keyboard, pressed the FIND button, and showed him the name displayed on the small screen.

"Arturo Domingues Guteriez"

"Katy came face-to-face with a man named Guteriez. She said he had a long face, prominent features, and a gold tooth. Arturo has those. He's a big-time drug importer, and gets the Denver dealers—the Bloods and Hells Angels are really big there—to pass out cocaine to kids like it's candy. His advice is to hook 'em before age twelve. All of that's known among the federal narcs, yet no one can pin him with anything."

Link shook his head. "I have the same argument as before. Katy's squeaky clean with drugs. Why would Guteriez or anyone like him be after her?"

"Got me," Maggie said truthfully. "She's either done, seen, or knows something to make her a threat. Right now let's find out if this particular Guteriez was one of the terrorists, and see if your fancy telephone's bugged. Kill both of those birds with one big hairy rock."

"Explain your hairy rock."

"We plant a lie. Call Erin on your sat phone and give her Guteriez's name. Tell her we found a message he left for the FBI. That he's agreed to expose everything that went on in Steamboat if they give him amnesty."

Link was looking troubled.

"Don't tell me you're concerned about a slimeball who's getting rich by ruining other people's lives."

"Erin and I don't lie to one another. That's our covenant." He brightened, onto a thought, opened the flip-top phone and made the call. Leading off, he mentioned someone named Jester, a fighter pilot buddy from way back. After a pause he said, "Yeah, *that* Jester, from the war." He then passed the information about Arturo Domingues Guteriez leaving a note for the FBI.

"Keep it to yourself for now," he told Erin. They spoke for a while longer but he did not mention Maggie. When done he pressed the OFF button, looking thoughtful. "That should work."

"So who's this Jester?"

"The code word our squadron used during Desert Storm when we thought Saddam's people were listening to our radio calls. She knows about it."

Maggie was considering that she deserved some more

cuddling. Thinking she'd picked a dumb time to fall in love. It seemed too sudden. Maybe it was just adrenaline.

"Erin's been talking with Gordon," he said. "The arsonist wasn't carrying identification, and he's not talking. Not even asking for a lawyer. Just stares at walls and ignores everyone. They've faxed his prints to Washington."

"I'm getting the feeling things are moving." *So let's slow down together.*

"What's next?"

"We need someone to witness what happens to Guteriez." Maggie did a FIND with her electronic organizer to pull up a phone number. She used the kitchen telephone to dial the number of another former student at Quantico, now a detective lieutenant in the Denver PD.

When he came on the line she used her married name.

Maggie did not enlighten the lieutenant that she was no longer with the FBI, nor did she claim to be an agent. If he had asked, she would have told him. He did not. She did not.

She gave the Cherry Creek address and said she'd gotten information that "the owner" was involved in something big that might be happening today. Real quick. After a couple of queries by the lieutenant followed by her silences, he realized she was not going to explain.

"If you decide to send anyone, make sure they have a lot of backup," she suggested, "and tell them to not take chances. Some extremely dangerous people may be involved."

"In what?" He was growing impatient.

She remained quiet.

"They see or hear something, should my people go in?"

"Lieutenant, I'm just telling you there's a situation. Everything else is your call. You also get credit for anything that comes out of it."

The lieutenant wasn't jumping. "Can't be anything good or the bureau would grab it."

"The bureau doesn't even know I'm calling. It's a no-lose situation for you. Tell me you don't want it and I'll call someone who does."

"I'll take it." His ho-hum tone made her wish she had picked someone else.

Maggie went to the bathroom and coughed more soot from her system. As she returned to the sofa, Link was examining his sheepskin. Using a wet towel to scrub at various smudges.

"You'll make it worse. Wear something else until you can get it dry-cleaned."

He took her advice, went into his bedroom, and returned in a down-filled parka. "How long will we have to wait?"

"My guess is not long. These aren't charitable people who give folks the benefit of the doubt. Not even solid citizens like Honest Art Guteriez."

"And if no one shows up at his place, my phone's secure."

"Either that or I picked the wrong Guteriez."

He buttoned the parka. "I'll be gone for a while. I want to share some of this with Gordon."

Maggie turned on a high-beam smile. "We're friends? And I'm still under contract?"

He gave her a look like she might be trying to sell him *another* used car. "Yes, and yes."

"Then could I get you to pick up a few things, since everything I brought was burned up?"

10:20 A.M.—Cherry Creek, Denver

As Maggie Tatro wrote down everything she recalled from the destroyed e-mail message, one hundred twenty air miles eastward the hard-eyed men and women were receiving their briefing. Without introduction, except to give his first name, Axel showed videos of Katy Dubois, and explained that she was the Kitten-bitch, their target.

He made his points clearly, for they were not mental wizards. The person who killed the Kitten-bitch would be set up like a prince. All who were helpful toward that end would also be rewarded. They were better off than the authorities. Axel had a special source of information and knew everything they did. And *nothing* would be known about them. Only after the girl was killed could they depart. Any slightest disobedience would be dealt with quickly and severely.

They asked questions, and were advised to just follow orders and shut up.

He explained what had happened at Steamboat. They were here to finish the job. As soon as the girl was located they'd muscle their way in and kill her. This time it would be violent from the start. Forget finesse or people they hurt. Make blood as necessary. Don't worry about killing police, just do it. Same with civilians that got in the way.

Weapons would be distributed when they went after the girl. Until then refrain from using product and remain alert.

They would take new four-wheelers—Tahoes, 4-Runners, Expeditions, Land Cruisers, and Monteros—from dealerships owned by Guteriez. Go to Interstate 25 North, then west on I-70 for two hundred miles to Glenwood Springs. Drivers would be provided with maps.

Axel observed his army of rabble, many of whom the day before had been leaning on street dealers to keep their product moving. Some of them dealing or even running.

He whispered a small prayer to Huitzilopóchtli, and pointed to the man suggested by the Voice. "Come up here." The offering narrowed his eyes warily, and came forward.

"What is this?" Axel reached into his shirt pocket.

"Jus' my pipe."

"Did you hear me tell you about no product?"

"Sure. You say don't use it, I don't."

He delved deeper and pulled out a baggie. "Were you told not to bring this?"

He shrugged. "Jus' pot. No crack or nothin'."

Axel placed his long arm around his shoulder. "Do you hear him talking back?"

"Hey man." The guy shook his head, eyes bulging. "I ain't . . ."

Pop. He wilted, dead before he touched the floor. Axel

holding the ornate pistol that was so small it was hardly visible in his hand.

People looked around uneasily. There were sounds as paraphernalia hit the floor.

"Like I told you," said Axel, "do not use product while you are here, or we will talk like this." He doubted he'd have trouble from them for a while. Just the rest of the world.

Start with Sergeant Santos. Thus far he'd killed the wrong man at the hotel, started a destructive house fire but failed to kill the occupant, and been arrested by firemen. What else could go wrong? Then five minutes earlier Axel had learned that a sedan had just pulled in and parked near the entrance of Guteriez's driveway with two plainclothes detectives inside.

Coincidence or not, he was not yet sure of the appropriate reaction. The group should soon start trickling out in ones and twos, and mustn't be followed.

Guteriez would remain behind because of his broken arm. Axel motioned him over and said he'd decided to let a few vehicles depart to gauge the reaction. If the police tried to tail them, he would call on him to create a diversion.

A cell phone buzzed in its holster. "Axel," he responded in his gravel voice. He walked a few steps away. It was the contact from T-Can East. "It was a mixup at Steamboat," she said. "Santos killed the person sent by the Voice to kill the same guy he was trying for."

"Explain all that later." He disconnected. Were they being purposefully funny.

T-Can West called. "Now the police are looking for a naked woman who . . ."

Axel was not sure he had heard correctly. "What?"

"A nude woman was pulled from the burning house by her husband. No names yet, but the firemen report she's small and has a good figure, and her husband's dark-haired and tall. He wrapped her in his sheepskin coat and drove away, and they haven't seen them since."

A chill of anger trembled through Axel. Anderson was tall and wore a sheepskin. Was he interfering, turning it all into a circus?

"So far Santos refuses to tell the police anything."

"He won't." Axel would make sure of it.

"One more thing from Steamboat. I just listened to the tape to verify it. Guteriez left a message for the FBI, promising cooperation if they'd offer him amnesty."

Axel's eyes snapped to Guteriez, who was speaking to one of his household staff.

"The information's good," said the contact. "It's from Anderson's sat phone."

"I do not trust Anderson."

"It's real. They don't believe we can monitor their satellite phones."

Yesterday Guteriez had visited his doctor to have the bone set. Had he contacted the police? Was that the reason for the car at the gate? He thought not. If the authorities believed the terrorists from Steamboat were here, they'd have brought the whole police force. *Still . . .*

"I'll handle the matter," Axel told the contact. "Advise the Voice to pick his replacement. I also want you to isolate the plainclothes detail parked outside. Do not allow them to call out."

Axel holstered the cell phone as he returned to the ragtag group. He told them to collect their gear, proceed to the vehicles parked outside, and to depart in two-minute intervals. After the second vehicle, they should wait for him to come out.

As they were leaving the room, Axel went over to Guteriez. "I wish to speak to you and your staff. We will need the diversion after all."

His host was pleased to help. As Guteriez gathered his people, Axel whispered, "Accept my offerings, oh Huitzilopóchtli."

10:45 A.M.

The detectives, one of each gender, both newly assigned and unaccustomed to being out of uniform, occupied the front of the unmarked but obviously official sedan. They had the engine running for warmth, a window cracked so carbon monoxide wouldn't accumulate, and had been parked across from the electrified gate that controlled access to the sweeping-arc driveway for the past half hour. Already they were bored out of their minds.

When they'd first arrived and noted the big house that was mostly hidden by foliage, they'd tried to determine what they were watching. The lieutenant had not enlightened them. So far all they'd found was that it was the address of Arturo Guteriez, no wife listed.

A sport utility vehicle departed. The female took photos while the male used binoculars to take down the license number. "Dopers," the woman announced as she lowered the camera. They'd both seen their share. After another vehicle departed they had not changed their minds. It was a gathering of particularly slack-jawed, don't-give-a-shit dopers.

During the following lull the male detective began to fool with the windshield-mounted video camera, which did not please the female detective who was trying to repair a nail.

"We oughta have this thing going," he said.

"Quit shaking the car."

He finished adjusting and sat back. "Might as well use it if we got it."

She didn't respond. Her lips were pursed as she continued her artistry.

They'd established their banter on a previous surveillance. He gave her a mock leer. "Kinda like your fundamental equipment. No reason to let that sweet thing get musty."

"Before I'd let you anywhere near it, I'd sew it up. Here comes another one."

He lifted the binoculars.

She looked up from her nail. "You got the video camera on?"

"Yeah. The winking light there means it's running."

She used the 35 millimeter anyway. "Get the plate number?"

He continued staring. "Hey, I got eyes like a hawk, a memory like a bear trap, and a fundamental organ like a stallion. Package deal. You oughta try it."

She snorted. "Makes my toes curl in anticipation."

He wrote the license number on the notepad.

"It's bigger than the last Jeep."

"That was a Pathfinder, for God's sake. Made by Nissan. I'm thinking of getting one."

"They're all Jeeps."

"This one's a Land Cruiser. Toyota made 'em for military use way back during the Korean War and they got popular."

"Jesus but I'm impressed. Learning all kinds of useless bullshit."

The vehicle pulled up just before them, and the man in the passenger's seat emerged. He was tall and angular, mostly knees and elbows, and ambled toward them almost comically, looking around like he was scoping the area.

"I don't like this," said the woman, pausing in her repair job and squinting.

"You don't like anything," said her partner as he rolled down his window. "Help you?" he asked, his voice conversational like he was a citizen who happened to be parked there.

The man took in the notepad on the seat, the 35 millimeter camera beside it. He gave a slight nod, then leisurely pulled his right hand from his jacket pocket.

"Gun!" the female cried, scrambling.

Pop, pop. Another round would be necessary. The first had killed the man, but the second punched a small hole in the woman's jawbone that made her twist and shriek. She grasped the door handle, desperate to get away. *Pop.*

The angular man opened the door, pulled out the two

bodies and placed them into a T, with their arms pulled in neatly at their sides. Then he took the camera and notepad and returned to the Land Cruiser, unaware that both his approach and departure had been captured on videotape.

24

Link was obviously not the kind to deliberate on articles of women's lingerie unless they were filled with the real thing. He'd enlisted the support of the two women working the desk of the Snowflower Condominiums, promising a reward so inviting that they'd turned the desk over to a maintenance man, then hurried to Ski Town and scrambled from one upscale shop to the next.

When Maggie lay aside pen and notepad to answer their knock at the door, they marched inside with armloads of packages.

"If you're Margaret, this stuff's for you," one said.

She looked on in amazement.

"You have a nice friend," the woman said in a happy Colorado drawl as she deposited her armload. "I was you, I'd keep him."

Maggie started to close the door behind them, but two men entered and deposited a collection of suitcases, some of which, judging from their weight, were filled. They nodded pleasantly and left.

The first woman pulled a small box from her purse. "He said to buy like you'd lost everything. There's a watch and a few sets of earrings in that one." She handed over a Visa card and an envelope stuffed with receipts. "Most fun I've

had in years. He was right, by the way. There's no spending
limit on the card."

Maggie read the totals and gave a gasp.

"He also said don't worry, it's a company card."

"Did he tip you?"

"Even better. Now we go back and pick up the outfits
we're getting for *ourselves*."

The instant the door closed, Maggie began pawing
through sweaters, skirts, and dresses, jumpsuits and slacks,
a knockout ski outfit. She paused to admire a nightgown
and black see-through peignoir. A makeup case from the
luggage was filled with essential toiletries, a variety of
scents, lipsticks, and makeup. Much of it in her shades. She
held up a 34 double D bra, her size, a tribute to Lincoln's
powers of observation. The room service at the Snowflower
was great, and so was he. She grinned like a thief as she
carted the loot into her bedroom.

Maggie took her time preparing, even pulled a chair in from
the kitchen so she could sit before the dresser mirror and do
it right. She cleansed, powdered, deodorized, and perfumed. Used a light layer of neutral base on her face, added
a hint of blush, and took time with her eyes.

Cat eyes. Green, with a hint of hazel, now accented with
mascara and long eyelashes. Eyebrows plucked and shaped.
Longish rust-colored hair giving off fiery glints. When he
arrived, she intended to give Link a kiss and hug he would
not forget. After all, he *had* saved her life, and after two
days of continuous intensity, they needed a small interlude.
She leaned forward to reshape her upper lip just a bit. Glanced
at her new Seiko. He could return at any moment.

A wicked thought flickered. Margaret Ann Tatro smiled
impishly, went to the bed, and reached past the one-piece
jumpsuit.

She drew on the sheer peignoir, with nothing but Maggie
underneath, went back into the bathroom, and examined.
Her breasts were clearly outlined, even the shadow of her
love triangle was visible under the dark gauzy material.

Nothing about the vision could be called subtle. She wondered about his reaction, recalling the scene in the bathtub when he'd been unable to draw his eyes away from her breasts. She wanted him to look at her like that again. Put the yearning back into his eyes.

She toyed with the idea of greeting him in the gauzy robe and whispering something like, "I want you, you fool." No. "I *need* you," she whispered throatily. She'd never said anything like it to anyone, but then, Lincoln affected her differently than other men. The first time she'd felt weak-kneed around him had been at age ten when she'd envisioned him as her prince. He was still strong and sure, with something added that made her want to nurture him.

As Maggie tried to make up her mind she tidied the bedroom, put suitcases and boxes into closets, even pulled the covers back very neatly, so it would be inviting. "Bed me, you delicious man," she tried in the seductive tone, and realized that despite the humor, it was what she really wanted. And her female intuition had been hinting that the feeling might be mutual.

As she switched off the bedroom's overhead light, someone rapped on the door. A thrill of trepidation shuddered through her as his key rattled in the lock. *Had* to be him. No one else had a key. She cracked the bedroom door. "I need you," she practiced under her breath as the front door opened.

Maggie heard him walk into the suite, and chickened out.

The husky man with the pigtail and gold earring entered quietly, but found no one in the living room. Perhaps she was resting in her bedroom. Possibly going through the things Anderson said some ladies bought for her.

"Maggie," he called in a low voice, not wanting to draw the attention of someone in another suite. He took another tentative step and was preparing to call again, when a bedroom door swung partway open. A woman stepped out wearing the sheerest robe imaginable.

His jaw drooped. She was *gorgeous*. Breasts thrust

boldly forward, lips parted and glistening, hair done to perfection. A picture so sexy that a saint would have been stirred.

Her voice emerged in a sultry whisper. "Bed me, you . . ." She froze. "Oh, *shit*!" The door slammed, loud as a gunshot.

He shook his head just once, hard. "Mr. Anderson said to bring a few things and hurry, ma'am. He'll explain downstairs." His voice was unnaturally high.

She said something about he'd damn well *better* explain. Then, "I'm supposed to pack?"

"Dress warmly and bring a change of clothes. We'll come back for the rest."

"Why?"

"Well, ma'am, he said the police are on their way to *arrest* you."

The copilot went into Link Anderson's bedroom. As he rummaged through the closet and then the bathroom, dropping various items into a gym bag, he tried to push the image of the woman from his mind. He did not succeed, nor could he erase his grin.

12:45 P.M.—Glenwood Springs, Colorado

Axel had arrived in a helicopter only an hour earlier, and despite his anger at all the things that had been going wrong, was pleased with the new base of operations. The unfinished resort was two miles off the Interstate, nestled into a small and secluded canyon. The contractors who had been working on finishing touches had been told to pack up and leave, so the rooms remained unpainted and without furnishings. That was no problem.

While there were more than enough bedrooms to handle everyone, they would use only five: for the two helicopter pilots, the television technician and announcer, and himself. There was a large, barren main room with a rock fireplace covering an entire wall. Fifty cots had been piled up in the center of the room. When they arrived, the ragtags would have to prepare their own cots, linens, and meals, do their own cleaning. He saw no reason to see to their comforts. Axel's army, he joked inwardly.

They'd moved the two helicopters—these painted a bright industrial orange—into a large maintenance shed. When the girl was located they could be pushed out and airborne within minutes. The armada of four-wheelers would follow, hauling the meanest human scum imaginable, ready to take over anything he required. Kill anyone he wanted.

A cell phone buzzed. The contact from T-Can West. "The remainder of your people will be there in two and a half more hours," he was told.

"Any interesting calls to the eight hundred number?"

"Not as many as at first. I'm on top of it. If anyone has anything real, like a location or a ransom demand, I'll take over."

"Just make certain the FBI doesn't suspect."

"They'll get a hang-up tone. Even if they suspect a problem, we'll have the girl's location and you can be on your way." He paused, went off the air for a few seconds. "We have another interesting intercept from Ski Town. Anderson had two desk clerks buy clothes for a woman in his suite. Everything, like she'd lost it all in a fire. I believe we've found the woman with the big tetons.

"Confirm their location," he rasped, and broke the connection. If she had read the e-mail message from Mexico City she knew too much, and Anderson had posed a danger from the beginning. Fortunately he had kept Captain Torré in reserve for the task. But should he use his last asset?

The T-Can East contact called. "I have the background information on Anderson."

"Tell me about him," Axel said immediately. He was avidly curious about his enemy.

12:55 P.M.—Basement Parking Lot, Snowflower Condominiums, Ski Town

Link waited impatiently in one of the several swivel chairs in the rear of the big diesel-powered Grumman van. Removed in two sections from the cargo bay of the MCP airplane, it now had the outward appearance of a quite large RV that had somehow been wedged into the basement.

Earlier, Link had found Gordon Tower in the busy Sheraton conference room, and shared Maggie's suspicions.

Randall, the foundation's chief investigator, had been in and out of the conference room, nervous and paranoiac, trying to discover why his room had been picked as the location to kill the dope dealer. He offered all sorts of rationales, the latest that the dealer had come to provide information and been silenced.

The MCP copilot had arrived with Steffie Footwine, the NSA expert. They'd checked the equipment at both airports and were excited about what they'd found but before they could give details, one of Gordon Tower's agents arrived with the news that the local police wanted to arrest Maggie and question Link. It was deemed prudent that they withdraw to the van and think things over.

Now Link waited impatiently. "I'd better see what's holding them up."

"Agent Tower said to stay out of sight," Steffie Footwine advised from up front. She was seriously nerdish and sensible.

Link had no time to respond since the door at the front of the vehicle opened and Maggie climbed aboard, closely followed by the copilot, who tossed in Link's gym bag, then struggled to deposit a heavy suitcase. Maggie marched back and took a swivel chair. Stone-faced.

As soon as the copilot settled into the driver's seat, he put the big vehicle in gear and crept toward the basement exit.

Link reached over to give Maggie a reassuring pat, but she pulled away as if he were in the infectious stage of a rare disease.

"What took so long?" Link asked.

When she refused to respond, the copilot spoke up. "The lady wasn't ready."

"I had to change," she snapped, and from her tone Link knew there'd be no explanation. "Now, *where* are you taking me?" she asked nastily as the copilot turned onto the street.

"The Gondola parking lot, ma'am. It's close and its unlikely anyone will look for you there."

"And who are you?" she asked the man with the pigtail. Her voice still indignant.

"John Rabeni, ma'am. Mr. Anderson's copilot. I was a test pilot and project engineer at Lockheed-Martin. If the Weyland Foundation buys the MCP airplane, I've got a full-time job with them. If not, I'll try out with the next bidder."

"A kindred soul," said Maggie. "Your job at the foundation's as shaky as mine." She looked around. "It's certainly large enough."

"Sleeps six," said the copilot. "Those are communications and mapping consoles along the side. Farther back are a couple of couches, a pull-down galley, and a bathroom."

She was mellowing, and Link wondered what had riled her. The clothes selection? She looked nice enough, wearing a forest green jumpsuit under a color-coordinated ski jacket, but something was definitely wrong with her world.

The copilot drove into the gondola lot, and parked in an open area at the back. The van took four regular spaces of the sparsely populated lot. When he'd set the brake, Gordon Tower clambered aboard, told Rabeni to lock the door behind him, and settled into an empty swivel chair. "I got a courier off to Washington with messages for the Bureau, the CIA, the NSA and whoever's in charge at the White House today."

He turned to Maggie. "Anyone see you get in the van?"

"No, but why am I hiding, Gordon? Mr. Rabeni mentioned the police wanted me?"

"Yeah. The local cops suspect the jerk who tried to burn

you up is one of the terrorists, but they're also curious as to where you and Link fit in."

"Then they haven't identified us?"

"They're onto Link, and it won't be long for you either. You left your rental car at the Crows', remember. Also, a reporter covering the fire got a few photographs."

"Oh God," she said.

"You were wearing Link's coat."

The copilot tried humor. "Before that, I hear no one looked once at your face."

She gave him a look that could freeze Popsicles without refrigeration.

"Er, sorry, ma'am."

She sighed. "Aw hell, take me to the station and I'll answer their dumb questions."

"The local cops aren't the only ones trying to get their hands on you," said Gordon. "You were right, Maggie. The bad guys were listening to Link's sat phone."

She brightened. "The setup in Denver worked?"

"Yeah, but the news isn't good. The lieutenant you called sent two green detectives, and someone killed them. Same with Guteriez and his maids and limo driver. All done execution-style using a small-caliber pistol."

She looked shocked. "Two cops were killed?"

"Link said you warned them. It's not your fault the lieutenant wouldn't listen. Trouble was, when he learned you'd left the Bureau, he said you'd represented yourself as an agent and pressured him."

"The liar."

"Link's your witness, and at some point I'll step in and wave the bullshit flag," said Tower. "But until we figure things out, we don't dare say a whole lot on the local phones."

Link was eyeing her. "So we're stuck together in the van for a while."

Maggie tried another glare that didn't quite come off, since a smile was competing at the corners of her lips. "Can we send someone for the rest of my clothes?"

"Better not," the copilot said from up front. "A police cruiser just pulled in at the condo."

"The clothes were okay?" Link asked.

Her voice softened. "Yeah. Thanks, Lincoln." That quickly her mood had changed.

Maggie listened with interest as Steffie Footwine explained the modules she and the copilot had discovered at the airports.

"Siedl MK 4,000s" she said. "They aren't marked, but I know the model."

"Made in the Czech Republic," Maggie interjected.

Steffie looked surprised. "You're right."

"That's the manufacturer I was told Axel Nevas prefers. Did Link tell you about him?"

"Yeah, a few years ago the NSA knew about Senõr Nevas and the Agencia operating in Washington, but they weren't considered a threat. He was blackmailing politicians, which we aren't interested in. The Agencia had moldy old equipment and such a low budget the we wrote them off as nonplayers in the espionage business."

"That's changed. Consider that Nevas has enormous resources."

"He must. MK 4,000s run a hundred thousand each, and it takes a large number to put together even a modest network. They're definitely players."

"I doubt it's the Agencia. More likely just Axel."

"Nope. Siedl's restricted from selling to anyone except government agencies in countries on a NATO-approved list. That keeps modules out of the hands of people like Saddam and Khaddafi, and away from private firms trying to trash the competition."

"Could they have been bought from salvage?"

"The MK 4,000's too new and too advanced. Target lines and trigger words are remotely programmed. Intelligence is gathered, stored, and sent back in FIPO."

"What in the world is fee-poe?" Maggie asked.

"First In, Priority Out. Data is sent to the listening post in prioritized order. Older models are FIFO, meaning it's sent in the order it's received."

"Could they have been stolen from the US Government?" Maggie tried.

"We don't use them. NSA buys American so we can control the design."

"You're saying," said Gordon, "that the Mexican Government is involved."

"It's nothing new. China, Israel, and France feel it's their *right* to spy on us. Mostly they're after industrial secrets, but they get more when they can. Why not Mexico?"

Tower released a sigh. "We just learned they're listening to Link's sat phone, and that's bad with a capital B. How widespread is it? How paranoid do we have to be?"

"That's according to the number of modules they planted, and where," said Steffie Footwine. "Finding them will be like searching for a worm in a noodle factory."

"Can't you find out from the captured terrorist?" asked the copilot.

"He's not talking," said Agent Tower. "He was a real surprise, by the way. We thought they'd escaped. Axel obviously left him behind for dirty work."

Maggie wondered. "Be nice to know if there are more like him."

"No telling."

"We can try to lure them out." She gave Link a nudge. "Care to join me as the cheese in the mouse trap?"

Twenty-five minutes later the others had gone—John the copilot and Steffie the spook to look for modules at the cellular towers and telephone switching center, Gordon Tower to continue the search for Katy—and Maggie was left alone with Link. Cheese on the trap, together.

Before they'd departed, Gordon had made a major decision. If modules were discovered they would be left undisturbed. In the meanwhile, the FBI would concentrate on a plan to locate the listening posts.

Axel had mentioned two *offices*, one in Atlanta and another he'd called the local one.

"Atlanta and Denver," said Steffie Footwine. "The primary telephone centrals. Forty long-distance carriers operate out of two adjacent buildings in Denver. Most telephones in the western US are switched there. Same with Atlanta in the East. Securitywise it's scary, but Ma Bell set it up like that a long time ago, and that's the way it's stayed. If Axel has his listening posts there, it means he has access to a nationwide network."

Since Maggie had accepted the fact of modules and listening stations, it was no big jump to realize the purpose was the distribution of drugs. Gordon Tower agreed. It made sense when they considered the advances made by the Mexicans in the trade—how they were aware of every move made by the authorities.

"We've got to find the listening posts," said Gordon.

"If they know you're getting close," Steffie said, "they'll just shut down the modules, move their LPs to new locations, and resume operations."

When the others had departed, Gordon Tower paused at the door to give Maggie a thoughtful look. Like something about her had changed. Then, like the others, he left.

Link made sure the forward door was secured, and the privacy curtain drawn. When he returned to the rear, Maggie had removed her ski jacket. When he took his seat, she moved behind him.

"You're tense." She massaged his neck muscles.

He groaned at a sensation, then said, "That's nice."

"Be quiet for a few minutes." Maggie did not explain, just continued with her thumbs, then moved her fingers in concert until the muscle had loosened.

He was thinking how they'd be alone for the next few hours when something very soft, like her lips, brushed the nape of his neck.

Link felt his body begin to respond, and hastily shifted his mind to business at hand. How they would entice any left-behind terrorists to attack the suite they'd vacated. There would be a series of "careless" telephone calls. Nibbles, to make Axel Nevas think they were in the suite. Once in a while they'd be *seen* there. A platoon of FBI agents were involved.

She stopped with her fingers.

"My turn," he tried to tell her, but his voice emerged in a sort of croak.

"Yeah." She spoke in a throaty whisper and took his hand. "Let's go back and you can show me the couch."

"Now?"

"I am not in a mood for that answer, Lincoln. You are dealing with a needful woman who just went through the embarrassment of her life. Everyone out there knows what we're doing, and I see no reason to prove them wrong." She pulled harder. He went reluctantly.

People were dying. Terrorists were loose upon the land.

All arguments faded as she turned and smiled, and quite slowly pulled down the zipper of her jumpsuit.

25

Shag arrived earlier than she'd expected, and Annie felt like having the fool wait in the cold until she was done making the place presentable, and would have if Leroy hadn't answered the door. Then Leroy made a big thing about him, like he was special and not just another ex-con skinhead showing up for free beer.

"What's all the mystery about?" Shag Creech asked as he came in.

"Money," Leroy told him. Which got the fool's attention and made him scratch his ass and wonder if it wasn't important after all, because then Leroy said there'd be no beer or pot until they made up the plan. He wanted them to be clearheaded.

Annie finished cleaning, which mostly meant emptying the ashtrays into a can and setting it outside, and shoving the mess that didn't have a place into the adjacent empty bedroom. She found an open can of Frito-Lay bean dip on a shelf, opened a new jar of Cheez Whiz with Jalapeno they'd got for the occasion, and unrolled a couple of half-filled bags of potato chips. The chips were stale and Leroy had forgotten to get more when he'd gone to the store for beer and Cheez Whiz. He said it didn't matter, which would likely be true after they downed a few beers.

As soon as Shag took a seat, Leroy changed his mind and

had her bring out the beer despite his pledge, then told her to just shut up while the men talked or he'd run her ass off to the back bedroom. Annie thought it was bullshit but she didn't argue.

Leroy showed Shag the Colt Python .44 magnum he had stolen from a place in Aspen, and told him about taking it to the last Aryan Brotherhood meeting, which Shag had missed. Not that he cared for niggers, greasers, kikes, queers, cops, and such. He did not, but he thought the Aryan brothers were dumb shits too. Shag didn't much like *anyone*.

When they'd finished that first beer, Leroy told Annie to bring in Shag's share of the money she'd got from the dealer in Cheyenne.

Shag opened the envelope and frowned. "That's all? Shee-it, Annie, that was a fuckin' Harley. I could of taken it to Denver and got two thousand dollars."

"That's all he'd give me," she said.

"You fat-assed cow. Next time . . ."

Leroy lifted the Colt and aimed squarely into Shag's left eye. He cocked the hammer.

"Aw, Leroy." Shag breathed his words.

"Tell her you didden mean it."

Shag mumbled he was sorry as shit.

"Annie's the one brought the payday coming up."

Leroy put the gun down, but Annie could tell Shag was upset and thinking about attacking. When she pulled the pistol over like she was looking at it, Shag settled some. He *knew* she wouldn't hesitate to shoot his sorry ass.

Leroy saw it was time and switched on the television. "Watch," he told Shag.

"We gonna look at TV, open another beer."

Leroy became exasperated. "Just watch the fuckin' thing." He did not appreciate being questioned.

So they all watched as the announcement came on the air that had been running for the past day. It opened with a couple of composite drawings. Like Annie had told Leroy, they looked a little like the cops who had checked her rig.

Next the kid's photo was shown.

Shag belched, said he'd like to get hold of some fresh pussy like that. "Eatin' stuff, man."

"Shit," said Leroy. "I got her right outside."

Shag started grinning like he was kidding.

"She's in Annie's rig, in the sleeper. Listen to the television."

The announcer encouraged anyone with information to call the 800 number on the screen. A reward was offered to the person or persons who provided information about her whereabouts, and a *substantial* amount to those contributing to her safe return.

"What's substan—that word?" Shag asked.

Leroy motioned at Annie, like such things were beneath him.

"It means a *whole lot,*" she said. "Her daddy's the richest man in the world."

"You shitting me?"

"That's why we're here," Leroy told them. "So we can figure out how much we're gonna sell her back to her daddy for, that sorta shit."

"She look like her TV pitcher?" asked Shag.

"Looks *just* like the pitcher," Annie confirmed.

He grinned. "I say we start by bringin' her in an havin' some fun." Shag was so horny they sometimes called him Bubba, after the President. He hung out at the Cowboy and kept track of which truckers were on the road so he could hit on their women.

Leroy shrugged. "Hell, we could fuck her brains out, but I doubt she'd be worth as much to her daddy." Annie and Leroy had talked about it between loving sessions the previous night.

Shag frowned, thinking it over.

"If I could, don't you think I'd be screwin' her instead of this ol' fat twat?"

Annie tried to mask her hurt. It was not the first time.

Leroy shrugged. Then, " 'Course, once we got his money an' things are goin' okay, you can bang her till she thinks she's died and gone to *heaven.*"

Leroy was first to snicker. Then Shag, with his fat braid jiggling. Finally they were both laughing so hard Annie thought they'd hurt themselves, howling about getting the money and the girl too—about spending the rich guy's cash, probably a Jew, right?—while they shoved it to his daughter. Make a call and hold *him* up, then hold her down, and knock *her* up. Fuck 'em both. Him in the pocket and her in the puss.

It was a while before they died down to a periodic snort and giggle.

Leroy recovered first. Snorted and blew his nose on the floor. "Problem is, no matter what they call it *before* they get her back, afterward they'll sure as shit call it kidnapping."

"So we kill her when we're done?" asked Shag, conversationally.

"Whatever we decide on. We gotta figure how're we going to do it and get away."

Last night, while they'd talked and loved, Leroy had figured once he had his hands on the money—two million dollars was an easy number to remember—they would leave the kid with Shag. When the police found the girl, or more likely her body, Leroy and Annie'd be in the wilds of Humboldt County in Northern California. They had biker and skinhead friends who grew pot there in places the authorities feared to go. He'd let his hair grow and she'd lose weight and get real pretty. With money you could do that sort of thing, no problem.

Annie was so happy it was all she'd been able to think about.

"So what do you think?" Leroy was saying to Shag.

"I don't understand why we can't fuck her and still call her daddy."

Leroy glared like he was getting impatient. "You know how much we're talking about? You ever *seen* a couple hundred thousand? That's your cut. You want to screw it up so you and me don't get *any* of it, just so you can have a piece of ass? What I'm sayin' is, we tell her daddy if he hurries with the money, then we *won't* fuck her."

* * *

The only way Katy could tell the day from night was to measure the light filtering through the port on the roof of the sleeper. The only human contact had been during the two visits by Annie, who had said little and would no longer let her see her face, as if Katy might possibly forget her.

Last night Annie'd had Katy turn away as she'd removed the stink pot, which was full of her waste. "Call my parents," she'd pleaded. "They'll pay a reward."

Annie hadn't responded. When Katy heard the hatch close, she'd found a large, empty mason jar—which she assumed was for urine and feces—a Pepsi and two chocolate candy bars.

Katy seldom ate candy bars. She knew what they would do to her teeth and figure. But she'd devoured the candy in a heartbeat. While the Pepsi tasted good she knew water was what she needed, but no one had returned so she could ask.

It had been so cold during the night that the small built-in heater had been unable to keep up. Still, the chill did not concern her as much as the dry throat and lack of water.

This morning when Annie had come by, she'd pleaded for water and toilet paper.

"Yer lucky to get what you do," she was told, and was left another Pepsi and a small box of dry cereal. Annie had replaced the waste jar, but the stench was so hideous that Katy doubted she'd ever regain her olfactory senses.

If she escaped the sleeper.

Annie thought the men were awfully slow in their planning, and wished they'd get it done. She was anxious to become rich.

Leroy tipped his beer bottle and chugged down half, belched grandly, and picked up where they'd left off. How in a while he and Shag would drive to Grand Junction, sixty-six miles north of the turnoff in Montrose, to make the first call. Leave the kid behind that time and just set things up. Later on call from someplace else and have the kid along so she could tell her daddy she was miserable, but she was alive and they hadn't been screwing her none.

Shag guffawed. "Yet."

And Annie said to herself, go ahead and laugh, sucker.

Shag would make all the phone calls, because Leroy was setting it up so if something went wrong he could say he'd had no part in it. Like Annie was the one handling the kid's food and shit. She'd decided it didn't really matter, so long as the two of them split for California with the money. He tried to change *that* part, she'd shoot the sorry bastard.

Annie stayed in the kitchen, keeping her yap shut as the men planned and talked. She'd started thinking about the money and what she'd do with her part, how she'd wear her new watch and the bracelet and buy more stuff like that.

Annie tried to do a calculation. If they got two million, and if Shag got two hundred thousand of it, what would be her half of what was left? She got out pencil and paper and tried to figure it, but did not know how many zeros to put in. Still, it ought to be a lot of money.

They'd agreed to wait a little longer to call, so Annie pulled more beers from the fridge. Leroy and Shag started a chugalug race that Shag won handily because he could suck down a bottle in three hard gulps. Then Shag challenged her, and she won the five bucks Leroy had lost.

Which was when Shag asked for the keys to the rig, saying he wanted to go out and take a look at the girl. When there was no reaction from Leroy, he sort of nonchalantly added, "Feel around some and see what she's got?"

"It ain't a good idea," Annie told him. "Let her be till we got the money." Thinking Shag might not stop himself once he got his hands on the kid, and then Leroy might want to join in.

"You oughta train Annie better," Shag complained.

She started to give a sassy reply when Leroy gave her a shove. "Quit arguin'."

"Dammit, Leroy," Annie began, "how come you're changing . . ."

Leroy slapped her so hard her head flew back hard, and she slammed against the kitchen counter.

"I tol' you to shut up. Now get us a *beer*!"

Annie limped to the fridge, whimpering because her side hurt like fire. Wondering if she'd busted a rib on the counter, like had happened another time. After she took the men their beers, she opened one for herself, careful not to look at Leroy. He got like this, sometimes little things would set him off.

When Shag brought up how he wanted to haul the girl out and take a look, Leroy just shrugged and said he guessed it wouldn't hurt none if she was good and scared.

"Give him the keys," Leroy told her.

Shag took a beer with him.

Katy carefully replaced the top on the jar. She had a terrible rash from the lack of basic sanitation and toilet paper. There had been a centerfold out of a man's magazine—she doubted even Annie would have chosen a photo of a nude sitting with knees wide apart and holding up impossibly large breasts—half of which she'd used the day before. During the night she'd been attacked by "old Montezuma," like her father described it when they visit South America. She'd splashed into the wide-mouth mason jar, and used the remainder of the centerfold and then candy bar wrappers for paper.

What a mess! And even more stench had been added to the rest. The good news was that she really did believe she would be released. Annie had proven her greed the way she'd taken the bracelet and watch, and her parents would be offering large rewards. The question was when?

Although it had been only a day since she'd carried a real conversation with another person, she craved such discourse. Which was precisely what she was thinking when she heard sounds from outside.

Rap, rap, rap.

"You in there?" A man's rough and demanding tone.

1:15 P.M.—Glenwood Springs

Axel's army had still not arrived from Denver when the T-Can West contact called to provide an update. Lots of things happening.

Axel asked what was being passed on to the Voice.

Action in Minneapolis, where the previous night a hundred kilos of high-grade coke had been moved under the police's nose. Also a truckload of meth. The DEA had raided a block away. The Voice was pleased with the way things were going in Minneapolis.

Axel impatiently asked for the latest on STOPPER.

Only a few new calls to the 800 number about the Kittenbitch. Mostly gossip about neighbors. The Denver police were still in the air about the murders at Guteriez's, but they'd mentioned a man in a police videotape.

A development was passed on from Mexico City concerning the "patient" who had authored the e-mail message. The way he paused between utterances, Axel could tell the contact was relaying the words as he listened to a report over his headset.

Input: They had the name of the woman to whom the message was sent. Margaret Brown, who was no longer an FBI agent as she'd been when the patient had known her. It was unlikely the patient lied. He no longer had teeth, and was getting a manicure so they could learn what else he knew about the Agencia. Two fingers removed so far.

Conclusion: Margaret Brown was the same M. A. Brown who had asked the Denver police lieutenant to observe Guteriez's. She was also Maggie Tatro, and had eluded them in the room in Steamboat Springs. She was with Anderson.

Input: Santos was still not talking to the police in Steamboat Springs. The FBI had forwarded his fingerprints to Washington but could not get a match.

The contact asked if Axel had new instructions, and he told him to place the Tatro-Brown woman's name back on the list.

He was warned there were so many trigger-words on the Colorado region modules that they were approaching saturation. Information was already being received more slowly than desired.

"Add her name," he ordered.

Then another input concerning Miss Grand Tetons, the woman from the fire. The police had searched the suite where she had been taken and discovered the new clothing. The T-Can contact felt she was close by.

"Yes, you fool. Grand Tetons is Maggie Tatro! That's why she must be watched."

Axel disconnected, feeling disconcerted.

Should he take the next step? Thus far they'd not overheard the woman talking to anyone about the contents of the e-mail, so he wondered if she had read the message. Was her removal worth jeopardizing Captain Torré, his only remaining asset in Steamboat Springs?

Then he thought of the man with the Tatro woman. Anderson, whom he'd come to despise even more now that he knew about him. Born on a Montana Indian Reservation with the mysterious name "Ghost of Black Wolf." Half Piegan, which was a tribe of the Blackfoot nation. Adopted at age four by a military family. An athletic teenager who had attended the Air Force Academy. Fighter pilot in the Persian Gulf War. After his discharge he had idled in Montana, working at highly physical jobs, until going to work for his close friend at the Weyland Foundation.

Except for the fact that he was descended from an inferior stone-age tribe of savages, there was nothing unique in that background. A military person of no great distinction. Yet Axel's emotions were still stirred when his mind heard the name, and even now he felt his hatred being charged with new intensity.

Another fact: Anderson's close friend was the father of the Kitten-bitch.

No more delay. Both Anderson and the Tatro woman were definitely dangers to his plan. He called Captain Torré on a cell phone, and told him to prepare for the assassinations. If he had commanded a hundred more killers in Steamboat, he would have sent them all.

Axel broke the connection feeling pleased. The offerings might be made in absentia, but one of the victims was a true enemy. "Great Huitzilopóchtli, I offer Lincoln Anderson."

Black Canyon

Leroy had brought out a bag of pot he called Mendocino Sunshine, and while Annie knew it was twiggy crap grown in a garage in town, they passed a joint back and forth. Annie was floating, happy as a clam, alternating between helping Leroy with the joint and chugging beer.

Leroy reared up like he was coming out of a fog and said he and Shag should get started for Grand Junction. "We oughtn't to wait much more."

Annie sucked on the roach and peered out the window. "Might piss off Shag if he cain't finish what he started."

Leroy gave his head a little shiver to clear it, although Annie knew he could shake all over like a yellow dog and not be sober. "Finish what?"

"Ain't you heard the yellin'? He got the girl's top mostly off, but she keeps squirmin' and kickin' so he cain't get her pants down."

Leroy's brow furrowed. "Thought he was just goin' for a feel."

Annie snorted, thinking if he believed that he'd believe anything.

"Go tell him to put her back in the rig," Leroy told her.

"He ain't gonna like it, and he won't listen to me nohow."

Leroy looked at her like he could not fathom that she'd spoken back. He narrowed his vision, still staring, and tried to get up.

Annie wasn't *that* nuts. She scrambled to her feet, reeled around some when she went into the kitchen for the Colt, and then headed for the door.

Outside she yelled, "Leroy wants her back in the rig!"

When he ignored her, she held the magnum with both hands, and fired a round into the snow. The sound reverberated from the mountains. "In the rig, dammit."

Shag looked at her like he was studying a problem, which he was.

"Don't listen, I'll walk down close an' shoot you square in the balls."

He gave a slow nod. He believed her.

Annie remained to watch the entertainment, and was not let down. It was ten more minutes before Shag shoved the screaming and kicking kid into the cab and got both legs crammed into the sleeper. Finally, at that late moment in the tussle, he got in a hard smack with his big fist that took the fight out of her. The kid went limp, dazed and moaning with hurt. Shag drew back again, but Annie went closer and yelled, "Hit her and I'll blow off yer nuts like I said," and he stopped, staring at the kid, huffing and sorely angry.

Then Shag grabbed the kid with a big hand to hold her up, and gave her bare breasts a series of such violent squeezes and pulls that made Annie's own tits hurt from watching. The kid screamed loud as any two police sirens, and Annie knew she was hurting so bad she'd have given in to whatever Shag wanted.

Which seemed funny as hell. So floating on the cloud of pot and beer, Annie laughed long and loud, thinking about the change in Little Miss Purepants' attitude.

Shag stuffed the kid into the sleeper and slammed the door. "Bitch!"

"Was it worth it?" Annie called out as she headed back in.

Shag followed with a morose look. There were bloody furrows on both sides of his neck where the kid had raked him, and he limped from being repeatedly kicked. But of course, he was a whole lot better off than the kid.

Back in the house, Shag settled by the couch, rolling a joint from the cheap pot and eyeing Leroy, who had his head back and was snoring loud. When he partied like this he'd sleep an hour, wake up and drink more beer and smoke more dope, then sleep again.

"We ain't goin' nowhere for a while," Shag said, observing Leroy.

Annie kept hold of the Colt in case he got an idea about killing them and taking the girl.

Shag lit up, pulled in a long drag, then coughed it out. "Got more beer?"

"We run out. Best if you two wait till morning now anyway," said Annie, not telling him about the case of Dog in the bedroom.

Shag got back on his feet, saying he'd head for the Cowboy.

"Don't be talkin' 'bout the kid," Annie yelled after him. "An' if any of us are gonna be rich, you two better start out first thing in th' mornin'."

26

They had mated urgently, yet the lovemaking held a spark of wonder as they'd moved together like long-time lovers—she periodically crying out—until finally, spent and drained, they'd collapsed together.

They kissed almost chastely as they settled back, still breathing harshly, and Maggie said she wished she had a come-down cigarette. She laughed about it for she hadn't smoked in years. For Link's part, he was still slightly puzzled, wondering how they'd allowed themselves to become so carried away. Yet he was feeling very warm thoughts toward Margaret Ann Tatro.

"The timing was bad," he said aloud.

She laughed. "Why, Lincoln. Are you a stuffed shirt?"

"Of course not."

"Then don't complain about something so wonderful. I just wish I had a cigarette."

"What brand," he asked, and she told him the ones she'd smoked several years ago.

At that moment he would have done anything for her, including hopping around trying to leap over buildings, but there were other justifications. They were to be seen periodically to lure the terrorists, of course—and while he resented being considered a "stuffed shirt," he felt he had succumbed too quickly to sexual appetites, with all of the emergencies about.

After all, there was a time for everything, and . . . what did she mean, stuffed shirt?

He pulled on sweats and went to the door. She looked pleased.

"Make sure you lock up behind me."

Outside, Link set up a moderate pace as he jogged past the Snowflower and then the Snowbird Condos, then slowed and crossed the street to a small outdoor mall. Feeling alive after the sexual release, letting his muscles stretch. Ready to turn back if something seemed amiss, yet perversely hoping he would draw a response from the terrorists.

He bought a pack of cigarettes in a minimart. There were two other shoppers, both males, neither acting particularly interested in him. As far as he could tell no one followed when he left.

Link trotted back past both condominium buildings and turned the final corner, slowed to negotiate a patch of ice at the edge of the Gondola parking lot, then ran swiftly to the van.

He paused at the door for a prudent last look about.

A man in a pickup fifty yards distant was the FBI agent in charge of the protection detail. There should be two others in the lot.

He thumped on the door.

Maggie looked out the thick glass window. "Sorry, mister. We don't want any of your damn Girl Scout cookies."

Link was chuckling as she slid the door open. And did not see the head that at that precise moment extended around a corner of the Snowbird condos. Or the eyes that scanned carefully, taking in much.

"No place like home in a mobile command post, huh?" Maggie squeezed his arm to her breast as she opened the pack and tamped out a cigarette. She'd found an ashtray.

"Awful habit," Link told her. He was no fanatic. Even when he'd been a young child everyone had known smoking was bad for you, so he wondered about the righteous fervor.

"Yeah," she said as he lit her with a match. She took two drags, sighed, and stubbed it out. Smiling so enigmatically, that he knew precisely what had made Mona Lisa glow.

She stepped into his arms, lay her head against his chest, and he thought she felt natural there. For the first time since his fiancée's death, lovemaking had not evoked guilt.

And he was *not* a damned stuffed shirt!

"Guess what?" She stretched up, kissed his jaw. "I thought you were cute when we were kids, and while you were gone just now I decided I was right."

"I've always tried so hard to be cute." Her breast rested against his forearm and he could feel the nipple stiffen. "If we were smart we'd be considering what to do if the terrorists attack."

"I've got a better idea, and this time let's not hurry," she said as she double-checked doors and drew the privacy curtain. She pulled him toward the back.

Link tried to argue a couple of times during the short trek, yet somehow most of their clothing had been shed by the time they reached the couch.

2:30 P.M.

Torré took his time, for hurrying could bring discovery. It was likely that Santos had been caught because of his compulsiveness. He'd told him to be methodical, but as soon as the sergeant had driven out of sight Torré had grabbed his duffel bag and driven the old pickup to a ramshackle range cabin that was on no one's map but his own. He had not trusted Santos to succeed. The sergeant was far too spontaneous and such a terrible shot that unless he used a shotgun he could not hit anything smaller than a house. He only thought he was very good.

After following the dark-haired tall man from the minimart and observing the parking lot long enough to realize he had to have gone to ground nearby, he'd returned to the outdoor mall and the old pickup. He'd pulled out the duffel and walked back, entered the side of the Snowbird's basement, but rather than going up to the suites, continued walking out the front.

Looking like he'd just checked out of the condo as he put down his bag at the bus stop.

It was a good lookout, with a view of the gondola parking lot, the entrances of both condo buildings, and the street. So he settled like a tourist waiting on a bus, hoping the dark-haired man would show again and lead him to the woman.

He must kill them both. Axel had sounded fervent about it.

On his drive in, the contact had called. Torré had worked for Axel for the past five years, and knew all about the T-Can listening posts.

The contact said there had been another sighting of the target woman and dark-haired man at the Snowbird Condos, and provided detailed descriptions of both. The contact paused. Then said there had just been a sighting at an outdoor mall across from the Snowflower.

Neither the contact nor Torré had known that both inputs had come from FBI agents speaking purposefully on the phones. Nor did the FBI agents realize they'd planted a seed that would bring the terrorist face-to-face with Lincoln Anderson.

As Torré stood at the bus stop, thinking about what he had seen when he'd first peered around the corner and wondering if it had been his imagination that there'd been movement at the large recreation vehicle, his eyes were drawn to an idling pickup and the shape of a man inside who was fastidiously *not* looking around.

Torré was a captain with the Mexican federal police, on extended leave of absence, and had policeman's eyes. Farther across the parking lot, near the gondola building, a woman stood idly, looking up at the ski hill. Waiting. Balancing skis on her shoulder like she was about to go to the gondola that ran from the opposite side of the building.

He was no skier, but during the last week he'd learned that they did not wear fuzzy boots on the slopes. They wore klunky ski boots, and she had none in sight. He decided it was a surveillance crew. It made sense. The police were looking for the same man and woman. Maybe they'd even received the same tips. What did not make sense was the fact that he was certain Anderson had rounded the corner and disappeared somewhere in their view.

Torré idly rested his foot on the duffel. He'd noticed tourists with such bags awaiting buses that periodically arrived to take them to Old Town or the airport. He should probably be carrying a ski bag as well, but some tourists rented skis and boots, so it was not required.

His cell phone buzzed. He switched it on, and was told that Anderson had been identified by an off-duty fireman who had been in the same store as Torré. He was wearing sweats, and had disappeared around the corner of the Snowflower.

Verification of what he'd seen, Torré thought. His problem remained as before. If the two in the lot were looking for Anderson, wouldn't they have seen and apprehended him?

He asked the contact if he knew about an ongoing surveillance detail.

Nothing, except the town police would send someone to the Snowflower Condo to check out the new leads. They were undermanned and in no hurry. Probably thirty minutes away.

Torré considered. If the man and woman in the parking lot weren't surveillance, he would eat his knit hat. He regarded the huge RV, and decided that was where Anderson had gone, and the woman might be there too.

He told the contact he'd be off the phone for a short while to handle business. Not to call unless it was urgent. He put the cell phone away, and purposefully looked out with a bored expression, hands stuffed in coat pockets and caressing metal.

The captain was a large, muscular man with a pleasant face. He wore a turtleneck, heavy slacks, and a short, bulky

overcoat. In the right pocket was a silenced Czech-made
7.65 millimeter Skorpion, fold-out stock removed so it was
configured as a stubby machine pistol. He carried an extra
clip in each hip pocket. In the left coat pocket was a .380
semiautomatic. Cheaply made and firing a lighter round
than he preferred, but Santos had insisted on borrowing his
.45 caliber.

But there were compensations. Unlike Santos, Torré was
a calm and deadly shot.

The fake woman skier looked about casually, did not
dwell on the van or the truck, but took in Torré. She put the
skis down and balanced them as she huddled to ward off the
cold. The man in the pickup scanned around the lot, also
rested his eyes on Torré, who craned his neck and looked
down the street, and shook his head helplessly over the tar-
diness of the bus.

All the while trying to figure how he could eliminate the
surveillers, then the man and woman in the van.

Axel had mentioned that he would then be called on to
eliminate an investigator that Santos had missed, but Torré
felt this was enough for now. If he had time, he would take
the small woman back to the cabin. Warm up with her, as
he'd done with the tourist with the long hair. Everyone had
their weaknesses. Santos's was impetuosity. Torre's was an
overpowering lust for women. Not whores or girlfriends but
those who had to be forced. Like the tourist. Halfway
through the rape he'd told her Santos had killed her husband, and kept pressing into her as she had sobbed. The image was indelibly stored, but it was time to replace it with
another. The short woman with the large bust would do.

Kill her man and remind her of it when he got her to the
cabin. Kill her as he finished. The thought was so appealing
Torré had to force himself to concentrate on his plan of
attack.

He mentally measured distances, and decided he would
walk out to the lookout in the pickup and show the ID taken
from the dead deputy. Announce himself loud enough for
the woman agent to hear so she too would relax. Then pull

the silenced Skorpion and shoot them both. The woman first, since she was mobile. Then the man in the truck. Both quickly without a sound. *Then* tend to the couple in the van, and return to the cabin. With the busty woman if the situation was just right.

Torré thought it through some more, honing it down, thinking it was not an imaginative plan, but a solid one. He determined the precise route he would take, and visualized it again.

It would work.

He took a final scan, then began strolling out, sure of himself, looking friendly and like he belonged. Halfway to the pickup he took in another spotter. A small man in a sedan. Close enough to the pickup that Torré figured, while still on the move, no changes were necessary.

First kill the woman who was now eyeing him, then the two in the vehicles.

The cell phone buzzed. He stopped, still thirty yards from the pickup, and drew it out of his pocket. The contact spoke urgently. "There is a protection effort by *someone*. Look for a very large van. They're maintaining radio silence, but we overheard . . ."

Torré switched off the instrument without lowering it from his face, and said something apologetic, like he'd try to be home on time. He said "good-bye" into the dead cell phone loud enough to be heard, dropped it into his pants pocket, and pushed his hands back into the coat.

He smiled, engaging the agent's eyes as he pulled the police ID folder from his left pocket, resting his right hand on the grip of the silenced Skorpion.

Link only vaguely heard the knocking sound that filtered through his consciousness.

"Not yet," Maggie whispered, her gentle tone matching the moment. She rocked slowly, cantaloupe breasts brushing his chest as she leaned forward, hot vagina enveloping him as she drew back. She had soared countless times. He had released early, the second time for the day, and was again close.

"Now you," Maggie whispered, and he turned over onto her. He set up a slow stroke. No hurry about it, more like they'd been lovers for years. His flesh was engorged, her sheath velvet, face glowing and flushed. Maggie made a purring sound, rising to climax once more as he began to release. She grasped him as he finished in a burst of energy. Both of them wordless, knowing they'd provided what the other needed. Unashamed and sated.

They lay back, panting together as the rapping noises again filtered through their awareness, telling them there was a world out there somewhere. "Let them eat cake," Maggie whispered, ignoring a louder series of knocks.

Link began dressing, feeling all the appropriate caveman instincts, happier than he'd been in months. Needing what they had done as much as she and uncaring that the timing might be inappropriate for others, since it had been so right for them.

"We should ignore them," she said impishly. "Keep at it until we've made up for all the years we weren't together."

He had on shirt and trousers, and was pulling on socks as a troublesome thought arose. "Think it's the police?"

"No. They'd be yelling and announcing and acting even more obnoxious. It's probably Gordon, but it doesn't matter. Anyone tries to interrupt my postcoital smoke is history."

He drew on his boots, straightened himself some more, and went forward. Pushed past the privacy curtain and looked out the glass above the sliding door, expecting Supervising Agent Gordon Tower.

It was one of the men he'd seen at the minimart. He was muscular and fit, and held up a leather case with an FBI badge. "Special Agent Hollings," he said. "I've got more people out here, and they want me to show you the new setup." There was a definite accent in his voice.

Link looked past the man at the parking lot, feeling the adrenaline that had begun to flow. Considered the situation for another few heartbeats, then unlocked the door and pushed it open.

The cheese in the trap.

"Gordon send you?" He stepped down onto the pavement.

"Yeah, Gordon."

Link determined that he wouldn't know Gordon Tower from a pomegranate. He slid the door firmly forward, heard the latch click and lock. From what he saw it was one-on-one. He was eager to take the man and ask some questions—like why they were after Katy Dubois—and apply enough pressure that he'd get answers.

The agent-in-charge's name was Hollings. This was definitely not him.

"Any sign of the killers?" Link asked conversationally. Looking around to verify he was alone—in his peripheral vision seeing the man drop the ID and draw his right hand from his coat pocket. Fast and sure. The gentle expression changing to raw determination.

Link's reaction was immediate, faster yet. He swept his left arm in a violent arc, catching the assassin's hand as the muzzle of a stubby machine pistol cleared the pocket.

The muted explosions were hardly audible over the metallic clacking of the mechanism. Rounds spewed wildly, impacting high on the van's side before the killer lost his grip and the Skorpion flew from his hand. Sailed in an arc that he watched with astonishment.

In the same fluid motion Link drew his right hand fully back to his chest, knuckles extended, tensed, hard as stone. He slammed the ridge of knuckles forward, twisting just as they smashed into the killer's sternum. Impacting with such force he felt something give. Not wanting to kill but certainly to immobilize.

Angghh. The killer reeled, dropped to his knees. Jaw dropping and unable to draw in a breath after the furious blow. Yet the eyes were still hard, the stare so intense it seemed inhuman.

Link took a step forward, then slowed as the killer's left hand lifted from the coat pocket bearing a small automatic.

Erk-erk, sounded from the killer's throat as he tried to draw a breath, yet the weapon's muzzle came level, wavered once as the finger curled about the trigger.

Link dove toward the van.

Bam! The pistol was small, but deadly. Also unsilenced and much louder.

Link scrambled beneath the big vehicle.

Bam! A round skittered past him on the pavement. Immediately followed by *Erk! Erk! Erk!* as the man continued to try to regain his breath.

Link heard the van's door slide open.

"Maggie!" he cried. "Lock the door."

"Unhhhhhhh," as the killer drew a gasp of air.

"Oh, God!" Maggie cried in falsetto. Then, after a pause, "He's coming inside!"

Link scrambled back under the van, rolled out just in time to see the assassin disappear inside.

"Unhhhhhh." Another long intake.

"Drop it, dummy." Maggie's voice had changed. No more fright, and now very sure. "I'm aiming at your eye, and I don't miss."

Link heard yet another *Unhhhh* of painfully drawn breath.

"You don't drop it, you're dead."

"You don't do it, they will," the man said. A resigned tone.

Bam!

"Dumb shit! I told you I don't miss."

Link hurried inside. The killer was sprawled at the entrance, his left eye replaced by a gout of blood.

Maggie's face was pasty. She held her small pistol in both hands.

"Link? Maggie?" they heard from outside, along with the huffing sound of someone who had been running.

"Dumb shit," Maggie hissed again, staring.

Gordon Tower appeared at the door, pistol drawn.

"It's over," Link said. "Maggie got him."

"I tried to tell him," she said, still staring. Tears coursing down her cheeks.

Another agent hurried up and spoke in Gordon's ear. Tower nodded grimly, and Link heard him mention the word bodybags.

"Was he the only bad guy?" Link asked.

"You tell me," said Tower.

"He's all I saw. He used the name of your agent-in-charge and showed his badge. I thought I had him until he pulled a second weapon. I should have hit him a little harder."

Tower leaned inside and took in the body, then Maggie.

"I had to lure him in," she explained. "He might have killed Lincoln." Her nose wrinkled and she began to cry. Still holding the pistol.

"If you hadn't stopped him, he would have killed both of you."

"I know." She kept crying. Quietly, but with a few deep sobs. An emotional release.

Gordon motioned at Link, then the body. "Help me get him out. And, Maggie," he said, careful not to stare, "you really ought to get dressed."

She immediately stopped crying and looked down in amazement, like she'd not been aware she had on only bra and panties, and fled behind the privacy curtain.

27

After they'd deposited the killer's body outside, Gordon held an impromptu briefing with his senior agents, explaining he was exercising his authority under the DT executive order, which provided him with decision-making powers during ongoing acts of domestic terrorism.

Exclude anything sensitive from telephone and radio conversations. Take a single roll of film for later, then bag the bodies of the two agents and the terrorist. At the hospital, stonewall about how Agent Hollings had been wounded. He needed time to think up the right cover stories to avoid alerting Axel Nevas.

They did not question, just started yelling at a covey of arriving agents to help.

"And don't let *anyone* near the van," Gordon told them. He retrieved a sheaf of paper he'd dropped, and brandished them at Link on the way inside. "I was bringing these sitreps over to bounce off Maggie. Your girlfriend's still the best analyst in the business."

Link did not argue. In the entry, he cleaned up the gout of blood with paper towels, then sat at the console with Gordon for a few quiet moments, coming off the adrenaline high. Maggie joined them, scrubbed and composed, wearing the jumpsuit. She stared where the dead terrorist had lain, then looked at the supervising agent. "Was he the second guy in the composites?"

"Looks something like him."

She slowly nodded, still thoughtful. "Axel knew where to send him. It's hard to fool someone who's listening to your phones, radios, e-mail, and maybe everything in between."

"We've got to find the damned listening posts, but we've also got to stop blabbing on the phones until we do. So far I've contacted the local authorities and state police, the National Guard—the general says some brass from the Pentagon's landing shortly, so that's another briefing—and sent couriers to the Hoover Building and our field offices in New York, Atlanta, and Denver. Anyone I'm missing?"

"You're just telling them the phone lines may be insecure?"

"That and not to let the media in on any of it yet."

Maggie raised a devil's advocate's eyebrow. "Perhaps you should include the media. Tell them it's for the safety of citizens that they suppress anything they hear."

"That sort of reporters' honor stopped fifty years ago. They'd say it's their job to keep the public informed, not to protect them, and Axel Nevas would tell them thank you and shut down."

"They'll get it sooner or later."

"Hopefully just after we find the listening posts."

"Why hasn't Nevas already shut them down?" said Link. "He knows Maggie received the e-mail."

"Not true," said Maggie. "All he knows was that it was sent. Lots of mail goes unread. Also, the story's out that I'm wanted by the police. He wouldn't've sent the shooter if he'd known I'd talked to the FBI."

Maggie leaned back in her chair, stretching out her full five-two which meant her toes touched the floor, nodding as she made points. "Let's give Axel the benefit of the doubt and say he knows everything spoken over telephones—which is giving him too much, because the way I understand it, they only know what's programmed into the modules."

"Meaning," said Gordon, "we've got to continue making Axel think you're a fugitive. Otherwise he'll suspect we know about the eavesdropping."

"Not enough," said Maggie. "He knows Link was with me at the fire. I'm betting this last shooter was sent after both of us."

"We'll let the word out that you're both fugitives?"

"Still not enough. You've got to kill us. Axel only left two shooters behind, so . . ."

"Just how do you figure that?"

"The first time he sent a single because I'm a smallish mere woman, and you males underestimate us. When the first guy fouled up, Axel still wanted me dead, but along with Link, too. In fact I *heard* Axel say Link was dangerous. If he'd had more people, he'd have sent more. And now that he's out of people here, what does that mean?"

Gordon was thinking so hard that his forehead had grown ridges and valleys. He glanced at Link. "This is what she's good at. Analyzing situations and giving me headaches. Maggie belongs in the Bureau."

"Not with Bozo the Ex there. I hear the President really likes his briefings."

"Yeah, so what does that say about both of them?" He returned to work. "If Axel sent his last shooter after you, you're saying . . . ?" His voice trailed off, waiting for her to continue.

"Steffie told us the modules and listening posts are programmed to look for certain information, and I'm saying that right now it's focused on us. He wants to know if and when we tell you about the e-mail, because the message explains his setup. Sooo . . ."

Gordon nodded. "So the longer he stays tuned in on you two, the better his odds are of learning he was scammed about Guteriez and we know about his eavesdropping."

"And like Steffie said, he'd shut down and move the LPs, and we'd never find him. You have to kill us off so he'll stop worrying about who we're talking to. Give him a warm, fuzzy feeling about us being off his back."

The three of them went over the wording of the messages. Gordon's people would begin with a call to the Washington hierarchy, telling them the killer had taken out two individuals: Abraham Lincoln Anderson and Margaret Ann Tatro. Then that the killer had been slain.

By the time the press were allowed near the scene, the body bags had been tagged with the appropriate names and moved to the opposite end of the parking lot from the big van.

Glenwood Springs

Axel waited impatiently, unable to suppress the nervous thought that something important was happening about which he could only guess. The lack of news was not always bad. For instance, so far the listening posts had no indication that the FBI knew about the e-mail message. But if Captain Torré failed to silence Tatro and Anderson, and without another assassin to send forth, he would have to assume that his network would be compromised.

That was the rational side of his desire for wanting Torré to succeed, but there was another, based in the primeval yearning he could not describe. For the past hour Anderson's name had reverberated in his mind. Over and over it resounded, although he tried to subdue it, connected somehow with his innate hatred of the man.

The instant the cell phone buzzed, Axel was clawing it from its holster.

"News from Steamboat," said the T-Can West contact. "An FBI after-action report."

Axel waited expectantly.

"A team of FBI agents set a trap for Anderson and the Tatro woman. They'd just taken them into custody when Torré arrived."

Axel began to grow petulant.

"He got them both. Anderson and Tatro were killed before they could be questioned."

Axel released a single, loud note of laughter. "What about Captain Torré?"

"They killed him. I would like to alter the priorities," said the T-Can West contact. "The dangerous one there now is the Footwine woman from the NSA. She's very intelligent."

"Keep track of her, but remain focused on finding Kitten." Ah how he wished he could have seen Anderson die. His enemy was dead!

"Good," T-Can was saying. "I want to take another close look at the truckers."

Ski Town

The two were alone in the van again, an intimate and easy air between them. Like something was very right. As they waited for the copilot and Steffie Footwine to return with their verdict on the eavesdropping, Link looked out a porthole at the meeting of police and senior FBI agents at the other end of the lot. Gordon Tower briefing his cover story. Three body bags were arranged in a neat row in front of the Snowflower condominiums. A growing number of newsmen were gathering beyond the crime scene tape, looking uneasily at the bags. Taking footage.

Maggie was leafing through the situation reports Gordon had left. Humming happily,

Link gained her attention, pinned her with a look and pointed a mean finger. "Don't ever, *ever* lure another guy in like that again."

"Hey, I was scared for you too." She winced under the weight of his glare. "Okay, gotcha. Never again." Was there a hint of amusement? "Mmm. Did I tell you that last sex was great?"

"I'm glad we were able to work it in between murders."

"That just adds spice to the stew."

Link still couldn't believe what they'd done, or rather *when* they'd done it. He looked out and saw that Gordon Tower was now with newspeople. Pointing around and waving his hands. Recreating the lie. Cameramen were shooting him and the area. None looking at the distant van.

Someone rapped on the sliding door, and they froze. Then they smiled at their silliness. "Can't be another one," she said, but Link was cautious as he went forward.

The MCP copilot and the NSA expert slipped inside.

Steffie Footwine held up five fingers, and ticked off where they'd located the latest eavesdropping modules. The telephone switching office, the cell tower, and the radio antenna coupling for the police base station. "It's everything I feared. If they've planted them in other small cities like this, we're talking about thousands of things. If they only have the two listening posts, they've got to have three or four supercomputers running full-time to keep up."

"Are the modules live?" asked Maggie.

"I measured with a field magnometer. They're operating full blast."

There was a period of silence as they digested the news. While it was what they'd feared and expected, it was not what they'd wanted to hear.

Gordon came in from his briefings, and they brought him up to speed.

"I take it it's going to be difficult to locate the listening posts without them knowing we're looking?"

Steffie pressed her glasses back with a finger. "Next to impossible."

"I've sent couriers to Atlanta and Denver with orders to set up the search."

"Great." She smiled. "What are they looking for?"

Gordon looked around for support.

"A room with three or four large computers?" asked Maggie. "Located in one of the buildings you told us about in Atlanta and Denver?"

"That's pretty good. You just described half the offices in those buildings. Make that in the entire cities. If you don't mind, I'll send a note to NSA with your next courier explaining everything and asking them to provide technical help at both locations."

"Mind?" Gordon asked, smiling as though someone had just offered to save his life.

"I'll also send a Tempest notification, so they'll set up procedures to protect classified government information. In the meanwhile, we've got to find a form of secure communications."

"You can do that?"

"It won't be easy," said the nerdish woman with her finger still to her glasses, "but we have to try. Axel Nevas used manipulation of information to kill a hundred citizens. God knows what the girl Katy faces, but Axel's not done there either and I fear for anyone who gets in the way."

"You don't think they have Katy?"

"No way. The modules are running at capacity, so they're in the middle of an operation. Getting her is so important they're jeopardizing the entire hundred-million-dollar network. They're listening and waiting for their chance to get her."

"Think there'll be more terrorism?" Maggie asked.

"Sure. They got away with it last time, so they're encouraged to do it again."

"I agree," said Maggie. "But where are they?"

"That I don't know. But when you find Katy they'll come after her. She's key to everything. Find out why they want her so badly and you've got real answers."

Steffie Footwine looked up suddenly. Excited by a thought. "Look, I'm only a middling senior supervisor at the NSA. Anyone here have a whole lot of leverage in Washington?"

28

The brigadier general who commanded the Colorado National Guard dropped by the big van, escorted by two stern-faced FBI agents. He listened to what they had to say, agreed with most of their plan, and made several inputs of his own.

When he arrived back at the Sheraton, the general spoke with the wing commander at Buckley Field over an unsecure telephone line, and made a rather mundane request. It was not the first time a combat airplane had been diverted to a civilian field.

Minutes later an F-15E Strike Eagle that had taken off on a training flight received a radio call. The weapons systems officer set HDN into the military global positioning system, and the aircraft commander altered course for Hayden Airport.

4:16 P.M.

The general's big H-53 helicopter dropped John Rabeni and Steffie Footwine off at the Steamboat airport, then proceeded to Hayden Airport with four other passengers.

Link deplaned at the side of the operations building, noted

the two-place Strike Eagle had already landed, and hurried inside, leading a somewhat perplexed chief investigator.

After all of the previous excitement the gruff airport manager now agreed to not mention the impromptu exchange of crew members over telephone or radio. "Broke all the other rules, so why not one more," he said.

The F-15 aircrew—call signs Zack and Ringo—waited in the flight planning room, where Link took the helmet from the weapons systems officer and apologized for the inconvenience.

"Better take my g-suit too," said Ringo. He handed over an inflatable rubber and canvas garment that resembled cowboy's chaps. Link thanked him. "You're filed for Albuquerque?"

"Yes, sir. Like we were told."

Link waved in the FBI agents who would escort the WSO to Ski Town, set him up in a hotel, and provide room service. He would be allowed to make a single telephone call to tell his family he would return tomorrow. Such announcements were routine in the life of aviators.

Link briefed the F-15 aircraft commander, call sign Zack, as they watched with some humor as Randall attempted to strap on the g-suit. He'd managed to put the first leg on backward when the major took pity on the investigator and pointed out the error.

The helmet fit Randall loosely, so Link took up the tension on the oxygen mask and chin straps. All the while explaining route and timing to the major.

"Got it," said Zack, the aircraft commander. He smiled at the investigator. "Let's git."

Zack was one of few full-time air guard members, a graduate of the elite fighter weapons school at Nellis, in Las Vegas. In other words, he was one of the best. While he might normally have enjoyed hotdogging just a little when taking off from a civilian field, like pulling the nose straight up and heading for the wildest blue, this time he did nothing to attract undue attention.

After flying south for fifty nautical miles, he called Denver Center, asking to alter his route and proceed to Washington, DC via Kansas City and Pittsburgh. When he'd made the turn he pushed the throttles forward until they were scorching along at six hundred knots, just under the verboten speed of sound so they wouldn't create a sonic boom and break landlubber eardrums.

Chief Investigator Randall held on for dear life.

4:30 P.M.

John Rabeni had ensconced Steffie Footwine in the MCP's right cockpit seat for takeoff, and after a very few minutes she was manipulating the controls of the exotic radars like a fascinated pro. She was also full of questions. "There's absolutely nothing back in the cargo bay."

"The computerized consoles are in the van. When it's loaded on the airplane, the radars can be operated from in back. Unloaded we use FM data link to connect the van's console with the airplane's radars and . . ."

She listened with an avid grin, getting a technological fix, and remained captivated all the way to Colorado Springs. Noting that their call sign was Whiskey Foxtrot Five-One.

"This is where we do our rabbit from the hat act," said Rabeni.

Steffie pointed at the radar screen. "An airplane is approaching from our left, descending."

"Meet Garth One-Nine. A military cargo bird assigned to the Air National Guard."

John Rabeni began to climb to the altitude just vacated by the other aircraft.

When Garth One-Nine changed to *their* IFF code, John turned off their own civilian Identification Friend or Foe system, and switched on the second system, activating the military IFF-SIF military code of Garth One-Nine. He turned hard right—the other aircraft turned left.

Denver Center warned that the two airplanes were converging. John called that Garth One-Nine had the other airplane in sight. The military transport that had just been Garth One-Nine called that Whiskey Foxtrot Five-One had the other aircraft in sight. The transformation was complete. The two aircraft had exchanged altitudes, headings, and identities.

5:05 P.M.—Glenwood Springs, Colorado

Axel's rabble army was being instructed on how to unfold the cots. He watched with little interest, waiting for something he could not comprehend. Troubled by something unknown. He had thought that Anderson's death would bring a sense of well-being, yet he felt that something was amiss.

To T-Can West's chagrin he'd added Anderson and the Tatro woman back to the list. Was Axel being overly paranoid? Did dead people pose a danger?

Anderson's birth name was periodically whispered in a recess of his mind, eerily, like a passing breeze. *Ghost of Black Wolf.* What kind of name was that? Did it mean he was the incarnation of wolves? The Piegan Blackfeet had been backward savages compared to the culture of his own ancestry.

He was wondering why he still thought so often of Anderson, even after the man was dead, when his cell phone buzzed.

The T-Can West contact said the Weyland Foundation's MCP airplane was flying eastward. "Footwine is aboard. The expert from the NSA? Do you want me to look into it?"

Axel sighed with displeasure, upset at the unwarranted interruption. "You wanted deletions. She's out of the picture, so remove her from the list. Focus on finding the Katybitch and go back to work." Axel disconnected, his mind already returning to Anderson.

6:55 P.M.—North of Fort Huachuca, Arizona

Rabeni radioed the Fort Huachuca tower at two hundred miles out, using Garth One-Nine. Adding that they had a code five, which was sure to gain at least mild attention, for it indicated a general officer was aboard. For security's sake the curious tower operator would not ask for a name.

John decided that he would likely spend the remainder of his natural life in another fort, named Leavenworth. But the code five procedure had been decided upon by Steffie Footwine and the National Guard general to gain the Fort Huachuca commander's attention.

They were cleared for landing following a straight in approach.

Steffie, with her thick eyeglasses and serious mien, looked back and forth at the tunable aperture radar return and the runway lights two miles below. Clearly shown on the display were four images that she knew were Boeing commercial jets modified for military usage and called T-43s by the U.S. Air Force. They were taxiing, converging on a row of buildings at the end of the parking area that she remembered were ugly, brown, and plain.

The fort, situated in a hot and bleak area of southern Arizona, housed a plethora of state-of-the-art items produced by the cooperation of military and high tech industry. Some were brainchildren of the Defense Advanced Research Projects Agency. Among DARPA's achievements were the development of the first useful digital computer, grandma of the PC, and the programmable memory chip. Also the Internet, established to work around the massive loss of communications expected in the event of general—meaning nuclear—war.

DARPA dealt with pure research involving advanced sciences. But there had been times when that research provided relatively inexpensive answers to difficult challenges, and the commander of the Army's Research and Development

Center at Fort Huachuca provided limited funding for limited production.

The normal *military specifications* requirement (mentioned with disdain by most military men since their civilian leaders, and not they, are the reasons for eight-hundred-dollar wrenches and thousand-dollar coffeepots) was bypassed. The results were a number of low-cost, technically advanced answers to some very big problems. Such as someone manipulating the national communications net. The solutions were called Work Around Comm Systems, or WACS, and involved use of expert systems—better known as artificial intelligence—and broadcasting over six frequencies that were forbidden by the FCC except in the event of *national emergency.*

There were sixty WACS base units, and she had locations for every one of them. Major American cities, the Pentagon, and so forth. In fact, she could have used more units.

Steffie Footwine had once been one of the NSA's liaison persons at Fort Huachuca, and had visited often and made it a point to remain aware of the various capabilities. She also knew how to work the bureaucracy, but this one posed a major hurdle. The chief investigator, Randall, should be landing at Bolling Air Force Base at any moment, carrying with him the requests from Link Anderson and Gordon Tower, and meeting with the only person who could make it happen.

9:00 P.M. EDT—Bolling AFB, Washington, DC

The chairman of the Weyland Foundation had known precisely what had been meant by Gordon Tower when he had called him in New York.

"Lieutenant Jester just confirmed that Link was killed," Tower had told him sadly. "Shot to pieces by a killer we believe is one of the terrorists."

Jester was the code word used by Captains Anderson and

Dubois in the Gulf War, when Saddam was intercepting their radio calls. It meant to not believe what was said.

"Terrible," Frank Dubois had responded. *"To pieces?"* Gordon was overacting.

Gordon had said the body would be shipped via "Eagle Air" to Bolling Field.

Which was where Frank met the F-15E Strike Eagle, and the chief investigator who climbed from the back seat looking so pale he almost glowed in the dark. Randall descended the ladder, started to walk toward Frank's wheelchair, then hurried to the edge of the grass.

He puked, took great breaths, then bent over and released another torrent.

Frank waited patiently beside the car, eyeing the sleek F-15 as the aircraft commander, a major the flight plan identified as Zack, handed him a leather brief. "Mr. Anderson said this was to go to you, sir."

Frank eyed his Desert Storm shoulder patch as he pulled out the first sheet of paper. "Link and I both flew fighters in the Gulf War. We were in the 355th, deployed from Davis Monthan."

"I was with the 36th Wing. F-15s at Bitburg." They shook hands.

Frank scanned the page, nodded at what he'd read, and looked up. "As soon as he's able to say something without vomiting, it appears Mr. Randall and I will head for the White House. Ever been there?"

"No, sir."

"The president just returned from Japan. Care to meet him?"

"No, sir." Zack modified his brusque reply. "I'm sure he has more important business."

"Then we'll drop you off at the BOQ so you can get some sleep. When can you transport my investigator back to Steamboat?"

"The rule is eight hours." Zack looked at his watch. "Three a.m.?"

"That works. He'll be here with bells on. Thank you very much, by the way."

"A pleasure, sir." The major offered a smile and a salute.

7:10 P.M.—Fort Huachuca, Arizona

Rabeni landed the MCP on Fort Huachuca's primary runway, turned off, and was escorted toward the gathered T-43s, which were the fastest in the Air Force's fleet within a thousand-mile radius and were also large enough to carry the WACS units. They had been requested by priority—but not classified—message from the Air Education and Training Command, supposedly to provide "emergency assistance for victims of mudslides in California."

The brigadier general who commanded Fort Huachuca as well as its technical function, stepped from his staff car and met John Rabeni, who shuffled and cleared his throat.

They'd met previously, when Lockheed-Martin had been trying to sell the MCP to the army. The one-star had not then been, nor was he now, enamored of either John's informality or his long hair. He stared at the gold earring and spoke icily. "You have a two-star aboard?"

Rabeni motioned awkwardly at Steffie. "It's her show, sir. I'd like to introduce . . ."

"Steffie Footwine," the general finished his sentence on a happier note. "How are you?"

Footwine liked the brigadier general who shared her technical bent, but she had little time, and immediately briefed him on recent events in Colorado. "The WACS units were the only options I could think of," she concluded. "We've also sent to Washington for authorization to release them, along with personnel to operate them."

He looked uneasy, and dropped his bombshell. "They're gone, Steffie."

She looked at him with drooping jaw.

"Last year we received an order to hand them over to—ah—a foreign government."

"But you had *sixty* of them."

"Fifty-four were tested and packaged and sent to Beijing. We would have sent the other six units, but they didn't check out and they only wanted the best."

She was aghast. "They went out in foreign military sales?"

He shook his head sadly. "Not even that. They were gifts from the President, along with other sensitive technologies ranging from unmanned air vehicles to missile booster propellant."

"All of them crown jewels." Steffie bit her lip, trying to think it out. "How about the WACS telephone instruments?" They'd had several hundred.

"None of the miniatures." He brightened. "I do have a few dozen old field phones we could reprogram, but they're awfully big and heavy." He gave her a neutral look. "And of course they're no good without operable WACS base units."

She looked at him squarely. "I'd like access to the six faulty base units and all the telephone instruments you can spare."

He smiled. "Sorry but you're not from the People's Liberation Army."

Steffie exploded: "Surely, you're . . ."

"Darn. You win the argument." He smiled as he motioned to a lieutenant colonel standing nearby. "Call in two dozen of our best people from the electronics group. Tell them to be prepared to work all night and then travel for a few days."

Steffie smiled. "Thank you, sir."

"Bull. I'm tired of doing the wrong thing for the wrong reasons and the wrong boss. If you don't get authorization, I was a darn good lieutenant and I can be one again." They walked toward the warehouse. "We'll have to repair, modify, and fine-tune them, you know."

"Yes, sir."

"If I recall, you're MIT?"

"Double-E, Class of '81. Also a master's in math and another in computer sciences."

"Ha. I have a Ph.D. in physics from the wild bunch at Cal Tech. We'll just see who can get the first unit up and running."

9:05 P.M.—Ski Town

In the MCP van, Maggie and Link waited for word about the WACS units. Since nothing could be said in the clear on telephones or fax, they'd decided on beeper messages—the beepers supplied by the FBI—using numbers for codes showing progress with the distribution of the WACS. The number 77 had just appeared in the window, meaning that Frank Dubois had done his part. They were authorized by the President to remove anything required from the stockpile of secrets at Fort Huachuca. So far there were no numbers showing units distributed, only the number 88, meaning NSA Agent Steffie Footwine was running into major technical problems.

To kill time, Maggie leafed through the latest situation reports—called sit-reps—left by Gordon Tower. She paused. "Listen to this, Lincoln. The line of trucks south of town?"

"I saw them. One of the drivers came up with the composites."

"It says here that two of the rigs weren't checked at all?"

He turned and frowned.

"That's all there is. We'll have to ask Gordon about it when he gets here."

She read how the Denver police were circulating a video of the man who had killed the two policemen. Quietly, though, since Gordon's courier had arrived with word about Guteriez's connection. She said spokesmen for the Weyland Foundation and FBI negotiators were working around the clock. The TV and radio spots had brought hundreds of calls, but nothing useful. Finally, the search around Steamboat Springs for Katy's body was continuing. The ski patrol, the park rangers, and mountain hospitality guides were all looking. So far, nil.

The FBI's Identity Division had information on everyone except the arsonist and the second shooter. No prints were on record for either. They'd sent names of the other dead terrorists, however. Gave backgrounds and arrest sheets. All had been involved with narcotics, most of them major distributors.

"It's *not* coincidence, Lincoln. Whatever Kay knows concerns the drug trade."

"It still doesn't seem right."

"But it is. And like Steffie said, whatever Katy saw or heard is the key to everything."

The FBI beeper buzzed. The numbers 41 and 92 were shown. The first two WACS base units were being deployed to Denver and Atlanta, for use in the search for the listening posts.

Only two units, out of sixty? "Wonder what's taking her so long," asked Maggie.

29

Katy was still hurting.

Vision: a hulking man opening the sleeper hatch and telling her to crawl out or he'd come in to join her. Katy scared out of her mind, but knowing if he got in, there'd be no escaping. Saying in her trembling voice that if he'd just open the hatch some more she'd crawl out. Then scooting through the opening and scrambling past the big ape, intending to get outside and run like the wind . . .

Her muscles had *refused*. It was like they were asleep because she hadn't gotten an ounce of exercise during all that time inside. So instead of running like the wind, a leg had crumpled, and before she could get up the ape was mauling her.

Ranting about throwing her on the ground—which was actually hard-pack snow—and fucking her brains out. Angry about her scrambling to run away.

There was no way she was going to willingly do it with him, *and* on the frozen ground. No way. And ugly? The guy's head was shaved and he had crude tattoos of lightning bolts and dripping blood going around his skull, except in back where there was a fat braid. To finish the portrait his face had been taut with lust and stupidity, and he was very, *very* big.

He'd grabbed and lifted her, turned her so she was facing

away, then grabbed a fistful of cloth, grunted and tore the front of her ski outfit apart along the zipper line. Not so strong, really, just big and fleshy, and breathing sour smells onto the side of her face as he began shucking her out of the suit, topfirst like he was skinning an animal. Ripping her silk thermals, then grasping flesh.

Which was when Katy had begun the fight of her life, deciding there was no way she'd give in to a human so gross. She'd lasted a long while too, knowing every second of delay was respite, kicking and clawing and trying to twist loose. In fact she might have succeeded in wearing him down enough to flee if Annie hadn't come out and threatened him.

Then, when he had her feet going into the sleeper, which she didn't fight much, hoping he'd cram her back in and leave her alone, the big man had screamed a new string of curses and hit her with his fist so hard the world had grown fuzzy and dark. Only half awake then as he held her and grasped and pulled her breasts like she was a milk cow. Stretching them impossibly, and hurting her more than she'd believed possible.

All the while beyond him she could see Annie, grinning in her soiled pink cowgirl outfit and looking like a fat and doughy child. Laughing uproariously when he stretched her breasts, like she was watching the funniest thing in the world.

Katy huddled on the smelly mattress, unable to touch the puffed side of her face because random bolts of pain still shot through her brain, and both breasts felt like swollen boils.

Time had passed, perhaps an hour—but it was getting no better. Worse, in fact, as blood continued to pump and throb. So intense was the pain that she tried to think of other things to take her mind off of it. To focus on anything except her misery.

She hardly cared what they did next to her, because she doubted she could hurt any more. But after an hour of hurting and crying and feeling sorry for herself because of the injustice, she began to busy her mind with other things. Katy thought about Link Anderson, and how she knew he and all kinds of others were looking for her. He'd find her. Maybe too late. Maybe he'd find her dead. But he would surely find her, and she imagined what he would do to the men who had handled her.

"I hope he tears off your heads," she said aloud, and enjoyed the images that arose in her mind. She thought of Link hitting the big slob, like the slob had done to her. He was fat and out of shape. Not Link. But all that was fine for dreaming, and while she had faith that Link and her father and even Maggie Tatro were looking and would eventually succeed, what should she do if the man came for her again?

Katy had trouble coming up with a proper answer. For instance, *should* she try to condition her muscles? While there was little room in the sleeper, there was enough for sit-ups and stretches. But wouldn't a workout make her suffer more from lack of proper sustenance? The few candy bars, which was all she'd had in the past two days, had given their sugar rushes, but an hour later she'd been ravenous.

Would working out only use up any energy she had?

She started doing situps, got halfway through the first one and almost shrieked at the bolts of pain that shuddered through her as her breasts contacted the fabric of her shredded thermal underwear. When the pain had subsided sufficiently, Katy very carefully shrugged and pulled until she was out of the top part of the ski suit and there was nothing to bind.

Very slowly then, she leaned forward, then lay back. Next put her hands out before herself and did it again. Yeah. Not so bad now.

Continuing with a purpose. Grunting as she sat, knowing it was helping the abdominal muscles. Not pausing to think about the thirst that would come. That was the trade-off she'd already considered.

Touch her shoulders back to the mat, then raise herself. Over and over, until it finally became easier. After a while she changed, now just sitting up straight and tightening her muscles until they quivered in protest. Isometric exercises, like she practiced on a long airline flight or in an automobile.

Tighten her feet. Count off fifteen seconds. Next her calves. *One-two-three* . . . Her thighs. Working her way up and then back down her body and trying to include all the muscles.

Then after a while, thinking of another matter while she tensed and counted. *Why* had the killers come for her? Axel and Lu for Lucille and Guteriez and the others. Why did they want to silence her?

She had time. She'd recall everything that had happened that was anything at all out of the ordinary. Then dissect every one of those. Because Katy Dubois knew that even if the people here released her, there were still others out there who wanted to kill her.

10:45 P.M.—Glenwood Springs

The rabble were bored, some talking and smoking, a few arguing about inconsequentials like how the other guy lived in a shitty place. Periodically a fight broke out, but Axel seldom interfered. Those were to be expected with the kind of people he had amassed here.

He'd slept in his bedroom for two hours, just enough to take off the jagged edge. Now he was awake again, in the main room watching another knife fight erupt and wondering if all this wasn't a mistake, whether his plan might be flawed.

Not because of the kind of people he had gathered, for they were perfect for his purpose. Expendable. He could offer any of them, as he willed. He could send them to die. Desert them and leave them. They could be readily replaced with others just as greedy and bloodthirsty.

One of the fighters called another a motherfucker then shrieked that he'd been cut.

Axel smiled and watched, but his mind wandered.

The contact from T-Can East, the Atlanta office, called

with an update. After giving him the news about *the trade* that had been provided to the Voice, she mentioned that Frank Dubois had visited the White House. Nothing new or exciting there. This President was more corrupt than any Axel had seen in Mexico. Dubois was rich and had access.

The White House had placed a call to Fort Huachuca, Arizona. Nothing to worry about there either, he told her, and disconnected. The second phone was buzzing.

The T-Can West contact asked if he could remove Anderson from the list since he was confirmed dead. "We *need* deletions. The system is saturating, and we have a ninety-second delay in some module transmission times. We need to delete more names and lines."

Axel wondered why his doubts lingered about Anderson. Surely the FBI had properly identified the Weyland Foundation executive as the one who had been killed, but . . . He found himself saying, "Not yet."

A sigh. "The woman with the grand tetons? She's *dead,* Axel, and we . . ."

"Go ahead." He would give him that much.

"Good. I'm deleting Margaret A. Brown, Maggie Brown, M. A. Brown, Margaret A. Tatro, Maggie Tatro, and M. A. Tatro." Pause. "I've removed her voice print. Now, if I had a few dozen more deletions like that. Such as the members of the city council?"

"They may be the first to hear when the Kitten-bitch is found."

"Then how about some of the target lines? Do we need . . . ?"

"That's enough for now."

Another sigh. Axel disconnected.

The other cell phone buzzed. T-Can East. The two listening posts were competing to see who could provide better information. Normally Axel did not allow it, but he needed every hint.

The Voice had sent a message to all dealers and distributors, large and small, to report any news about Katy Dubois. The T-Can East contact said she had a possible result.

"A dealer in western Colorado called to tell us about a man named Creech. He said Creech isn't reliable, but he had scratches he said were caused by a girl kept in a truck."

A truck? Axel stopped pacing the floor. Cocked his head. "Western Colorado?"

"A town called Montrose. This Creech was bragging about really putting the kid in her place. That she was out at *Leroy's*. When our dealer got back to the bar he was gone."

Something about it sounded right. "Is Montrose far from Steamboat?"

"Two hundred miles distant, at the southwestern corner of the state. I told the dealer to wait until I'd called the Voice."

"I told you to give it to *me* first!" He felt his anger rise. "What did she say?"

"To contact you. Sorry, Axel."

If there was nothing better by morning, he decided to find out where *Leroy* lived, and send someone for a look. He disconnected and looked out into the large room, at the scores of cots and the milling men—and women, although they were the sorriest examples of femininity he'd ever observed. In Mexico such specimens would be found in the worst parts of cities, offering themselves for coins. Here they were loud and angry. The men were even worse. Animals would be apt descriptions. Just after their arrival an especially nasty fight had erupted. Two had been beaten to the floor, and the victors had taken turns urinating on them. How, he wondered, could he rely on such humans, who had no humanity? He smiled at the wittiness of his thought.

A man who had been sleeping looked up with an irritated expression. He smelled bad, and slept with an open knife in his hand for protection.

Axel returned to the bedroom and lay down to sleep. Tomorrow he would make another offering to hasten things along. Perhaps send someone to Montrose for a look.

A short while later he was awakened by sounds of men struggling and cursing near his door. Axel rolled out of bed, picked up his small pistol, and padded over. When he pulled

it open, he found two men wrestling, fighting for control of
a slender stiletto.

"You woke me," Axel said almost amiably.

They struggled on.

"Great Huitzilopóchtli, accept these humble offerings,"
said Axel. Smiling, for there was no reason to wait. There
were plenty more like them who were available.

11:25 P.M.—Fifth Street, Denver

Two hundred miles distant, four FBI agents parked and prepared a panel truck marked WILSON BROS. JANITORIAL SER-
VICES. Beside the wiretap console, which was not in use,
rested a large box-like unit measuring three feet by four
feet, and painted olive drab. On its side was stenciled: WACS
BASE UNIT NBR. 43. Seated before it were an army second
lieutenant and a specialist first class, who were manually
tuning errant frequencies that drifted off.

There was another van and base unit in Atlanta, parked at
a similar-looking building. Those technicians were having
similar difficulties.

The FBI agent seated beside the WACS unit operators
had a list of offices before him, showing the two hundred
eight telecommunications and related companies that occupied the building. Beside that were the locations of Wilson
Bros. janitors who mopped and cleaned the corridors and
periodically reported to the stakeout truck.

Wilson Bros. did exist as a company, and held the contract to clean the buildings. But the logo on the panel truck
was freshly painted, and the present cleaning personnel
held juris doctorate degrees and were agents of the FBI. The
most complex systems the Wilson Bros. had previously
fielded were triple-brush floor waxers. The same was not
true for the agents and army specialists in the panel truck.

The WACS station controlled and connected a total of
sixteen hand-held telephones, and when all were up and
running, would relay between other base stations hundreds

of miles distant. Yet the sound was crisp and clear. The highest frequency was above that of most radars, so high it approached that of infrared light, the lowest frequency just slightly higher than household alternating current. The frequencies were switched every two to eight seconds at the behest of a complex algorithm. Smart enough to select the best frequencies for a particular range and function. If a listener were to tune in any of the frequencies, and could possibly demodulate it, he or she would hear an odd series of beeps, growls and squeaks.

The intercepted communications were indecipherable using any decoding system known to man. Except, of course, to the Chinese People's Army, who were offering copies for sale to Iran, Libya, and North Korea for many millions of dollars.

They made their first observation. "Second floor," called the agent-in-charge who sat by the army specialist. "Any luck?"

The second-floor crew had inserted a video viewing device into the crack under an office door. The FBI team and the NSA agent accompanying them were watching two people, one working on a telephone switching module, the other on a laptop hooked into the Internet. The FBI agents had believed they'd found the LP on their first look!

"Just another small comm business," said the NSA agent. "Putting in overtime."

"Go to the next office." The agent-in-charge marked a slash beside the company name. A *doubtful*. If nothing else was found, they would come back and check them again.

They had several different detection devices available. An aural detector could tell if humans were present. One required a small hole to be bored into a wall or door, and a video wand. Another involved a sensitive device that could replicate video and audio from the emanations of a computer monitor. A device was employed from the surrounding buildings, and cast a laser beam at any glass window.

The vibrations of the glass were measured and demodulated, and sounds and signals from within were recorded.

A call came in from Supervising Agent Gordon Tower, from the WACS unit just set up in Steamboat. He was the man in charge, operating under the authority of a plan called the DT.

"Can you hear me, Denver?" Tower asked.

"Loud and clear," answered the woman agent-in-charge. "We ironed out our problems with the WACS unit and checked our first office. Only two hundred and seven to go."

Not said cheerfully. Seventy agents were presently working in and around the building. Her husband and daughter were at home sleeping. She wished she were there too.

"Keep at it. Any progress, Atlanta?"

"We've looked at four suites so far," said Atlanta. "I agree with Denver. It's going to be a long night. Maybe two or three days long."

"For your information there'll only be a total of five WACS units. New York and Washington should be coming on line any time now. You two are the keys to everything. We're paralyzed until you locate the listening posts."

11:53 P.M.—Ski Town

Link answered the door, and let Gordon inside. The FBI supervisor growled a weary greeting, accepted the cup of coffee, sat back, and rubbed his brow.

"It's slow-going," he lamented. "Unless we're lucky it's going to be a long night." He looked at Maggie. "Get a chance to go over all the sit-reps?"

"From what I read you're covering all the angles."

"Ask about the trucks," Link reminded her.

"Can you believe two of 'em got through without being checked?" Gordon asked. "The highway patrol didn't fess up until a short time ago. I put it in there because I might need your help."

"How did it happen," Maggie asked.

"The HP set up a roadblock at the Interstate, and the very first driver refused to open an equipment box. They held him up while they checked with Denver about legalities and jurisdictions, then there was a shift change and he was waved through by mistake. No follow-up, and now he's home in Salt Lake City. His background: shaky. Fines and suspensions going way back for faking manifests. An opportunist. Nothing really bad in his past, but if he has Katy, visions of big money can change a lot of things."

"How large is the equipment box?"

"Large enough for a body. The other rig that got through belonged to a woman from Montrose, way over on the west side of the state. *Ba-ad* girl. Two arrests for driving under the influence. Several old ones for prostitution. One for battery when she got into a bar room brawl with a man. Three for possession of stolen property. Suspected by the DOT for transporting illegal goods. To round out her sweetness, she associates with members of a neo-Nazi skinhead group with ties to the Klan."

"And the police didn't inspect her rig?"

"She told the patrolman a cat had died in the sleeper, and the trooper said the odor was so overpowering he thought it was still in there. He confessed he was leery she might somehow pass on something he didn't cherish getting."

"What's the follow-up?"

"Since Link's got not much else to do, being dead and all, I figured he could fly one of my agents to Salt Lake, then to Montrose, so we can check them out."

"Okay if I go along?" Maggie asked.

Gordon Tower gave her a wry look. "Actually, I sort of expected it."

Link started to say that no one had asked him, but judiciously did not.

The supervising agent removed a video cassette from his briefcase, went over to the VCR/TV at the console, and plugged it in.

"We received this from Denver about an hour ago."

He switched it on.

The video was color, but of mediocre quality. Grainy and moving in jerks. The image showed a gated driveway, with high hedges to either side. Snow on the surfaces.

"It was taken by a tattletale camera in the unmarked car where the two cops were killed."

The wrought-iron gate swung open as a Toyota Land Cruiser emerged into view. The SUV crossed the street and was parked in front of the police car.

"Meet the killer."

An angular man got out of the passenger side. Tall and thin, with limbs like those of an articulated stick man. He neither smiled nor frowned, just walked toward the driver's side of the patrol car. When he disappeared from view, Gordon reversed the video so the man walked backward. He froze on a relatively clear frame.

The killer looked intense, and had a thin blade of a nose. Like a hatchet.

"Any ideas who it might be."

Link stared hard, feeling the unsettled sensation.

"Axel Nevas," said Maggie. "I saw his photograph once."

Gordon nodded. "I thought so."

Link Anderson had seen him face to face, across the service road just a few blocks from where they were parked. Axel had wielded a rifle. The fervent expression was precisely as he remembered it.

The face of evil.

PART 3

The Uncompahgre Plateau

30

It was moonless and dark when Link drove the MCP van
into the Steamboat airport. As they passed a lighted hangar,
he pointed out the Piper Colt. "Swiss cheese," he told her, "but
they'll repair it. It's a tough little airplane."

They were on their way to Salt Lake City and Montrose,
where an agent would check out the two truckers and their
rigs. The MCP airplane was unavailable. Only four WACS
base units had been deployed and set up thus far, and Steffie
Footwine was doggedly working to get the other two—the
total had diminished from sixty for some unknown reason—
up and running.

The FBI agent was bringing a WACS telephone, despite
the limitations of the devices. They were better than nothing, since they provided security, but offered a big step back
from the normal capabilities offered by American communications industries.

Link parked the big van at an unoccupied part of the airport parking lot, and pulled out his and Maggie's bags. They
walked together toward the idle terminal, caught themselves looking at one another, and smiled.

The airport had been built for tourists shuttling in from
Denver and Salt Lake City. Just as the facilities had been
completed, the primary airline that was to service them had

gone under. Now it was an airport in waiting, unused except for a few private airplanes, and during the past few days, government-owned aircraft like the Piper Saratoga parked in front.

Link confirmed the tail number stenciled under the decal of the American flag, and placed their small overnight bags into the compartment aft of the big single engine.

A man hurried from the terminal, a bag in each hand, clad in a mountain of cold weather gear. "I'm your passenger. Special Agent . . ." His shivering made his already impossible last name sound like a crunching sound. Crzksa, or perhaps Kurzecksay, or something in between. "Call me George." He did a little dance, shuddered. "Man it is *cold* out here."

Link managed to stuff one of the agent's large suitcases into the baggage compartment, and place the other one behind the second tier of seats as Maggie introduced them. Using first names only since Tower had killed them off.

"We'll go to Salt Lake City first," George managed, and brandished a bulky WACS phone. "When we're done there, I'd like to return close enough to contact Supervising Agent Tower, and . . ."

His voice continued as a numbing sensation tingled through Link. With it he felt the fear for someone close. Katy, he knew. He closed his eyes and visualized their destination. The city, the lake, the spired tabernacle. Majestic white mountains to the south, north, and east.

Something about it was not right.

Special Agent George was droning on about using the airplane's altitude to check in on the WACS before they looked for the woman trucker in Montrose. "The units are line-of-sight," he said knowledgeably.

Link broke in. "Describe Montrose," he said.

"Never been there," said George, but Maggie spoke up. "Mountains in the distance. Uncompahgre Plateau to the west and Rockies to the east. I'd imagine there's snow on the ground."

That did not sound right either. Link beheld a mental image of mountains, not large but very close. Then a feeling of being trapped in something dark and cramped.

As quickly as they'd come, the sensations and images left him. He felt a wave of fatigue, and made himself relax. Tried not to think that Katy might be inside . . . a coffin.

George had noticed nothing amiss, but Maggie watched Link with narrowed eyes and concern. He gave a small shake of his head, to tell her all was okay. The FBI agent started telling them he hated to fly in anything smaller than a 747. George worked in the audit office of the Miami field office. He'd been sent to help, and was willing enough, but this was stretching it.

Link pulled a small flashlight from his pocket and completed a walk-around inspection of the airplane. Pleased that it was an R-model, meaning it had retractable gear, which would add twenty miles per hour to the cruising speed. He climbed onto the wing and opened the hatch. Examined the instruments and controls. All the standard stuff, plus a state-of-the-art navigation panel with a military-version GPS.

"Do you know how to start it?" George called out in a somewhat hesitant tone.

"I think so," said Link, with tongue firmly in cheek.

"Then you've flown this model before?"

"Something sort of close. Starting and flying it shouldn't be a problem," said Link, "but sometimes stopping these babies can be a real challenge."

"Oh," said George, as if mollified. Maggie rolled her eyes.

"Come on in and get warm while I file the flight plan."

Link led the way into the terminal, and spoke to the fixed base operator, the same man who had dealt with the helicopters. He looked over the computerized printout of the night IFR/VFR flight request, and said, "Looks good."

"Weather's on the way," said the man. "Don't get caught in the stuff."

"How bad?"

"Sleet, snow. High winds. Another storm of the century according to the Denver TV, like they say two or three times a year so tourists won't realize it's a regular thing."

"It's headed here?" Link asked.

"Predicted south of us again, but you saw what happened last week. The front should hit Grand Junction about noon. Aspen about one. There's some CAT out in front of the storm."

Link took off at five-thirty-five, when it was still pitch dark. He lifted the gear and remained at full power through the climb, and commented that it was a sweet running bird.

They ran into the forecast *CAT,* or air turbulence, not long after leveling at ten thousand feet, and George immediately began filling the first barf bag. Link observed with sympathy as the agent drew in a breath and vomited some more.

There was an odd *honk,* and after a moment's confusion, Maggie reached back for the heavy WACS phone. She found the ON button and spoke, then handed it over. "For you."

Erin's voice was loud and clear. "We just got our WACS unit here in New York. How're you doing, pardner?" They'd not spoken since he'd used the Jester code word.

He explained what they were up to. "You?"

"I've had the computers working on Axel Nevas since we got Gordon's courier message. He's a walking contradiction, smart enough on the technical details but a certifiable weirdo with the Aztec thing. One college friend said he'd fried his brain with LSD and chemicals, and another said he was just plain nuts. I'm coming up with a profile, but it's slow. Unbelievable how much we humans rely on electronic communications."

"We just saw his video."

I heard Maggie identified the killer as Nevas. Something you should be aware of. There's been an effort to find out everything possible about you. Birth data, childhood, all of it. I think it's for him."

"Maggie overheard him saying I was dangerous."

"Hmm. If he's got a fixation, maybe there's something we can use. Gordon explained how he planted the report about you getting knocked off. I'll do some what-ifs with Axel's mental profile. See how he'd react if we brought you back to life?"

"But not Maggie," Link said forcefully. "She's been through enough."

"I understand. Congratulations, by the way. She's nice."

Congratulations?

"I'll think some more about all this while you're in Salt Lake. Here, Frank wants to talk before you get out of range of your base station. We're in his office."

"Anything about Katy?" was his friend's immediate question.

"So far nothing, but I still don't think the terrorists have her."

"Gordon thinks it may be a kidnapping, but not by the terrorists. If there's a phone call, our negotiators have instructions to ensure her safety *first*. It's a helpless feeling, Link."

"Hang in a while longer, Frank. We're doing everything we can." He told him about Maggie's contributions. Freezing in the snowdrift. The fire. Shooting the terrorist.

"Gordon said you two are close. Thank her for me," Frank told him.

The connection became intermittent. "We'll contact you around noontime, when we're back in range." Link shut off, and handed the phone back.

"I'm officially employed again?" Maggie asked.

"Yeah." He grimaced. "And everyone in the universe knows what we did in the van."

"Great."

He started to extol the merits of privacy, but just muttered, "Too quick."

"Mmm." She grew a smile. "It was just right."

"I mean it happened—you know. The timing was poor?"

"No, I *don't* know." Her look was turning darker and he wished the subject hadn't arisen. They flew on, trying to ignore the sounds of Special Agent George barfing into the bag.

8:42 A.M.—Grand Junction, Colorado

As they entered the city, Leroy J. Manners looked over at Shag, who was at the wheel of Annie's tittie pink rig. "You know what to say?" His head ached.

"Yeah, yeah." Shag muttered something under his breath. He'd been in the foul mood since Leroy had called and awakened him.

While Leroy had waited for him to show up at Black Canyon, Annie had whined about wanting to come along, saying that was the original plan—to go to Grand Junction without the kid the first time—until he'd got sick of telling her they'd do it all at once, and decided to hit something to make his head better. She'd swallowed a tooth and was braying like a mule when Shag arrived and he went out to join him.

Once they were in the truck, while Shag was still trying to figure out the gears, Leroy had banged on the sleeper hatch. "You back there?" he'd yelled.

"Let me out. Please?" The kid's voice was hoarse and raspy.

"Yeah," he said. "We're gonna do that in a little while."

Shag had got the rig started, and after about ten seconds of warm-up had pulled forward and ripped the plug-in unit out of the side of the cabin.

The drive to Grand Junction had taken two hours, mostly because Shag screwed up every time he shifted, sometimes using too high a gear, usually too low. At the traffic light in Montrose he'd found reverse, and they'd damn near backed over a car.

Now, getting close to where they were going, Leroy cracked open the sleeper. "Need anything back there?"

She spoke in a dry croak. "Water, and something to eat beside a candy bar."

Leroy closed the hatch and pointed out the Conoco station ahead. The sign called it: EARLY'S PIT STOP — GASOLINE AND MARKET — SANDWICHES.

When Shag was parked, Leroy went inside. A few minutes later he emerged with a bologna sandwich, a box of Cheese Nips, and a bottle of spring water.

He opened the hatch and held them inside, careful she couldn't see his face. When the kid took them he made his voice pleasant. "We're gonna let you talk to your daddy."

"Thank you! Oh God, *thank* you!"

"Won't be long," he told her, and closed the hatch.

He lowered his voice. "Pull up close to the phone booth," he told Shag.

"You do the talkin'," Shag decided.

"You want a hunnert thousand dollars, you gotta earn it."

"I drove here, didden I?" He was still sullen.

Leroy considered if he shouldn't kill the bastard on the way back. But then he wondered what was the harm? How would they know who was doing the talking?

He pointed. "Go 'head and pull up."

Shag found a gear too high, and they lurched across the blacktop. He managed to stop when Leroy's side was a foot distant from the booth, and shut off the engine. "Close enough?"

Make yourself busy and tape the kid's arms behin' her and her legs so she can't run." Leroy squeezed out and looked around. It was a good setup. The kid would be shielded from the view of passersby when they pulled her out to talk.

He got out the 800 number Annie had written down the day before, slid into the booth, and dropped the quarter.

9:06 A.M.—Fifth Street, Denver

The T-Can contact was trying to relax. It had been a long night at the computer. With Axel refusing to add more people—wanting to keep their numbers to a minimum—only four were left to handle each twelve-hour shift. They'd been on the headphones for eleven hours straight, and were ready for a break. Axel had been wrong. The project they'd called STOPPER—finding and dealing with Katy Dubois—had added greatly to their workload.

And while the money was good, there was far too little free time to spend it.

The woman at the opposite end of the table was typing an e-mail to the Voice. Telling her about a scheduled police raid in West L.A. She sent a message every thirty minutes, even if there was only a "negative action" report.

The contact leaned back, yawned, and almost missed the flickering yellow light.

He selected the special 800 line.

". . . don't worry who I am. I got the girl with me. You wanna tawk with her?"

"Yes, very much." This FBI negotiator had a particularly smooth, sincere voice. The contact had practice and could mimic them all. This one was a favorite.

"She wants to tawk with her daddy in a couple of minutes. He there?"

The voice scanner was on. The patterns of the caller's voice did not match any of those stored. He was not a previous caller and he sounded real. Interesting, thought the contact, as he turned on the scrambler that screwed up the FBI's Caller ID.

"I can have her father on the line in seconds," said the FBI negotiator. "Would you like to hold for him?"

"No way. I know how you people can trace a call if I stay on too long."

The contact examined the readout: Grand Junction, CO—Early's Conoco—92555 Highway 50 S. He had a premonition. This one was genuine.

Yes, he decided, and made the switch, shutting off the FBI negotiator and taking over.

"I can't trace your call. You must be calling from some special phone," he said, mimicking the negotiator's voice and adding some bullshit.

"Tell the kid's ol' man—Frank somethin', right?—I'll

call back in five minutes, and he can talk to his kid. I wan' him to have two million dollars ready."

"I'll pass it on to Mr. Dubois. That's a lot of money, however." He determined that he was not speaking to a mental giant.

"Dammit, two million. Wan' us to hurt the kid?"

"Of course not," said the contact, who did not care if he ground her into hamburger.

"Have him at the phone in five minutes." The person at Early's Conoco Station hung up.

9:08 A.M.—Steamboat

Gordon Tower was in his hotel room with his senior agents and the chief of the second hostage rescue team—going over options. Talking periodically on the WACS to a team of executives at the Hoover Building in Washington who were huddled in a similar meeting.

Steffie Footwine now had five base units up and running. He'd heard she might not be able to repair the sixth.

The heavy telephone honked obnoxiously, and Gordon picked up. Thinking it was one of the deputy directors they'd been brainstorming with.

It was the senior negotiator, in Denver to work with the Weyland Foundation representative and help handle calls to the 800 number.

"Shoot," Gordon said, then turned grim. He nodded several times, and said, "Stay in touch." Then he switched off and faced the others. "Two minutes ago they got what he thought was a valid ransom call. A man said he had Katy. Then the line went dead."

"A hangup?" asked J. B. Stone.

"He thinks the bad guys shut him off. The same's happened twice before, but this time he's got a feeling it was the real thing."

"So we may be missing the ransom call."

"Yeah." Gordon turned to the HRT chief. "Make sure

your people are ready. If the terrorists return, I want to kick their asses and do it quickly."

"We're ready," was the resolute answer.

9:09 A.M.—Glenwood Springs

Axel had noted the empty cots that morning, and sent out a search party. Two of his rabble had walked off toward town. Now they were doing a fast-talk shuffle.

He was palming the little pistol, thinking it was not yet time for another offering after the two the previous night. He had only just received their replacements, crack dealers driven in from the baddest streets of Denver.

"We was going to walk some, then come on back. No shit, man."

A cell phone sounded, and he took a few steps away since the man continued jabbering. "Axel," he answered in his deep voice.

"We got a ransom call. I think it's real."

"Where?" he said, walking to the map.

"Grand Junction."

Axel put his finger on the small city to the west. It was not at all close to Steamboat. If it was real, the Kitten-bitch had been moved. He moved his finger southward on the map. The previous night they'd gotten the tip about Montrose. The two were not far apart.

"When will you know?" he asked.

"A couple of minutes. They're going to put the girl on the phone."

Axel covered the mouthpiece and motioned to the ones holding the two men. "Let them go, and tell the pilots to get ready to fly."

Then to the T-Can West contact. "Check her voice print and make sure."

When he disconnected, he found that his pulse was racing.

9:12 A.M.—Fifth Street, Denver

The contact kept the line isolated. No calls could be made to the phone booth in Grand Junction. All outgoing calls would be routed through the listening post.

"I'm tired," said one of his people. She looked it. A new data dump came in from Phoenix, and she wearily went to work listening to the conversations.

The yellow light blinked—the contact pressed the mouse button. "Hello?" Using the FBI negotiator's mellow voice.

"Daddy?" It was a girl. Sounding sad and frightened.

"Your father isn't here yet, Katy. Are you okay?" He stared at the voice scan, and waited.

WORKING—NO MATCH—INSUFFICIENT DATA

"I'm . . . I'm okay so far."

WORKING—NO MATCH—INSUFFICIENT DATA

"I'm just a little sick because I'm not getting . . ."

MATCH—KATHERINE DUBOIS

"Here!" The kidnapper's snarling voice took over from the girl. "Your choice. You wan' her alive? Wan' her fucked by a hunnered guys? Wan' her cut up in pieces?"

Actually, thought the contact, that would solve the problem. But, "No!" he responded in a horrified voice. "Mr. Dubois will be here in one hour, and he'll have your money ready. You can arrange everything then."

"Yeah?" The kidnapper sounded surprised. "No games?" The crude voice was lighter, as if he were very pleased.

"Of course not. That phone is very clear, by the way."

"Good. I'll call back."

When the light went off, the contact was already on the line with Axel.

9:16 A.M.—Glenwood Springs

As Axel awaited confirmation, his excitement mounted. A pilot and four men were already out at the first helicopter, which others were pulling from the big garage. All clad in cold weather clothing. The pilot examining a flight map, determining his best route to Grand Junction. The four dealers reaching into opened crates of weapons and ammunition.

When Axel finally took the call, he allowed himself to smile.

"Go!" he cried in an exultant voice, and laughed uproariously. "We have her!"

Someone yelled for the first helicopter to start up and lift off.

It was the double offering from the night before. Axel was sure of it! "Thank you Huitzilopóchtli," he cried, and drew odd looks. "The rest of you! Get warm clothing and weapons. Take all the ammunition. There will be bonuses for everyone."

As they cheered and hurried, Axel ordered them to leave for Grand Junction in the four-by-fours, told them that they would receive directions while en route.

As soon as they were dispatched, he would board the second helicopter and direct the battle. The endgame had begun.

31

Leroy and Shag were across the highway from the Conoco Station, drinking coffee and finishing their stacks of pancakes. Leroy trying to envision two million dollars and wondering if that much money wouldn't fill a cardboard box. Thinking of killing Shag when they got back to the cabin. He might have considered doing it before then, but he would likely have even more trouble with the gears on Annie's rig.

Another trick was fooling with his mind, how at the cabin he should do both Shag and Annie, and blame the kidnapping on them. It was difficult thinking with the hangover.

"How's he gonna get the money here?" Shag asked.

"Not so loud." He figured the kid's daddy would have a way.

Shag started giving the waitress a hard time about the bill, like he wasn't going to pay because the pancakes were doughy, but Leroy told him to lay off. "It ain't a good time to be givin' people shit," he said.

"Yer jus' full of orders, ain'tcha."

They each counted out enough to cover the food, then went outside at just about the designated time. Across the street a group of teenagers were converging on the phone booth.

Thankfully they'd parked the truck behind the café or one of them might've heard the kid yelling.

"Use another phone," said Shag. He was increasingly interested in the money.

Leroy was about to give him grief when they heard a whup-whup-whup-sound, and turned to watch a helicopter descending from up high. It neither veered nor paused, just kept coming, and pitched up and hovered over the Conoco Station, low and so close he could look right inside. The back door was partway open, and hard-faced uglies with headbands and pigtails were looking around, carrying artillery and acting like they wanted to use it.

Leroy and Shag took off together, fast-walking around the side of the café to where they'd left Annie's rig. Knowing that whoever was in the helicopter was looking for *them*.

Airborne, West of Glenwood Springs

Axel was in the right seat of the second helicopter, scanning out over the mountains, remembering the last time he'd crossed them. Glancing at his watch as seconds ticked by.

Let her be dead!

He answered the cell phone. The pilot reported that they were hovering near the booth. "All there are down there are some goggle-eyed teenagers."

"Back off so you don't scare anyone away," said Axel. He paused, thinking it was too much to hope they would use the same phone, but he felt they were close.

A minute later there was still nothing from T-Can, so he called the helo pilot again.

"Look around. Tell me what you see, as if you're my eyes. People? Vehicles?"

"There's traffic coming out of the city."

"Forget it. What's pulling out and heading away from you."

"There's a motorcycle and a new VW bug. Oh yeah, a

U-Haul moving van about to leave the service station going north."

A possibility, Axel thought. "Anything else?"

"A semitrailer's pulling out of the café parking lot across the highway. You know, the kind used to haul a big trailer, only there isn't a trailer."

Axel felt an electric jolt. "Is there a sleeper cab?"

Pause. "Yeah, but it doesn't look like it was made for the tractor. More like an add on. The whole thing is strange-looking—painted pink."

Where had he heard that before? "Which way's it headed?"

"South."

Toward Montrose, Axel thought, and his mind clicked and it all came together. The Kitten-bitch was in the pink truck. He felt a shot of elation. Remembered Sergeant Santos laughing over the radio about an ugly woman and a pink truck in the lineup at Steamboat. Thought about the dealer last night who had heard of the girl in a truck at "Leroy's."

He spoke calmly. "Follow it. Stay out of their sight, but don't lose track."

Axel kept the telephone line open, thinking. Deciding. His mind clicked.

The plan was simple. As soon as the truck reached an uninhabited stretch of highway—and there was plenty of that between Grand Junction and Montrose—he would have the helicopter land up ahead, get the shooters to dismount and wait with weapons ready, and then riddle the rig with bullets. Have them pull out the Kitten-bitch. When he arrived he wanted to see her body. Desecrate it. Offer it to his god. Send it to the Voice in small pieces.

Axel found himself smiling, thinking how he would exult to the Voice. Talk to the dead man and tell him his worries were over.

"How far is the truck from Grand Junction?" he asked after a moment.

"Three or four miles."

"And the traffic?"

"Light. You think she's in the truck?"

"I *know* it!" Axel outlined his plan. Told the pilot how he would have him land in front of the truck, and have the shooters dismount.

"Ahh, maybe we'd better wait."

Axel frowned. "Is there a problem?"

"There's patches of ground fog and a low overcast. Up ahead it gets even . . ."

"Fly in front of the truck on the highway and put it down—now!"

"Maybe," but the pilot's tone was hesitant.

Axel was seething. "Why didn't you *tell* me?"

"It's just now moving in." Pause. "Can't land in front of the truck. Ahh, it looks awfully solid. It's even heavier off to the right, like this is the leading edge of a front."

Axel's mind raced. He did not dare lose her again. Think! His voice emerged calmly. "Forget everything before. Land at Montrose Airport."

"We may have trouble getting permission in this stuff. Maybe we better . . ."

"I said to *land there!*" He was shouting, angry. "Tell the idiots with you to take over the airport. Kill anyone you have to, but make sure no one drives or flies in or out. I'll hold *you* responsible when I arrive there."

"I understand." The pilot voice was uneasy. "We'll see you at the airport."

Axel was instantly calm. "Thank you." He had known deep inside that it would come to another blood-letting. It was why he had prepared as he'd done. After all, great Huitzilopóchtli was the god of *war*. It was Axel's fate, to be victorious in war.

The only thing missing was his great enemy—Anderson.

He called the T-Can West listening post and spoke with the contact. "Direct everyone to Montrose. We will meet at the airport. And have your people find out where a man named Leroy lives. I believe it is very close to Montrose."

"There will be a lot of Leroys."

"This one has an acquaintance named Shag who drinks too much, and an ugly woman with a pink truck."

Montrose would be easier than Steamboat. He had an abundance of people, all expendable. He would block the airport and all roads leading out of the city, and neutralize the authorities. No one on the outside would know, for T-Can would shut down communications, commercial radio and television. They could bottle up the town and plug the cork.

The truck was headed to Leroy's with the Kitten-bitch. And so was he.

U.S. Highway 50

Leroy J. Manners was hunched down, looking back through the mirror. For more than half an hour there'd been nothing except fog. But before the fog, there had been the orange insect in the sky, holding back and coming closer as the visibility grew worse. He was thinking about the way the fog had come along to hide them, like the weather was on his side.

"They still back there?" Shag asked.

"Maybe, but I can't see nothin' but crud."

"They get us for kidnapping—you and me, with our records—they won't screw around. They'd put us away and keep us there. We oughta stop and break the kid's neck. Throw her out. Who'd know it was us?"

There was no *way* Leroy was going to throw away two million dollars. He was going to be *rich*. He'd felt it down deep when he'd first realized Annie was bringing the kid home.

Leroy explained something to Shag. "Them wasn't cops in the helicopter. Not with long hair and nose hardware. You see the guns? Them wasn't cop guns."

Shag thought about it, then spoke in a near-whisper. "The bastards are after the kid and our *money*."

"Yeah." The thought of it made Leroy burst out cursing. "I only saw four and th' pilot. We can take 'em."

As they passed the airport turnoff, they heard loud rotor sounds and got a glimpse of the large, orange helicopter as it descended through the gloom.

"Stop at the Cowboy up ahead," said Leroy.

As soon as Shag had pulled to a stop, Leroy took the keys from the ignition, jumped out, and went inside. Annie was in a booth at the side of the barroom, drinking a beer and sulking.

"My mouf hurts." She held her swollen jaw, wearing an aggrieved expression.

"Go on home," he told her. "We gotta problem."

Her eyes narrowed. "The cops find out about the kid?"

"Not the cops. Somebody else. They show up, I wanna be ready. Drop by Bubba's and tell him to come over. We might need his help."

"I ain't gonna split *my* part of the money, Leroy. Not even with my blood nephew."

"Tell him we got beer an' he'll come runnin'." Bubba Hartinger was as dim as a ten-watt bulb, but he had not been known to pass up many alcoholic drinks."

Annie slid out of the booth and they hurried to the door.

Leroy crawled back into the cab with Shag and passed him the keys. He might have gone with Annie except the girl was in the truck and he didn't want to risk her being stolen.

Shag watched Annie get into her old pickup. "How come you got the cow?"

"She knows a couple things," he said. "Le's git."

Black Canyon

As soon as they'd parked at the cabin, the men went around back and started digging in the snow. "Think they'll find us all the way out here?" Shag asked.

"Don't wanna find out, unless we're ready."

Leroy kept a few handguns, shotguns, and hunting rifles

in the cabin, but it might not be enough for thieves who could afford a helicopter. Beneath the snow at their feet, and a layer of plywood, and a foot of earth, was Leroy's real arsenal, which he felt could stop about anything short of the Royal Marines, which Shag said was the toughest group on earth. Leroy did not know which marines he meant, but he admitted they sounded awfully professional.

Annie drove up and parked next to the cabin. For a while she just sat and watched them dig. Finally she got out and went inside. Still acting upset. "She oughta help," Shag complained, but Leroy didn't answer. Just looked at the time and hurried faster. It was noon, and while he did not think the thieves could be there that quickly, he did not trust them.

It began to snow, lightly but enough to allow Leroy to relax some, since no helicopters were going to spot anything. He felt the shovel strike something solid. "We're there."

It was two in the afternoon before a pickup rattled down the lane. Bubba Hartinger had towed a trailer with two snowmobiles loaded aboard, and brought his wife.

Leroy snorted in disgust. "He just had to bring the titless wonder."

The mixologist came over for a look at the huge M-2 heavy barrel machine gun they'd placed on the heavy steel base-plate at the corner of the cabin. It was World War II vintage, and they'd been working with motor oil and rags to remove the rust, since it had been buried improperly and water had seeped in.

Shag was trying to rub rust from the back latch and trigger pin mechanism. He motioned his head at the bartender. "Leroy says you ain't good for nothing but warmin' his ears with your ankles, but you can get your ass over here and help."

Her husband laughed as if Shag were joking. Bubba was younger than the other two men, and sort of pudgy. While he looked not at all threatening, he kept his head shaved and had elaborate tattoos, like a child trying to be one of the big boys. He would not have survived if he hadn't been able to claim Leroy as a sort of relative.

Leroy grabbed hold of the charging lever. Pulled with considerable effort. *Clack.* He pressed the trigger and there was a muffled *thunk.* "Works," he said proudly.

Annie came out to look at the weather. She went closer and stared at the gun.

"We'd been here earlier but Honey had to get off," said Bubba to his blood aunt.

Annie gave the mixologist a hard look. The two were not friends. She had heard the ear warmer jokes too many times and knew they were truth.

Leroy was snapping the belted .50 caliber rounds together. "Help me with these."

"Get more rust off the feed or it'll jam for sure." The only time they'd fired it, she'd helped by repairing the plunger solenoid, without which it was a single-shot cannon.

"Who's all the people up on the highway?" the titless wonder asked out of the blue.

"Huh?" blurted Leroy.

"Yeah," said Annie's nephew. "They was going real slow along the highway when we drove in."

"They got long hair?" Leroy asked.

"Yeah. Ain't cops or skinheads or nobody I know. You got a beer, Aunt Annie."

"How many of 'em?" Leroy asked, working to keep his voice steady.

"Four cars, maybe," said Bubba.

"Go ahead and unload them things," Leroy asked, jabbing a finger at the snowmobiles. "Then one of you go take a look." He paused. "May be phone people lookin' for their money."

"Don't look like any telephone people I ever seen." Bubba grinned. "Aunt Annie. Git me that beer and I'll go ask what they want."

"Tell 'em we ain't here," said Leroy. Shag was glaring toward the highway.

While Annie retrieved beer and Bubba unloaded snowmobiles, Leroy dug into the half-frozen dirt, trying to find the garbage sack with three hand grenades he'd buried last summer.

Katy huddled in the sleeper cab, teeth chattering and getting colder by the minute. Shag had bound her securely before letting her out to talk on the phone. While she'd managed to untie her feet, the tape that bound her wrists behind her back was impossible to loosen.

She recognized the voice of Shag. Also Leroy and Annie. There were others as well, but she doubted they could or would do anything to help.

Twice that morning she'd had to pass up chances to escape. When Leroy had first opened the hatch, she'd been too dehydrated and weak. Then, when she'd been on the phone, she'd been securely bound, and Leroy had maintained a firm grasp on her arm.

She had dared to believe she was about to be released when he'd overheard Shag saying they should cut her throat and leave her by the road. So now, even with all of the commotion outside, she was as ready to escape as she'd ever be.

Katy had strong legs, Her swimming coach said her endurance was incredible. Her legs would help get her free, and then she'd use them to run like the wind.

She sat with back braced on the wall opposite the hatch, feet resting on the closed hatch. When the next person cracked it open, she would kick out with all her might. *That* should give the person a proper headache. They might cut her throat, beat her, or rape her or force her to perform an obscenity, but there was something they could engrave on her tombstone right now:

"This one did not go willingly."

She heard Shag and Leroy talking, whispering in hoarse voices next to the cab so someone else couldn't hear.

"Assholes."

"Out at the highway. Not police."

"They're after the girl," she heard.

The terrorists? Katy felt a chill that was not caused by the cold.

She kept both feet poised on the hatch. Waiting for her chance. Praying she got it.

32

Special Agent George had wanted Link to fly close enough to Steamboat that he could call Gordon Tower on the WACS. Now they were there, but he showed no interest. On the takeoff roll he'd begun to fill his third barf bag of the day. He was working on his fourth.

"We should be within range," Link told Maggie.

She tried the phone. Got nothing. Tried again, and after a hiss of static, received the Steamboat base unit operator loud and clear. It was either all the way bad or all the way good.

Gordon came on, sounding tired. When she told him George had checked the trucker in Salt Lake City, he sounded puzzled. "George?"

"Your agent. The trucker started to give him a bad time, and I thought we'd have to pull him off. He's good at the bad cop stuff."

It was more like sick cop stuff. George had been in no mood to trifle with.

"How's the storm?" Gordon asked her.

"We shouldn't get the brunt of it until after we land at Montrose."

"We're still searching for the listening posts. Eighty percent done in Atlanta and seventy percent in Denver, and so far nothing. You wouldn't believe how paranoid these companies are. Using white noise so we can't listen, steel in the walls so we can't poke a pinhole through, that sort of thing."

"Gee," she said, "I wonder why?"

"We've got to find the LPs." Gordon released a weary sigh. "Sounds like you'd better sit out the weather in Montrose."

Maggie looked at her pilot and thought of snuggling. "We just may do that."

"Let me speak to my agent. Sounds like I should congratulate him."

"Sorry, but George is indisposed. Anyway, Lincoln wants to check in with Erin, then beat the worst of the storm to Montrose."

Maggie got through to Erin, and handed the phone over. Link spoke to his assistant using his customary few words. He was turning for Montrose when he handed the phone back.

"She wants to talk with you."

Erin said she was finishing her computer profile of Axel Nevas. "So far he appears to be a classic paranoid schizophrenic."

Maggie agreed. "That's my take on him except I'd replace classic with extreme. Delusions of greatness and absolutely no empathy for others. I'm pretty sure he's responsible for a lot of murders in the drug trade. Multiples so he can arrange them in geometric figures."

"I've looked that up. The only Aztec connection I get with the geometric dead folks are heiroglyphics showing one particular god." She spelled Huitzilopóchtli. "He was the worst of the lot. Loved war. Preferred the sacrifice of war captives, but here's the important part. He *really* loathed and feared his enemies. It was personal with him, a love-hate thing. And Axel tries to think like Huitzilopóchtli, and believes Link is his born enemy."

Maggie found herself nodding along. Then she stopped, knowing what was next.

"Since we killed Link off in Axel's mind, I propose we bring him back to life. That ought to warp his little Aztec mind, and the more we can preoccupy him while we're closing in on the LPs the better." She paused. "Agreed?"

Maggie looked over at the man she'd fallen so hard for. Her heart screamed, *Not him!* "Yeah," she said. "I agree."

She broke the connection, feeling glum. "Erin says they're resurrecting you."

Link nodded. "Gordon's going to make the announcement."

"Anything else from Erin?"

"She's gone over Katy's schedule before she left for Steamboat, and came up with only two times that she was without her bodyguards. Both were meetings of her ski group."

"That should narrow it down," Maggie said.

"Erin's looking at who attended, where the meetings were held, and so on."

They flew on in silence, trying to tune out Special Agent George's gross sounds.

Link tried to raise the Montrose airport, then switched to the alternate frequency shown in the pilot's "en route supplement" handbook. Neither worked.

They heard a Southwest Airlines pilot calling for Montrose. Then a United Express bird.

Link raised the Southwest pilot on the radio and was about to question him further when a voice boomed on the primary frequency.

"All aircraft trying to contact Montrose Airport be advised that we are below weather minimums and both runways are closed. I repeat, we are below weather minimums and both runways are closed. Do not attempt landing. We are experiencing radio difficulties."

That was all.

The Southwest pilot attempted to raise Montrose again, but was unable. Finally he said he was diverting to Colorado Springs.

"I thought you just said the weathers's not all that bad," said Maggie.

"Bad but not awful," said Link. "I've used instruments to land in a lot worse."

He had a map out, and was examining the symbols around Montrose.

"Ever meet a crusty guy named Tom DeBerre?" he asked.

"He was one of the old timers I met at Steamboat. He said he lived near Montrose."

"I knew him before he got out of the AIr Force. He bought some property here with an untended airstrip." He tapped a symbol on the map. "Here it is. DeBerre."

"And you're going to land there."

"Maybe." He dialed coordinates into the GPS and pressed an ENTER button. "We'll make a low pass and see if there's too much snow to land."

"You can't raise him on the radio?"

"It doesn't list one. It's only a small grass and dirt strip."

Special Agent George lowered the barf bag. He was pasty-faced and shaken.

"Gordon Tower said congratulations for the good work," Maggie told him.

He looked out with horror as Link began to descend into the weather, and pulled the bag back up to his mouth.

Black Canyon

Axel was taking his time driving in the poor visibility. The T-Can West contact had given him the approximate location of "Leroy's cabin" and he'd sent several vehicles full of men ahead to locate it while he prepared. Things were progressing, and he wanted no mistakes.

He could have taken any of the many rental vehicles offered by the agencies after they'd taken over the airport, but the dump truck from the airport maintenance garage—with the tailgate removed—seemed perfect for his needs.

The highway appeared spectral, for to either side were only swirls of snow and gray fog. He slowed when he came to a gathering of vehicles, and pulled off into a nondescript driveway that disappeared into haze and forest.

Twenty or so of his rabble milled about, staring at something in their midst, laughing and carrying their weapons in sloppy poses. When Axel crawled down from the dump truck, two of them dragged over a pudgy young man. A lightning bolt was tattooed around one side of his shaven head, a spider web on the other. Both eyes were swollen together and his mouth drooped. He had been so badly beaten that he was unable to walk.

"We were looking for the road here when he drove up on his snowmobile and asked what we were doing," said one of Axel's soldiers. "He likes to talk. Says there's people and the pink truck and the cabin up the road."

"Whose cabin."

The soldier brandished a heavy lug wrench, the business end already glistening with red. "Who owns the cabin, my man?" He thumped him squarely in the face with the wrench, making blood and spittle fly.

The prisoner moaned and sobbed. "Leroy Manners."

Leroy's cabin. Axel smiled.

"He says they got an old machine gun in there they're trying to fix."

"Do they know you're here?"

"Yeah. They know. He told them and then they sent him for another look."

"Did you ask about the Kitten-bitch?"

"He didn't see her."

All the while Axel stared down the lane into the fog.

He told his rabble what he wanted done with the captured skinhead. When they complied, Axel was surprised that the man could still scream so loudly.

He gathered them, and spoke over the constant shrieking of the prisoner. Preparing his army for battle! Asking if they had ammunition, which they did. Telling them what was expected. As he finished, some looked excited, others nervous.

Huitzilopóchtli would be proud.

The chosen seven—a most holy number for Huitzilopóchtli priests—climbed into the bed of the dump truck.

The others remained behind to kill anyone who tried to escape.

Leroy J. Manners had the hundred-round belt properly inserted when they heard the rumble of a heavy engine revving from the direction of the highway.

"They're comin'," yelled Shag, aiming his bolt-action rifle into the fog.

The bartender had been huddling in horror since they'd heard the first screams from the highway. Leroy telling her the sounds were likely coming from an animal being beaten to death to spook them.

"Move off the road," Leroy called, for Shag was in the middle of the lane.

"Fuckers want my money, they gotta go *over* me," he roared. Excited and grinning.

"Get outa the way so I can shoot 'em when they come."

"Gotta cock it," Annie advised. Looking at the machine gun with a critical eye.

Leroy pulled back on the charging lever, and released it. *Clunk*.

Shag looked back, then hastily moved out of his firing path.

The engine sounds grew more pronounced, until they saw the squat shape of a truck coming around the big bend, obscured by distance and snowfall.

"I ain't moving," Shag repeated, just before he took his first shot at the truck.

The same terrible squeal continued.

"Get the machine gun working!" Annie yelled.

There were two terrifically loud explosions as a pair of fifty-caliber rounds issued from the M-2. Then it jammed.

The truck materialized in more detail. Became a dump truck. Then became a Mack, and all gunfire ceased. Spread-eagle and staked across the grill was Annie's nephew. Naked, face puffed and bloody. Eyes swollen closed. Chest and belly slashed open and intestines trailing as he squealed at the top of his lungs.

"Jesus," Leroy muttered, firing his rifle until it emptied, then drawing the Python.

The truck kept coming, steadily and not slowing.

"Get out of the road!" Leroy yelled to Shag, who was shooting, walking forward, shooting again. He noticed the truck was close, turned to flee, and was run over.

The dump truck rocked to a halt. Human forms were dropping from the back. *Bra-a-a-at. Ch-ch-ch-ch-ch! Bra-aa-aat!*

Leroy fired the Colt Python four more times, clicked on an empty and threw it aside.

But even in all the excitement Leroy did not forget about the kid and the two million dollars. He ran for Annie's truck, and pulled the door open.

"I'm going to get you out of there," he yelled to the kid, meaning for her to get ready, not realizing he had just increased her fright level even more. He opened the hatch, leaned close and started to swing it back.

The metal door slammed into his face with such fury and force that for a split second Leroy J. Manners' entire body was airborne. His head twisted and smacked into the metal CB unit so hard the radio was ripped from its mount.

He dropped soundlessly. Unmindful when a slight form slithered over him.

Axel did not join the shooting. Two of his rabble had been picked off as they'd run around the side of the truck. The remaining five fired wildly, spewing 9 millimeter and 7.65 millimeter rounds into the cabin, the truck, and the trees.

Bra-aa-aa-aa-at. Ch-ch-ch-ch-ch-ch.

"Don't let anyone get away," Axel yelled angrily.

New movement caught his eye, a snowmobile speeding toward the safety of the forest. The figure was slight—similar in size to the Katy-bitch.

"Shoot her," he cried, pointing, and weapons blasted and roared. The small figure crouched low, disappeared into the gloomy fog, and the receding guttural roar of the engine mocked him.

Had it been her? Would kidnappers, even those with as little intelligence as these, allow her near a snowmobile?

Ch-ch-ch-ch. Braa-aa-aa-aat. Ch-ch-ch.

The skinhead he had run over was vomiting a rush of blood, trying to crawl away.

"Wait!" Axel yelled, but one of his rabble pressed a silenced Skorpion to the man's head. *Ch-ch-ch-ch.*

"Check the truck," Axel called out, pointing to the rig. "Find the Kitten-bitch!"

Someone yanked open a door. "We got a live one." It took three of them to drag a mountain-sized man from the pink tractor's cab, and drop him onto the ground. He was huge, and since there were no apparent wounds, Axel wondered why he wasn't fighting or running. Instead he remained on all fours, now and then jerking his head to one side in a small spasm.

One of his soldiers dragged a fleshy woman from the cabin. She was wounded and bloody, wore a dirty pink shirt and pink jeans, and her face was swollen.

Axel went to her. "Where's the girl?" he asked. "Katy?"

She began with a shrewd look, like she wanted to bargain. Then grew wide-eyed as she saw the big man on all fours. "Leroy?" The woman tried to go to him, and when they restrained her, she began to cry.

Axel pulled the small pistol from his belt and walked over. Placed the muzzle against the back of the man's head.

"Please," crooned the woman.

"Where's the girl?" he asked.

"In the sleeper cab."

"Check it," Axel said, motioning with the pistol.

One of the men who had mounted the skinhead on the dump truck went to look. He complained about the awful smell, then said, "She's not there."

A string of barely audible curses issued from the man on all fours.

"Leroy," Axel said conversationally. "I'm about to kill you."

"You cain't." The voice was a low croak. "The kid already done it."

Axel started to smile, but noticed that the man's head hung at an odd angle. Leroy gave a final lurch, released a low sigh, and his bowels and bladder loosened as he leaned forward onto the ground. In repose, the broken neck was obvious.

"She kilt him!" the woman in pink screamed. "That no-good rich bitch kilt him."

Axel put the gun to her head and popped her. As she fell and convulsed, he walked away, wondering how the girl had managed to escape—again.

On the snowmobile? He had brought a detailed area map—and unfolded it onto the back of the pink semi. After a moment he answered one of the cell phones.

"Axel."

T-Can West: "There's something very odd. I've checked it three times now to be sure."

"Go on." Axel was irritated enough with events.

"One of the body bags at Steamboat is empty."

Axel drew in a harsh breath. Waited for him to go on.

"The FBI's acting like Anderson isn't dead. The airport operator at Steamboat swears he took off in one of their airplanes this morning."

Axel very slowly looked around in the obscuring fog and snow. Anderson was indeed mystical, just as his Indian name implied. A foe worthy of the great Huitzilopóchtli, and of his servant.

A lesser man might even fear Anderson.

"It's got to be a mistake, Axel. I shouldn't even have bothered you with it."

It was no mistake. Axel had felt it before, and now. His great enemy was alive again.

"The Voice called," continued the contact. "Do you have the girl?"

"No, but she was here." Axel steadied his voice. "We'll stay until we find her. Do your part. Turn off all their communications here. I do not want a whisper getting out. Not over radios, telephones, or anything else."

Axel put the cell phone away and attached a radio microphone to his jacket lapel.

One of the distributors was waiting for his call.

"Close it down," Axel said. Meaning the city of Montrose, Colorado. How he wished that Anderson was here so he could congratulate and face and kill him. Honor him with death.

He did not realize that his facial features had become mobile and were constantly changing, switching between serenity and fear and peace and rage as if a toggle switch were being levered back and forth.

Only slowly did the condition pass.

33

Link touched down, and braked gingerly. At the end of the run, he swung the bird around and taxied back toward the heavy Ford pickup and the lone figure beside it. On his second try, Link had pulled up because he'd seen him in another vehicle making a high-speed pass down the runway, smoothing the snow with a blade attachment.

He had landed on his third approach.

Link parked and shut down the engine. In back, Special Agent George literally threw open his door and fell out. Making happy sounds to show how grateful he was to be on the ground.

Old Tom DeBerre watched George with a curious expression, then, as Link and Maggie climbed out, looked up. "Storm's just about here," he muttered. "You got baggage?"

"Yes, sir."

"Put 'em in the pickup. You won't be going anywhere till this storm leaves us, and that'll be a couple days. We'll put your things in the house."

"We don't mean to impose."

"No child of Lucky Anderson or Turk Tatro is imposing when they stay here. Now hurry before we all freeze."

"Yes!" cried Special Agent George. "Thank you."

Tom DeBerre, retired lieutenant colonel of the United States Air Force, eyed George like he might be from another planet. "I've known them since they were pups. Who are *you*?"

"I'm a federal agent. FBI. I need to rent a vehicle."

"I'm not in the business," DeBerre snapped, and the subject was closed. He took a bag from Link and swung it into the pickup's bed.

Link remembered more about Tom DeBerre. He had not been a pilot, but a backseater in F-4 Phantoms who had flown a good deal of combat and gained a reputation for being capable. He'd also been known as one of the crotchetiest men in the service.

"Would you mind if I borrowed your pickup?" Link asked, hauling more bags.

"Might as well. I won't be using it," said DeBerre.

"What if I loaned it to George?"

"Up to you. I also got that old white CJ-5 Jeep you saw with a snowplow if you want to go your own way, which after viewing his behavior I would suggest."

DeBerre took Maggie and George to the house while Link put the airplane to bed. Chocking the wheels and tying it down. Taking a canvas cover from in back and strapping it in place over the engine. When DeBerre returned, sans passengers and luggage, Link crawled in, but the old airman just stared and let the engine idle. "Before we head in," he said, "would you mind tellin' me what the Sam Hell's goin' on."

Black Canyon

Katy Dubois had not been on the snowmobile. Following the mightiest kick of her life, she'd slithered headfirst over Leroy—hands still taped behind her—and stared in awe at Axel Nevas's oncoming army. Men had screamed, bullets had twanged, and there'd seemed nowhere to go.

She'd considered running, but knew she would not make it for ten feet. Instead she'd crawled under the tractor and huddled as bullets pinged through the metal and created eruptions in the snow.

Then she'd looked up at the undercarriage and pulled in a breath of salvation. Inches above her head was a steel-encased well, large enough to contain not one but two truck tires—presently unoccupied since Annie did not carry a spare.

There had been no hesitation. Katy had raised up and awkwardly wedged herself into the meager space, drawn in her legs and pressed herself against the rear of the well, and then remained still, starting now and then as a bullet skittered beneath or punctured the metal. There were a few bullets holes at the very back, but she doubted she could be seen.

She'd waited as the shooting slowed to an occasional boom, then heard the sound of the snowmobile racing away followed by another cacophony of gunfire. She remained perfectly still then as the world outside became quieter, waiting with bated breath for one of them to crawl underneath to inspect. Heard Annie's voice crying about someone being "kilt."

Then there was the deep voice that she recalled so vividly, and she'd been returned to the world she'd tried to escape at Steamboat. Axel was following her, still wanted her dead.

She smelled smoke, and then more, until she was certain they were burning the cabin.

Axel, said to not leave anything behind that could be driven. More gunfire then. Long bursts of it mixed with laughter. The tractor where she hid lurched and shuddered as it was riddled even more. She waited for a bullet to penetrate her lair, but as the shooting died down she remained unharmed. Then another peril, for diesel ran freely onto the snow where the fuel tank had been pierced.

And all the while, she kept hearing over and over, the deep voice exhorting them all to keep looking for the Kittenbitch. Katy knew who they meant. She waited, praying no one would ignite the fuel that saturated the snow. Also hoping no one would crawl under the rig.

"Ten miles from here to Montrose." Axel's distinctive voice. "That's where she's going on the snowmobile."

Another conversed with Axel. They spoke about cutting off the town. Roadblocks. No TV or radio. No telephones. No flights. Twenty of their people already inside the police station. They'd encountered five officers, cut them off, and were waiting them out.

"That's all good," Axel kept repeating. "But we've still got to find the Kitten-bitch. And Anderson. Look for Anderson. He is more than a human. He can disappear like a ghost."

Axel was ranting and babbling. Katy shifted enough to look out a jagged group of bullet holes. He appeared obsessed. Eyes blazing. Tall and angular, with a thin and cruel nose.

"Everyone take one more look around," shouted Axel in his deep tone.

Behind him the cabin was ablaze. When the flames reached the puddle of diesel Katy would either be forced from her hiding place, or burn.

She prayed they would soon leave, for the fire was getting closer.

Tom DeBerre's

Old Tom tried to phone the airport to tell them the Piper had landed. He pressed the button a few times. "No dial tone. Probably the storm."

"Mind if I borrow that pickup?" asked Special Agent George. "I'd like to check the woman's truck before the weather gets worse."

DeBerre gave him a frown that confirmed his determination that he was a fool, and handed the key to Link. "Pump the gas twice before you start up when it's cold."

Link passed the key to George. "Pump the gas twice. Do you have her address?"

The agent read from a notepad. "Twelve miles east of Montrose on Highway 50."

DeBerre humphed. "Black Canyon. Tell him that's government land. Anyone lives there is squatters."

"Yeah," said Special Agent George. "Tell him I already know all that."

Tom DeBerre gave directions to the destination. "While he's there, tell him to shoot a guy named Leroy Manners and do us all a favor. Damned government agents gotta be good for something more than stealing our money."

Link felt there was a misunderstanding. "George isn't IRS. He's with the FBI."

DeBerre turned and peered. "It's hard to imagine."

"I'm looking for a woman trucker named Annie Hartinger. Know her?"

"She and Leroy live together."

Link regarded the agent. "Maybe I'd better go along."

"I don't like little airplanes, but I can handle a questioning and a truck inspection." He bundled up until only his nose was showing, and departed.

Link pulled his own coat back on. "Tom. If you don't mind I'd like to drive over to the airport and make sure they know we're down."

"I'd like to come," Maggie immediately told him.

Tom DeBerre motioned. "Jeep's in the barn. Take it easy in this stuff. No speed records." He settled on the couch to watch television, muttering about the storm. After repeatedly switching the remote control and getting only static and test patterns, he threw up his hands. "Can you believe that? Telephone's out, and the television station's on the blink."

"We'll go now," Link said.

"Yeah. By the way, it's awfully good having you pups here."

Link had opened the door and started out, when he turned back. "The place where George's going. What's it like?"

"Black Canyon's nice, which is why they made it a state park. Makes it all the more of a shame for Leroy and his woman to squat there."

"Trees?"

"Sure. Rugged, low hills, a few mesas, and some spruce and pines."

The description matched Link's mental image. "Thanks," he said.

"Hold up a minute. TV's coming on."

An image of a news studio and a grim-faced, heavily madeup woman.

"Never noticed her before," said Tom DeBerre.

She began immediately. Talking in monotone: "Montrose area residents are advised that the storm is intense, and expected to worsen. Telephone service is interrupted, and repairs are estimated to take several hours. All local schools are closed as of this time, and no buses will be allowed to run due to icing conditions. Students will be provided emergency shelter, and parents should not attempt to pick them up. Until further notice, all routes from the city are closed. The Colorado State Highway Patrol has issued warnings and recommendations to delay all travel."

The newscaster stared solemnly at the camera. "Finally, law enforcement officers will be visiting as many residences as possible to assist in emergencies. Please cooperate."

A popular soap came onto the screen.

Tom DeBerre had gotten up and was peering outside. "Doesn't seem that bad," he said. "I'm on a plateau here, and I usually get the worst of the weather first."

"They'll have a better report at the airport," Link said.

"I'll be interested," said DeBerre.

Link went out, and Maggie followed. "When we're done at the airport, I want to take a look at Black Canyon."

"Where George is headed?"

"Yeah. Just a feeling that won't go away."

The aging Jeep, with its raised snowplow blade, roll bar, and canvas top, started easily. After a period of warm-up, Link eased forward, then got out and closed the doors behind them.

Maggie switched on the radio as they drove through the yard and out the gate. The announcements were much as they'd heard from the television newscaster, and in fact sounded as if they were being read by the same person.

"It seems almost unreal," Maggie said as they started down the side of the plateau.

Montrose was at the bottom of the incline. The municipal airport was north on Highway 50, which was the main drag.

Snow had begun to fall in such big obscuring flakes that Maggie had to point out the airport turnoff sign. "Turn now," she said, and Link did so out of faith alone, for his vision was reduced to a few feet. They crept along slowly, not wanting to ram another vehicle, windshield wipers working busily to clear the accumulating snow.

"Now I understand what the newscaster meant about it being a bad storm," said Maggie.

"Her announcements were premature," Link said.

"You're just jumpy after what happened in Steamboat."

"Maybe." He barely saw the red road cones and the airport policeman in time to stop. The cones were strung across the roadway, and the man in uniform held out a restraining hand.

"Airport's closed," he said when Link rolled down his window.

"I'd like to go in and check the meteorology."

The man frowned as if he didn't understand.

"A weather forecast? I'm a pilot."

"Just a minute." The airport cop stepped away, speaking into a collar microphone.

Maggie whispered, "Something's not right."

Link put the manual transmission into reverse.

There was a wild gust of wind, and for a moment the visibility cleared just enough to see the nearest parked airplanes. Two orange helicopters without markings. A man there, looking toward the policeman and talking into his own lapel.

"That's all right, Officer," Link said, and began to accelerate in reverse.

"Hey, wait up!" By then the guard had become indistinct in the blowing snow.

Link swung the wheel, and slid around in a 180. Threw the Jeep into first gear, and accelerated toward the highway.

Maggie was crouched in her seat, making herself smaller than she was. "Know what I noticed? Airport cops don't carry Czech-built Skorpions with built-in silencers."

"And airport cops know what meteorology means. And he was talking with a guy standing just fifty feet away next to two helicopters. Different colors, but the same Bell 212 model they used at Steamboat. *And* they had no markings, which is illegal."

He slowed down some as he turned south, now headed back toward the city of Montrose.

She was silent for a while as he drove. Then drew a breath and said, "How's this? Katy was brought here in the woman's truck. Someone made the ransom call Gordon told us about, and one of Axel's listening post's took it. Now the terrorists are here looking for her."

"That's a lot of ifs and conjecture."

"True."

"I can't think of anything better," he said.

"And *now* I'm concerned about what we heard on television and the radio. If they're stopping help from getting in, and Katy from getting out." She looked at him.

He wished he had left her at Tom DeBerre's.

"We'd better warn the police, then check out Black Canyon," Maggie said.

They continued ahead until they saw an arrow and sign announcing the police station. It was to their left, on the Gunnison Highway. US 50, labeled the loneliest road in America, also went past Black Canyon.

He saw the reflection of flashing blue and red lights at the intersection, and slowed down.

A police cruiser was pulled crosswise to form a roadblock. Link braked behind two other vehicles. Uniformed policemen were going through the first car.

"We don't have to go looking," Maggie said. "The police found us."

"Maybe," said Link. He rolled down the window just a

few inches as a man approached. He was in police uniform, but the shirt fit poorly and he sported a pair of gold rings in his left nostril. He was grinning, holding a Skorpion machine pistol.

They felt a nudge as a pickup's bumper made contact from the rear.

They were tightly sandwiched, front and back.

"Got anybody in there, my man?" The faux cop was peering in.

"Just the two of us," Link said, keeping his voice light. Friendly.

"Seen a blond bitch? Sixteen? Little mole on her cheek?"

Link was staring beyond him, at the half-obscured face of a comically articulated stick man. The stick man came closer, his gaze intense, his visage transforming from a frown into a beaming smile.

Axel Nevas stepped up beside the opened window and Link felt no surprise when a small pistol was thrust through the window and pressed to the side of his head. The bladed-nosed man spoke in a rumble. "Welcome to Montrose, Mr. Anderson. Or is it Ghost of Black Wolf? You wouldn't believe how pleased I am to meet you again."

34

Axel held the pistol firmly to the side of Link's head. "Where is Katherine Dubois?"

"Have you tried calling her at home?"

"Intelligent people do not make light of serious questions."

"I'm serious. The last time I saw her was in Manhattan."

Axel regarded Maggie, "I see the woman with the grand tetons is with you. It appears that both of you survived."

"*What* did you call me?" Maggie said, voice sharp.

Axel ignored her outburst. He cocked his head shrewdly. "You fooled the FBI, Mr. Ghost of Black Wolf. But of course I too am a high priest and know how such things are done."

In the past days, Axel had changed. When Link had viewed him across the deadly street in Steamboat he had seemed sure of himself. In the video, only a single day later, he had appeared troubled. Now it was as if he displayed every slightest inner emotion on a countenance that rippled through the spectrum of human passions.

He had called him Ghost of Black Wolf. Link had all but forgotten the Blackfoot name of his birth—honoring a distant ancestor.—which had been discarded by age four. Had Erin's games with Link's resurrection driven Axel over the brink? He tried to think of a way to put it to use—to do anything possible to save Maggie.

Axel spoke in his gravel tone. "Let me repose my question, Mr. Anderson. You know Katy well. Once again, this time with the life of the lady beside you at stake, where would she have gone? To meet you?"

"Possibly," Link said, trying to buy time. Looking for vulnerability.

He tried a new twist. "Let the women live, and I will share my secret of life." Using a mysterious tone.

Axel froze into place, like a statue of stone, yet his face continued to reflect the gamut of emotions and turmoil. A long moment passed before he returned to life and gave a nudge of the gun barrel. "Get out," he said. "Both of you."

They had only seconds to live.

Think! Link badgered himself. In the periphery of his vision he noted that before them there was now only a single light Toyota pickup. The first vehicle had been driven away.

Which was precisely when Maggie looked forward, widened her eyes, and gasped.

The instant Axel's eyes flickered toward the front of the Jeep, Link jammed the accelerator full down, at the same time twisting his head to the left.

Capturing the terrorist's gun hand.

Bam! The sound was loud in the enclosure—regardless that it was small-bore. The muzzle blast emitted a shower of gritty niter, but as the Jeep leapt forward and Axel's forearm was drawn with it, another firing was unlikely.

They slammed into the small pickup, catching it with the raised snowplow, shoving it along before themselves. Also dragging Axel, who shrieked as his elbow was twisted in the unnatural direction. The pistol dropped behind Link's back. The elbow snapped with the sound of a broken twig and the arm bent almost double as Axel was dragged for ten, fifteen, and twenty feet before sufficient bones were crushed and sinews and muscles torn that his arm—undulating as if made of gelatin—flopped free.

The pickup was shoved off to their right, and they crashed into the patrol car, which spun crazily as they pushed on through.

A look in the side mirror showed Axel falling to the snow-covered pavement, mouth open in a scream that Link could not hear. A glance at the other side showed another gunman, dropped into a crouch and aiming his Skorpion. Three rounds bored through the plastic back window, scoring a triangle of hits squarely in the middle of the Jeep's windshield.

Link took a hard left at the intersection, felt the Jeep skittering, and prayed it would not lose traction. To do so meant rolling over, which they could ill afford. The vehicle fishtailed and the tires dug for purchase, and after a precarious tilt, caught. They corrected, and were speeding eastward on Highway 50.

They were going too fast for the available visibility, but he dared not slow. After a long two minutes the snow diminished in another rare lull, and again in the dim distance there were reflections of blue-red flashing strobes.

Another roadblock! Link turned off, made a series of random right and left turns, and slowed down. And almost plowed into a 4-Runner and Suburban, both with engines idling and doors open. As he spun the steering wheel and they went around them, he took in three toughs gathered on either side of the street. Brandishing weapons—he saw Skorpians and shotguns—in threatening manners. On one side they had a family out in the snow, bullying them. On the other an hysterical woman was screaming, and a much younger blond girl lay facedown in snow that blossomed crimson. Too young to be Katy, he saw.

Link accelerated past, and after a block almost ran into another four-wheeler. Two of the second group wore uniforms, but as before it was easy to tell they were not real police.

They passed into the gloom too quickly for the terrorists to react.

They had just witnessed two door-to-door searches. Looking for Katy. The girl likely slain because she'd had the misfortune of being young and blond.

Link made another random turn, stopped, and backed

into an empty driveway. He killed the engine. They stared ahead, mouths drooping.

"They're here."

"Oh *God*, are they here," she said in a strained voice. "And Axel's gone over the edge."

"Thanks for the diversion back there."

They were still as a four-wheeler passed, going fast.

He patted her shoulder, and she took his hand. Squeezed it. Like they were a pretty darn good team.

"I still want a look around Black Canyon."

"The newscaster said all major routes out of town are shut off."

"I think the television announcer's one of them. Or maybe it was a tape they ran."

"It's even bigger than Steamboat, Link. And no one outside has a clue it's happening. We've got to get the word out."

He reached into his shirt pocket and pulled out the flip-top phone.

"They'll overhear you and shut you off."

"Yeah, but that'll take them a few seconds. I just need to get Erin's attention. Blurt out something like, Montrose was taken by terrorists. What's that take, two or three seconds?"

"It's worth a try."

Link switched the sat phone on, then pressed MEM and then 1.

The response was a hissing sound. He tried again, with the same result.

He huffed a dismal sigh. "The entire system's down."

"We're cut off from the world like everyone else."

He tried the engine. It started easily. It was unlikely they'd damaged anything critical.

"So what's the plan?" Maggie asked.

"If the snow's not too deep, we'll go around their road-block and take a look at Black Canyon."

They paralleled the highway, using back roads and crossing fields and hillocks where necessary, and once discovered themselves approaching a sheer drop-off.

The good news was they could see the strobe lights of the roadblock on the highway, half a mile back. The bad news was that Link drove straight forward and down the embankment, and Maggie couldn't suppress a frightened squeal.

"Tell me when you're going to do that," she said as they slid the final few feet.

"I thought you'd try to talk me out of it."

"Darn right. Sometimes you need guidance, Lincoln."

They returned to the highway, crawled onto the shoulder, and the snow immediately began dropping in tremendous flakes.

"We're past them," she said, leaning forward to peer past the furiously working wipers. He drove ever slower as drifts of several inches became commonplace. It was wet snow that clung to everything, including signs and distance markers.

They came to a turnoff, the road to their left barely visible, and Link slowed even more.

"This isn't the right driveway," Maggie observed. "We've only come six miles."

He pulled over, stopped, and climbed out. "I'm looking for the alternate way back to Montrose DeBerre mentioned."

"He called it Preston Road," she said from the Jeep.

"Yea," Link knocked snow from the street sign. "This is it."

"The cabin's still four miles from here," Maggie said.

He started for the Jeep.

And almost didn't hear the sound of a hesitant voice.

"Link?"

He stopped and looked back.

"Link!" A vague shape rose from the side of the road, and slowly came forth.

"Katy?" He hardly dared to believe his eyes, but the slight shape kept coming toward him, stumbling and beginning to sob.

35

Katy appeared both physically and mentally exhausted. She would not respond to his questions, just sobbed and stayed close. There had been too much for too long.

Her arms had been taped behind her back at both elbow and wrist. Link used his pocketknife to free her, then held her for a while, standing on the lonely highway, letting her cry and hoping she could get at least a portion of the emotion out of her system.

Maggie was first to hear engine sounds from the direction of town. "Someone's coming."

Link hefted Katy and hurried to the open door. When he deposited her on the backseat and Maggie slid in beside her, Katy looked out with wide-eyed trepidation. He hurried around, threw the Jeep into gear, and drove onto the side road.

It was a close encounter, for a Suburban immediately rushed past the intersection.

"Did they see us?" Maggie asked from the back.

"I don't believe so. How is she?"

Maggie's voice turned soft. "Battered and very frightened."

Link's mind spun with problems and possibilities. Two things were paramount. They had to get word out about the terrorists, and take Katy to safety. The highway just behind them went on to Gunnison. If the vehicle they'd just seen held no terrorists, it would be an option.

Too big an if. He mentally eliminated the highway as an escape route, for it might also be closed due to the storm.

From the back he heard: "You're going to be safe, honey."

Protective instincts mushed around inside Abraham Lincoln Anderson as he continued on Preston Road toward the dangerous city.

"Where are we going?" Maggie asked.

"Back to Tom DeBerre's," said Link

"Through the city again?"

"I don't know of any safe places, and I want to get to the airplane."

"You can fly in this terrible weather?"

"No, but it's equipped with a VHF radio, and we can call airliners."

"I heard them talking," Katy said. Regaining her voice. "They said they were going to close down the town."

"Welcome back," Maggie said.

"I knew you'd come for me."

Link drove slowly as Katy described her time in hell. She spoke haltingly at first, then faster, as if a dam were bursting.

"Did they hurt you?" Maggie asked quietly.

"Yeah. But I hurt one of them too."

Link told them to help look for reflections of strobe lights.

"You'd think they'd turn off all those lights," Katy said.

"Maybe they don't want anyone running over them," said Link.

Maggie added, "We aren't dealing with intellectuals."

"I don't know. Axel seems smart," Katy said. "Every time I turn around, he's back. This time I saw his face."

"So did we." Maggie described the incident at the roadblock.

"You did that to Axel?" Katy asked, grinning gleefully.

Link started to respond, then muttered, "Damn!" and pulled over. The familiar glow of roadblock lights was directly ahead.

"How far?" Maggie asked, keeping her voice low.

"Hard to tell. A hundred yards?"

A semi went by, not speeding, but not moving slowly either. They heard the blast of an air horn and the squeal of brakes. A moment later an angry voice sounded, asking what the hell they were doing.

Link used the diversion to drive off the road and into a field populated with scrub brush and growing snowdrifts. Using four-wheel low range, and going slow. They were well past the roadblock and headed back for the highway when they heard shotgun blasts. He felt a stab of regret, regardless that he'd not had time to wave the rig down.

Back on the roadway he continued to drive slowly, lest they encounter more unfriendlies.

The town seemed deserted. "We've got to be careful," Link told them.

"I've been holding my breath for the past five minutes," Katy said.

3:25 P.M.—Montrose Hospital

The terrified doctor's hand trembled. He dropped the developed X-ray film, hastily retrieved it and clipped it onto the back-lit viewing glass.

"It's bad," the doctor muttered, sweat formed in beads on his forehead.

Axel understood the usefulness of cruelty to instill obedience. When a medical technician had dawdled at the entrance to the emergency room, one of the rabble army had beaten her senseless. Another had found a doctor trying to get away, and kicked him until he'd howled for mercy. This one had come willingly.

"It's very badly broken," said the doctor in a near whisper, wiping a trickle of perspiration from his nose. "I count two dozen fractures. We'd have to cut to get to them." He was pointing at the X-ray.

Axel did not endure pain well, and had shrieked and cried during the drive from the roadblock. He knew he was in shock for he had vomited all the way and his head grew so giddy that he'd felt himself slipping toward unconsciousness. Yet he'd had the presence to demand only enough morphine to eliminate the worst of the searing pain and still be able to think clearly.

Observation: From the elbow down the arm was puffed and blue, the hand swollen three times its normal size, fingers looking like fat blood sausages.

He had been considering his next move. Avoiding the obvious, to call the Voice and tell her he was incapacitated. That the Kitten-bitch still lived and the listening posts and his half-billion dollar network were in jeopardy.

The Voice, who the distributors feared. Marta Fuentes, a vapid robot who had only to react to the information Axel's listening posts provided. All-knowing only because his people presented her with the secrets of their enemies. A minor player in the game.

But Amado, her brother, was truly sprung from the fount of greatness. An Aztec warrior-king who had listened to his priest and wrested power and control of all North America. Then he had "died." Gone into seclusion in a massive home in Florida, and begun his real transformation by losing thirty pounds the old-fashioned way, through diet and exercise.

Three years ago he had quite logically believed that nothing could get in his way. Then the DEA and FBI had lured scores of the Mexican bankers and investors in his money-laundering group—the backbone of the Mexican financial world—to a celebration at the Casablanca Club in Las Vegas where they had arrested one hundred fifty-seven of them and indicted an even larger number.

The dead man had been stunned. *Why hadn't he been warned?*

Answer: Operation Casablanca had been planned in the US without telling the Mexicans for fear of a leak that might endanger American agents. They'd known not to trust their southern counterparts, who were under Amado's influence and control.

The President of the United States had called the President of Mexico, apologized for violating the sovereignty of such a wonderful neighbor, and promised it would not happen again.

Yet Amado had seethed. In Mexico no one had moved without his knowledge. Every telephone and radio conversation were monitored by the Agencia, and all was available to Amado. He had decided that he must have the same capability in the United States.

Axel had set up the listening posts, planted modules in telephone and radio facilities in target cities across the continent. With a virtually limitless budget, he had purchased more modules from the Seidl factory than any European country, his orders so huge that the company had to expand its facilities.

The move into North America was so effective that the dead man again, and with reason, felt invulnerable. He'd toyed with extending his business worldwide, and met with the man who would be instrumental in making it happen.

An important man, who would be even more important. A politician who had slept many nights in the Lincoln Bedroom, and dined with the British Prime Minister.

And at the meeting, Amado, who had still possessed that highly distinctive feature, had come *nose to nose* with Katy Dubois.

Even shrouded by the numbing morphine, Axel periodically shuddered. It was time to tell the Voice that the listening posts might be compromised.

Yet he continued to hesitate.

Time to call. He stared down at his useless arm for another few seconds, then with his left reached about and picked out the second cell phone on his belt.

When he had punched in the numbers he sat a little straighter, feeling a new tingling of pain. The Voice answered.

"Axel," he said, squinting at the doctor and trying to focus.

"Did you finish the job?" The Voice sounded pleased to hear from him. Since their arrival in Montrose, all communications had been through the T-Can listening posts.

Axel started to tell her, but stopped himself. "We're closer," was all he said.

"Call when she is dead." Her voice was curt. The connection was broken.

Axel regarded the mangled arm.

"I want you to remove it," he told the physician, and immediately knew it was the proper decision. While he did best with the right hand, he was not awkward with his left. He would get by. And rather than suffering for weeks, it would be over with quickly.

Before the doctor could respond, Axel motioned at a distributor—Luis Gomez—who had gone through the Steamboat war. "You are in charge until they awaken me. Stay at my side and watch him. If he makes a mistake, kill him and bring in another surgeon."

Axel regarded the doctor. "As soon as it's done, I must be awakened. I want the arm to be gone, and the pain as well. I have much to do."

"We can't guarantee . . ." the doctor started, then he looked at the irrational fervor in the penetrating eyes and sprang to work, telling nurses to prepare an operating room.

Axel pondered: *How did Anderson and the woman get here?* The answer was, of course, that they'd flown. Anderson knew magic, but he could also fly an airplane. So where had they landed, with the airport closed? He spoke to Gomez. "Send a few of our best people to visit all of the small airfields, and tell them to destroy every airplane they find."

There! They could not get away.

Axel next called the T-Can West listening post. They

were to monitor local aircraft radio frequencies for Lincoln Anderson's voiceprint.

As the nurses prepared the gurney to be taken into the operating room, he took a radio call. They'd captured an FBI agent. His first name was George, his second name unpronounceable. Axel ordered them to hold him. When he emerged, an offering would be appropriate. With that in mind he made his last transmission.

If anyone were to locate Anderson or the woman, hold them too. What an offering that would be! As they moved him into the operating room, Axel thought how killing such an honored enemy would be like experiencing the fragile taste of a fine vintage wine.

3:37 P.M.

There'd been only the one roadblock. Now they were on the west side of the small city, the Jeep having no problem negotiating the road up the side of the plateau, despite the snow.

Katy was increasingly talkative. "I've been trying to think why they want to kill me."

She had their attention.

"My friend Julie Cordellons was my vice president in the ski club, but she didn't come to the last meeting. Her mother said she'd had to return to Mexico, but she sounded odd and sad. I think something's wrong. We should look for Julie." She took a breath. "I hope she's okay."

"Then you think this is about Julie?" Maggie asked.

"I don't know. It's the only strange happening I've been able to come up with."

"Consider this?" Maggie tried. "Everyone involved with the terrorists is in the drug trade. The ones in Steamboat were, and I'd bet my purse the ones here are too."

Katy shrugged. "I have a few friends that tried pot, and an *ex*-friend who sniffed methamphetamine. But I didn't do any of it. I've got better things planned for my future."

"How about your friend Julie?"

"She was like me. We stayed away from kids who used drugs."

"Let's go back. What happened the last time you saw Julie?"

"We had our Sno-Bunny meeting at Sharon's house to discuss the ski trip. That was all. Nothing out of the ordinary."

"How about before the meeting?"

"We were running late so I picked up Julie, and we . . ." Katy stopped.

"What?"

Katy spoke more slowly. "We were hurrying out and took the back entrance. That's where we saw Julie's father and another man."

"Julie's father?" Maggie asked.

"Ambassador Cordellons. Mexico's UN representative."

Maggie bubbled with excitement. "Also the odds-on favorite to be the next secretary general. Who was the other man?"

"It's hard to remember. It was just for an instant."

"Was he dark or light?"

Katy held her eyes almost closed, thinking hard.

At the top of the plateau, Link turned into Tom DeBerre's driveway.

They slid to a halt and he ambled out to greet them. As the women climbed from the Jeep, the retired lieutenant colonel took in the badly battered snowplow.

"Somebody get in your way?"

"As a matter of fact. Has Special Agent George shown up?"

"Nope. Phones are out, TV's wacky, and I heard shooting from town. Earlier you said you're here to check out a woman trucker but there's got to be more. What the hell's going on?"

"Climb in and I'll try to explain while we drive out to the airplane.

"Mind if Katy and I raid your kitchen?" Maggie asked. "She's starved."

"Go right ahead." DeBerre sniffed and gave Katy a look. "Might want to borrow the shower and a scrub brush too."

"Wonderful!" Katy announced.

As they departed, Tom DeBerre eyed Link. "That the girl they've been showin' on TV?"

"Yes, and a lot of people are trying to do her harm." On the drive to the airstrip, Link gave old Tom a condensed version of events.

"Be damned," DeBerre said a few times. When Link explained how the FBI were in charge he grumbled, "And all they sent us was that sorry George?"

The airplane was sheathed in a layer of ice that Link laboriously chipped away at. As soon as he could open the pilot's door, he slid in, switched on the battery and the VHF radio, and dialed in an en route frequency. Without waiting, he called: "This is an emergency radio transmission from Montrose, Colorado. We have a terrorist attack in prog . . ."

A booming voice came over the speaker. "This is Montrose ground control. That was a test. Disregard the last transmission."

Other loud calls, "American Seven-Nine reports light turbulence at flight level . . ."

"US Air Eight Six Zero requests to deviate from filed flight plan, and climb . . ."

"Southwest five-one-eight is at ten miles, inbound from the . . ."

"Recordings," Link said in disgust as more conversations joined in, effectively jamming the frequency. He switched to 121.5, the radio setting reserved for emergency use.

"You *know* they'll be waiting on that one," said DeBerre. "And something else. If they were that quick, they were waitin' and probably using an RDF on your transmission."

The newest radio direction finders were fast and accurate. The intersection of lines drawn from any two RDFs at different locations would show their position.

DeBerre was looking through the falling snow in the direction of Montrose and the newest sounds of distant gunfire. "They'll be on the way. Think you can fly out of here?"

"It would be a challenge," Link said honestly. Visibility was intermittently poor, and the icing conditions remained extremely hazardous.

"There's no back doors on this plateau, so the only alternative would be to hold them off. I've got a couple deer rifles, but nothing fancy."

"*They've* got automatic weapons, and there are a lot of them. Katy says they wiped out Leroy's bunch in less than a minute."

"Then start deicing this thing and get it ready to fly. I'll go after the ladies."

3:52 P.M.

Oscar and another dealer from South L.A. shared the seats of a GMC Yukon, leaving the driving to one of the few women. She was unkempt, and smelled as bad as the men.

They had been sent out to locate all the small airfields and . . .

Oscar took a radio call from Luis Gomez, his boss back in L.A., who had been placed in charge. "Anderson just tried to radio from his airplane. I'll have his location in a minute!"

Anderson was the pilot they were looking for. They'd been given descriptions of him and a short woman, both of whom were to be caught and held. Axel wanted them for his own purposes, the poor bastards.

Gomez again: "The pilots just called from the airport. Anderson's on a flat-top mountain six miles west of town."

"Does he have the Katy-bitch or the woman with him?"

"No way to tell. I doubt he's going anywhere in this weather, but you should go up there after him."

Oscar had the driver turn around, and radioed another

team to meet him at the main intersection in town. They would go together. His concern was that when they arrived at the plateau, the others would kill indiscriminately. They were an undisciplined and violent group.

36

4:00 P.M.—Tom DeBerre's

Link was working desperately to make the airplane airworthy. He swept snow from wings and fuselage, pulled the canvas off the engine, and went to work with the scraper.

The Jeep returned, and the women dismounted. "Where's Tom?" he asked.

"He checked me out on the snow blade, then grabbed a rifle and told us to go on. I think he went down the hill to stop them. Link, there's something I remembered to help Gordon's people search for the listening posts. Axel mentioned someone called T-Can."

"Tell him when we get there."

Maggie waved at the runway. "Where do I plow?"

He pointed. "All the way to the end. One pass down and back, then get on board."

"Gotcha," she said, crawling into the idling Jeep. The damaged blade moved tediously and in jerks and starts as it lowered.

New gunfire erupted. A staggered series of rifle shots, these closer than before.

Old Tom DeBerre on the hillside road, trying to buy them time?

Maggie drove forward, the blade angled just slightly, bumping along and pushing the snow aside, headed toward the distant dropoff at the rim of the plateau. "Get in and buckle up," Link yelled to Katy, and did not have to repeat himself.

He used the ice scraper on a new deposit of clear ice he discovered on the right wing, increasingly convinced the flight was a bad idea. If a logical alternative had presented itself, he would have jumped at it. There were none he could think of.

The chatter of automatic weapons fire interrupted the lonesome rifle shots. Then more joined in and Link waited vainly for a response from Tom. He grimly made sure the wheel chocks were clear, opened the hatch and was scrambling into the pilot's seat when the gunfire diminished.

Link worked the controls, found them sluggish—meaning there was remaining icing—but at least they responded. The snowfall diminished in another rare lull. Maggie was visible halfway to the end of the runway when he started the engine turning over. *Crank, crank.*

Prop just turning slowly. "Come on," he encouraged. *Crank, crank, crank,*

''Come on," Katy joined in from the seat behind him.

Link stopped. Checked engine and fuel settings to make sure all was proper.

Crank, crank, crank. The engine caught, and the propeller fluttered for a half-dozen tries. The engine quit.

Maggie had arrived at the far end of the strip—shoved the snow on over the edge, then laboriously turned around and started back.

Crank, crank, crank. "Come on, engine," Katy crooned.
Crank, crank, crank. "Hurry, Maggie," she added.
Crank, crank, crank. Another false start, this time lasting longer.

Link stopped. Adjusted everything again.

"What's wrong with this thing!" Katy asked anxiously.

"Nothing. It's just the cold."

Crank, crank, crank. Maggie was almost halfway back. Driving faster now that she had the knack. Plowing a straight line that would be easy to follow.

Crank, crank—the engine caught. This time sounding

lustier. It revved slowly to speed. Coughed twice in protest, but kept running.

They heard only vaguely as Maggie pressed down on the Jeep's horn.

"Why's she doing that?" Katy asked from the second row of seats.

Link guessed, turned, and confirmed his fear. Two four-wheelers were passing the barn, one behind the other, coming directly across the field.

He revved the engine until the airplane strained against the brakes. Almost taxied closer so Maggie wouldn't have so far to drive, but reconsidered. At their altitude and considering the conditions, the airplane would need all the runway to get off the ground.

"Hurry, Maggie!" Katy too had seen the vehicles, which were churning through the thick snow only three hundred yards distant.

While they waited, Link continued to work the controls so they wouldn't freeze up. He reached over and unlatched the passenger's door. Maggie would have little time.

She came on, faster, closer.

Waved urgently to motion them on, and did not slow down as she passed. Just began raising the snow blade and continued directly toward the utility vehicles.

"What's she doing!" Katy cried.

Link's heart was too heavy to answer. He pulled the throttle full open and the engine roared. The Piper creaked as it budged, the sounds of reluctant wheels becoming unfrozen.

"Maggie," Katy cried mournfully.

"Bend forward and hold on to your legs," he yelled above the roar.

They were accelerating down the path Maggie had carved for them.

"She's back there!" Katy cried.

"She did it so we could get away," he said. "It's our job to survive. Now damn it, hold onto your legs and stay down. That way if we hit something you've got a chance."

A look to the rear showed the four-wheelers still coming,

but now with Maggie headed directly at their leader. She was fifty yards and closing.

Link brought his eyes back and silently urged the aircraft on, for while they were moving ever faster they were not nearly at takeoff speed.

He looked back in time to see two four-wheelers scatter like frightened quail as the Jeep continued through without wavering from course.

Maggie had done her part.

The precipice was only a hundred yards distant yet they were still too slow! He held the throttle open, willing more speed as they passed the point of no return. It was do or die, for with their momentum there was no longer room to stop. V-2, they called it in the military. He held that idle thought, and drew the yoke just slightly back as they approached the edge.

There was a final bump, and the Saratoga staggered through the air like a drunken pigeon, with insufficient air speed to gain grace. Too heavy with ice! Yet Link could feel the airplane struggling, *trying* to fly.

The ice accumulated on wings and fuselage was steadily growing thicker and heavier. The altimeter showed that they were steadily sinking earthward.

Link started the landing gear coming up, yet they continued to lose height. Below he could see only swirling snow, but the ground was in there somewhere and they would not be long meeting if he did nothing.

He cautiously tried to maneuver, but had difficulty trying to turn right. Then he discovered that he could not draw the nose up. Icing on both the rudder and ailerons, and fast getting worse. A different person might have cursed or prayed. But Link had no time for that, and busied his mind with solutions—and decided upon a desperate gamble.

The airplane had crashed. Oscar had watched them go over the ledge and drop from view, and guessed at what had happened. After all, ice had formed on all the other metal surfaces.

Wouldn't it be as thick on the airplane that had just disappeared into the murk?

The driver was venturing too close to the edge, so he yelled out for her to stop, and then to back up. Oscar despised heights. He dismounted and stared out at the gloom. Thought he heard the faint buzz of an engine, but doubted it was the case. When they'd been ambushed by a rifleman on the way up, the gunfire had partially deafened him.

A woman had been driving the Jeep that had darted toward them and made them turn away. Whether it was the short one they looked for he did not know, and for the moment at least, she had eluded them. He called the men in the vehicle he'd left to block the road at the bottom of the plateau, and told them she'd be coming.

Finally he radioed Gomez about the airplane. "He went off the end of the runway and crashed in the valley," he said. "All we could see was the guy inside. No way he could have lived."

"Too bad," said Gomez. "The doctor says Axel will be back with us in another half hour and he sure wanted Anderson alive. How about the woman?"

"We've got a chance of getting her alive if none of the apes shoot her. Everyone hear that? The woman's coming down the hill, and *nobody's* supposed to shoot her."

Oscar crawled into the Yukon, and told the driver to return down the hill.

Link kept the nose just slightly downward, wanting to increase airflow over the control surfaces. With the engine turning at maximum torque, they also gained airspeed.

There was no more time to think about it and wonder . . . .

He twisted the yoke, rolling violently to the left for a full revolution, then slammed the controls back to center, halting the roll so abruptly that he *felt* the ice being flung free. The aileron controls were still not smooth, but were instantly better.

He wanted to roll hard right as well, but there was no time. The single slinging maneuver had to be enough, and as he sensed the snowy surface rushing up to meet them he desperately hauled the yoke back; and discerned the spectral vision of looming cottonwood branches.

"Hold on!" he yelled to Katy as they thumped into treetops—and he still held the controls back as the ground rose before them. Hoping they were ice-free. Betting their lives on it.

The Saratoga was a proven design, but was not built to withstand the g-forces of a fighter. As they shuddered under the full power pullout, the bird struggled gamely—continuing in its great arc—and they leveled just a few feet above an icebound creek that meandered through the valley. For the next minute they were quiet, letting their hearts recover as Link steadily gained altitude. Finally Katy released a long sigh, and said, "Wow."

Throughout the climb-out they remained silent, Link checking power and climb angle and working the controls so they wouldn't freeze again. They were through eight, then nine thousand feet. Yet he did not contact the flight center, and kept the IFF turned off.

He leveled, and set the letters H-D-N into the global positioning satellite system. The GPS immediately showed heading and distance for Hayden County Airport. When they drew closer he would turn for Steamboat.

First things first. He asked Katy to hand up the WACS phone.

He connected with the base unit operator at Steamboat, and asked to be connected with New York. A moment later he handed the WACS phone to Katy. "Your father's on the line." At which time Katy Dubois broke down and began to cry uncontrollably.

"She'll be with you in a minute, Frank," Link said softly.

37

It had not snowed at Steamboat. This time the storm had indeed passed to the south. White-clad members of the reconstituted FBI Hostage Rescue Team were visibly positioned at intervals along the length of the runway when they landed at dusk. Link let the airplane run out so they could all get a look at Katy before he turned and taxied back.

Individual agents raised their fists in symbols of victory. Katy waved back.

Link parked and shut down in front of the terminal he'd departed only twelve hours earlier, and Gordon Tower met them as they deplaned. He and Link had been talking for the past half hour, grappling with the problem at Montrose, but Tower's first words were for Katy.

"Your parents are aboard a Gulfstream, on their way. They say for you not to move, and for me to sit on you until they get here."

That did not get a smile from Katy, who had been glum since watching Maggie raise the snowplow blade and head for the terrorists. Neither did she argue as she was ushered toward the terminal building, a phalanx of special agents and Foundation bodyguards on either side.

Before she went in through the door which was held open for her, she turned. "Thanks, Link," she called out almost shyly.

As she disappeared inside, Link told Gordon, "I'm going back for Maggie."

"Soon enough. Right now we've got to talk about what they've got at Montrose, and make some tough decisions. There's been a lot of changes since you left."

"I'll be right with you," said Link. He found an uninhabited area of the terminal, and used the WACS phone to call Erin Frechette in New York.

"Hi, pardner," she said, and congratulated him on finding Katy. "Too bad about Maggie. Did she have a chance of getting away?"

He'd kept himself numbed on the subject, just as he had done when he'd flown combat and friends had been lost. "Not much of one." He paused, thinking it was harder than combat. "She thought she was onto something after she talked with Katy."

He told her about the man at the Mexican ambassador's home, and how on the flight Katy had remembered that he'd had medium-dark skin, mean eyes, and a bulbous nose.

"Maggie felt he might be the one behind all this," Link said.

Erin was interested, and said she would run with it.

The men—Gordon, the state police commissioner, and the National Guard general—were among those in the MCP van, drinking strong coffee and considering what Link told them about the terrorists. A critical question was the strength and placement of terrorist forces.

"I *want* those guys," the general kept repeating, reflecting all of their thoughts.

They studied their individual video monitors, viewing digital maps of Montrose. John Rabeni had returned with the MCP airplane and a fatigued Steffie Footwine, and was showing them how to use the consoles built into the side of the van. Included was a stored digital map of the world, including all cities, major and minor. But he was anxious to get into the air and fly near Montrose, and augment the maps with detailed radar pictures of the situation.

Link touched an electronic pen to the digital map, explaining the roadblocks and terrorist search teams. Red marks appeared on all of those positions. "They were moving south and west through town, looking for Katy," he said of the search teams.

They decided the task could take the terrorists all night. There was also the factor that they might learn that Katy was no longer in Montrose. Either Tom DeBerre or Maggie Tatro could reveal that fact, if taken alive. But the terrorists obviously did not yet know for they had not pulled out.

"We've got to get in there and protect the citizens," said the police commissioner.

"But we do it right. I do *not* want them to escape so they can do this again," said the FBI agent. They would wait at least a while longer to try to find the listening posts.

Gordon took a call on his WACS phone, and looked pleased. "That was Judge Marian DeVera," he said, naming the new director of the FBI. "Congress just lifted any remaining restrictions. The terrorists are declared a danger to society."

The general had received much the same information, as had the police commissioner.

They were encouraged to work together. To coordinate with Washington if and when possible. To locate the listening posts—still an ongoing effort—and stop the illegal COMINT. To neutralize the terrorists, who were declared a danger to society. Deadly force was authorized—be the terrorist man, woman, or child. If one of them threatened a law enforcer or citizen, they could be destroyed. Bang.

Congress was in emergency closed session, their stated purpose to compromise on a revised spending plan to rejuvenate the economy. Contrary to what Gordon Tower had believed, the senior members of the media had also been briefed on the situation, and were honoring the silence as had not been done since their forebears had kept the secrets of the D-Day invasion. Everyone was coming together as a part of a massive game to rescue the people of Montrose.

Only the weather was not cooperating, for the storm was worsening.

Gordon took another call on the WACS phone. He listened raptly and brightened perceptibly. He turned to the others.

"We just got a bingo on the Atlanta listening post. They've inserted a video camera. Five people inside, all working with supercomputers and saying all the right words. Mentioning Montrose and the Voice a whole lot."

Congratulations came from different sources and voices.

"Maggie's the one we've gotta thank for remembering the name T-Can. It was located a full block from where we were looking, but the sign on the door reads Tin Can Communications, and they just *happen* to have an office in Denver."

"When can you go in?" the general asked.

"We'll take down both offices simultaneously. Do it so fast they can't shut off or disable their system, or get the word out."

"So, when?"

"We can be ready before ten o'clock. I wish it could be even quicker because our people have been in and out of the two buildings so much they've got to be suspicious."

Link spoke up. "It might be nice if you had a diversion for Axel, so he'd have other things on his mind." When he had first described the arm injury, Gordon had doubted the terrorist would be able to carry on. Link had convinced him differently. Axel was driven. Also nuts.

"What kind of diversion are you thinking about?"

"Anything to keep his mind off the listening posts."

They began to lay out the timetable.

The military would contain the terrorists and not let them escape. The FBI would clear Montrose with their HRT. The state police would converge by highway from all directions.

"We can't promise that there won't be casualties," said the general.

"As long as they're terrorists, who gives a good damn."

The general used a joystick to slue the electronic map a

few miles north of town. He zoomed in on the airport and turned to Link. "Where were their helicopters?"

"Out a bit, so I can see the highway?"

He zoomed out.

Link traced the route he and Maggie had taken in the heavy snow, when she'd had to call out the turn to the airport. He put the pen to the screen. A red dot appeared where the guard had stopped them. He made small X's where he'd seen the helicopters.

"Only the two helicopters?"

"There may be more, but those were parked separately and had a guard."

Rabeni raised his voice. "And they may have moved them. I can show you precisely what they have if you'll let me get up there with the MCP. It's got the best precision ground-mapping radar this side of J-STARS, and you can observe it all from here in the van."

As they continued, Link Anderson stepped behind the curtains at the rear of the van. There he pulled on his battered sheepskin and hat, transferred a holstered Smith & Wesson revolver from his kit bag to a small pack, slipped past the others, and went to the front of the van. "Will they know you're up there?" Gordon was asking Rabeni.

"Not unless someone screws up on the phone or radio," the test pilot replied.

"Let him go," said the general. "We need all the help we can get."

"I'll give you a call on the WACS phone." Rabeni bolted for the door.

Outside he met Steffie Footwine, who was stumbling tired, but bent on joining them in the van. "I'm taking the MCP back up," he told her.

Without hesitation she said she would go along, to help operate the radars.

Link, only a few feet distant, overheard their discussion. Her determination reminded him of someone he missed very badly. As for the decision-makers in the MCP van, he'd told them everything they needed.

He entered the terminal, where he found the Weyland Foundation's chief investigator talking to the tactical leader of the Hostage Rescue Team. It took Randall only a moment to collect the things Link required. He dropped the small carton into the pack, ignored the investigator's questions, and went out and jogged toward the ungainly MCP airplane.

The test pilot was surprised when he climbed aboard. "You're coming?"

"Part of the way," said Link. "And don't announce my presence."

He had decided upon the proper diversion for Axel Nevas.

Montrose

Axel had trouble remembering the flow of events over the past hour.

When he had awakened in the recovery room, the surgeon and Gomez had been waiting expectantly. He'd said little in response to the doctor's questions, feeling dry-mouthed and confused, still floating from the drugs and anesthetic.

Status briefing: Anderson had died trying to take off in an airplane. The woman had eluded them. The search teams had not yet found the Katy-bitch. It was hard to assimilate it all, but he had felt sadness that Anderson was dead. As if something remained unfinished.

Two nurses had helped him sit up, as he'd told them he wanted.

His first thought was that he felt dizzy. His second was that he was off balance without the weight of the arm on the right side. Then he had moved and there'd been a violent twinge of sensation.

"It *hurts*," he remembered crying out.

"I don't dare give you more morphine," said the frightened doctor.

"My pistol," Axel had demanded of Gomez, and was

handed the small secondary weapon taken from his ankle holster. He'd wavered, then shot the doctor, who howled with pain as the bullet pierced his shoulder. Axel fired again and again, until he'd exhausted the clip. The surgeon continued to scream and crawl about.

Axel had growled instructions, and terrified nurses had wheeled him from the room and the noisy doctor. All of that had happened an hour before, and Axel had remained in a terrible mood since. Wafting in and out of full awareness, outraged because they were unable to locate the Katy-bitch. Seething because of the disfigurement Anderson had caused. Feeling cheated and wishing his enemy were alive so he could kill him.

Now Axel looked out at the men going from door to door, pushing their way through the homes and frustrated in their search. He was in a Suburban being driven by Gomez, attended by one of the terrified nurses from the hospital. She'd given him another shot of morphine, and had brought more.

He looked out, noting that it was already very dark.

In back the captured FBI agent moaned in pain. Axel had had him beaten and tortured for information—found he'd arrived in the airplane with Anderson and the woman and knew nothing about the Katy-bitch. He had made sure they'd stopped short of killing him.

He received a new radio call from Oscar. "We just caught the small woman."

A giddy wave of delight swept over Axel. "Bring her to me," he replied. He felt the features of his face working as various emotions shuddered through him.

The MCP was at six thousand feet, throttled back so they were hardly flying, the cockpit lights turned to a subdued red glow so they would not destroy night vision. But those were not visible from the back, where Lincoln Anderson stood at the open hatch, looking into the black and stormy night. Feeling the sharp chill of the subfreezing wind despite his parka and heavy-knit snow mask.

"The plateau's coming up in twenty seconds," Steffie

Footwine announced on intercom. "You'll be fifteen hundred feet above the ground."

Link leaned forward in anticipation, and placed gloved hands on the sides of the opening.

"Five seconds," she intoned.

Link counted down, and rolled forward into the void. The icy blast cut into his core, instantly dropping his body temperature. He waited for a count of three to pull the chute cord. The big canopy inflated almost instantaneously, and he felt the jar to his toes.

He swung in a large arc once, twice, then again, and crooked his knees slightly and looked down into the blowing snow to discern the earth before . . .

The impact was sudden and unexpected. He rolled in a poorly executed parachute landing fall, then rather than trying to rein in the chute and risk being dragged about by the whims of the storm, he unfastened the releases and let the thing blow free.

He removed the knit mask, pulled his hat out of the small pack, poked and shaped it best he could, and placed it on his head. Finally he strapped on the .357 magnum Smith & Wesson revolver with its heavy "highway patrolman" frame, and loaded enough ammunition into the pockets of the sheepskin to wage a moderate-sized gun battle.

Link Anderson began to walk toward the south edge of the plateau where he knew he would find Tom DeBerre's house. While he did not hope to find the man there—or Maggie Tatro, for that matter—he must begin somewhere.

38

The note was handed to the senior on-duty controller, who read it with near disbelief.

"Put the word out to all of our people," his superior quietly told him.

The senior controller stared at him for a moment, then rose from his console and went down the row of radar controllers, stopping to show each one the note.

> **This is not an exercise. A counterterrorist operation is under way in Montrose. All radios and telephones are being monitored, so do not mention military aircraft flying from Steamboat, Buckley Field, and Peterson AFB, and progressing to and from Montrose. Until otherwise directed, divert all other air traffic from those restricted corridors.**

There were puzzled looks and confused shrugs, but the controllers remembered the atrocities at Steamboat, and complied without comment.

Buckley Field, Colorado

Six Special Operations C-130s had lined up for takeoff. There were three variant models, so dissimilar they could easily be mistaken for entirely different aircraft. Most were new, but under the skin they were the same reliable Hercules that Lockheed had manufactured for fifty years. When the lead MC-130 pilot pushed up power and the big airplane rumbled down the runway, the twenty camo-painted marine recon specialists in the rear began to get the butterflies that accompany all operations. The same was true of the US Army Rangers in the next three birds.

The final two aircraft were of different breeds, as were their crews. The EC-130 carried a foursome of electronics and media specialists, including—of all things—a baritone-voiced announcer. The AC-130 was an airborne artillery post, sporting a 40-millimeter cannon and a mini-gatling gun. These were only some of the ingredients that went into special operations.

Bob Adams Airport, Steamboat

That morning four helicopters had been flown in from Fort Polk, Louisiana, by the United States Army, and placed at the disposal of the FBI. The forty-eight special agents of the replacement Hostage Rescue Team, thoroughly briefed and prepared, all wearing white camouflage, boarded three of the MH-53 aircraft. Each carried a sidearm of his choice, and either a silenced Ingram machine pistol or M-16 automatic rifle. Four sported Remington 700 bull barrel rifles with low-light scopes. All wore lightweight packs, with miscellaneous gear that included handheld GPS receivers and low-light scopes. Two carried man-radars, which like the helicopters were on loan from the army. All had radios, and when en route would put an earphone in one ear and attach boom mikes to their lapels. The radios were to remain off until authorized by the team leader.

Gordon Tower and his senior FBI agents boarded the fourth and final helicopter, and strapped into the web seats that lined the sides of the interior.

Barring a major emergency, there would be no turning back.

He had jitters from wanting to get on with it, but no second thoughts. He wondered about Link Anderson. The MCP test pilot had called back that he had parachuted into Montrose. A parachute-qualified specialist with the HRT said it was foolhardy dangerous in the midst of a storm. That he might still be floating around in updrafts. Yet Gordon understood.

Maggie and Link had found each other when they'd both believed it might be too late. They seemed just about perfect for one another.

The last time he had spoken with Erin, she'd told Tower that the duel had become more of a personal thing. If Axel Nevas survived the mutilation of his arm, he would kill innocents just to spite Link. Especially his friends. And *most* especially, his loved ones.

And there was another reason for his going, for as they had brainstormed he had mentioned that it would be nice to have a diversion. Link *was* the diversion. He had relayed a message through the MCP test pilot that he would meet Gordon at the Montrose airport.

One by one the jets began to whine, and the rotors came to life.

8:00 P.M.—Montrose

Link had found nothing in the deserted farmhouse. No slightest sign that Tom DeBerre or Maggie had returned since they'd departed. He had walked to the home next door and found it just as empty, but located the keys to a big and shiny new tractor in the barn, with a snowplow on front that was much larger that the one mounted on the Jeep. He had climbed on, checked that the fuel tank was full, and then driven to the house, where he had filled a ten-gallon jug of water and taken it along, down the twisting road to town.

It was particularly and bitterly cold, and he hoped the water would not freeze.

Halfway down the hill, when butterflies fluttered about in his stomach, Link stopped the tractor cold in the road. Looked out into the blowing blizzard and tried to make himself harder, tougher. He thought of Maggie and lost all doubts.

The snow continued falling as he proceeded to the main intersection in town, wondering if the terrorists still operated the roadblock there. Thinking: Use the tactic of surprise!

The tractor's headlights were very bright and illuminated the startled eyes of two terrorists, seated in the police cruiser parked in the middle of the street, engine running for warmth. As he slowed to a crawl, one got out and shielded his eyes.

"Where you think you're going, my man?"

"Watch," Link said, and lurched forward. The big John Deere plowed headlong into the terrorist, then into the cruiser, then compressed it all into a major mess which he plowed into the side of a brick building.

He backed off a few feet, climbed off, and peered into several vehicles that had been pulled over. Some contained bodies of citizens. None contained life.

Link crawled back on the tractor and had gone east on Highway 50 for only a block when he heard a series of gunshots. He turned immediately, turned onto another side street when he saw the glow of headlights, and pulled up to an SUV. *Use surprise!*

Someone screamed shrilly from the other side of the street. He climbed off, unstrapped and drew the big S&W, and stalked over. Heard the sounds of fists thumping into flesh. Grunts and groans. There was a shape of a man astraddle and beating another. Two others stood about.

One turned to flash a light toward Link. He wore a policeman's shirt, bloody where the original owner had been shot.

Link fired two rounds that echoed like great explosions. The two standing men were blown several feet back. He moved up to the one straddling the other.

"Oh shit."

Link swept the heavy revolver in an arc and knocked him from his perch. Then he gingerly hauled up the victim on the ground. "You okay?"

"Bastards hurt my *wife*!" He fell on the terrorist and began pounding.

Link pulled the SUV into a vacant driveway and killed the engine. When he checked again, the citizen was still slugging and cursing. He returned to the tractor and went on.

Two blocks farther he found a group of four terrorists, beating on a door and demanding entrance. Just as the ones before, these hardly noticed his approach. He shot one who tried to raise his Skorpion, and marched the others to the street.

When he left a few minutes later, they were pleading for him to return.

Ten minutes later two more terrorists were dead, and four more were begging him to come back.

He caught three taking turns with a girl, forcing her parents to look on. When Link stopped them, the father went inside for his rifle, but when he returned, Link had already taken all three away. A few moments later they too were asking him to return.

Axel did not like what he heard. "What do you mean, they don't answer?"

Oscar was leaning on the door of the Suburban, nodding emphatically. "Fifteen, maybe twenty aren't answering."

"The radio batteries," said Gomez, who was sitting in front. "Bet all the batteries went bad."

"Maybe," said Oscar. "I never thought of that."

Axel cocked his head, wondering if that could happen. It was something he would normally know, but not now, not on this stormy night while in the morphine fog.

The little woman with the large tetons began to moan in the very back.

"Shut her up!" he snapped, and heard a loud crack as one of the men back there slapped her. She was not very alive, but enough to cry out. The FBI agent named George had not made a sound for a while. Axel hoped he was alive as well, but Grand Tetons was Anderson's woman, and must suffer greatly before he offered her to Huitzilopóchtli.

"Don't kill her!" he called back. They seemed confused when he alternated between telling them to beat her, then not to kill her. Then to mistreat her some more.

The T-Can West contact phoned. "Axel, we intercepted a scary conversation a few minutes ago. A company here in the building called the police about unauthorized people hanging around. We've been seeing workers who don't belong."

Axel narrowed his eyes. Wondering.

"I think we should shut off . . ."

"Axel!" Gomez had turned around to him, looking upset. "There's someone on the radio calling for you."

"One moment," Axel told the T-Can contact, and switched on the radio.

"I'm sorry. Oh God, I'm sorry, oh God!" Then the sound of the same man sobbing. "Don't leave me. Please don't leave me."

"Axel?" A softer, calmer tone.

His heart began to pound.

"I'm back," said the voice of Lincoln Anderson. "Come and get your men." A gunshot sounded. Not close but not far.

"Go there!" Axel cried out to Gomez. "Find him! I want him *dead*!"

Gomez drove toward the gunshot source, Oscar following with more men in a Yukon.

The cell phone rang repeatedly. "Yes!" Axel shouted into the mouthpiece.

"What should we do?" asked the T-Can West contact. "We have a . . ."

"Be quiet, you fool. I'm busy!"

They'd driven for what seemed an eternity before they found the first of the frozen men.

Sitting on the street corner. Arms and legs bound before him around the base of a metal lamp post. Tied securely with plastic lock cuffs like grocers used to cinch up cardboard boxes.

Another man tied to the next post down the street. Then another and another. Big tough men. Twelve of them in all. Still wearing heavy coats and gloves. No signs of mistreatment.

Alive, crying. Trousers and undershorts pulled to their ankles. Ice sheathing their legs, which had turned a dark and unhealthy shade of blue.

It was terribly cold—the temperature holding at ten degrees below zero. Anderson had tied them securely, and poured water on their genitalia. They were frozen fast to the metal posts and did not dare to stand. When Axel had a few of them pried loose they screamed in agony.

Axel left the rest to die, for none were of use to him if they could not walk.

Grand Junction

The Grand Junction airport had been closed off and on by the storm, but for the past hour the closure had been dictated by the National Weather Service, who claimed that "inverted wind shear conditions" existed in a rectangle that reached from Denver to Grand Junction to Durango to Colorado Springs. All traffic, except for NWS aircraft, were restricted from the area.

The disclosures were baffling. Were the weather satellites that precise, to pick up inverted wind shears, whatever those were? What kind of aircraft were flown by the National Weather Service? In the midst of the discussion, the airport manager heard the sounds of multiple jet helicopters passing over. Large ones, making a great deal of noise.

The airport manager called the flight operations section, and was advised that Denver Center had confirmed that Na-

tional Weather Service aircraft were operating in the area.
The manager said he didn't realize that NWS airplanes flew
in blizzards like they did in hurricanes.

An old, grizzled, and unemployed pilot named Glenn
Davis—several of them hung around the airport trying to
act important—said he'd never heard of such a ridiculous
thing.

Three minutes later the airport terminal building shuddered as a large propeller-driven airplane flew over very
low. Then another, and another.

"What the hell?" asked the manager as three more
passed over.

"Them wasn't helicopters," Davis said knowledgeably.

They waited, and blew out collective sighs when the
quiet continued.

"Guess that's all," said the manager, just before the building almost rattled off its foundation, and they heard the re-
verberating and lusty roar of a big jet fighter, flying low.

"For God's sake," yelled the manager.

Old Glenn Davis was staring out at the falling snow as he
nodded sagely. "Looks like the National Weather Service
got themselves a proper air force."

9:40 P.M.—Atlanta, Georgia

Fourteen FBI agents were in the hallway, pistols drawn with
muzzles held aloft, two of them crouched on either side of a
door marked TIN CAN COMMUNICATIONS, LTD.

The agent in charge watched the seconds tick down, and
nodded. All turned away lest a spray of wood or shrapnel be
released, and he depressed the detonation button. The noise
from the four small shaped charges—three for hinges and
one for the lock—was sharp. *Crack!*

An agent stepped forward and kicked the door, which fell
inward.

The agent-in-charge tossed in a stun grenade. They
crouched and held their ears.

9:40 P.M.—Denver, Colorado

Precisely the same scenario was followed in the somewhat smaller office suite in Denver. The stun grenade went off with a brilliant flash and clap of thunder, and a second later the first agents rushed in, guns aimed squarely at four people who sat with mouths agape and eyes wide.

"FBI! Do not move a muscle. If you do, you're meat." It was a female agent, whose chest rose and fell with such healthy vigor that they believed her. They froze, just as she'd said.

"Stand up *ver*-y slowly. Do not touch your mouse or keyboard. Do not touch *anything*. Otherwise I will shoot you, and that is a promise. That's it. Nice and slow."

She reached forth and pulled the headphones off all four of them, one at a time. An agent stepped up behind each operator and took them by the arm.

The agent-in-charge put her sidearm away. "Take 'em into the hall and keep 'em there so they'll be handy if we need a question answered." She motioned at the four spooks on loan from the National Security Agency, two men and two woman, all of whom looked like—and were—computer nerds. They took their seats and examined the state-of the-art scopes and video monitors and switches, smiling as if studying flavors in an ice cream shop.

9:40 P.M.—Montrose

The Combat Talon version of the C-130 was at five hundred feet over the first drop zone when the ten members of the first marine recon team stepped off the rear platform and into the stormy night in two-second intervals.

"They're out," the drop master said over intercom, and the pilot turned ten degrees right. Fifteen seconds and one mile farther, the green lamp came on once more.

The second well-bundled team began to jump into the blowing snow and bitter cold.

All members of both teams landed in open fields, within three hundred feet of one another, a feat for a night weather drop. It was a matter of practice. The men had an average of four hundred jumps, and the aircrew had dropped more than a thousand troopers.

The three other MC-130s fared almost as well with the remaining six teams. The ranger insertion went without a hitch. The worst foul-up came during the third Hercules second drop, when a SEAL came down on the roof of a garage and broke his leg in the process of falling off. The good news was that a medic had landed only fifty yards away.

The various teams remained quietly in place until nine-forty-four, when a call was made over their radios. "Form up." The LPs in Denver and Atlanta had been taken and radio silence was no longer required. The teams completed their individual joins-ups without incident. Then they made their way to their respective blocking positions on all sides of the city.

Montrose Airport

From beginning to end, the battle for the Montrose airport took precisely ten seconds.

The two helicopter pilots were in the terminal lounge, drinking coffee and wishing Axel would hurry so they could get the hell out of Dodge. Two of the more reliable dealers had been left to ensure that no harm came to the only persons who could get them out when the getting was called for. They wore ill-fitting airport police uniforms and had spent the day blocking access to the terminal.

When they'd arrived en masse, they'd rounded up the few passengers and airport employees. Then, until the others departed, they'd spent their time beating the males and molesting the women. The two left-behind dealers had toyed with the idea of killing them all so they wouldn't be a bother. Finally they'd incarcerated them in an employee locker room.

Now all four were together in the lounge, waiting for Axel's signal. They'd been told to keep a guard on the helicopters, but were tired and hungry and out of sorts.

The battle began when a man in sheepskin coat and western hat walked into the lounge, holding a very large revolver with the muzzle upward, in what the police called the port arms position. "Don't be foolish," was all he said.

Since he did not have the pistol pointed at anyone in particular, one of the dealers did not take him seriously. He was in midair, diving for the machine pistol that he had left on a nearby table, when a magnum-driven bullet impacted, shattered, and almost severed his left leg. He rolled into a ball in immediate shock.

The others prudently tossed their weapons on the floor.

Ten seconds from start to finish.

The man in the sheepskin turned the terrorists over to the unkind care of the airport employees they'd molested and beaten, and drove the SUV commandeered from the men he had frozen, to the base operations building.

There Link slumped against the wheel and waited. His diversions were over. He felt the bruises from the lousy parachute landing, allowed himself to feel the excitement and fear that he had suppressed during the fury, and realized just how lucky he had been.

He had hoped his surprise tactics would prevail, and they had. He had neutralized a goodly number of terrorists. Any more would be most difficult, for they would be expecting him. It was time for the professionals to step in.

He had prayed he might come across Maggie. Now, as he waited in the darkness for Gordon Tower and the others, he feared the worst.

39

The first three MH-53s swept in from the north, and one after the next landed on the highway at the eastern edge of the city. As they deplaned, the FBI agents formed into twelve four-person parties. There was no pep talk, just the HRT tactical team chief walking out before them and pointing into the blowing snowfall.

"It's seven miles to the other side of town. Does anyone have questions?"

There were no takers.

"See you on the other side."

The fourth helicopter landed at the Montrose airport, in front of base operations, and Gordon Tower was first to emerge.

Link Anderson walked out to meet him, endured a confrontation with a half-dozen FBI agents clad in camouflage, then greeted Gordon with a handshake.

"How did it go?" Tower asked.

"I stung a few."

"Maggie?"

"Nothing yet."

Tower was concerned about the HRT agents. They'd decided the best way to sanitize the town was by foot. Flush out the terrorists as they went, neutralize the ones they could, and drive the remainder into the military net enveloping the town. It would be dangerous, but the agents were highly trained and capable.

But that was not all of the plan.

As soon as the first helicopters had dropped off the Hostage Rescue Team, they took off again, and the crew chiefs loaded audiotape loops provided by the EC-130 baritone announcer. The words were broadcast over public address speakers directed earthward, so loud that the sounds of jets and rotor blades were muted. "Citizens of Montrose, you are under attack by an organized group using terrorist tactics. Please turn your televisions to Channel 4."

Five thousand feet above the rooftops, the EC-130 flew in a constant orbit. In the back the baritone announcer watched the current television broadcast on Channel 4, a sitcom of dubious quality. A senior airman technician switched on a signal inverter, and carefully worked frequency and amplitude controls. The picture faded as its signal were canceled.

Some televisions were on cable, others antenna or dish. It did not matter. The new signal on Channel 4 was so overpowering, due to the directional antenna of the EC-130, that the crewmembers liked to say they could fry all the eggs in the refrigerators.

The baritone broadcaster looked gravely into the camera. "I am Air Force Technical Sergeant Roger Stiles, and we are broadcasting live." He went on to advise them that they were under attack by terrorists, known not to balk at murder.

The terrorists were searching for a girl named Katy Dubois. "As you will see, Miss Dubois is in our custody many miles from here."

Video footage showed Katy in Steamboat, surrounded by hawk-eyed agents.

"The terrorists are cut off from the outside world. Our orders are to use lethal force as necessary. If they do not have a death wish, they will give themselves up."

In the EC-130, a VHF radio scanner picked up a ground conversation that was neither FBI nor military: "You hear the fuckin' TV?"

The captain pointed at the signal on the screen with his forefinger. The technician turned on a jammer, and moved the jagged spike squarely over the radio signal. A moment later another signal popped up on another frequency. The technician covered that one too.

The terrorists could no longer communicate. Those who heard about the announcement tried to radio Axel for guidance, and received only jamming. A few drove aimlessly, looking for leadership. Others headed for the nearest road out of town.

The first terrorist casualties were inflicted by a SEAL team operating on the northern perimeter, when a Chevolet Blazer careered around a corner and ignored the uniformed man trying to wave him to a halt. When the Blazer ran over the spike strips laid out on the street, all four tires were blown. The vehicle skidded and almost toppled as it came to a halt.

Four persons piled out, cursing angrily, asking what the hell was going on. Thinking it was one of their own roadblocks.

"Raise your hands," said the SEAL team leader.

"Aww, fuck off," said the driver, leaning down to examine the tires. He had not seen the SEAL clearly.

"You didn't hear the television announcement?" asked the SEAL leader.

"Yeah. You believe that shit?"

"They've got a couple of young girls in the backseat," said a SEAL. His voice was flat.

"They're pretty well used," said one of the terrorists, "but you can have 'em if . . ."

"Oh shit," yelled the driver as he approached close enough to note that these were not their brethren. He turned and dove toward the Blazer, and dropped as a silenced Ingram made a metallic rattling sound. Five seconds later there were no surviving terrorists.

The sat phone buzzed in Link's pocket. "Hi, pardner," said Erin. "Where are you?"

"Waiting in a helicopter with Gordon and his senior people."

"I've been working with the information from Katy about the Mexican ambassador and the guy with the big nose. So far I'm batting zero. I just got authorization from the FBI to connect into the supercomputers at both listening posts, so maybe I'll find something there."

"Sounds like it's going to be a long night for you."

"Yeah. One last thing before I get to work on it. Link, it's imperative that they take Axel Nevas alive. Don't let them kill him. He's the one with the answers."

10:45 P.M.—Tin Can Communications, Fifth Street, Denver

The NSA agent in the leftmost seat of the listening post took the call. "Go ahead." he said.

A rumbling voice responded. "This is Axel. We have intruders. Call the Voice and ask her to send the spare helicopter."

The agent regarded the Voice Scan: MATCH—AXEL

He looked at his cheat sheet, and found: "Axel—Axel Nevas—deep voice." Beside the enty was a list of pertinent questions. He was a very big fish.

"How many do you have with you ?" the agent asked.

"Only myself and Gomez. Now call the Voice."

They did not yet know who the Voice was, or how to contact her. "What's your location?" he tried.

"What? Oh, for the helicopter?"

"Yes," the agent ad-libbed. "I'll need to know where to send it."

"Ten miles southwest of the city. Our radio's being jammed, so we'll flash a light."

The NSA agent couldn't believe his fortune. "Sure. Just a minute."

He delayed—as if going off line to talk to this *Voice*—grinned at the FBI agent-in-charge, who was monitoring on a headset, and moved his hands like he was reeling in a trout.

The agent-in-charge did not look nearly as impressed.

The NSA agent flipped the switch, reconnecting with Axel. "The Voice says the helicopter's on the way."

"Do you have a time of arrival?"

"Half an hour." He walled his eyes, thinking up more trash. "Flash your light three times when you hear it coming."

"I will do that." The connection was broken.

The NSA agent chuckled at his cleverness as the FBI agent-in-charge called Supervising Agent Gordon Tower.

11:00 P.M.—Montrose

Tower lowered his cell phone and thought for a moment before motioning Link over. Wondering if he wasn't too emotionally involved because of Maggie,

The two lovers had been almost transparent about the way they'd fallen for one another. He'd never seen Maggie acting that zany. And Link?

He decided he had no choice. If the man responsible for destroying his own loved ones was about to be taken, he would expect a friend to let him participate.

A call came in from Washington. A deputy director saying more helicopters were on the way from Denver along with busloads of federal agents and marshals. His forces would continue to build, regardless of the storm.

"Send more medical personnel," he told him. "We're finding a lot of injured."

Gordon hung up, and told Link about the call from the listening post. "My agent-in-charge there didn't like everything she heard," he added. "She feels Axel may be setting us up."

Link's eyes shone in anticipation.

Gordon Tower pulled over his senior agents, and gave them five minutes to argue out a plan of attack. Then he approved it, for it was simple enough that it might work.

Eight agents would accompany them. Everyone would wear radios and all would be closely coordinated. Once they found Axel and whoever was with him, the pilot would hover, then turn on the landing lights to dazzle them. The agents would rappel down fore-and-aft ropes, and overpower them.

One, two, three.

40

Link stood at the forward door, looking down at the swirling snow at the base of the stark mountains, wondering where the terrorist leader might be. So far there was nothing. No blinking light. In fact no lights at all after leaving the town.

They were ten miles southwest of Montrose, at the location Axel had proclaimed, and had very gingerly descended to just 200 feet above the terrain. While that seemed especially low when facing an armed enemy, if they flew higher they would be unable to see the ground. The snowfall had diminished, but vision remained murky.

A status report was broadcast over radio. So far twelve terrorists had been taken prisoner. Twenty dead. Fourteen requiring medical attention. Too bad all the ambulances were being used to transport injured citizens. No one felt pity for the killers.

"I'm dropping down to one-fifty feet," said the pilot over intercom.

The aircraft had begun its descent when Link pressed the mike switch. "I see automobile headlights at two o'clock."

They flew closer. The lights winked off. "Anything?" the pilot asked, but no one answered. He slowed near where the lights had appeared. They turned and set up an orbit.

Nothing.

The lights came on again. *Blink-blink-blink.* The lights

again turned off, but Link could make out the fuzzy outline of a vehicle, and not far from it a number of hazy shapes in the snow. Nothing was distinct in the gray fog of particles that swirled and blew in the downdraft.

The pilot began to descend toward the vehicle. Announcing the height. One hundred feet, seventy-five; everything beneath them obscured by the manmade haze. At fifty feet, the pilot pulled back, and the craft hovered.

Almost time for the blinding light and the deployment.

The odd shapes Link had seen appeared like crude arrows in the snow, all pointed in the same direction.

"Now!" Gordon Tower called over the radio, and the brilliant landing lights came on, augmented by two five-thousand watt searchlights trained on the vehicle and figures.

Rappelling lines were cast out forward and aft doors.

"Hold everything," announced SSA Gordon Tower.

Link had experienced the horrors of combat. He knew to harden himself so he could continue functioning. Yet no one could be unmoved by the scene illuminated below.

The arrow shapes were human, legs and arms extended 45 degrees from their sides, blood blossoming from the heads like emphasis marks.

Made to lie down and then executed. Two and three abreast. Ahead of each was another. And yet another. A dozen of them. One of the bodies was clad in bulky clothing as Special Agent George had been. Another had only one arm.

The human pointers were aligned toward an objective.

Two persons standing together. A man wearing a ski mask, holding a small woman upright by a fist of hair. His other hand holding a pistol to the side of her head. The man's feet were firmly set, and he was squinting up at the helicopter. Tall, like Axel. Wearing dark clothing like Link had seem him in.

He slowly turned Maggie about so there would be no doubt about who he held. Her face was bloody, her jaw and eyes puffed and swollen. He swung her about again so her predicament and condition were obvious.

"Bastard," exploded an agent over the radio.

"Don't do anything rash," intoned Gordon Tower.

Axel motioned with the pistol for the chopper pilot to descend, and aimed it at a flat expanse where he wanted him to land.

"Should I?" asked the pilot.

"I can take him out without hitting her," said an agent with a rifle.

"You didn't listen," Gordon snapped. "We have to take him alive."

Down below, Axel again pointed at the flat expanse.

"I don't think we have a choice," said Tower.

The big chopper eased forward.

"Wait," said Link over the radio. "Keep the lights on." He leaned toward Gordon Tower, shouted, and told him what he intended.

Tower did not look at him, just kept staring at Axel below. Finally he gave a single nod. Not, Link knew, because his idea was perfect, but because in their desperation something must be done—and quickly.

Link hurried to the open rear door and pushed past the four agents there. He looked out.

They were still at fifty feet. Below them the terrorist remained poised, the gun held to Maggie's head. Avoiding looking up at the helicopter that cast such brilliant light.

Emotion trembled through Link. *Take him alive,* his mind reasoned. You *need* him alive.

Link took a rappelling clip from an agent who did not argue. He tugged to ensure that it was attached to the rope, then turned and poised at the lip of the door, looking back at the void.

When he dropped out and squeezed the clip he would slide down the rope. When he released his grasp the device would catch and hold. He went through it in his mind.

Resist temptation. Link unsnapped the holster from his belt, and handed it, still containing the heavy Smith & Wesson revolver, to the nearest agent. Taking Axel alive was more important than his own life.

The agent took it, looking surprised and as if wondering what to do with the weapon.

"Now," said Gordon Tower.

Landing and floodlights switched off at the same instant—hopefully leaving Axel temporarily blinded—and the helicopter immediately backed off twenty feet..

Link fell back and out the door, let the rappelling clip run for a count of two, let it catch and swung. The second time he released the clip he impacted the ground and tumbled onto his side.

Pain shot through his chest from the impact as he disconnected and crouched. Moved to a position beside a low bush before Axel's eyes could possibly adjust, his sounds masked by the roar of the helicopter's jets and rotors.

He became still. Waiting. Using the tactic of stealth that he'd learned so well.

Axel shuffled closer, his dark form dragging Maggie's.

Link remained as immobile as the bush beside him, an irregular shadow in a world of those. Human attention was drawn by movement and symmetry, by things not a part of nature.

The big helicopter moved again, this time churning even farther away.

"What are they *doing*?" Axel muttered, stopping again to look. His words faint in the roar of the engines. Something was amiss, but Link could not quite pin it down.

There was still nothing from Maggie, and the way he was handling her made Link wonder if she was alive. Although he'd tried to numb his mind from sensitivities, it was a difficult thought that the terrorist might be using her lifeless body as a prop.

Axel was ten feet distant. Almost close enough to rush and take down before he could kill Maggie. If she was indeed still alive.

Link heard the faint buzz of a cell phone. Gordon Tower trying to contact Axel through the listening post, as he had asked him to do. When Axel answered it might distract him enough to allow Link his moment.

Axel took a step toward the helicopter, still holding on to Maggie. Acting confused.

The cell phone buzzed, sounding as if it came from beyond Axel, but sounds were deceiving in the mantle of snow. It buzzed again. Again Axel ignored it.

There would be no distraction. Link would have to improvise. He rose. Took a cautious step. Then another. Then paused, for Axel was turning as if he'd sensed a presence.

Go for the gun, was Link's thought as he lunged. He threw his arms about the terrorist and slid them downward, drawing the gun hand with them, then slammed his shoulder hard into his opponent's back. Jolting him with such impetus that Maggie would have been torn from his grasp if his hand had not been so entwined in her hair. Instead she was dragged along, limp as a sack of flour.

The man in Link's hold bellowed with outrage—but not in Axel's guttural tone. Another disparity; he had full use of the arm that had been twisted.

This wasn't Axel!

Link found the gun hand, then the barrel. But the man was surprisingly strong, and with effort was able to twist away, dragging both Maggie and the gun from Link's grasp.

The terrorist took two more steps, then turned to face him, intent on bringing the automatic up to bear. But Link again wrapped his arms about his prey, and this time bowled him over. The killer, Maggie, and Link sprawled in a melee of arms and legs.

Neutralize the gun! Over and over the refrain repeated in Link's mind.

The man freed himself from Maggie, and shoved her away as he gained his feet—Link hanging on and following. Then it was he and the killer, face-to-face and torso to torso, grappling for possession of the weapon. A stalemate, until Link again found the pistol's barrel. He twisted his entire body, levering and tearing the autoloader from his foe's grasp. The terrorist immediately retaliated, lashing out with such impetus that the pistol was flung into the darkness.

Again they stood immobilized, fingers enmeshed, muscles straining as each tried to gain advantage. The helicopter had returned overhead, and their clothing flapped and fluttered in the downdraft. Then the lights beamed once more and their world became brilliant white.

Link sensed danger, and twisted aside as his opponent savagely rammed his forehead forward. The man's head missed, and he became off balance. An opening! Link slammed his knuckles into the killer's rib cage. He staggered and groaned. Link drew his hand back to his side, and again unleashed the stone-hard knuckles, twisted them as they were propelled forward—striking in the same spot and feeling ribs give.

As the terrorist began to fall away Link saw new motion in a corner of his vision. As he turned, a searing needle screamed through the muscles of his shoulder, accompanied by the *pop* of a small-caliber round. He finished turning, drawing his gasping opponent along with him.

And came face-to-face with Axel Nevas, with his thin blade of a nose, lips drawn into a snarl as he sighted a small automatic at Link's face.

Link thrust his former opponent forward as he dropped.

Pop.

"You shot *me*!" cried the man he had just fought.

Link scooped Maggie into his arms.

Pop! A miss.

He ran with her into the murk, veered to change directions, and lost his footing on slippery ice. *Pop.* That round also missed, but he was falling headlong. Sliding helplessly, all the while trying to cradle Maggie in the protective basket of his arms.

The side of Link's head smacked hard into something large and dark and solid. His world spun away, and his focus narrowed until it became a pinpoint in the darkness.

Someone placed a thumb and forefinger on his neck. "He's got a pulse."

Link slowly rolled over, and laboriously rose onto all fours.

"You took a header into a big rock so take it easy, buddy," said a second voice.

Both agents were breathing hard, as if they'd just run a long distance. He had obviously not been unconscious for long.

The helicopter had landed on the road beyond the vehicle, cutting off that route of escape. The chopper was not distant, yet the shape was vague. The snow was falling in earnest. Big flakes, coming down so heavily that with the darkness it was difficult to see anything.

"Both terrorists are gone," said the first agent. "You see where they went?"

"No." Link stared at Maggie. The second agent was kneeling over her, examining her with a flashlight. Her face was a mass of bruises and lumps, and she breathed in shallow wheezes. Blood frothed at the corners of her mouth.

"We have to get her to help. She's got a rib penetrating her lung," said the agent.

"Take good care of her," Link said as he carefully gained his feet. Keeping his voice even. He could not allow himself to feel the fury, lest it interfere with his task.

"Hey, you're hurt too," said an agent.

"And the SAC wants to talk with you," said the other. "He'll be right . . ."

Link walked in the direction away from the helicopter, into the darkness, and past the sprawled and posed bodies. After two-dozen paces he knelt and ran his hands over the snow. Lightly and quickly. He came across the lost pistol, but left it. Worked his way around in a large arc until he found the depressions that he sought.

He measured the human tracks and determined there'd been only the two of them. One taking larger steps than the other. The one he'd fought, who Axel had shot, was not moving fast.

Link continued to follow. He did not hurry, but neither did he dare to go slowly lest they escape. Axel had intended to hijack the helicopter, using Maggie as bait. That option had failed so he'd go on to the next. Another vehicle? He'd had all of those victims—the offerings—plus the man and Maggie, yet there had only been one four by four?

Link heard his name being called from far behind. Gordon Tower's voice. He went on, taking his time, making sure he remained on track. The bullet's path through the fleshy part of his shoulder stung, but it was not life-threatening. If it had been, he would have done the same.

Tracking and trying not to think about Maggie and what had been done to her. About the fact that Axel must be taken alive. Far behind he heard the FBI agents forming a tracking team. They were not quiet about it. He went on.

Gordon Tower looked out in disgust. Snow was coming down so hard that a couple more inches had accumulated since they'd deplaned.

All of Axel's victims, some of them obviously citizens, others more likely terrorists, had been shot, but three of them—not counting Maggie Trato, who was not expected to survive unless she received timely medical attention—were alive.

Special Agent George Krzecajt, who had accompanied Link and Maggie on the flights to Salt Lake City and Montrose, had been terribly beaten before the shooting. The bullet had gone through his neck and emerged on the left side of his throat. Condition: critical.

Another, an older man identified as Thomas DeBerre, had been dealt with in haste. The bullet had been fired from a couple of feet, and had been deflected by the thick bone of his skull. He was disoriented, had an atrocious headache, and was asking for whiskey to deaden the pain. Condition: fair.

The last of the live ones was a woman with so many rings in her tongue that Tower could not understand how she could eat more than soup. She had been shot twice, but neither was in a fatal spot. She spent her time cursing in a shrill voice, using the filthiest words the agents had ever heard. Gordon believed her to be one of the terrorists. Condition: foul.

The immediate problem was the weather, which was so bad they could not fly the injured to the hospital.

The agents who had gone out to search had followed tracks to the rocky hillside where the trail had become too difficult. They were staying put until more agents arrived to assist in the search.

As they waited for a lull, SSA Tower kept the remaining agents in the helicopter with the victims, exercising the limits of their first-aid training. When the weather broke they'd take out the wounded and haul in the group of man-trackers forming in town.

Pop. A gunshot.

"Was that from town?" an agent asked.

"No way. Town's ten miles from here."

"It sounded like a small-caliber."

The search party radioed that they'd heard the shot too.

Damn! thought Gordon Tower. *Where was Link?*

More reports came in from Montrose. A total of forty-seven terrorists had been neutralized. Despite requests to stay out of it, citizens had joined in the search. Three of the killers had been shot and killed trying to break into homes to hide.

The chopper pilot came aft. "Get buckled in. I'm going to lift her straight up, head directly for the hospital, and put her straight down."

Gordon Tower did not argue. The injured needed immediate attention.

The pilot returned forward, and after a moment the jet engines surged. At the same time Tower received a radio call that the search party had heard more shots.

Foothills, Uncompahgre Plateau

Axel discerned a sound from directly behind, turned, and fired. *Pop!* He stood still, peering into the darkness as if he might see something if he stared. As the morphine continued to wear off, the missing arm ached incessantly, and every few minutes a sharp pang coursed into his very core, like someone was driving a spike into him.

Gomez stumbled along behind, crying and holding his arms about himself. Axel would have killed him if he hadn't believed he might serve some other purpose.

"Why did you shoot me?" Gomez whined.

"Quiet. We're being followed."

Gomez fell, tried to rise, and fell again. He reached up. "Help me," he said.

Axel looked at the shadows, considered, then turned uphill. He moved cautiously, treading on bare rock where possible. Anderson was not the only one who could play the stealth game. He revered Jaguar, who was part god and moved invisibly, and held no doubt that he would escape. Eleven humans had been offered for Huitzilopóchtli. Mictlantecuhtli, lord of death, would be pleased as well, but he was not as strong.

The listening posts had been discovered, and his network compromised. He'd known as soon as he had heard the strange voice. Now the FBI agents thought he was trapped, but for a man of Axel's shrewdness there was always a back door.

He had prepositioned a vehicle, should the attempt to take the helicopter fail.

He heard a crackling noise in the darkness. He knew it was Anderson.

With that thought still echoing he heard a ghostlike voice.

"You won't get away." Soft and contained. Coming from everywhere.

Axel remained very still, the small pistol ready.

"I have heard that you mimic your ancestors."

"They were great priests," he breathed. He felt vulnerable, which was unnatural for him. "The Aztec were mighty and powerful, and great Huitzilopóchtli was their god of war."

"And a handful of Spaniards defeated their entire nation and made them lick their boots." The voice was filled with disdain.

"Through trickery." Axel looked warily about. "You come from backward savages."

"My ancestors numbered a thousandth of what your Aztec did, yet every enemy who dared to fight them lost. Cree, Flathead, Sioux, Crow, Snake—all of them. Not even the US Army defeated the Piegan Blackfeet in battle." He laughed easily, mockingly. "They would have barbecued Hernando Cortes in his fancy tin suit."

Axel slowly revolved, the execution weapon held before himself. Anxious to destroy the savage who dared to disparage his proud people.

"The Piegan were especially cruel to anyone who harmed their people."

Axel fired at the source of the voice. Then again and again. He turned and hurried upward. The Blackfeet had been ignorant aborigines when his people . . .

Even as he was fleeing, the soft voice came, as if it surrounded him. "You should not have hurt my friends, Axel. You chose the old ways, so I will do the same."

Axel ran faster, which made him stumble and then fall into a shallow roadside ditch. He whimpered as he pushed himself to his feet and scrambled on up the slope. He realized that he'd lost the pistol but did not dare go back.

He hurried on, peering into the snow, and almost passed by the Jeep Cherokee he'd left on the hillside road only an hour before. Axel stopped, huffing with exertion, and felt a giddy rush of relief. He opened the driver's door, heart pounding and anxious to depart before Anderson could get to him, slid inside, and reached into his pocket for the key.

He had made it!

But as he searched for the ignition, a hand grasped his own.

His shriek was involuntary. Anderson was inside the car with him!

Axel forced himself to relax, and let a sigh bleed from his lips. He smiled.

They would provide medical attention and more morphine. He would make no statements other than to demand fairness, and wait for Don Amado to provide a massive legal defense fund. There would be dozens of lawyers. Amado needed him for business, and the list of things that his money could not buy was a short one.

"Am I under arrest?" he asked calmly.

"It's not that easy," said Lincoln Anderson.

Axel did not understand, but he was not concerned. The thing that still baffled him was the failure of his offering to Huitzilopóchtli. A thought arose in his mind. Then he smiled as the answer came to him. ''Eleven weren't enough!'' he blurted. "He needs more blood."

Anderson was quiet for a moment, and when he finally spoke, Axel was surprised that he understood. "Yes," he said. "You need to make more offerings."

41

The owner was sleeping hard. He'd been troubled by the pressure bandages swathing his face, and had taken four times the normal dosage of Ambien, a heavy-duty sleeping pill.

"Wake up!" Marta pleaded, and shook him harder.

He groaned and shifted, and finally regarded her through groggy eyes.

"The listening posts aren't sending their messages."

He muttered something incomprehensible.

"They've missed five times now!"

"Call them."

"It is impossible that they'd both miss like that unless something is very wrong, Don Amado."

He turned to her with a harsher gaze.

"I am sorry. I know you are now Carlos David, but this is very, very serious."

"Umm. Call Axel. He'll know what is wrong."

"I tried but there's no answer." She was actually wringing her hands with concern. "Then I tried some of the others with him. Nothing. I can talk to our distributors everywhere else but there's nothing from the Tin Can listening posts."

"Axel doesn't answer?" he parroted, and wondered.

"We must leave!" she cried.

"Calm yourself, Marta. We will go. After all, you are the

Voice and powerful men tremble at your tone." He slapped her, hard. "But do not *ever* call me Amado again."

He began to dress.

3:35 A.M.—Montrose Hospital, Montrose, Colorado

Maggie was alive. Terribly beaten, prognosis still iffy, but alive. Supervising Special Agent Gordon Tower had been allowed to peek into the recovery room following the initial surgery, and she had looked awful, but she fought death valiantly.

He had set up temporary headquarters down the hall in a large empty office, where he and several assistants spoke on phones and radios and continued to run the mop-up operation. Montrose remained bottled up by military forces, and FBI agents still searched although it appeared that the final terrorists had been taken.

A senior agent came in, took a seat, and released a weary breath. He'd just returned from the Uncompahgre where fifty agents now searched. Four hours had passed since Link had disappeared, and all they had found was one unnamed terrorist who had collapsed on the trail. Shot in the abdomen, and now waiting his turn in the ER.

"Anything on either Anderson or Nevas?" Tower asked.

"Nothing. The snow's accumulating, and any tracks they left are covered."

Another senior agent came in and settled.

"How about you. Everything running smoothly?" Tower asked.

"Yes, sir. What happened here wasn't as one-sided as we thought. Everyone didn't just roll over. There were entire neighborhoods the terrorists couldn't penetrate and got shot up for trying. The people are thankful we came, but most are convinced they would have driven them out by morning."

"Identifications of the terrorists?"

"They're starting to give their names. Two or three big-shot distributors and a lot of small-fry dealers."

Gordon Tower motioned at the door. "Like the lady in the operating room has been trying to tell us all this time."

"How's she doing?" The agents were rooting hard.

Tower told him.

The senior agent took his feet to leave. "I'm picking up more trackers and heading back up there. They're bringing in dogs from Grand Junction."

"Dogs aren't much good when it's this cold," said Gordon.

His cell phone buzzed, and he picked up.

"Gordon, Erin Frechette."

Link's assistant at the Weyland Foundation had been authorized to delve into the supercomputers at the listening posts.

"Have you been able to pull anything out yet?" he asked.

"A lot, but that's not why I called. Link just contacted me on his sat phone."

Tower rushed his words. "Where is he?"

"Safe. I told him how Maggie's last operation went well and he asked if we'd keep an eye on her until he gets back."

"Back from where?"

"Actually, he didn't say."

He frowned, wondering. "What about Axel?"

"Link said Axel isn't in the mountains any longer."

"We need him, Erin, to find out what it's all about."

"Tell me what you'd ask Axel Nevas, and I'll see if I've got answers."

"What is this? Some kind of a game?"

"Come on. What would you have liked to have gotten out of Axel?"

"To lead off: Who does he work for? Who is the Voice?"

"He worked for a fellow named Amado Fuentes."

Gordon sat back. "Impossible. Fuentes had been dead for three years."

"Nope. He lives with his sister, Marta. The drug lords call her the Voice, and they're scared to death of her. If she gets upset, Axel pays a visit and makes an offering. At least he did."

He cocked his head, wondering. "I'll buy. Where are Fuentes and his sister?"

"You really want to know?"

"Of course. If he's really alive, Amado's one of the most wanted people in the world. And if he's behind this terrorism we'll want him even more."

"He's behind it. He also controls most of the dope coming into the US and he's so ungodly rich that if he snaps his fingers the President of Mexico—or maybe any President—bows. Axel Nevas's eavesdropping cost him half a billion dollars, and he didn't blink an eye."

"Why wouldn't I want to know where he is?"

"What if I said he'd been in Boca Raton dieting and getting over his plastic surgery while his sister ran the business?" She gave him an address. "But if they're following procedures, which you can bet they are, they're flying home right now."

"Where's home?"

"Likely the same place they operated their business out of for years while the Mexican Government protected them, and wouldn't even let our airplanes fly over."

He remembered. Before his "death" it was said that units of the Mexican Army protected Amado Fuentes.

"Come on, Gordon. Do you think they're going to let you go after him down there?"

"Maybe," he tried.

"Ten percent of the trucks crossing the border under NAFTA are also hauling dope. Seventy percent of our illegal drugs come through Mexico, but our President's promised that we'd never, ever encroach on their sovereignty again, and they're banking on it."

"What about Ambassador Cordellons in New York?"

"You can't arrest him. I doubt you can even have him sent home, because it might embarrass someone. Anyway, it's Katy's word against his that he met with anyone."

Gordon Tower asked the real question. "Did Link get all this from Axel?"

"Here's where I'm supposed to say: Get what? Link felt it

would be best if you just forgot most of this, along with the fact that he was ever there."

"I've got a problem with that, Erin. Until we nail Axel, Katy's in jeopardy."

"Link said for you not to be concerned. It will handle itself."

"Where is he, Erin?"

"Forget he was there, would you please?"

He hesitated. "I'll have to run all of that past our new Bureau director."

"Link spoke with her. Judge DeVera is a close family friend. She knows and trust him. We're asking you to do the same."

How could he argue? "Like you said, what conversation? Who's Link Anderson?"

"More good news, Gordon. I've been stripping the super-computers in Atlanta and Denver, and getting a long list. Small dealers and large, and distribution points. The trade should be wounded for a while."

She was right, thought Gordon Tower. Still, he wondered what had happened to Axel Nevas, and where he might be.

At 6 A.M. the medical team working on Maggie Tatro upgraded her condition from critical to serious. Unless there were complications, she was expected to recover.

At daylight that morning a Lear jet 65 landed on a just-plowed runway nearby. The strip was owned by an old fellow named Tom DeBerre, who had refused to remain in the hospital and was in the house sleeping off an encounter with a bottle of Johnny Walker Black whiskey.

When the Lear jet's hatch was opened, two figures emerged from a nearby Jeep Cherokee. The leader was hawk-eyed and gaunt. The other had only one arm, and stumbled quite a lot.

Once aboard, the gaunt man checked a gun case to ensure that a Browning hunting rifle was oiled and ready. After ensuring that the passenger could not move about freely, he went forward and took the captain's seat.

The copilot had filed a flight plan for another small and private airfield, not far west of Mexico City. It had been arranged that the customs official sent to examine the airplane and its cargo would arrive half an hour after they landed.

42

The gaunt man had lain in the same position with little movement for the past three days. He was the same dusty color as the earth, and human eyes that swept over the mound of boulders would not distinguish him from other natural features of the llano. Neither would they distinguish the one-armed man lying beside him.

Now and then the one-armed man whispered in a deep croaking voice that he needed food or water, or complained that he was uncomfortable or that his missing arm was hurting. The gaunt man generally ignored him, although he periodically permitted him to drink sparingly from a water bladder. They had not brought food, and he did not care about a lack of comforts.

The previous week a salesman of fabrics had visited the merchants and asked questions of the people in the nearby village. He was friendly and outgoing, and even the policemen of the special detachment and employees of the rancho who frequented the local cantina enjoyed his company. He had left with several orders and his suitcases of samples, returned to Mexico City, and briefed the gaunt man in meticulous detail.

In was no secret that Rancho Fuentes had received an important guest. Señor Carlos David (pronounced

Duh-'veed by his hosts) was an immensely wealthy businessman from the Bahamas who was considering purchasing the
place. He was relatively youthful and, except for a small bandage across his nose from some mishap, appeared handsome.
Every few mornings—at random times for security sake—he
rode one of the rancho's fine thoroughbreds on a jaunt across
the llano, accompanied by numerous well-armed guards and
a woman with severely swept salt-and-pepper hair.

The rancho had once belonged to Don Amado Fuentes, a
legendary Robin Hood figure in the gringo drug trade who
had died three years earlier. Even after his death, the rancho
people maintained such airtight security that not a coyote or
wild pig could penetrate the perimeter without setting off
alarms and being observed by video cameras and having a
security detail dispatched. Of course there were periodic
maintenance problems, like the previous week when a segment in a remote area was disabled for half an hour, but
those were few.

The gaunt man waited patiently at the rocky outcropping,
protected from the elements by a dust-laden cloth tied about
his head and arranged to shield his face from the sun. His
pastime had been watching two scorpions that periodically
dueled over the right to remain in the shade of a stone. An
iguana approached and eyed him curiously, as if wondering
if he was alive or another dusty landmark, and left without
haste.

The one-armed man began to babble again. Talking about
the gods of the Aztecs and how one—the god of strife and
warriors—was particularly demanding. He was utterly mad,
the symptoms of his severe schizophrenia heightening with
each passing day, fueled by the unnerving silence of the gaunt
man, and his own knowledge that he had asked too much
from Huitzilpóchtli while offering too little. The god of war
needed *blood*. Not merely from normal humans, but also
from humans of greatness and wealth, who wielded tremendous power.

He needed the lifeblood of royalty.

Then the one-armed man would be freed, and regain all

that he had lost. In his deep and guttural voice he expounded happily upon those things whenever he was allowed to speak.

"They will come today," interrupted the gaunt man. He had spoken little since they'd arrived, except to tell him what must be done. His senses were tuned to their surroundings, and he could percieve things such as the distant sounds of riders.

The one-armed man stopped talking and grew a crafty expression.

The sun was an hour above the horizon when they heard the approach of many humans. First laughter, then when they were closer a man's loud voice boasting about a bull he had purchased from a breeder in Switzerland. The one-armed man recognized the great man's voice.

Sound carried easily on the bleak-featured llano, and they could hear him lecture how modern cattle were so much larger and hardier than their ancestors. He spoke English, which they had not heard during the past few days. The riders who had periodically come by, checking every bush and blade of grass but not seeing them, used only Spanish. But the man who rode at the fore of this group spoke English with just a hint of British Caribbean islander. As he well should, since a language tutor had worked with him for the past year.

The woman with severely swept hair rode beside and just behind him. Then came a score of alert men who constantly swiveled their heads. Big men, who looked capable and sure.

The gaunt man moved subtly, bringing the dusty rifle upright in front of the one-armed man, then thumbing down hinged scope covers at front and rear. He knew the precise distances to every bush and large stone. The riders were at four hundred yards, coming at a brisk walk.

He set the scope to 4X power, looked out at the riders one last time—waited patiently until they were three hundred yards distant—and said, "You know what to do."

*   *   *

Since their arrival they'd gone through the exercise precisely one hundred times daily, and the gaunt man had described it so often that when the one-armed man leaned forward and looked through the eyepiece, it was just as he had mentally viewed it. He gripped the Browning autoloader with his one hand, pressing the stock firmly to his shoulder, and waited.

Don't fire until they pass the large cactus, the gaunt man had instructed him.

He felt the great pleasure that he did when making an offering, and did not notice that the gaunt man had slipped away.

Two of the humans were especially important. More wealthy and powerful than any previous Aztec royalty. He would shoot them first, then perhaps some of the others.

They approached the large cactus, and he said in his gravel-tone, "For you, great Huitzilopóchtli, I offer a king and a queen."

The man in front was first. He shot him in the small bandage across his nose. Then the woman beside him as she started to scream.

Epilogue

Abraham Lincoln Anderson picked up the news magazine and scanned the contents, noting that the pages were filled with the events of the previous month in Colorado. The terrorists were described as drug traffickers, but nowhere was a connection with Mexico mentioned. The FBI was investigating the rationale behind the attacks, while the press conjectured that the mountain communities may have been the battlefields of a turf war between white supremacists and drug distributors. The President had flown to both Steamboat and Montrose, and was seen sympathizing with locals, and the White House had issued a statement promising to get to the bottom of the tragedy and present the truth to the public sooner rather than later.

The prisoners were not close-mouthed. It seemed like a footrace for who could tell the most about the atrocities and get the best deals from prosecutors, brokered by the flood of America's top lawyers who were pouring into Colorado to take their money. A number of the terrorist leaders, who were major distributors in various large cities, spoke of someone called the Voice and a violent killer named Axel. Their stories were confusing and nonverified.

Appearing in this week's issue of the news magazine were other topics as well. For instance, in the Crime section, the past week had netted more drug busts than the DEA had

claimed in the past year. Also, the price of illegal drugs had
jumped by twenty percent.

In the International section, an article presented the fact
that Mexico's UN Ambassador Antonio José Cordellons had
withdrawn his name from consideration as the new secretary-
general, claiming pressing family commitments. Also in
International was a smaller article describing the deaths of a
Bahaman man named Carlos David, his female companion,
and two others in an apparent hunting tragedy in Mexico.
David was said to be extremely wealthy. There had been
doubt as to his identity until his fingerprints were taken and
matched those on record.

"Good to have you back, pardner," said Erin, coming in from
the outer office with fresh mugs of coffee and interrupting
his reading. "Ready to go to work after your vacation?"

Link closed the news magazine and leaned back. Looking weathered and lean. "I promised Maggie I'd drop by the
hospital this morning."

"You'll want to be on time. While you were away a single
doctor started hanging around, and I can certify he's one
sexy dude. Then there's Randall, the chief investigator . . ."

"You're joking. She thought he was a Neanderthal."

"Things change. That's the price you pay for courting
America's heroine."

The public liked the story of the feisty ex-FBI agent, and
various publishers were trying to sign her for a book deal.
There'd been no mention of Link Anderson in the media except as the pilot who had flown her and Special Agent
George to Montrose.

Erin laughed at his discomfiture. "Maggie's expecting
you at nine. She wants to ask about your apartment to see if
her china fits the décor."

After going over the latest correspondence, Link and Erin
looked out the window together, sipping coffee and idly
commenting on such things as why normal humans might
choose to live and work in New York.